The Dante Inferno

The Dante Dynasty Series

Books 1-3

By

Day Leclaire

USA Today Bestselling Author

Please Note:

This is a work of fiction. Names, characters, places, and incidents either are the product of the author's imagination or are used fictitiously, and any resemblance to actual persons, living or dead, business establishments, events or locales is entirely coincidental.

Boxset Cover Design by Adrienne G. Smith, 2021

For more information, visit my website at: _http://www.DayLeclaire.com_

Thank you!

Table of Contents

Book Descriptions

*Some blazes, once ignited, can't be
extinguished.
Just one burning touch connects a
Dante with his soul mate.
The Inferno ... curse or blessing?*

Sev's Blackmailed Bride, Book #1

One scorching touch connects Sev Dante
with lovely jewelry designer, Francesca
Sommers. One passionate night together
changes their lives forever. One painful
secret will tear them apart and destroy
both their lives.

As the powerful, take-charge CEO of
Dantes jewelry empire, Sev never
believed in The Inferno until it sweeps
through him like wildfire. According to
family legend, to ignore The Inferno
guarantees disaster. To succumb, a life
of bliss. But what happens when the
woman The Inferno chooses works for
his competitor and creates a stunning
jewelry collection that threatens to
destroy his plans to rebuild his family's
empire? The only option available:

blackmail her to work for him and become his bride.

Francesca Sommers has her dream job, working for her father, even if he's unaware of her existence. Her life is almost perfect … until Sev changes her with a single touch. She can't resist him or his relentless seduction. Has no choice but to surrender to his raw passion. To give him everything and anything he demands. Even to be forced into marriage.

But surrendering to Sev means losing both her budding relationship with her father and her career. And when Sev discovers what she did to even the scales and protect her father's business from his hostile takeover, she will lose him, too.

Will The Inferno be enough to save them? Or will its relentless fire consume them both?

Marco's Stolen Wife, Book #2

A fierce contest between twins…

One scorching touch between sexy international businessman Marco Dante and gorgeous Dantes CFO, Caitlyn Vaughn and The Inferno explodes. Until Marco's twin brother, Lazz, parts them, planning to make Caitlyn his own. But he hasn't counted on The Inferno or Marco's determination to win his Inferno mate, no matter what.

Posing as his brother, Marco switches identities and sweeps Caitlyn off for a romantic weekend, seducing her first into becoming his wife and then into his bed for a night of passion unlike any other. The weekend is perfect ... until a fatal mistake on Marco's part reveals the truth.

She married the wrong man.

Or did she? Marco claims it's some bizarre family myth called The Inferno, where soul mates connect with a single touch. But she couldn't possibly love a man she only met one time, for all of five minutes. How can the lust she feels for a relative stranger far outstrip the chaste relationship she had with his brother? And yet, that's exactly what's happened.

Now Caitlyn finds herself married to Marco for better or worse. The better, she finds in his arms and bed. The worse occurs when their marital mix-up is leaked to the press.

Can she find a way to prove both the existence of The Inferno ... and that Marco is the only man for her? Or is their relationship doomed if The Inferno is demonstrated to be nothing more than a myth?

Nicolò's Wedding Deception, Book #3

A liar and a thief ... or his Inferno mate?

When Kiley O'Dell claims to own half the mines that contain Dantes legendary fire diamonds, the family sends the most ruthless and cynical of the brothers, Nicolò Dante, the family troubleshooter, to negotiate with her. Neither expect the legendary Inferno to strike, sending both up in flames.

Nicolò suspects Kiley's claim is a con. And he'll do whatever necessary to get to the truth, even chase a panicked and fleeing Kiley. To his horror, she darts into traffic and is hit by a cab before he can save her. After she wakes, she insists she has amnesia. Now he's certain she's conning him, and he has a way to prove it.

Turning the tables on Kiley, Nicolò claims she's his wife. What he doesn't expect is for The Inferno to tumble them into a fierce love affair. Which is the real Kiley? The sweet, passionate woman in his bed, someone he'd do anything to keep, or the crafty con artist he first met? And what will happen when she discovers they're not married at all, that far from being her loving husband, Nicolò is out for vengeance?

Lover or liar? Devious or delectable? Only The Inferno can determine which.

Other Titles by Day Leclaire

The Wacky Women Series

In the world of Wacky Women, nothing ever goes according to plan!
From one disaster to the next, these women will do anything to find true love.
Heartwarming, hilarious, and unexpectedly poignant, Fall into laughter while you fall in love.

Once Upon a Cowboy (Book #1)
Once Upon a Jinx (Book #2)
Once Upon a Time (Book #3)
Once Upon a Ghost (Book #4)
Once Upon an Enchantment (Book #5)

The Dante Inferno:
The Dante Dynasty Series

Some blazes, once ignited, can't be extinguished. Just one burning touch connects a Dante with his soul mate. The Inferno ... curse or blessing?

Sev's Blackmailed Bride, Book #1
Marco's Stolen Wife, Book #2
Nicolò's Wedding Deception, Book #3
Lazz's Contract Marriage, Book #4
Luc's Unwilling Wife, Book #5
Rafe's Temporary Fiancée, Book #6
Draco's Marriage Pact, Book #7

Gianna's Honor-Bound Husband, Book #8
Becoming Dante: Gabe, Book #9
Dante's Dilemma: Romero, Book #10
Forever Dante: Lucia, Book #11

The Cinderella Ball Series

Married by Midnight!
You're invited to a wedding . . .
your own!
Come to the Cinderella Ball single . . .
leave happily wed.

Fairy Tale Husband
Fairy Tale Wife
Fairy Tale Wedding
Fairy Tale Marriage
The Cinderella Ball (Books 1-4)

The Salvatore Brothers

Six sexy Italian-American brothers,
ready to win their soul mates.
The Salvatore Brothers will charm,
tempt, seduce ... or even wed and bed.
They'll do whatever it takes to find their
bride.
And when they say whatever it takes,
they mean absolutely anything!

HOW TO: Hide a Baby
HOW TO: Bare Your Bride
HOW TO: Ensnare Your Lover
HOW TO: Marry Christmas
HOW TO: Seduce Your Wife
HOW TO: Lure Your Mate

Sev's Blackmailed Bride

The Dante Dynasty Series:
Book #1

By

Day Leclaire

USA Today Bestselling Author

Dedication

To my own soul mate, Frank, with much
love for your
constant patience, encouragement, and
sense of humor.
It just keeps getting better!

Prologue

He refused to lose.

He refused to allow anything—or anyone—to get in the way of his rebuilding Dantes into the formidable empire it had once been.

Severo Dante fought for the calm control that typified his business dealings as he regarded his brothers. He found it more difficult than usual to maintain an impassive facade, perhaps because the next few business decisions would prove vital to their overall future. Passion was the hallmark of the Dante name, of the Dante image. But the head of the company couldn't afford to allow emotion to overrule intellect. Too much depended on his ability to handle all that went on behind the scenes.

Where others provided the creativity that turned the sparkle and glitter of gemstones into the world's most coveted wedding rings, Sev utilized logic and business acumen to drag Dantes back from the brink of ruin and propel its return to the public acclaim it had once known. At least, that had been the plan until he hit this latest roadblock.

Sev turned from the panoramic view of downtown San Francisco and faced his brothers. "Timeless Heirlooms was in the perfect position for acquisition. Dantes should already have it tucked beneath our corporate umbrella. What the hell happened?" he demanded.

The Dante twins, Marco and Lazzaro, shrugged as one. "New designer," Marco explained.

"It's revitalized their company," Lazz added.

"Who is this designer? What's his name? Where did he come from?" To Sev's frustration, no one answered. "We need to find out. Now. Timeless Heirlooms belonged to Dantes until we were forced to sell it off after Dad died. Now that I've solidified our financial position, I want TH back. And I want it back *now*."

Marco paced restlessly. "Maybe we should reconsider taking over Timeless. Since we're global again, I'd rather go head-to-head with them and crush them where they stand. We've been cautious long enough. Let's get moving," he persisted. "Expand from our wedding ring market into the areas we once owned—not just heirloom and estate jewelry, but all jewelry needs. Earrings, bracelets, necklaces. Hell, tiaras, if there's a demand for them."

Sev shook his head. "It's too soon. We need a really spectacular collection to launch us, and we don't have that collection, or anything close to one. Nor do we have a suitable marketing campaign, even if one should fall into our laps. By taking over TH we corner that particular market in one simple move. Once solidified there, we'll choose our next target. Something bigger and more impressive." He turned his attention to Lazz. "What's our best approach for finding this new designer?"

"TH is having a spring showing—" Lazz checked his notes with typical thoroughness "—tomorrow night. The Fontaines will be featuring their latest designs, as well as the creative geniuses behind them. One of them has created quite a buzz. Once we have the designer's name, we can order a background check. Find his or her vulnerability."

A cunning gleam appeared in Marco's eyes. "Better yet, we can hire him out from under the Fontaines. He'd make a fine addition to Dantes. Then when we've bought out Timeless Heirlooms, he can go right back to what he's doing now—designing contemporary pieces with the look and feel of heirloom and estate jewelry." A hint of ruthlessness colored his words.

"Only he'll do it for TH's new owners. *Us.*"

"That's a distinct possibility." Sev considered his options before reaching a decision. "Here's what I want. It might look suspicious if we all attend TH's show. Lazz, you handle the background check and give us something to go on. Marco, you're the people person. You and I will attend the showing. I'll speak to the Fontaines directly."

Marco smiled. "While I use my natural charm and sex appeal to get the latest gossip."

Lazz groaned. "The worst part is . . . he's right. I've never understood how we can look exactly alike and yet women who won't give me the time of day are all over Marco."

A knock sounded at the door, interrupting a discussion that had been ongoing since the twins had crawled out of their respective cradles. Their youngest brother, Nicolò, walked in. Long considered the family "trouble-shooter," he took charge when creative answers were needed to sort out a family dilemma. Nicolò often claimed that he didn't believe in problems, only solutions.

"Primo sent me," Nicolò said, referring to their grandfather. "He thought you might have a job for me."

Sev nodded. "I want you working with Lazz. He'll fill you in on the latest developments with Timeless Heirlooms. We may need some innovative suggestions in the near future."

Nicolò inclined his head, his expression reflecting both his interest and his fierce determination. "I'll get right on it."

Sev folded his arms across his chest. "When Dad died and we discovered that Dantes teetered on the verge of bankruptcy, we were faced with some unpleasant choices—"

"You were faced," Lazz interrupted. "You were the one forced to make the tough decisions and sell off all the various subsidiaries of Dantes."

"Selling off the secondary holdings saved the core business and allowed us time to recover and rebuild." Sev eyed each brother in turn. "It's been a long road back, but now we're in a position to reclaim what we once lost. I won't allow anything to stand in the way of doing that. We all agreed that the first business we return to the fold is the heirloom and estate jewelry. That's Timeless Heirlooms. If this new designer is all that stands between us and reacquiring TH, then we either find a way to take them over . . ." His expression fell into merciless lines. "Or take them out."

Chapter One

Francesca Sommers ran a critical eye over the sumptuous ballroom in Nob Hill's exclusive five-star hotel, Le Premier, and struggled to suppress a severe case of nerves. In a little over twenty-four hours she'd have her very first showing. She couldn't believe her good fortune, both in being offered the opportunity to work with Tina and Kurt Fontaine, as well as having her designs among those featured at Timeless Heirlooms' spring show.

As though sensing Francesca's nervousness, Tina came up beside her and slipped an arm around her waist. "You can stop worrying right now," she said. "You'll see. Your pieces will be the hit of the evening. Not to take anything away from Cliff or Deborah's talent and skill—they're both good designers—it's your collection that will take everyone's breath away. It offers the perfect blend of romantic elegance and timeless appeal that are hallmarks of my company."

Francesca relaxed ever so slightly, smiling in delight at the compliment.

"Are you sure you don't mean old-fashioned?" she asked with a laugh.

Tina lifted a dark eyebrow, which gave her exotic features an imperious cast. "Period pieces are a Fontaine specialty. We're at the leading edge of the resurgence in popularity for jewelry like this. You'll see. Tomorrow night's showing will put us over the top."

Francesca shook her head. "Catching Juliet Bloom's eye will put us over the top. I don't suppose she's responded to our invitation?"

"Her agent contacted us. She's still out of the country wrapping her latest film. But her agency's sending a representative. And I've learned that Juliet's next movie is another period piece. If this rep likes what she sees . . ." Tina lifted a shoulder. "We've all done the best we can. The rest is up to fate, as well as those stunning pieces you've designed."

Kurt entered the room and Tina murmured an excuse before joining her husband. Francesca pretended to give her full attention to the various displays currently under construction, but in reality, she studied her employers with an intense yearning.

As the brilliant and creative owner of Timeless Heirlooms, Tina couldn't be more different from her husband of nearly thirty years. Small, dark, and vivacious, she hurtled through her days, whereas Kurt took life in stride. He also qualified as one of the most strikingly handsome men Francesca had ever met, towering over Tina, his Nordic appearance the polar opposite of his wife's.

Although he held the title of Director of Operations for TH, his real job consisted of supporting Tina and keeping the nuts and bolts of the business end of the company running smoothly. With his calm, reassuring demeanor, he excelled at both, even during stressful and frantic periods such as this.

Francesca gripped her hands together. Right now, Timeless Heirlooms desperately needed Kurt's soothing touch. Despite the Fontaines' attempts to keep everyone in the dark, rumors had reached Francesca of their financial difficulties. They were counting on her—or rather, her designs—to help them recover their footing in the volatile world of jewelry sales. In response, she'd thrown herself, heart and soul, into her job, giving the Fontaines every ounce of her talent and skill. But would that be enough?

For as long as Francesca could remember, she'd wanted to work for one of Dantes' subsidiaries, mainly because it offered an unparalleled opportunity to advance her career and bring her designs to life. But when the Fontaines bought out TH, a far different reason drew her to apply to them for a job, instead of Dantes. A reason she kept tucked close to her heart.

It gave her the opportunity to get to know her father.

Sev's plans for the evening of the Fontaines' show seemed perfect, right up until he saw her.

For some inexplicable reason, she drew his gaze the moment he walked into the ballroom and the impact from that one look struck with all the power and sizzle of a lightning bolt flung from on high. Every business plan, every thought about taking over TH, of tracking down this new designer and acquiring him for Dantes, leaked from Sev's brain and puddled at his feet. In its place one imperative remained.

Get. The. Woman.

She stood in the midst of a group of people, a tall, golden swan surrounded by sparrows. Everything about her spoke of old-time grace and elegance, the very embodiment of Timeless Heirlooms' motto—jewelry that mates past with present. He knew many beautiful women, but something about this one captivated him on a visceral level.

Unremitting desire entangled him in an unbreakable web and refused to let go no matter how hard he struggled to break the bond.

For a split second Sev forgot why he'd come or what he hoped to accomplish. Instead, he felt compelled to follow that primal tug. He would have, too, if Marco hadn't grabbed his arm.

"Hey, where are you going? The Fontaines are in the other direction." He glanced toward the section of the room that held Sev's attention and grinned in sudden understanding. *"Bella,* yes?"

"Yes." The single word—one riddled with desire—betrayed him and Sev shook his head in an effort to clear it. What the hell was happening to him? He never lost focus like this. Nothing ever came between him and business. Nothing. Not even a drop-dead gorgeous woman whose very presence sang with all the promise and allure of a Greek Siren.

Marco straightened his suit jacket. "Since my assignment is to mingle with the guests while you see what information the Fontaines are willing to cough up, I believe the lady in question is on my list." He clapped his brother on the back. "Looks like you're out of luck, Sev."

The mere thought of his brother getting anywhere close to this particular woman had Sev seeing red. Marco, the charmer. Marco, who could entice any and all women into his bed with a single look. Marco, who had never met a woman he hadn't enjoyed to the fullest, before discarding. Marco, with his golden swan.

A faint roaring filled Sev's ears, a noise that deafened him to everything but one increasingly urgent demand. *Get. The. Woman.* "Not her," he ordered. It amazed him that he could still speak coherently, considering the compulsion that infected him and drove him to react in ways in complete and utter contrast to his normal character. "Stay away from her."

Marco still didn't get it. "You're not playing fair," he protested. "Why don't we let the lady decide who she prefers?"

Sev simply turned and looked at his brother. "Not her," he repeated.

Marco held up his hands, the humor fading from his expression. "Fine, fine. But if she approaches me, I'm not sending her away. Not even for you."

Sev's hands collapsed into fists and it took every ounce of effort to keep from using one of them to rearrange Marco's features, arresting features that attracted women to him with lifelong ease, not to mention unparalleled success. "If she approaches you, send her over to me."

Marco frowned. "Have you met this woman before? Do you have a history with her? You know I don't poach my brothers' women. Not unless your relationship's over." His smile glimmered again. "I don't suppose it's over by any chance?"

"It's not over. In fact, it hasn't started. Yet." His gaze fixed on his quarry. "I'm just staking my claim. Now are we clear, or do I have to spell it out with my fists?"

"No, it's not clear. Stake your claim? Spell it out with fists?" Marco's frown deepened. "Have you lost your mind? When have you ever spoken about a woman like that? What's gotten into you?"

Sev drew in a slow breath, fighting to clear his head, with only limited success. What *had* gotten into him? Marco was right. He never reacted like this over a woman. Nothing and no one came ahead of business. But another glance in the blonde's direction caused the desire to erupt in messy waves of molten heat. It filled him with a whispered demand to go to her. To seduce her. To take her and make her his, no matter who or what stood in his way. It overshadowed all else, rooting into his very soul and sending out powerful tentacles that latched on to every part of him and refused to let go.

"Hey! Wake up, big brother." Marco snapped his fingers in front of Sev's nose, concern bleeding into his voice and expression. "I'll tell you what. Why don't we check out the new designs before we get to work? See what we're up against."

"Good idea," Sev managed to say.

Despite the arm his brother dropped on Sev's shoulder, it took every ounce of self-control at his command to turn his back on the blonde and walk away. With every step, he could feel the quicksand of need sucking at his feet and legs. It didn't matter how much distance he put between them, he could still sense her on every level, and that awareness unsettled him more than he cared to admit.

They found the spring collection staged on sweeps of raw silk and took their time studying the pieces. Models also roamed the ballroom, their beauty enhanced by the glitter of diamonds and colored gems. Marco flirted with the models, while Sev assessed the displays. He kept hoping the blonde might gravitate this way. Since she wore one of the premier sets, he assumed she must be a model, as well, especially with her height and regal bearing. But she kept her distance and he couldn't decide whether to be relieved or annoyed.

Marco ended his conversation with a leggy redhead wearing a solid three million dollars' worth of high-quality stones and returned to Sev's side. "I don't get it. Nothing I've seen so far is enough to save Timeless from going under," he said in an undertone. "It's all the same old thing."

"No, not all of it. Not this, for instance."

Sev paused by a display unique in its simplicity. Not that the jewelry needed a fancy backdrop to make it stand out. The pieces spoke for themselves. White gold, diamonds and jet formed a sweeping pattern as elegant and sophisticated as any in recent memory. And yet, an air of romance permeated each item, a promise that by gifting this necklace, or this ring, or this bracelet, the recipient would receive a tangible expression of utter love and devotion.

An image of the blonde wearing the gems flashed through his mind. He could see the delicate strands of the necklace encircling her throat, the graceful length accentuated by the simple drop earrings. It would look perfect on her, particularly when complemented by acres of pale, creamy skin and a simple black silk sheath.

"Aw, hell. This is the first I've seen of this designer's work. It's just the sort of collection I had in mind for Dantes' expansion," Marco said. "We are so screwed."

In more ways than one. If Sev didn't get his mind back on business, he might as well kiss Timeless Heirlooms goodbye. "Find out who designed these and get the information to Lazz and Nicolò," he instructed his brother. "I'll go talk to the Fontaines. Maybe I'll learn something helpful."

Or maybe he should head for the kitchen, grab a bucket of ice and pour it over his head in the hope of dousing the heat rampaging through his system. Damn it to hell! What had that blonde done to him and how had she done it?

Marco grimaced. "Whatever you learn better be helpful, because I have a feeling they no longer need to sell TH."

Unfortunately, Sev had a nasty feeling his brother was right. Still, his conversation with the Fontaines elicited a few interesting facts. They had, indeed, hired three new designers for the express purpose of revitalizing TH. And they had some big deal in the offing, all very hush-hush. Whatever the deal, the Fontaines were convinced it would catapult them into the big times.

Yet, Sev caught the hint of desperation Tina couldn't quite conceal, which told him all he needed to know. Despite tonight's success, they were still vulnerable. He just needed to uncover the source of that vulnerability and exploit it.

He headed for the far end of the room where French doors opened onto a shadowed balcony with a stunning view of San Francisco. The light breeze held a final nip of winter's chill, but he found it a welcome relief after the perfumed warmth of the ballroom. Removing his cell phone from his jacket pocket and hit a button to connect with Lazz.

A few seconds later the call went through. "Sev?" A rapid clicking bled through the line, indicating his brother was typing as he spoke. Ever the multitasker. "I just spoke to Marco."

"And?"

Lazz sighed. "You're both at the same party. So why am I the one keeping you two up-to-date?"

"Do I really need to answer that?"

"Okay, okay. Marco has two names for you so far. There's a Clifton Paris and a Deborah Leighton. He's working on the third one, but everyone's being very mysterious. He thinks it's because they're planning some huge announcement in regard to this final designer."

"Which means he's the one we're after."

"Probably. Marco said there's some special deal TH is about to close, also involving this particular designer."

"The Fontaines said the same thing. Does Marco know what the deal is or which designer?"

"Actually, he does, at least in part. They're about to sign a big-name actress."

Sev fought for patience. "There's a lot of big-name actresses out there. Which one are we looking at?"

"Don't know, yet. But the rumor is, she's at the very top. If they do sign someone like Julia Roberts or Jennifer Lawrence or Juliet Bloom, it'll be huge for them. And it'll effectively prevent both a buyout and, quite possibly, our ability to compete with them on the open market."

Sev grimaced at his brother's all-too-accurate assessment. "I need to find out who they're courting and get the agreement delayed. Put Nicolò on it."

"Right away."

"We also need leverage. Call that PI we hired last year—Rufio—and have him start an immediate investigation of the designers Marco's already identified. Then call Marco and tell him I want that third name ASAP. Tell him to alert me the minute he has it."

"Check."

Sev pocketed his phone. Time to gather himself for round two. He glanced toward the glow of lights, where the subdued chatter of voices wafted from the ballroom. To his relief, his reaction to the blonde had eased somewhat. Five minutes and counting without a single image of her short-circuiting his brain and sending the rest of him into overdrive.

Or so he thought until she appeared in the doorway and stared straight at him. For a split second he believed she came in search of him, that the ever-tightening tendrils between them were acting on a subliminal level and drawing her to him. Then he realized that her eyes hadn't adjusted to the darkness that cloaked him. He nearly groaned. She couldn't see him at all. Did she even sense him? Doubtful. This was his insanity, not hers.

She hesitated while light streamed around her, capturing her in its warm embrace. She'd dressed simply, in a silk sheath of palest lilac. No doubt the color had been selected to complement the jewelry she wore, the set unquestionably the work of TH's mystery designer. A delicate rope of silver, studded with the unmistakable glitter of diamonds and Verdonian amethysts, hugged the base of her neck while a simple confection of the same stones flashed discreetly on the lobes of her ears. Understated. Stylish. Sophisticated.

With a sigh of relief, she stepped onto the balcony. The light from the ballroom gave her a final caress, slipping through the thin silk to reveal a womanly shape that nearly brought Sev to his knees. Full breasts strained against the low-cut bodice, while a nipped waist and shapely hips gave the simple dress an impressive definition.

She crossed to the balustrade and stared out at the view, absently rubbing her bare arms against the spring chill. Sev found he couldn't move. The rational part of his brain ordered him to return to the gathering and finish the job at hand. But an overwhelming need eclipsed that small voice of sanity. It was as though some primeval part of himself dominated reason and rationale. He'd become a creature of instinct. And instinct demanded that he inhale her very essence and imprint it on his mind and body and soul.

Her instincts must have been as finely tuned as his own, for she lifted her head as though scenting the air. Then, with unerring accuracy, she spun to face him and her gaze collided with his.

"I've been waiting for you," he said.

Francesca froze, every nerve ending sizzling to life in an instinctive fight-or-flight reaction. She couldn't say what alerted her to the man's presence. One second she believed herself alone and in the next heartbeat she sensed him on a purely intuitive level.

She stared at him and the breath hitched from her lungs. He blended into his shroud of shadows so completely that the ebony richness of his hair and suit melted into his surroundings, making him appear part of the night. Only his eyes were at odds with the endless darkness, glittering like antique gold against a palette of black. As though aware of her apprehension, he stepped into a swath of light coming from the ballroom to enable her to get a better look.

His height impressed her. He stood a full two or three inches over six feet with an imposing expanse of shoulders and long, powerful legs. For the first time since childhood, she felt downright petite. Reflected light cut across his features, throwing the patrician lines of his face into sharp relief. Heaven help her. She couldn't remember the last time she'd seen such a gorgeous man.

But something stunned her even more than his appearance—the emotional turmoil he triggered. She'd never responded to a man like this before. Never experienced such an intense, uncontrollable physical reaction. She stood before him, filled with a feminine helplessness utterly foreign to her nature. Desire shook her, the intensity so absolute that she could only stare in bewilderment when he offered his hand.

"You've been waiting for me?" she finally managed to say. "Why?"

"I noticed you when I first arrived and hoped we'd eventually meet. My name's Severo. Sev, for short."

"Francesca Sommers." She took the hand he offered before snatching it back with a startled exclamation. "Good Lord. What was that?"

He appeared equally stunned. "Static electricity?"

She'd felt static electricity before. Who hadn't? In fact, as a child she and the other foster children had often delighted in scuffing their socks on the carpet before chasing through the house in order to shock each other. That brief zap of electricity bore no similarity to this.

She scrubbed her palm across her hip, but after that initial searing of flesh against flesh, the sensation changed. It scored her palm like a brand, though unlike a brand, it didn't hurt. It sank deep into her bones—part tingle combined with a peculiar ticklish itch. She didn't know what to make of it.

"Maybe we should try that again," Sev said.

She took a swift step backward. "Maybe we shouldn't."

His mouth tilted to one side. "I'm sorry. I have no idea how or why that happened. You sure we can't try this again?" He held out his hand. "I promise, if anything bad occurs, I'll keep my distance."

She hesitated for an instant, then reluctantly slipped her hand into his. "So far, so good."

The previous sensation didn't happen again, true. Instead, another one took its place. It felt as though some part of him seeped from his hand to hers and sank into her pores before being lapped up by her veins. It slid deeper with every beat of her heart, imbuing her with his essence. Worse, each beat filled her with forbidden desire.

She fought the sensation, fought to speak naturally. "So, what brings you to the showing, Sev? Are you a buyer?"

"Not exactly, although the set you're wearing is something I wouldn't mind acquiring. May I have a closer look?"

No more than a few feet separated them. The single step he took in her direction shrank that distance to mere inches and magnified her reaction to him. Drawing in a deep breath, she tilted her head to one side so he could get a better look at her design, praying he wouldn't take long so she could escape into the relative safety of the shadows surrounding them. The next instant she found escape the last thing on her mind.

His hand brushed her collarbone as he traced the curve of her necklace with his fingertips, branding her with fire. "Stunning. Absolutely stunning."

On the surface his comment sounded simple enough, yet a heavy, old-world lyricism underscored it, filled with the flavor of foreign climes. She could hear the faint strains of a glorious Italian aria, smell the tart richness of ripening grapes, soak in the heat and humidity of a Tuscan summer.

Unable to help herself, she swayed toward him and whispered his name. His response came in a frantic explosion of movement. He swept her into his arms, locking her against him. Hips and thighs collided, then melded. Hands sought purchase before hers tunneled into the thick waves of his hair and his spread across her hip and spine, flooding her with a heavy liquid warmth. Lips brushed. Once. Twice. Finally, their mouths mated, the fit sheer perfection.

She practically inhaled him, unable to get enough. Not of his taste. Not of his scent. Not of his touch. His hands drifted upward, igniting a path of fire in their wake. The most peculiar awareness filled her as he touched her. Though his caress aroused her, she didn't get the impression his actions were a form of foreplay. Instead, it almost felt as though he were committing the shape and feel of her to memory, imprinting her on his brain.

She pulled back slightly, fighting for breath. "I don't understand any of this. We've only just met. And yet, I can't keep my hands off of you."

"I can't explain it, either." Desire blazed across his face, giving him a taut, hungry appearance. "But, it's happening, and right now that's all that matters. Fortunately, that also makes it easy to fix."

Yes. Thank goodness they could fix this terrifying reaction and make it go away. "Fine. Let's get it taken care of."

He caught her hand in his. "Let's go."

"Go?" She resisted his pull, not that it got her anywhere. He simply towed her along. "Go where?"

"I'll pay for a room here at Le Premier, and we'll spend the night working this out of our systems. Come morning, we go our separate ways, flame extinguished."

Francesca fought to think straight. "This is crazy." Severo, a man she'd met just five minutes ago, had kissed her with a passion she'd never known existed and then casually suggested they book a room at a hotel for a night of mind-blowing sex. He seemed to have missed one vital point. "I don't do one-night stands."

He never even broke stride. "In the normal course of events, neither do I. For you, I'm willing to make an exception."

Under different circumstances she'd have found his comment amusing. Without the warmth generated by his embrace, the cool San Francisco air allowed her to regain an ounce of common sense and she pulled free of his grasp. "Wait. Just wait a minute."

She watched him fight for control. "I'm not sure I have a minute to spare." A swift grin lit his face with unexpected masculine beauty. "Will thirty seconds do?"

She thrust her hands into her hair, destroying the elegant little knot she'd taken such pains to fashion a few short hours ago. There was a reason she couldn't go with him. A really good reason, if only she could bring it to mind. "I can't be with you. I need to get back inside. I—I have obligations." That was it. Obligations. Obligations to . . . She released a silent groan. Why the *hell* couldn't she remember? "I think I'm obligated to do something important."

Sev shot a perplexed glance toward the ballroom. "As am I." His mouth tugged into another charming smile, one she found irresistible. It altered his entire appearance, transforming him from austere man-in-charge, to someone she'd very much like for a lover. "Since you don't know me, you won't appreciate what I'm about to say, but right now, I don't give a damn about obligation or duty or what I should be doing or saying or thinking. Right now, finding the nearest bedroom is all that matters."

"I'm not sure—"

He slid his arms around her, pulling her close, and her hands collided with the powerful expanse of his chest. Everything about him seduced her. The look in his eyes. The deep warmth of his voice. The heated imprint of his body against hers. "Perhaps this will convince you."

He lowered his head once again and captured her mouth with his. Where before his kiss had been slower and more careful, this time the joining was fast and certain and deliciously skillful. He teased her lips apart and then slid inward, initiating a duel that she wished could go on forever.

Her hands slid upward to grip the broad width of his shoulders. She could feel the barely leashed power of him rippling beneath her palms, could sense how tightly he held himself in check. And she found that she wanted to unleash that power and break through those protective safeguards. What would his embrace be like if he weren't holding back? The mere thought had her moaning in anticipation.

He must have heard the small sound because he tensed. A compelling combination of desire and determination poured off him. His kiss deepened as he shifted from enticement to an unmistakable taking. He wanted her, and he expressed that want with each escalating kiss. If they'd been anywhere else, she'd have done something outside her realm of expertise. She'd have surrendered to his seduction and given herself to him right then and there.

She'd never experienced anything that felt so right, not in all her twenty-six years. How could she have doubted? How could she have questioned being with this man? She belonged here in his arms and nowhere else. She wanted what only he could offer. More, she wanted to give him just as much in return. As though sensing the crumbling of her defenses, he lifted his head and stared down at her with dark, compelling eyes.

"Come with me," he insisted, and held out his hand. "Take the chance, Francesca."

How could she refuse him? Without another word of protest, she linked her fingers with his.

Chapter Two

Francesca remembered little of their passage from the balcony to the front desk of the hotel. She existed in a dreamlike bubble, every word and action touched with enchantment. From the moment she put her hand in Sev's, the insanity that invaded her earlier came crashing back with even greater intensity. After he collected a key card and made a brief stop at the gift shop for supplies, he led her to a private elevator that whisked them straight to the penthouse suite. It wasn't until she stepped inside that a modicum of common sense prevailed.

"Perhaps we could have a drink and get to know each other," she suggested. "Take this a little slower."

To her surprise, he didn't argue. Maybe he felt the same way she did, overwhelmed and off-kilter. Desperate to regain his footing in this strange new land they'd stumbled upon.

"Let me see what they have in stock." He checked the selection of wines and chuckled, the deep, rich sound tripping along her nerve endings. He hefted one of the bottles. "Well, would you look at this. Here's something you might enjoy. They actually carry one of my family's labels from Italy."

"You're vintners?" she asked in surprise.

"My extended family is." He smiled, the relaxed warmth and humor causing her system to react in the most peculiar way. "I have a huge extended family. You probably couldn't mention a single field of interest where I couldn't find one of my relatives in that business."

"Even the jewelry business?" she joked. Since he'd been at Timeless Heirlooms' showing, he must have some connection to the jewelry industry.

He gave her an odd look. "Especially the jewelry business."

Before she could ask the next logical question—why he'd been present at the showing—he handed her the wine. Their fingers brushed and she caught her breath, the sound a sharp, urgent reaction to his touch. The fragile glass trembled in her grasp and without a word she set it on the closest surface. Slowly, ever so slowly, her gaze shifted to meet his and time froze.

How was this possible? How could she experience such intense feelings for a man she knew nothing about? She'd always kept herself guarded, had made a point to develop previous relationships slowly and with great care. Emotional distance promised safety. This—whatever this was—promised excitement, yet threatened danger.

Spending the night with Sev would change her, mark her in some indelible fashion. And yet, even knowing all that, an uncontrollable yearning built within, sweeping relentlessly through her, a yearning she had no more power to resist than the tide could fight the forces that drove each wave toward shore.

She gave up the battle. Stepping into his arms, she surrendered to his embrace. Relief surged through her, catching her by surprise. It took an instant to identify the cause and realize that it felt wrong to be apart from him, that on some level she needed to touch him and have him touch her. That without him she felt adrift and incomplete.

Without a word, she helped him remove his suit jacket, the heavy silence broken only by the sigh of silk. His tie followed. She tackled the buttons of his shirt next. It felt so peculiar to stand before him and perform such an intimate, domestic chore. This should be a wife's pleasure. Or a lover's. She was neither. Or did a one-night stand qualify her as his lover?

His shirt parted, the crisp white of fine cotton juxtaposed against the tawny darkness of his skin. Her hands hovered for an instant, creating an additional contrast of cream against rich gold, before she flattened her palms against hard, bare flesh. She splayed her fingers across the rippled warmth and slid them upward, sweeping his shirt from his shoulders. Desire hummed through her veins and reverberated in her soft murmur of delight.

"Nice," she whispered.

"I plan to make it nicer."

A laugh escaped her. "I didn't notice before, but you have an accent."

His mouth curved to one side, an answering laugh turning his eyes to a dazzling gold. "Maybe it's because Italian was our first language, even though my brothers and I were born and raised in San Francisco."

She wanted to ask more questions, to learn everything possible about him. But more urgent demands took precedence. Unable to help herself, she feathered a line of kisses along the firm sweep of his jaw. It wasn't enough. Not nearly enough. Forking her hands into his crisp, dark hair she drew his head downward and found his mouth with hers.

With a moan of pleasure, she sank inward, tasting the single sip of wine he'd consumed before passion had overruled social niceties. He teased her with a series of gentle kisses, at distinct odds with the ones they had shared earlier.

These tempted. Suggested. Offered a dazzling promise of hot, sultry nights and endless pleasure. She pressed closer, her silk-covered breasts warm and heavy against the bare expanse of his chest. She reached for the zip to his trousers just as an insistent burr came from the cell phone he'd tucked into his pocket. Startled, she took a hasty step back.

"Wait." Sev fished out the phone and set it for voice mail before tossing it toward a nearby coffee table. It missed, clattering to the floor. "There. All taken care of."

"Don't you need to get that?" she asked.

"It's just my brother. It can wait until morning."

A slight frown creased his brow. Once upon a time he'd have taken Marco's call regardless of the circumstances. On some level he recognized the urgency of speaking to his brother. But that urgency faded to a dull, nagging sensation, one easily dismissed.

Nothing like this had ever happened to him before. Not this crazed need. Not taking time away from business for a sexual interlude. Not the haste and desperation of making this woman his.

From the minute they kissed, nothing else existed for him but a raw, desperate wanting, one he intended to satisfy.

"Forget about the phone." He cupped her neck and urged her closer, forking his fingers into her hair and tumbling the loosened strands into total disarray. "Forget about everything but right here and right now."

She relaxed against him and in the muted light her hair gleamed softly while her dark eyes held mysteries he longed to probe. He found the zip to her dress and lowered it the length of her spine. She released a sigh as the fabric parted. Inch by inch, the silk slid from her shoulders, revealing acres of smooth, pale skin. It skimmed her breasts before drifting downward to cling to her hips. A simple nudge sent the gown floating to the carpet, leaving her standing within his embrace wearing nothing but garter and stockings, panties and heels. And her jewelry. It glittered against a palate of cream.

He cupped her hips, supporting her as he sank downward, brushing a series of slow, openmouthed kisses from the pearled tips of her breasts to her soft belly. He slipped her heels from her feet and tossed them aside. Then he turned his attention to her stockings. It only took a moment to release the light-as-air nylons and roll them down the endless length of her legs, before disposing of her garter belt.

Damn, but she was sheer perfection, with narrow, coltish ankles, shapely calves and long, toned thighs. He paused where lilac silk acted as her final bastion of defense to press a kiss against the very heart of her. She trembled beneath his touch, sagging within his grasp.

"No more," she gasped. "I mean—"

"I know what you mean," he replied roughly.

And he did. If they didn't find the bedroom soon, they weren't going to make it there at all. He rose and her hands flew to his waistband, ripping at his belt and zipper. He backed her toward the bedroom as she fought to strip him, all the while snatching greedy, biting kisses. In the hallway, he kicked off his shoes and stepped free of his trousers. And then he swung her into his arms.

Sev reached the bed in three short steps and returned her to her feet. He cupped her face, his hands sweeping past the necklace she still wore. The feel of cool gemstones against his heated flesh allowed sanity to return for a brief instant, at least long enough for him to recognize his obligation to protect her jewelry from harm. With a practiced flick of his fingers, he removed necklace, bracelet and earrings and arranged them with due care on the nightstand table.

Satisfied, he returned his attention to Francesca, lowering her to the mattress. She lay in a tumble of creamy white against the darkness of the duvet. Opening the box he'd purchased at the gift store, he removed protection and put it within easy reach. Then he stripped off his boxers and joined Francesca on the bed. Lights from the city drifted through the unshaded windows opposite them, tinting her with an opalescent glow that battled the shadows attempting to conceal her from him.

The peaks of her naked breasts reflected the muted light, while darkness flung a protective arm low across her belly where her final scrap of clothing remained. She lay quietly beneath his scrutiny, her face turned toward his. Light and shadow worked its magic there, as well, the moon slicing a band of brightness across the ripe fullness of her bee-stung mouth, leaving her eyes—eyes the deep, rich brown of bittersweet chocolate—hidden from him.

He traced a path from moonlight to shadow, delving into the mysteries the dark kept hidden. Her eyes fluttered shut and filled him with an intense curiosity to know all she fought to hide. "What are you thinking?" he asked.

"I'm wondering how I came to be here." She shuddered beneath his touch and it took her a minute to finish. "One instant my life is simple and clear-cut and the next it has me so confused I can't think straight."

"Then don't think. Just feel."

He kissed her cupid's mouth. Unable to resist, he captured the plump bottom lip between his teeth and tugged ever so gently. His reward came in the low, helpless moan that escaped her.

"Do that again," she urged.

"All night long, if that's what you want."

He teased her lips once more, light, brushing strokes that promised without satisfying, suggested without delivering. To his amusement, she chased his wandering mouth in greedy pursuit. He finally let her catch him, delighting in the way she coaxed him into a deeper kiss. She gave both promise and satisfaction, delivering on all he'd suggested. He couldn't get enough of the taste of her, of the incredible parry and slide and nibble of lips and tongue and teeth.

With each exchange, the fever within burned higher and brighter, demanding instant gratification. Sev resisted, refusing to rush. Francesca deserved more. For that matter, so did he. He wanted to explore every inch of her, to delve over each luscious hill and into every valley. To commit her to memory, and then repeat the process in case he'd missed something.

"Why have you stopped?" The question came in a whisper, her confusion communicated through the growing tension in her shoulders and back. "Is something wrong?"

"I haven't stopped," he reassured. "I've just slowed down."

"Oh, I get it. You want to drive me crazy."

He chuckled. "Drive us both crazy."

Her tension changed in tenor, no longer a self-conscious nervousness, but a woman's driving desire, full-bodied and certain. A vibrating need sent a burst of urgency through him. Maybe he'd been kidding himself. Slow was guaranteed to kill him.

Her long graceful hands swept across his torso from shoulder to hip, exploring with open delight. Despite her eagerness, he sensed a tentativeness behind each touch, a newness that spoke of sweet inexperience, right up until her hand closed around him with gentle aggression. Okay, maybe not total inexperience. She found the foil packet he'd set aside for their use and ripped it open, sliding the condom over him with deliberate, torturous strokes. Unable to stand another second, he rolled her under him.

Her body gave as only a woman's body could, accommodating the press and slide of a man's passion. The moonlight shifted, fully baring her to his gaze. High, round breasts tempted his caress, the nipples already ripe and taut with need. He gave them his full attention, each sweep of tongue and hand causing her breath to hitch and her heartbeat to race. Drifting lower, he paused long enough to give due attention to an abdomen that combined the sheen of satin with the softness of down.

And then he eased her panties from her hips. He followed their path with a string of kisses, before drawing the scrap of silk and lace off and allowing it to drift to the floor behind him. With that final garment removed, it left nothing between them but heated air. Neatly cropped honeyed curls shielded the apex of her thighs and he cupped her there, drawing a single finger along the damp cleft, inciting a shudder of desperate yearning.

"It's been a while," she warned. He caught the hint of apprehension she struggled to control. "I haven't—"

He was quick to reassure. "I'll go slow. You can stop me if I do anything you don't like."

"I won't stop you." Her eyes darkened. "I can't."

"I'm relieved to hear it." He swept her loosened hair away from her eyes, the dark blond strands framing the face of an angel. "Slow and easy now, sweetheart. Open for me," he urged. "Let me in."

To his relief, she didn't hesitate. Her thighs parted, lifted, exposing her most private secrets to him. Ever so gently he teased the opening, tracing his thumb across the very center of her pleasure. She tensed, drawn bowstring-taut, and the breath escaped her lungs in a moan of sheer delight. Again he circled and swirled, until he sensed she teetered on the very edge, before he eased between her legs and sank into her.

She fisted around him, hot and slick and tight. He fought for control and a modicum of finesse, while instinct rode him, slashed through him, inciting him to take her hard and fast. To mate. To storm her defenses and shatter them once and for all. But he couldn't hurt her like that. She deserved better. Slowly, ever so slowly, he pressed inward. If she hadn't told him of her previous lover, he'd have sworn she'd come to him untouched.

"Am I hurting you?" The guttural tone of his voice shocked him. He could hear the raw, feral quality of a man teetering on the edge. "Do you want me to stop?"

"No. I need . . ." A rosy flush of want rode her cheekbones, and her expression in the moonlight revealed a vulnerability to him and him alone. She twined her arms and legs around him, her fingernails digging into his back. "More, please."

He didn't require any further encouragement. He drove home with a single powerful thrust. Her cry of astonished delight was everything he could have asked for and then some. She moved with him, finding the rhythm with impressive speed, riding the ferocity of the storm with him. He slid his hands beneath her, cupped her bottom and angled her in order to give her the most pleasure.

The storm intensified, howling through him with each stroke. Rational thought fled before a single inescapable imperative. *Take the woman.* Make her his. Put an indelible stamp on her, one that would bind them together from now through all eternity. She belonged to him now, just as he belonged to her. There was no changing that fact. No going back.

The storm reached its zenith, tearing at him, threatening to rip him apart. Even in the midst of the insanity, even at his most frantic, he remained focused on Francesca. Her needs. Her desires. She anchored him, even as she drove him onward, giving and gifting and surrendering. Her unique feminine perfume, the scent of passion, filled his nostrils. He could feel her approaching her climax and sealed her mouth with his. She arched upward as it hit, and he drank in her cry of ecstasy as though it were the sweetest of wines.

It was his turn after that, his release unlike any he'd ever experienced before. She'd done that to him. For him. With him. She'd marked him in some ineradicable fashion. Given him something uniquely hers to give, something he'd never known with any other woman.

"Oh, my," she murmured long afterward, the breath still hitching from her lungs. "That was . . . unexpected."

"Very." As unexpected as it was unforgettable.

Struggling to catch his own breath, he gathered her up and rolled with her to take the weight from her and transfer it to him. She curled close with a unique feline grace, entangling their limbs into an inescapable knot, part feminine silk, part masculine sinew. Full, round curves cushioned hard angles. With the sweet, gusty sigh of a woman well-satisfied, sleep claimed her.

He lay awake for a long time, holding her close. His palm still itched and burned from that first contact and he longed to rub it. He resisted, not wanting to disturb Francesca's slumber.

Their joining should have fulfilled him, satiated whatever fever fired his blood and drove him to make this woman his. It hadn't. Not by a long shot. It should be over now, the flame diminished to a mere flicker. It wasn't. It continued to roar like wildfire driven before a gale. Instead of ending things, their lovemaking had rooted the bond between them, weaving the fabric of their connection into a tight, inseparable warp and weft.

Whether she knew it yet or not, this night had made her his.

Francesca stirred beneath the benevolent rays of the early morning sunshine.

Lord, she felt incredible. Warm. Relaxed. Happy. She didn't know what had caused such an amazing sensation, but considering how fleeting such feelings could be, she didn't want to move in case it went away.

A heavy masculine hand skated down the length of her spine to cup her bottom, giving it a loving pat. "Mmm. Nice."

What the hell? Francesca's eyes flew open and she stared in horror at the gorgeous male relaxing inches from her nose. Sunlight marched boldly across the bed and openly caressed a man whose bone structure managed to combine both a masculine hardness and a mouth-watering allure. Thick, ebony hair framed high, sweeping cheekbones and an aristocratic nose. He smiled drowsily, his wide sensuous lips stirring images of all the places that mouth had been. Memory crashed down on her, overwhelming in its intensity.

What had she done? A better question might have been, what *hadn't* she done? In the brief time they'd spent together, they'd made love in every conceivable fashion. Of course, she'd reveled in every minute. Sev had proven an outstanding lover. But the romantic illusion cast by the glittering evening had faded beneath the harsh reality of morning light. She'd had a job to do last night at Le Premier, and instead she'd—

Francesca bolted upright in bed in a flat-out panic. *Her job!* Oh, damn. Damn, damn, *damn!* What had she done? How could she have been so foolish? The Fontaines were going to kill her when she arrived at the office. She scrubbed the heels of her hands across her face.

This was not good. What in the world would she say to them? How could she possibly explain what she'd chosen to do instead of representing Timeless Heirlooms at last night's showing? She needed to get home immediately and call them. But first, she needed to return the jewelry she'd worn last night before Tina went into total meltdown. Assuming she hadn't already.

Francesca thrust a tangle of curls from her face and looked desperately around for a clock, hyperventilating when she read the glowing digits that warned she had precisely half an hour to get to Timeless Heirlooms and explain herself to the Fontaines.

"Where are you going?" Sev asked in a sleep-roughened voice. He snagged her around the waist and tipped her back into his embrace. "I have the perfect way to start our morning." A slow smile built across his face. "Funny thing. It involves staying right here."

She wriggled against him. "No. Please let go. You don't understand."

"Mmm." He reacted to her movements in a way she'd have delighted in only hours before. "That feels good."

"I have to get to work."

His hold tightened, locking them together from abdomen to thigh. Heat exploded, and even knowing she may have destroyed her career thanks to one night of stupidity, desire awoke with a renewed ferocity that left her stunned. How was this possible? She squeezed her eyes shut. Why, oh why, did this temptation have to hit last night of all nights? And why hadn't their time together satisfied the unrelenting hunger that accompanied it?

Well, she knew one thing for certain. If she hesitated even one more second, she wouldn't get out of this bed anytime soon. Taking a deep breath, she planted both hands against his chest— Lord help her, what a chest—and shoved. To her surprise, she succeeded in freeing herself. One minute she lay cocooned in warmth and the next she stood beside the bed, naked, cold, and vaguely self-conscious. Sev lifted onto an elbow and studied her through narrowed, watchful eyes. Tension rippled through him, and a hint of something dangerous and predatory lurked in his expression.

"I have to get to work," she explained. "Assuming, after last night, I still have a job. I made a huge mistake leaving with you."

His tension increased ever so slightly, and he continued to remind her of a watchful panther debating whether or not to take down his prey. "Which was your mistake? Leaving with me?" He tilted his head to one side. "Or leaving with a couple mil worth of the Fontaines' jewelry? I suspect both the Fontaines, as well as your agency, won't be too pleased. If you'd like, I can place a couple of calls and get you off the hook."

Francesca frowned in confusion. "What agency?" she asked, before waving that aside. "Oh, never mind. More to the point, where's the jewelry?"

Sev gestured toward the diamond-and-amethyst pieces glittering on the bedside table. "Relax. Everything's safe and sound, and more importantly, undamaged."

"Thank God."

She scooped up the set with exquisite care. Since she didn't have the jewelry cases on her, she could only think of one safe place to put them, and swiftly fastened the pieces to her neck, wrist, and ears. It wasn't until she finished that she sensed Sev's gaze on her. His hungry look deepened and made her acutely aware that she stood before him wearing nothing but the designs she'd created. Tension filled the room, heating the air between them.

Her job! How could she have forgotten *again?* The thought propelled her to action. She caught a glimpse of lilac panties peeking from beneath the pleated edge of the dust ruffle and snatched them up before exiting the bedroom. To her dismay Sev followed right behind, wearing even less than she.

The instant they hit the living room, Sev's cell phone emitted a faint buzz from the direction of the coffee table. This time he picked it up and answered it. "What?" His gaze flickered in her direction. "Say that name again? You're certain?"

She spared him a swift glance, concerned by the sudden grimness lining his face. "What? What's wrong?"

He closed his phone with a snap and came after her. "Who are you?" he demanded.

She stepped into her panties and looked around for her dress. "I already told you. Francesca Sommers." She spotted her dress heaped in a silken pool a few feet shy of the couch. A vague memory of Sev's tossing it toward the cushioned back came to her. Clearly, he'd missed.

Before she could snatch it up, Sev caught her arm and spun her to face him. "You're not a model. You're Timeless Heirlooms' new designer."

His statement sounded more like an accusation. She carefully disengaged her arm from his grasp and bent to pick up her dress. It was ridiculous to feel self-conscious after the night they'd spent together. But something about the way Sev stared at her caused her to hold the gown tight against her breasts. "I never claimed to be a model. You must have jumped to that conclusion." She frowned. "What difference does it make, anyway?"

"Did the Fontaines put you up to this? Is that why you followed me onto the balcony last night?" The questions came at her, fast and sharp.

She stared at him in utter bewilderment, combined with a bubble of irritation. "I have no idea what you're talking about. All I know is that if I don't report in to work within the next twenty minutes, I won't have a job. Now, do you mind? I'd like to—"

He cut her off with a sweep of his hand. "I'm talking about a TH employee falling into bed with one of the owners of Dantes five minutes after meeting. I'm talking about you using the oldest trick in the book to gain inside information for the Fontaines."

She jerked backward as though slapped. "Dantes? You work for Dantes?"

"Sweetheart, I *own* Dantes."

The connection hit and hit hard. Her dress slipped from between fingers that had gone abruptly boneless. "You're a Dante?"

"Severo Dante. CEO and chairman of the board of Dantes."

"Oh, God." She was so fired. "I thought you were a buyer." She managed to add two and two, despite working with only half a brain. "You were at the showing last night to scope out the competition, weren't you?"

He looked around. Finding his trousers between the living room and the bedroom, he snatched them up and yanked them on. The man who stood before her now bore little resemblance to the one who'd made such passionate love to her only hours before. With the exception of the unbuttoned trousers riding low on his hips, he wore nothing but an endless expanse of bare flesh.

Desire still hummed between them, calling to her with even more strength and power than the night before. And she might have answered that call, too, if he hadn't used that one word, that single, appalling word—*Dantes*—that had her itching to run in the opposite direction as fast as her wobbly legs would take her.

She wriggled back into the dress she'd chosen with such care for her first showing. She didn't bother trying to hand-press the wrinkles. Nothing would salvage this mess other than a trip to the dry cleaner's. But at least now she could face him on an even footing, or at least on a somewhat even footing.

She planted her hands on her hips. "Okay, let's have this out. You think I came on to you last night so I could find out your plans in regard to TH?" she demanded. At his nod, she glared at him. "How about the possibility of your coming on to me so you could get the inside scoop on TH's plans? After all, you're trying to buy out the Fontaines, aren't you?"

He studied her for a long silent moment. "It would seem we have a problem."

"Oh, no, we don't." She found her shoes kicked under the wet bar and shoved her feet into the spiked heels. At the same time, she thrust her fingers through her hair in an attempt to restore order to utter disaster. "It's very simple from here on out. We avoid each other at all costs and we don't mention last night to anyone. *Anyone,*" she stressed. "If I'd known who you were last night, I'd never have taken off with you."

"Liar."

She closed her eyes, forcing herself to admit the painful truth. "Fine. That's a lie. But I wouldn't have gone with you because you're Severo Dante. It would have been despite that fact." She opened her eyes and fought to keep her gaze level and not betray the profound effect he had on her. "I owe the Fontaines more than I can possibly repay. Betraying them with their chief competitor isn't the sort of repayment I had in mind. So, from now on, we're through. Got it?"

He came for her again, closing the distance so that no more than a whisper of space separated them. It would have been so easy to push aside that cushion of air and take another delicious tumble into insanity. Just the mere thought had her body reacting, softening and loosening in anticipation. He was a Dante, she struggled to remind herself. She hadn't realized that fact before, and therefore couldn't blame herself for what happened the previous night. But now that she did know, she had a duty to keep her distance.

He brushed aside a lock of her hair. Just that slight a touch and she came totally unraveled. "It would seem we have a problem," he repeated.

No question about that. "I've been consorting with the enemy." Still consorted. Still wanted to consort. And then consort some more.

He shook his head. "It's a hell of a lot more complicated than that. Whatever this *thing* is between us? It isn't over." He traced his hand along the curve of her cheek, leaving behind a streak of fire. "It's only just begun."

Chapter Three

Severo left Le Premier, stopping at his apartment only long enough to change, before continuing to Sausalito to confront his grandfather about the events of the previous night. He had questions, questions only his grandfather could answer.

"Primo?" he called, stepping through their front door.

Silence greeted him, which meant Nonna was out and he should continue on toward the gated garden behind his grandparents' hillside home if he wanted to find the object of his search. Sev headed for the kitchen at the rear of the house and stepped from the cool dusky interior into a sunlit explosion of scent and color.

Sure enough, he found Primo hard at work on a bed of native Californian wildflowers. Thick gray hair escaped from beneath the brim of a canvas bucket hat and surrounded a noble, craggy face. At Sev's approach, Primo rocked back onto his heels, grunting in pain from the arthritis that had begun to plague him in recent years.

Fierce golden eyes, identical to Sev's own, fixed on him. "Do me a favor." He spoke in his native tongue, his Italian seasoned with the unique flavoring of his Tuscan birthplace. "Grab one of those bags of mulch and bring it over here. My ancient bones will be forever grateful."

Sev did as ordered. Stooping, he split the bag with a pair of gardening shears and set to work beside his grandfather. Memories from his childhood hovered, other days that mirrored this one, days filled with the scent of cool, salt-laden air combined with rich loamy earth. Long, industrious moments passed before Sev spoke.

"I'm in the mood for a story, Primo."

His grandfather's thick brows lifted in surprise. "You have a particular one in mind?"

Sev spread a generous layer of mulch around a bed that combined the striking colors of golden poppies, baby blue eyes, and beach strawberries. "As a matter of fact, I do." He paused in his endeavors. "Tell me what happened when you met Nonna."

"Ah." An odd smile played across the older man's face. "Are you asking out of simple academic interest, or is there a more personal reason behind your sudden interest?"

"Tell me."

Primo released a gruff laugh at the barked demand. "So. It is personal. You have finally felt the burn, have you, *nipote?*"

Sev wiped his brow before fixing his grandfather with an uncompromising stare. "I want to know what the *hell* happened to me and how to make it stop."

"What happened is what your ancestors always called the Dante Inferno," Primo answered simply. "Some consider it a family curse. I have always considered it a family blessing."

The name teased at a far-off memory. No, not a memory. More of a childhood story, carrying a grain of truth amid the more fantastical elements. "Explain."

Primo released his breath in a deep sigh. "Come. The story sits better with a beer in one hand and a cigar in the other."

Brushing plant detritus from his slacks, he stood and led the way into the kitchen. Cool and rustic, huge flagstones decorated the kitchen floor while rough-hewn redwood beams stretched across the twelve-foot plaster ceiling. A large, scarred table, perfect for a substantially sized family, took up one end of the room, while a full complement of the latest appliances filled the other. After washing up, the two men helped themselves to bottles of homemade honey beer and took a seat at the table. Primo produced a pair of cigars. Once they were clipped and lit, he leaned back in his chair and eyed his grandson through an aromatic haze of smoke.

"I did try and warn you," he began.

"You didn't issue a warning. You told us a fairy tale when we were impressionable children. Why would we put credence in something so implausible?"

"It was real. You just chose not to believe. Not to remember."

The quiet words held an unmistakable conviction, one that threw Sev. "So now I'm supposed to accept that you and Nonna took one look at each other and it was love at first sight? A love inspired by this . . . this *Inferno?*"

His grandfather shook his head. "No, youngling."

Youngling? At thirty-four? Sev just barely managed not to roll his eyes. "Then what happened?"

"I took one look at your grandmother and it was *lust* at first sight." He studied the burning tip of his cigar and his voice dropped to a husky whisper. "And then I touched her. That is when The Inferno struck in force. That is when the bond formed, a bond that has lasted our entire lives. Whether you are willing to believe it or not, it is a bond our family has experienced for as long as there have been Dantes."

"Lightning bolts. Love at first sight. Instant attraction." Sev shrugged. "All names for the same spice. How is our story any different from thousands of others? What makes it *The Inferno* versus the simple chemistry most lovers experience?"

Primo took his time responding. When he did, he came at his answer from a tangent. "Your grandmother belonged to another man. Did you know that?" Bittersweet memories stirred in his distinctive eyes. "She was engaged to him."

Aw, hell. "Not good."

"Now that is an understatement if ever I heard one," Primo said dryly, stabbing the tip of his cigar in Sev's direction. The ring drifted between them like the period to an exclamation point. Sev clenched his hand. Or like the ring of itchy fire centered in his palm. "You need to understand that all those years ago an engagement was as much a commitment as marriage vows, at least in our little village. So, we fled the country and came here."

"Have you ever regretted it?" Sev asked gently.

Primo's expression turned fierce, emphasizing the contours of his strong Roman nose and squared jawline. "Never. My only regret is the pain I caused this other man." His mouth compressed and he lifted his beer for a long swallow. "He was *mio amico*. No, not just my friend. My *best* friend. But once The Inferno strikes . . ." He gave the sort of shrug only a true Italian could pull off. "There is nothing that can stop it. Nothing that can come between those who have known the burn. Nothing to douse the insanity but to make that woman yours and keep her by your side while The Inferno burns evermore, never to ebb or douse. She is your soul mate. Your other half. To deny it will bring you nothing but grief, as your father discovered to his great misfortune."

Sev wanted to refute his grandfather's words, to dismiss them as an aging man's fantasy. But he hesitated, reluctant to say anything now that Primo had mentioned Sev's father. And one other fact held him silent. Everything Primo said precisely matched his reactions last night, which created a serious dilemma for him. He had plans for Francesca, plans other than taking her to bed. To restore Dantes to its former glory, he had no choice but to steal her away from the Fontaines.

"When you first saw Nonna—before you touched—what was it like?"

Primo hesitated as he considered and dug bony fingers into his right hand, massaging the palm. Over the years Sev had witnessed the habitual gesture more times than he could count, long ago assuming it resulted from arthritis or some other physical complaint. Now he knew better. Worse, he'd caught himself imitating the movement over the past few hours. Even now he could barely suppress the urge.

A far away expression entered Primo's ancient gaze. "I had been away at university and returned for *mio amico's* engagement party. I cut through a meadow on my way home and there she was, gathering wildflowers."

The mention of wildflowers made Sev think of Primo's garden. As long as he could recall it had overflowed with local flora. "That must have been a sight."

"You have no idea, boy." The long-ago memory dampened his eyes and his voice grew rough with longing. "She crouched beneath an orange tree in full blossom, singing beneath her breath, her hands like little, graceful hummingbirds darting among purple hyacinth and daises and brilliant, red poppies." He moved his own gnarled hands in slow, clumsy imitation. "So young. So young and innocent I thought God would stop the beat of my heart for daring to gaze upon such beauty and virtue."

Sev could see the image as though it moved before him. "Then what?" he demanded.

"The wind whispered to her, sending a shower of orange blossoms raining down on brown ringlets that tumbled all the way to her hips. She wore a thin cotton dress and the afternoon sun shot it full of golden rays, outlining—" Primo broke off abruptly and glared at his grandson. "Never you mind what it outlined, *nipote*. Suffice to say, the minute I set eyes on Nonna, it was as though we were connected. As though a ribbon of desire joined us. The closer we came, the stronger it grew. When we touched, the ribbon became stronger than a steel cable, binding us together so we could no longer distinguish my heartbeat from hers. We have beat as one ever since."

The story affected Sev more than he cared to admit, probably because it rang with such love and adoration and simple sincerity. True or not, Primo clearly believed every word. Not that the origins of his grandparents' romance helped with his current predicament. Okay, so he'd felt that connection, the shock and burn when they'd touched, that ribbon of lust, as he preferred to consider it. But ribbons could be cut.

"How do I get rid of it?" he demanded.

Primo drank down the last of his beer before setting the empty bottle on the table with enough power that the glass rang in protest. "You do not," he stated unequivocally. "Why would you want to?"

"Because she's the wrong woman for me. There are . . . complications."

Primo released a full-bodied laugh. "More complicated than her belonging to your best friend?" He swept his hand through the air, the gesture leaving behind a smoky contrail. "It is impossible to cut the connection. The Inferno has no respect for time or place or complication. It knows. It chooses. And it has done so for as long as there have been Dantes. You either accept the gift and revel in the blessing it offers, or you walk away and suffer the consequences."

Sev stilled. "What consequences?"

"You ignore The Inferno at your own peril, nipote." He leaned forward, each word stone-hard. "If you turn your back on it, you will never know true happiness. Look at what happened to your father."

"You think The Inferno killed him?" Sev demanded on a challenging note. "Are you that superstitious?"

Primo's expression softened. "No, it didn't kill Dominic. But because he chose with his head instead of his heart, because he married your mother instead of the woman chosen for him by The Inferno, he never found true happiness. And both our business and our family suffered as a result." He took a slow drag of his cigar, the tip flaming with an unholy red glow. "I am warning you, Severo Dante. If you follow in your father's footsteps you, too, will know only the curse, never the blessing."

Tina Fontaine threw herself into a chair near where Francesca sat at her drawing board, while Kurt filled the doorway leading into the small office. One look at their expressions warned Francesca that her previous night's indiscretion had left her career teetering on a knife's edge.

"You owe my dear husband a huge thank you for stopping me from calling the police last night," came Tina's opening volley.

Francesca stared in horror. "The police?"

Tina leaned forward, not bothering to disguise her fury. "It was your big night. And you disappeared with a bloody fortune in gems around your neck without bothering to tell anyone where you'd gone. What did you expect me to do?"

Francesca clasped her shaking hands together. "I'm sorry. Truly. I have no idea what came over me."

The ring of truth in Francesca's comment gave Tina pause. "Where the hell did you go?"

"I think I can guess," Kurt inserted. "Holed up somewhere clutching a wastebasket, were you?"

Francesca stared at him, utterly miserable. She didn't have any choice. She couldn't lie. She had to admit the truth and take whatever punishment they chose to dole out, even if it meant the end of her career at TH. "Not exactly. I—"

From behind Tina's back, Kurt gave a warning shake of his head. "But you were suffering from a severe case of nerves, I assume?" Before Francesca could reply, he continued, "It's the one excuse Tina can sympathize with, can't you, darling? It happened to her on the night of her first show, too."

Tina gave an irritable shrug. "Yes, fine. It happened to me when we opened our first jewelry store in Mendocino. Too many nerves, too much champagne, and too little intestinal fortitude." She shot Francesca an annoyed look. "Is that what happened?"

Francesca hesitated, before nodding despite nearly overwhelming guilt. "I'm so sorry. The crowd got to me and I decided to leave early." She kept her gaze fixed on Tina, but caught Kurt's small look of approval. "I promise it won't happen again."

"I suggest it doesn't. Next time I'll fire you." Tina continued to stare with uncomfortable intensity. "How in the world did you evade security? I need to know so in future our designers and models can't pull a similar stunt."

Francesca kept her gaze fixed on her drawing table. "There's an exit off the balcony," she whispered. "One of the guests escorted me."

"Go on."

Francesca swallowed. "As for the jewelry, I can't tell you how sorry I am that I worried you. I swear I kept it safe." Or rather Sev had. She'd been too far gone by that time to give a single thought to what damage their lovemaking might do to the delicate pieces.

"That's the only thing that saved your job," Tina said sternly. "If anything had happened to the jewelry, you'd be cooling your heels in jail."

Tina's assistant appeared before she could say anything further and leaned into the room around Kurt. "Call for you," she informed her boss. "It's Juliet Bloom's rep."

Tina came off the chair as though catapulted and flew toward the door. She paused at the last instant. "Fair warning, Francesca." She threw the admonition over her shoulder. "The rep wasn't happy when I couldn't produce you last night. If she's calling to blow off our deal because you were incapable of doing your job, you're gone."

Francesca fought to draw breath, seeing her career vanish before her eyes thanks to one night of utter foolishness. "I understand."

"And there's a call for you on line three, Francesca," the assistant added, with a hint of sympathy.

"Excuse me for a minute," she murmured to Kurt. She picked up the phone, not in the least surprised to hear Severo Dante's voice respond to her greeting. "How may I help you?" she asked in as businesslike a tone as she could manage.

"Huh." He paused as though giving it serious thought. "I'm not quite sure how to answer that. Most of the possibilities that come to mind would be interesting variations on last night's theme."

She didn't dare respond to the comment. She'd risked quite enough already, thanks to Sev. "I'm really busy right now. Could I get back to you in regard to that?"

"In regard to that, you can get back to me anytime you want. But I'm calling for a different reason, altogether. I want you to meet me for lunch at Fruits de Mer at one."

She spared Kurt a brief, uncomfortable glance. "That's not even remotely possible."

"In hot water, are you?"

"Yes."

"Then let's make it tomorrow."

"I'm sorry, that's quite impossible."

"Make it possible or I'll come by the office and let you explain my presence to the Fontaines. Or better yet, I'll explain everything to them. Personally."

Oh, God. If he did that, she'd be fired for sure. Painfully aware of her father listening in, she chose her words with care. "You are *such* a *gentleman.*" Let him read between those lines, or rather, lies.

He chuckled. "You're not alone, are you?" At her pointed silence, he added, "I'm serious. We need to talk. Will you come tomorrow?"

"It would seem I have no other choice. Now, I really have to go." She ended the conversation by returning the receiver to its cradle. "I'm sorry about that, Kurt."

He regarded her far too acutely. "I assume that was your young man from last night?" He held up a hand before she could reply. "I caught a glimpse of you and your mysterious friend leaving together."

Francesca stiffened in alarm. Had he recognized Sev? No, he couldn't have or he wouldn't be acting so understanding. "And that didn't worry you?" she asked hesitantly.

"Not when I consider some of the antics Tina and I got up to when we were first dating. I do, however, recommend in the future that you don't mix business with pleasure."

Embarrassed color warmed Francesca's cheeks. "I hope you know that I don't usually . . . I'm not—"

He waved that aside, but not before she saw his cheeks turn a ruddier shade than normal. "I helped you out of a tight spot this time because, quite frankly, we need you and what you can do for Timeless Heirlooms. But I won't bail you out again."

"I understand." It killed her to be having this conversation with her father. More than anything she hoped to win both his approval, as well as his friendship. Instead, he'd helped her lie to his wife and put their relationship at odds. "As I told Tina, it won't happen again."

"Listen to me, Francesca." He took the chair Tina had vacated. "Your six-month contract with Timeless Heirlooms is almost up. Tina and I are both very excited with what we've seen from you so far. Equally as important, we've enjoyed working with you."

She smiled in genuine pleasure. Receiving such a huge compliment from her father meant the world to her. "Thank you. I've enjoyed working with you, as well."

How could she not? She was living the dream of a lifetime, one she wanted more than anything. Thanks to the detective she'd hired, she'd been able to track down her father the minute she'd graduated from college and approach him without anyone being the wiser. To her delight, she discovered that he shared her passion. Even more incredible, the company he and Tina ran were actively hiring designers, if only on a trial basis.

"Tina and I were on the verge of making your position here permanent. But after last night, we simply can't take the risk. Not yet. You understand our predicament, don't you?"

Her smile died. In the past six months she'd struggled to prove herself as both a top-notch designer, as well as a woman he'd be proud to claim as his daughter. It had all gone so well. Until last night. And now she'd ruined everything.

"I do understand," she managed to say. "Kurt, I can't thank you and Tina enough for giving me this opportunity. I swear I'll make it up to you."

"I don't doubt that." He offered her a slow, generous smile, one that never failed to fill Francesca with an intense longing. He stood and held out his hand. "We'll give it another couple months. Maybe once we have Juliet Bloom under contract, we'll feel more comfortable offering you a permanent position with us."

Francesca slipped her hand into his bearlike grasp, fighting back tears. Determination filled her. It didn't matter what it took, she'd find a way to win his approval, as well as a permanent job at Timeless Heirlooms. If that meant avoiding Sev—well, after the lunch he'd forced on her—then that's what she'd do. Because nothing was more important than having the opportunity to get to know her father, even if she could never tell him the truth about their relationship.

"Thank you for offering me another chance," she said with as much composure as she could manage. "You won't regret it."

"All right," Francesca stated the minute she joined Sev at Fruits de Mer. She took the seat across from him and folded her arms across her chest. "You blackmailed me into coming here. What do you want?"

Sev studied her silently for a long moment. If he could peg her with a single word it would be defensive. From the moment she'd stepped foot in the restaurant and spotted him, she'd had trouble meeting his gaze. He could guess why. He'd seen this woman naked. Had taken her in his arms and made love to her, not once or twice, but three times during their night together, each occasion more passionate than the last. It should have ensured an ease between them. And maybe it would have, except for one vital detail.

Forty-eight hours ago they'd been total strangers.

And yet, nothing had changed. No. That wasn't true. If anything, the attraction between them had grown, become more palpable. He could see the hunger and desire lurking in the depths of her gaze, unwanted as it was undeniable. Her pulse throbbed in her throat and a heated flush touched her cheeks. Most damning of all, her body reacted to his presence. A heated flush touched her cheeks and her pulse throbbed in her throat. His gaze dipped downward briefly, not surprised to see the hard peak of her nipples against the thin silk of her blouse.

"You expected things to be different," he said. "Didn't you?"

She looked at him, the unremitting darkness of her eyes making a startling contrast to her pale complexion and honey-blond hair. "Today, you mean?" She gave him her full attention, a painful vulnerability lurking in her gaze. "Let's just say I'd hoped things would be different."

She'd changed toward him since their night together and he could guess the reason. Now that she'd discovered his identity, she'd decided to end things between them, something he refused to allow. "You hoped our reaction to each other would change now that you know who I am. Because you work for Timeless Heirlooms and I own Dantes, you thought that fact would put a stop to what we're experiencing."

"Yes." A slight frown creased her brow. With a swift glance toward nearby tables, she dropped her voice to a whisper. "I need to explain something. I don't know who that woman was two nights ago. I've never—" She took a deep breath. "I'm not making excuses."

"Of course not." He understood all too well. "But that doesn't alter the facts."

She retreated from him, icing over tension and longing with such speed he suspected she'd had many years of practice. "As far as I'm concerned, whatever happened between us has run its course."

He tilted his head to one side. "Because you say so? Because it would be so much more convenient on the work front?" He couldn't help laughing. "You're kidding, right? This isn't something you can cut off like a light switch."

"I think it is."

He studied her for a moment to assess her veracity. Satisfied she actually believed the nonsense she trotted out, he placed his hands flat on the table. He slid them across the linen-covered surface, inch by inch. When his hands came to within a foot of hers, she released a soft groan.

"Okay," she said, snatching her hands back. "Point made. Maybe this . . . this—"

"Attraction? Desire?" He lifted an eyebrow. "Lust?"

She waved the choices aside. "Those are just varying shades of the same thing."

"And you're still experiencing each of those shades, as well as every single one in between."

He caught the faint breathy sound of air escaping her lungs. "Whatever this is hasn't run its course at all, has it?" she asked.

"Not even a little." He massaged the tingle in his right palm. "I could feel you, you know."

Her brows shot up. "Feel me? What do you mean?"

"When you walked in the room, I didn't even have to see you," he admitted. "I could feel you."

Her brow wrinkled in confusion. "I don't understand any of this," she confessed. "How is that possible?"

He didn't answer. Couldn't answer. "Is it the same for you? Has it eased off any since that night?"

She wanted to lie, he could read it in the hint of desperation in those huge, defenseless eyes. "Maybe it has." She moistened her lips. "I'm sure it's not quite as bad as the other night. It can't be."

"There's an easy way to tell." He extended his hand across the table once again. "Go ahead. Touch me."

Francesca hesitated for a telling moment before splaying her fingers and linking them with Sev's. She gasped at the contact, going rigid with shock. The next instant everything about her softened and relaxed, sinking into what he could only describe as euphoria. Then the next wave hit. A hot tide of need lapped between them, singeing nerve endings and escalating desire.

"I want you again." He told her precisely how much with a single scorching look. "If anything, I want you even more than last time."

"We can't do this. Not again," Francesca protested. "I've already put my job in jeopardy by spending the night with you. If the Fontaines find out it was you at the show, that you were the reason I left, they'd fire me on the spot. I won't risk that. Working at TH is too important to me."

Didn't she get it? "You want me to stop?" He lifted their joined hands. "Tell me how. Because I'd love to know."

She leaned forward, speaking in a low, rapid voice. "What I want is an explanation. Maybe if I understood how and why, I could make it stop. Why do I feel such an odd sensation every time we join hands? Why does just a touch cause me to go all wonky inside?"

His mouth twitched toward a smile. "Wonky?"

She squeezed her eyes shut. "Hungry. Lusty. Horny as hell. God, I can't even believe I'm saying those things!"

He hesitated, loath to repeat the story Primo had told him. But she deserved some sort of answer, even one as far-fetched as The Inferno. He didn't believe they were experiencing anything to do with something so fantastical. Or that his grandfather's Inferno fairy tale belonged just there, in fairy tales. None of that mattered. Regardless of what he thought, she should know.

He forced himself to release her hands, despite an almost uncontrollable urge to sweep her up in his arms and bolt from the restaurant with her. More than anything he wanted to hole up somewhere with acres of bed, twenty-four-hour room service, and a suitcase full of condoms.

"Look, I think I can explain this, though the explanation is going to sound a bit crazy." Nor was this the venue he'd have chosen to tell a woman about The Inferno. But at least a crowded restaurant would give the illusion of safety once she'd fully ascertained the extent of his family's insanity. He gave it to her straight. "There's a Dante legend that my grandfather swears is true, about an Inferno that occurs when a man from my family touches the woman meant to be his."

Her eyes narrowed, but at least she didn't run screaming from the restaurant. "Somehow I don't think this is the sort of story we should hash out in public. Do you?"

"Not even a little. My place isn't far from here. We can talk there, if you'd prefer."

"Talk?" A swift laugh bubbled free and she regarded him with wry amusement. "That would make a nice change. I don't suppose you can promise that's all we're going to do?"

He shook his head. "I can't promise a thing where you're concerned." He leaned back, giving her enough room to breathe. Hell, giving them both enough room to think straight. "But I swear, I'll try. Will you trust me enough to come with me?"

She turned those bottomless dark eyes on him in silent assessment. He'd never met a woman quite so fascinating. She faced the world with elegance and strength and feminine dignity. And though he sensed they were integral parts of her, he also suspected they were a shield she used to protect herself from hurt.

Every so often he caught a glimpse of a waif peeking out, nose pressed to the glass, the want in her so huge and deep it amazed him that one person could contain it all. And yet, he also saw the steely determination that carried her through a life that—if he correctly read all she struggled to conceal—had slammed her with hardship while offering little joy to compensate.

After giving his offer a moment's thought, she nodded. "I promised to meet you this one last time before we parted company, and I will. Besides, I always did like fairy tales even though they never come true." A tragic smile played about her perfect bow mouth, tempting him beyond measure. Then she surprised him by lifting a hand and signaling the waiter. "But who knows. Maybe this one will be different."

Chapter Four

Ten short minutes later they arrived at his Pacific Heights Georgian residence. "This is your home?" Francesca asked, clearly stunned.

He could tell the size and grandeur unnerved her. Hell, as a child it had unnerved him, as well. Built in the 1920s, his grandparents purchased it during Dantes' heyday, when Primo controlled the reins of the company.

Sev had recently updated the house from top to bottom, taking a diamond in the rough and giving it the glitter and polish it deserved. While still on the formal side, he'd made a point to add a more welcoming feel to the place. From the two-story entry foyer, a curving staircase, complete with wrought-iron railing, swept toward the second story and an endless array of rooms perfect for entertaining.

"When I'm hosting guests, I stay here. More often I use my Nob Hill apartment. It's more compact. More to my taste." Unable to resist touching her, he slid his hand down her spine to the small hollow just above her buttocks and guided her toward the private den he kept exclusively for his own use. "This is my favorite room in the house."

Francesca visibly relaxed as she looked around. Light filtered in from a bank of windows that provided an unfettered view of the bay and Alcatraz Island. Two of the other walls bulged with books that overran the floor-to-ceiling mahogany cases. The final wall, at right angles to the windows, offered a cozy fireplace fronted by the most comfortable couch Sev had ever owned. He used the electronic controls to light the fire and gestured for her to have a seat.

It amused him that she took the precaution to sit as far from him as the couch cushions allowed. Understandable, but still humorous. "Okay, let me give it to you straight," he began.

She listened intently while he ran through Primo's explanation of The Inferno, refraining from asking any questions until he finished speaking. "You said that, in the past, your family experienced this Inferno," she said after a moment. "What about your brothers? Have they felt anything similar?"

"I'm the first," Sev replied.

Wariness crept into her gaze. "That suggests you buy in to all this."

"No, not really." And he didn't, despite Primo's insistence that legend matched reality. "I think it makes for a charming story, but a story, nonetheless."

"Then how would you explain what's happened to us?"

He'd given that a lot of thought and decided to believe the simplest explanation. "It's nothing more than lust. Given time, it'll fade."

Though she took his comment with apparent equanimity, a pulse kicked to life at the base of her throat, betraying her agitation. "But what if it's more than that? Has it ever infected the women in your family?"

"I don't understand. Which women?"

She made an impatient motion with her hands. "Haven't any of the Dante men had daughters? Have any of the Dante women experienced this Inferno?"

Sev shook his head. "There's only been one daughter in more generations than I can recall. My cousin, Gianna. Here, let me show you."

He circled the couch to a cluster of photos on a console table and picked up a panoramic photograph in a plain silver frame that showed a group shot of all the Dantes. Seated in the middle were

Nonna and Primo. Sev, his parents, and brothers stood to Primo's right, while his Aunt Elia, and Uncle Alessandro, with their brood of four, stood beside Nonna. He handed the picture to Francesca when she joined him, tapping the image of the only female of his generation, a striking young woman with Sev's coloring.

"If Gia's been cursed by The Inferno, she's never mentioned it."

A hint of laughter lightened Francesca's expression. "Cursed? I thought you said Primo called it a blessing."

He couldn't help himself. He leaned toward her, cupping her cheek. "Does it feel like a blessing to you?"

She shut him out by closing her eyes, concealing her inner thoughts. "No, this isn't a blessing. It's a complication I could live without." She eased back from his touch and opened her eyes again, at the same time slamming impenetrable barriers into place. "And what about the other women? The women who are the object of the Dante men's . . . blessing?"

"Like you and Nonna and Aunt Elia?"

"Yes. What choice do we have? How do we escape this Inferno?"

He gestured toward the image of his parents. "My father escaped by marrying someone else."

Francesca blinked in surprise. "Your mother wasn't an Inferno bride?"

Sev shook his head. "Shortly after they died, I discovered letters that indicated he'd been in love with one of his designers, but married my mother, instead."

"Why didn't he marry the woman he really loved?" she asked hesitantly. "Do you know?"

Sev shrugged. "When I confronted Primo about it, he admitted that my mother had invaluable contacts in the industry. It was more of a business arrangement than a true marriage. Not that it did either of them any good."

"What went wrong?"

Maybe it was the hint of compassion he heard in her voice, but he found himself opening up in way he never had with any other woman. "All of my mother's contacts couldn't make up for my father's lack of business savvy." He studied the photograph. God, they looked so youthful. Just six or seven years older than his own thirty-four, he suddenly realized. They also looked remote and unhappy, though how much of that related to their marriage and how much to business difficulties, he couldn't determine. "They were on the verge of a divorce when they died in a sailing accident."

"And you blame that on The Inferno?" she asked in patent disbelief.

"No. I blame it on bad luck." He couldn't tell her the rest. Couldn't admit that he blamed himself for what happened right before and immediately after his father's death. That piece of guilt he kept locked tightly away. "I'd just graduated from college. The day after their funeral, I stepped into my father's shoes. I spent the first year of my tenure dismantling Dantes and the last decade rebuilding it."

"I'm so sorry." She slipped her hand into his and squeezed. Just that, and yet it made all the difference. The connection between them intensified in some indefinable way. Before it had been sheer sex, or so he believed. Now another emotion crept in, one he resisted analyzing. She hesitated a split second before confessing, "I lost my mother, too. I know how painful that must have been for you."

That might explain some of the sorrow he'd seen lurking in her eyes. "How old were you?" he asked.

"Five." Soft. Abrupt. And a clear message that she had no interest in pursuing the conversation.

Not that he planned to drop it. He'd just approach the subject with more care. "It helped that my brothers and I were older, though at just sixteen, Nicolò had a tough time adapting. Fortunately, Primo and Nonna stepped in, which made a huge difference." He paused. "What about you? Did your father ever remarry?"

"My parents weren't together," she admitted, avoiding his gaze. "I went into foster care."

Oh, God. He tiptoed across eggshells. "Didn't the authorities contact him?"

"They didn't know who he was. I didn't find out myself until after I'd graduated from college and hired someone to locate him for me." She picked up the next picture in the line, putting a clear end to the discussion. A slight smile eased the strain building around the corners of her mouth. "Primo and Nonna on their wedding day, I assume?"

"They eloped right before immigrating to the U.S."

The ancient black-and-white showed a couple arrayed in wedding finery. They looked impossibly young and nervous, their hands joined in a white-knuckle grip. But the photographer managed to catch them in an unguarded moment, as they gathered themselves for a more formal pose. They glanced at each other, as though for reassurance, and the power of their love practically scorched the film.

"Nonna didn't want to escape The Inferno, did she?"

"No."

Francesca returned the photograph to the table with clear finality. "Well, I do." She paced restlessly toward the windows. Once there, she glanced over her shoulder. With the sunlight at her back, her expression fell into shadow. But he could hear the tension rippling through her voice. "I'm not interested in you or the Dante Inferno or having an affair with you. I just want to be left alone to pursue my career. This is a distraction I don't want or need."

"I wish it were that simple. That I could make it go away for you. But I can't."

He wanted to see her, to look into her eyes and know her thoughts. To touch her and reestablish the physical connection between them. Without conscious thought, he joined her at the windows. The instant he slid his palm across her warm, silken skin, his world righted itself.

"Why can't I just walk away from you and never look back?" she demanded. He heard the turmoil underscoring her question, while hunger battled common sense. And he understood what she felt since it mirrored his own reaction to their predicament. "Why can't I simply return to the life I built for myself?"

"You can. We both can." Steely determination enveloped him. "The minute we work this out of our systems."

Sev swept Francesca up into his arms and carried her to the couch. She murmured a token protest, one lost beneath the series of tiny, biting kisses he scattered along her throat. They tumbled onto cushions that molded to their entwined bodies and enfolded them in a private world of suede-covered down. The buttons of her silk blouse parted beneath his hands, revealing a feminine scrap of lace that struggled to contain her breasts. He couldn't help himself. He reared back, drinking in the sight.

Two nights ago, he'd seen her by moonlight and thought it impossible for her to look any more stunning than adorned in shades of silver and alabaster. But now, with her hair and skin gilded in sunlit gold, she robbed sense and sensibility with her beauty. Inch by inch, he lowered himself onto her. And inch by inch, the heat they generated soared, an inferno in the making. Given the number of promises he'd made and broken, he half expected her to push him away. Instead, she basked in that heat and wrapped him up in an ardent embrace.

It was as though they'd never left off from the night before last. He reacquainted himself with her mouth, plundering inward. She moaned in welcome and met him with a feminine aggression that sent him straight over the edge. There were too many clothes between them. He yanked at his tie and the first few buttons of his shirt, but somehow he'd lost the ability to work past the knot imprisoning him. Instead, he turned his attention to her and unhooked the front clasp of her bra. He filled his hands with her bountiful breasts and her breath escaped in a fevered rush.

"We were supposed to have worked this out of our systems by now," she gasped.

"We will." Maybe in a decade or two. "But until then I need your hands on me. I need to be inside you again."

He shifted a knee between her legs and slid the hem of her skirt upward, uncovering acres of smooth, creamy thigh and a tantalizing glimpse of butter-yellow panties. He itched to explore all that lay beneath that scrap of silk. To see those soft curls gilded with sunlight, as well. He ran a finger along the scalloped edging, stroking inward toward dewy warmth until he found the sweet heart of her.

Francesca groaned in response, a rich, feminine, keening sound that called to him on every level and drove him ever closer to the edge. He knew that sound, had heard her make it countless times during the night they'd spent together. But there was another sound he wanted to hear. Needed to hear. The sound she made when she climaxed in his arms.

She shuddered against his stroking touch and he couldn't stand it another minute. He needed her. Now. In a single swift move, he skimmed her panties down her thighs and tossed them aside. Next, he ripped his belt free and unfastened his trousers, pausing only long enough to remove the protection he'd had the foresight to stick in his pocket before their meeting. Her hands joined his, helping to free him from the restriction of his clothing. And then she cupped him, her touch cool against the burning length of him. Instead of easing the raging fire, it only served to intensify it.

He couldn't remember the last time he'd been so desperate to have a woman that he'd been unable to make it to the comfort of his bedroom. With Francesca, nothing mattered except to have her, right here and now. He lifted her and slid deep inside. Her legs closed around him as she welcomed him home.

His groan of pleasure mingled with hers, the heavy pounding of his heart in perfect tempo with hers. The breath exploded from her and then he heard her siren's song, signaling her scramble toward the highest of peaks. He joined her there, calling to her, mating with her, locking them together until he could no longer tell where her body ended and his began.

They moved in perfect harmony, continuing a dance that had begun their first night together. The tempo this time around quickened, turning fast and hard and greedy. He couldn't get enough of her, not how tightly she clenched around him or how she cushioned him against the softness of her woman's body or how she met each thrust with joyous abandon. Long before he was ready for the encounter to end, she spasmed beneath him, and he found he couldn't hold back, couldn't resist going up and over the peak with her before crashing down the other side, holding her tight within his arms.

Long minutes passed without either of them moving, maybe because movement proved a physical impossibility. Finally, the breath heaving from his lungs, Sev levered himself onto his elbows and gazed down at Francesca.

Heaven help him, but she was beautiful, her face delicately flushed with the ripeness of passion, her mouth moist and swollen from his kisses, her eyes heavy-lidded and slumberous. In that moment, his world rested within the warmth of her grasp. How had she come to mean so much to him in so short a time?

"I can't walk away from you, Francesca." Pure steel swept through the words. "And I won't."

She closed her eyes with a groan. "I shouldn't have agreed to have lunch with you. I should have known we'd end up like this again."

He caught the hint of regret and deliberately kissed it away, plying her with soft caresses and long, slow strokes until she trembled in his arms. "Something tells me we'll always end up like this."

Her eyes flew open, the sultry darkness lit with a want so deep and strong, she couldn't disguise it as anything else. "We can't. We can't do this again," she whispered through lips still red and swollen from his kisses. The scent of their passion enclosed them, belying her statement and he could feel the tension within her battling against the soft, hungry give of her body.

Sev wanted her again. Again and again and again. For the moment, he'd allow her to escape. But only for the moment. He eased himself up and off her. Holding out his hand, he assisted her from the couch and helped return a semblance of order to her clothing.

"I didn't give you a choice about lunch," he informed her. "And just so you know, I don't plan to give you a choice in the future, either."

She eyed him in open alarm, but didn't ask the question he suspected hovered on the tip of her tongue. Instead, she murmured, "Where's the bathroom?"

He directed her, then excused himself long enough to freshen up, as well. He returned to find her fully tucked and buttoned and preparing to leave. "There's something I want to ask you," he told her. "Actually, it's the reason I invited you to lunch."

A smile flirted with her mouth, a genuine one that filled him with fierce pleasure. "You mean, you didn't invite me so we could indulge in a wrestling match on your couch?"

He regarded her with a hint of laughter. "As delightful as that was, no." He crossed to her side. Unable to resist, he slipped a hand into her hair. Cupping the back of her head, he took her mouth in a swift, hungry kiss, a kiss she returned without hesitation. "Come work for me," he offered when they broke apart.

Her eyes were alight with a slumberous passion and he suspected she didn't assimilate his offer immediately. He saw the instant words connected with comprehension. The passion eked away, replaced by astonishment. "Work for you?" she repeated.

"I can offer you a far better salary than you receive at Timeless, excellent benefits, your own studio. You'll have the Dante name behind your designs." He pressed, determined she see how much more he could do for her than the Fontaines. "I can assist you become one of the most sought-after designers in the world. Best of all, we won't have to sneak around hiding our relationship from your employers."

She took a hasty step away from him, pulling free of his hold, if not the connection burning between them. It refused to release either one of them. "Let me get this straight. You're offering me a job so we can continue our affair?"

"Of course not." Honesty compelled him to admit, "Okay, fine. In part. But mostly because you're a damn good designer. Dantes would be lucky to have you."

Her eyes narrowed. "And what happens when we're no longer Infernoed?"

The word provoked a swift smile. "Infernoed?"

"Right now, the hot, southern climes of your anatomy are doing your thinking. Once that brilliant mind of yours kicks in, you'll regret any decisions you make while in the throes of this thing. And I'll have thrown away a job I love for a position at Dantes as the ex-mistress of the owner. How long do you think that'll work?"

He struggled not to take offense. Until two nights ago his southern climes had never before overruled the cooler, dispassionate northern half of his body. Yet, he suspected Francesca assumed it happened on a regular basis. It was part of the price he paid for having a Latin name. Emotion over intellect. Total nonsense, of course.

"I won't compromise the family business for anyone or anything," he stated. "My offer is genuine, Inferno or no Inferno. When our affair ends, you'll still have your job, and it'll be a hell of a lot more secure than your future at Timeless."

He could tell she didn't believe him. "Thank you, but I'm happy with the Fontaines."

"Would you at least allow me to make an official offer?"

She dismissed the idea with a swift shake of her head. "I have my reasons for staying at Timeless Heirlooms, and money isn't really one of them. I'm up for a permanent position there. In fact, I would have it already if I hadn't ruined my reputation by spending the night with you. The only saving grace is they don't know it's you."

He thought fast. "We can be discreet. They don't have to know."

She cut him off with a swift shake of her head. "Forget it. I won't make that sort of foolish mistake again or do anything to jeopardize my standing with the Fontaines. And just so we're clear? Being with you could get me fired and my job's more important than anything else." She spared a swift glance toward the couch where the cushions still showed the imprint of their entwined bodies. Still held the heat of their passion. "Even that."

"Francesca—"

She waved him silent. "Forget it, Sev. I agreed to meet with you this one last time. I think you'll agree it was a lovely way to conclude our affair. And that's all this is. A brief affair, now concluded. Now, I really need to go." She picked up her purse and slung it over her shoulder. "If I don't come back from lunch in a reasonable length of time, they'll start asking questions I can't answer."

It would be pointless to argue, he could tell. Better to find out what Nicolò and Lazz had dug up regarding the gorgeous Ms. Sommers. That way he'd be in a stronger position to formulate a new plan, one with a better chance of success. And it had to be quick, before his North surrendered to his South.

"I'll arrange for a cab," he limited himself to saying. "And I'll give you a call later this week."

She gave him a remote smile. "There's no need . . . on either count."

He watched the delicious sway of her hips as she exited the room, the view threatening to bring him to his knees. "Damn, woman," he muttered. "There's every need. And I plan to prove it to you."

But he'd better figure out how, and fast. Because if he'd learned nothing else as a result of the past few hours, he'd discovered how wrong he'd been about The Inferno and all matters related to it.

He'd been determined to woo Francesca away from the Fontaines and have her work for Dantes. To tempt her—not with sex—but with the financial advantages of working for Dantes. Or that had been his intention until he'd come face-to-face with one incontrovertible fact. A fact that sent his carefully laid plans crumbling to dust. There was no way in hell he could keep his hands off her now, or anytime in the near future. As of this minute, the plan changed.

Not only did he want to uproot her from Timeless Heirlooms so the company would be more vulnerable to a

Dantes' takeover, but he also wanted to transplant Francesca into his bed and keep her there.

At least until The Inferno burned itself out.

Chapter Five

Foolishly, Francesca assumed she'd seen the last of Sev.

The delusion lasted right up until she decided to eat lunch at her desk, ordering from her favorite deli, a place that offered fast delivery service and thick sandwiches, stuffed with every imaginable delicacy. Within thirty minutes her sandwich arrived, along with a sprig of vivid-blue forget-me-nots, their delicate scent sweetening the air in her tiny office.

"Thank you," she said to the delivery boy before burying her nose in the fragrant blossoms. "What a nice thing to do."

He eyed her speculatively. "Do I get an extra tip for bein' so nice?"

"Absolutely." She handed it over with a smile. "And thanks again."

"No sweat. The flowers weren't from me, by the way. There's a note that came with them. I stuck it in the bag with your sandwich." With a cheeky grin he darted from the office.

She couldn't help but laugh at his audacity. Then curiosity got the better of her. She opened the bag and found a business card tucked inside. She glanced at it and, to her dismay, her fingers trembled. Sure enough, the linen-colored pasteboard had Sev's name and business information typed on the front. On the back, he'd scrawled *Remember*.

Somehow, he'd figured out where she usually ordered lunch. And for some reason, she spent the rest of the day sniffing the forget-me-nots as she struggled to do as he asked and remember . . . remember that dating Sev promised a fast end to a short career. Worse, it would put an even faster end to her burgeoning relationship with her father. Her mouth firmed. She wouldn't allow anyone—not even a man as sexy as Severo Dante—to interfere with either of those two goals.

The next morning on her way to work, she swung into her favorite Starbucks, desperate for caffeine after a sleepless night of wishing she were in Sev's bed once more. To her dismay, the line stretched long and wide and she schooled herself to patience. Far ahead, toward the front, she caught a glimpse of a distinctive set of shoulders and striking ebony hair. Unbidden, her heart kicked up a notch and the air escaped her lungs in a soft rush.

It wasn't Severo Dante, she silently scolded, and constantly obsessing over him wasn't going to help matters. She refused to see Sev in every man with an impressive build and dark coloring. She needed to get a grip. Deliberately, she forced her gaze away only to catch herself peeking at him as he finished paying and turned to leave.

This time the breath exploded from her in an audible gasp as she realized it *was* Sev. He came directly toward her with the languid grace so uniquely his, carrying a pair of cappuccinos. He handed her one with a warm smile and a quiet, *"Tesoro mio,"* before continuing out the door.

"Oh, God," the woman behind her said with a groan. "Does that happen to you often?"

"No." Francesca stared at the cappuccino, then at the door through which Sev had vanished, before glancing at the woman behind her. "At least . . . not until recently."

"I don't suppose you know what *tesoro mio* means?" Before Francesca could respond, the woman shouted out, "Hey, who knows what *tesoro mio* means?"

"Italian. It means my treasure," an older woman toward the front of the line called back.

"Wow," Francesca's companion in line murmured. "Just, wow."

"I couldn't have said it better myself."

Francesca knocked back the drink Sev had given her in the vain hope it would pull her out of the sensual stupor fogging her brain. It didn't. Instead, she spent the next twenty-four hours daydreaming about him.

The next morning, Friday, she wasted her entire time in line searching in vain for Sev's distinctive build. She refused to be disappointed when she didn't spot him, and even came up with a handful of reasonable excuses for lingering in the small bistro while she sipped her drink. But he never showed.

When she arrived at work, she was stunned to discover a blown-glass vase sitting on her desk with a new flower to replace the forget-me-nots, this time a sprig of orange blossoms. The white star-shaped blooms caressed the flame-red glass, the contrast between the two colors quite striking. Unable to resist, she picked up the vase, the sweet perfume of the flowers flooding her senses while the delicate glasswork warmed within her hold.

It was an incredible piece with sinuous curves that flowed from base to stem and seemed to beg for her touch. Had Sev stroked it, just as she was now doing? Were her fingers tracing the same path his had taken? It was a distinct possibility, since no one who held this gorgeous creation could resist running their fingers along the flowing lines of the fiery glass.

"Oh. *My.*" Tina came to peer over Francesca's shoulder. "I've never seen anything so beautiful. Where did you get it?"

"It's a gift."

"And orange blossoms. *Très romantique!*"

"Really? I didn't know. I just love the scent."

"Mmm. They mean eternal love." Tina's eyes filled with laughter. "Or innocence. I'll let you decide which is more appropriate."

Definitely not innocence. Francesca hastily returned the vase to her desktop. She took a seat and pulled out her sketchpad, determined to get straight to work. Not that she accomplished much. More times than she could count she found herself staring into space with a reminiscent smile on her face while she stroked the vase and inhaled the sweet scent of orange blossoms.

Saturday came and Francesca assumed she wouldn't have to worry about Sev showing up at Starbucks, or sending her a gift at work, or finding some other way to tempt her into giving in to his blatant seduction. Or so she thought until she opened the door to her apartment to his latest surprise.

"What are you doing here?" she demanded.

Sev lowered the fist he'd been about to use on her door. "I came to talk to you."

"I thought we decided we weren't going to contact each other again," she said. "Nothing can come of this, you realize that, don't you? No matter how much I might want to see you, it means losing my job, and I won't risk that."

He stared down at her with such heat that it was a wonder it didn't turn the air to steam. "I'm well aware of that fact. Not that it changes anything." He glanced over her shoulder and into her apartment. "Aren't you going to invite me in?"

"No, I'm not."

"Please, Francesca."

Just those two words and she felt her resolve fading. "What's the point, Sev?" she whispered.

"This. This is the point."

He cupped her face and took her mouth in a passionate kiss. Francesca closed her eyes as Sev made his point, as well as several others, in ways sweeter and more generous than any that had gone before. She gave herself up to sheer rapture, surrendering to desire over common sense. Without even realizing it, she backed into her apartment and Sev kicked the door closed behind them. Endless minutes passed before she surfaced with a groan.

"I can't believe we're doing this again. It's not safe." She fisted her hands in his shirt. "Listen to me, Sev. I'm telling you straight out. You can't show up at Starbucks or send me flowers or any more gorgeous vases—thank you, by the way—or slip me notes in my lunch."

"Fine. I won't. Instead, why don't I steal you away for the weekend?"

She had to give him credit for sheer brazenness, if nothing else. "Forget it. I've already told you—"

He nodded impatiently. "Yeah, yeah. Heard it all before. That still doesn't change anything. We need time together in order to resolve our differences."

"We can't resolve our differences," she emphasized. "There are simply too many obstacles."

"Obstacles we haven't made any effort to overcome. I'd like to try and correct that oversight. I've made reservations. We'll be discreet. No one will find out we've been together."

"And if I say no?" she asked, lifting an eyebrow. "Will you blackmail me again?"

"Would that make it easier for you to surrender?" His voice dropped, reminding her of a certain moonlit night when he'd whispered the most outrageous suggestions in her ear, suggestions he'd then turned from proposition to action. "Come with me, Francesca. Or I swear I'll show up at Timeless and tell everyone who'll listen that we're lovers."

"I don't believe you. You're just saying that because—"

He leaned in, stopping her with another endless kiss. "Don't challenge me." There was no mistaking the warning in his dark eyes. "When have I ever failed to follow through on my word?"

"Right now," she informed him. "All this week. You said—" She hesitated, struggling to recall precisely what he had said when they last met. As far as she could remember, she'd done most of the talking that day. He gave her a knowing look and she blew out her breath in an aggravated sigh. "Okay, fine. You might not have come right out and said it, but you did agree to end the affair."

He tipped her face up to his. "Does it look like I agree with our ending things?"

Not even a little. "Without question."

His slow, knowing smile proved her undoing. "Go pack a bag. We can finish arguing about it in the car."

She turned without another word and crossed to her bedroom. Five minutes later she returned with an overnight bag, more certain with every step she took that she'd completely lost her mind. And maybe she had, but after five minutes with Sev, she no longer cared. One more weekend and then she'd put an end to their relationship, she promised herself. Just these two days together and then no more. After all, who would it hurt?

To her delight, Sev drove them into wine country, where he'd booked a room at a charming bed-and-breakfast. They spent the day at several of the local wineries sampling the wares before enjoying an impromptu picnic that consisted of generous slices of the local Sonoma Jack cheese and freshly baked bread. That night they dined out at a small, elegant restaurant specializing in French cuisine, their day together one of the most enchanting Francesca had ever experienced. The sun had long since set when they returned to their room and silently came together.

She'd been waiting for this from the moment she'd agreed to spend the weekend with Sev, had been anticipating it, desire fomenting with each passing hour. And now that the moment had arrived, she tumbled, falling headlong into his arms and into his bed, if not into his heart. Because she couldn't quite convince herself that what they felt could be anything more than physical.

"We can make this work," he told her, during the still hours between deepest night and earliest morning. "If we agree not to discuss anything job-related, this will work."

"For how long?" she protested.

"Look, I know TH is after a big-name actress to pull them out of their financial hole. Eventually, I'll find out who she is. I don't need you for that. There are far more interesting ways to spend my time with you."

She managed a smile, even though she continued to worry. "Our jobs mean everything to us, Sev. Even you can't deny that. They're as much a part of us as our flesh and bones. We won't be able to share that part of ourselves."

He conceded the point with a swift nod. "We'll discuss other things, instead."

"Like what?"

He rolled onto his side to face her. "Like, growing up in foster care. Coming from such a huge family, I can't begin to imagine it. Why were you never adopted?"

She tugged the sheet over her breasts and tucked it beneath her arms. A ridiculous reaction, she conceded, and more than a little telling. But talking about her childhood left her exposed. Any covering, even a sheet, helped compensate for that.

"I almost was," she said in answer to his question. "When I was eight. I'd been in foster care for three years by then."

He traced a scorching finger from the curve of her cheek down the length of her neck. As always, she flamed beneath his touch, her breath growing ragged. "What happened?"

Francesca shrugged. "They were about to adopt me when Carrie unexpectedly became pregnant with twins. The doctor ordered complete bed rest and her husband insisted I be placed elsewhere because it was too much for his wife. I heard him tell the social worker that taking care of me put their babies at risk, and that the babies were their most important consideration."

Sev swept her hair back from her face, regarding her with heartbreaking compassion. "What happened then?"

"I went through a succession of homes after that. Four, I think." She dismissed the memory with a careless smile and rolled over on top of him. His warmth became her warmth and helped diminish the coldness that streaked through her veins and sank into her bones. A coldness those particular memories always engendered. "Acting out, I guess, because I'd been foolish enough to imagine that Carrie and her husband might actually want me as much as the children they were about to have."

"I'm sorry." He released his breath in a rough sigh, causing the curls at her temples to swirl and dance. "That's such an inadequate thing to say. But I mean it."

"Like I said, don't feel sorry for me." Pity was the last thing she wanted from him. "I survived."

"And found your father. That must have helped." He studied her curiously. "You haven't told me anything about him. What's he like?"

"There's not much to tell," she claimed, aware of how evasive she sounded. "He . . . he had a one-night stand with my mother. Since he was married at the time—is still married—I didn't feel comfortable intruding in their lives."

Sev swore. "You just can't catch a break, can you?"

"What about you?" She deliberately changed the subject. "You've said that after your father's death you had to dismantle most of Dantes. I gather that included Timeless Heirlooms."

"Yes."

She could tell he didn't want to talk about it, but pushed, anyway. "Which explains why you're so determined to get it back again. That must have been as difficult for you as foster care was for me." She hesitated before asking, "Why has it become such an obsession? I mean, if your father was the one responsible for Dantes' decline—"

He wrapped his arms around her and reversed their positions, bracing himself on his forearms to lessen the press of weight on top of her. "Why have I become so obsessed with rebuilding it?"

He looked so fierce. So determined. "Yes."

"Because my father tried to tell me something about the business the day before he died." His words grew ragged. "And I was too impatient to listen to another of his crazy schemes. Maybe if I had—" He broke off, a muscle jerking in his cheek.

"What?" Her eyes widened in sudden comprehension. "You think he had an idea for saving Dantes? One that didn't involve dismantling the entire business?"

"I don't think. I know. He called it Dante's Heart. Even my mother thought it would work. I—*reluctantly*—agreed to meet with them the next day when they returned from their sailing excursion."

"Only they didn't return."

He closed his eyes, grief carving deep lines into his face. "No."

"Didn't he write down his idea? Leave some sort of clue behind?"

"I tore both home and office apart looking for it. There was nothing. Nothing except—"

She recalled what he'd told her when they'd visited his Pacific Heights house. "Letters detailing his affair with a designer."

"Yes." His mouth slid into a smile. Without fail, that simple quirk of his lips caused her body to quicken in anticipation. "Seems to run in the family."

She acknowledged his comment with a sad smile before returning to the heart of the matter. "You think if you'd only taken the time to listen to your father, you wouldn't have had to sell off all the Dante subsidiaries?"

His hands swept over her, settling on the softest of her curves. "If you're asking whether I blame myself, I'll make it easy for you. I do."

She fought to speak through her shiver of desire. "Seems we both have something to prove."

"So it does." He traced a path of kisses from the hollow of her throat downward. "The first thing I want to prove is how much I want you."

In the hours that followed he did precisely that. Their lovemaking took on a desperate edge, as though beneath the passion they sensed how much they needed one another.

Sev gave no quarter. He took with a ruthless power Francesca couldn't resist. He branded her with his fire, taking her to heights she'd never, ever experienced before, taking her in ways she'd never, ever experienced before. The level of intimacy should have terrified her, the knowledge he gained over her body, and even more overwhelming, her heart, allowing her nowhere to hide.

He forced her from hiding and into the light, forced her to connect with him on every possible level. She might have resisted, but for one thing. He gave every bit as much of himself as he took, baring himself to her need, her touch. Her desire. And in doing so, filling the emptiness within.

Their weekend together changed everything, convincing Francesca that maybe she could have it all. Despite the small warning voice, she couldn't quite silence, she allowed herself to be talked back into Sev's bed. Or blackmailed there, he frequently claimed with a teasing grin.

As the days slid into weeks, she became more and more certain Sev didn't have an ulterior motive, other than to get her in his bed as often as possible. But since that was her motivation, as well, nothing could make her happier. Of course, he continued to offer her a job at Dantes at regular intervals, making the tempting offers as such casual asides they felt more like a joke than a true offer. Foolishly, she even managed to convince herself he'd forgotten about identifying which actress Timeless Heirlooms hoped to sign as their spokeswoman.

Or so she believed until he picked her up one evening and handed her a brightly wrapped package. "This is for you. Fair warning, I want major good-guy points for this one."

"That depends." She picked up the box and shook it. "What did you get?"

"Something you mentioned last week. Go on and open it. It's just a DVD." His expression turned gloomy. "It has chick flick written all over it, but for you, I'm willing to take it like a man."

Ripping off the outer wrapping she realized he'd bought her the latest Juliet Bloom release. She stiffened, wondering if this was his subtle way of telling her he knew about the possibility of TH using Bloom as their spokeswoman. "Thanks," she murmured. She cleared her throat, forcing a more natural tone to her voice. "I can't wait to watch this."

"Then we'll do it tonight," he responded promptly. "We'll order in Chinese and crack open that bottle of Pinot Grigio my family sent over from Italy."

All through the beginning of the movie she remained on edge, praying she wouldn't do or say something to give away TH's plans. The entire time, Sev remained his normal self. As far as she could tell, he didn't watch her with any more intensity than usual. There were no double entendres or suspicious comments. Halfway through the film, she managed to relax and even enjoy herself, perhaps in part due to the glass of wine Sev kept topped off.

By the end of the movie, she was in her usual position whenever they watched a DVD, on the couch curled up in Sev's arms. Tears filled her eyes as the film reached its stunning climax, a scene in which the heroine stood before the villain, clothed in nothing but defiance and diamonds.

"It reminds me of our first night together," Sev murmured. "You were wearing your amethyst-and-diamond set, remember? Bloom would look stunning in one of your designs."

Francesca couldn't tear her eyes from the film. "Yes, she will," she murmured.

It took a full half-dozen heartbeats before she realized what she'd said. It took even less time to realize he'd understood the implications. She ripped free of his embrace and stood. "Oh, God."

Sev climbed slowly to his feet, holding up his hands in a placating gesture. "Honey, don't. Don't overreact. I swear to you, I already knew."

She shook her head, not believing him. "This was a setup, wasn't it?"

"Not even a little."

Tears of anger blurred her vision. "And I fell for it. I got complacent. Even when I saw which movie you'd chosen, I convinced myself not to read anything into it." The breath hitched in her throat as she looked around for her purse. "I have to go."

"No, you don't," he argued. "You need to stay so we can talk this through."

She ignored him, scooping her purse off the coffee table and crossing to the entryway to snatch her sweater from the antique armoire he used as a coat closet. "Just answer me one question, Sev." She spun to face him. "Are you going to use the information about Juliet Bloom to try and take down TH?"

At least he didn't lie to her. "Yes."

"Then there's nothing left to be said, is there?"

"There's more to be said than you can possibly imagine. But since you're in no mood to listen to me tonight, it can wait until tomorrow."

"You're wrong, Sev." She yanked open the door to his apartment and stepped through. "There is no tomorrow for us."

Chapter Six

The answer to Francesca's question—was Sev going to use the information she'd let slip?—came the next morning when she rushed in to work.

A message sat on her desk requesting she report to Tina's office at her earliest convenience. It didn't have anything to do with her slipup, she attempted to convince herself. Not this fast, nor this soon. He'd only had one night to track down the actress or her rep and cause trouble. He couldn't possibly have accomplished that so quickly.

But a feeling of impending doom clung to her as she sprinted up the steps to the executive level of Timeless Heirlooms. The Fontaines shared adjoining offices at one end of the floor and she could hear Tina's voice raised in anger coming from her side of the suite. Not unusual, given her volatile nature. But not welcome, either, all things considered. Kurt's placating voice rumbled in response to whatever Tina said, indicating the two were in there together.

Francesca knocked on the door, not in the least surprised when no one answered. She doubted they heard her over the shouting. Peeking around the door, she asked, "You wanted to see me?"

Kurt waved her in and toward a brilliant magenta sofa at one end of the room. She took a seat and waited. Outside, storm clouds marched across the city skyline, a perfect reflection of the Fontaines' mood.

"I'm serious, Kurt. Something has to be done about them."

"What do you suggest, honey?" He shoved a hand through hair a shade paler than Francesca's own honey-blond. "I've called Juliet Bloom's rep every day since the showing. She's polite, but refuses to commit."

"Because of those damn Dantes!"

Francesca stiffened at hearing her worst fears confirmed. "What have the Dantes got to do with Juliet Bloom?" As if she didn't know.

Tina swung around, only too happy to explain. "Surprise, surprise, they've approached her, too." She slammed her hands down on her desk. "They sell wedding rings, for God's sake, not jewelry sets. But because it's the Dante name, Bloom is listening."

Francesca's heart sank. Oh, God. He'd done it. Somehow, he'd used her slip of the tongue to wrestle the Bloom account away from the Fontaines. "When . . . when did this happen?"

"We're not sure. Bloom's been cagey ever since the show. Promising, but never quite committing. Then this morning we found out why."

Francesca closed her eyes to hide the guilt she knew must be readily apparent. This was all her fault. She should have been up front with the Fontaines from the start. She never should have allowed Sev to convince her to continue their affair, despite the hint of blackmail behind his insistence. But she'd wanted him, wanted him desperately. And so she'd caved when she should have held firm. If TH went under, she'd be the one responsible and they'd never forgive her. Hell, she'd never forgive herself.

"What are you going to do?" she finally asked.

Tina resumed her pacing. "What can we do? We're running out of time." She didn't need to add that a good portion of Timeless Heirlooms' future hung on the actress agreeing to be their spokeswoman and wear Francesca's creations in her next picture.

Kurt glanced at Francesca. "Severo Dante called," he murmured in an aside.

"He told us he was behind the delay and upped his offer for Timeless."

Tina glared in frustration. "I don't care what that SOB offers. I'm not selling." Her anger crumbled to panic and she barreled straight into Kurt's arms. "We're in this together, right? United we stand and all that? Because I couldn't do this without you. This place would fall apart if it weren't for you."

His arms tightened around his wife. "I'm not going anywhere. We'll figure something out."

Tears stung Francesca's eyes at the open display of affection. If only she'd had that sort of unconditional love and protection growing up. She shook her head, refusing to allow her thoughts to go there. It wouldn't serve any purpose other than to drive her crazy with futile longing. Kurt could never be her father. And Sev would never be anything more than her temporary lover.

After all, it didn't matter that she couldn't claim Kurt as her father, she decided then and there, or reveal her connection to him. She refused to do anything that might damage the Fontaines' marriage. And finding out that Kurt had not only indulged in an affair in the early years of their marriage, but also that a child had resulted from the affair, would do more than damage it. Knowing Tina, it could very well destroy thirty years of wedded bliss. Francesca could barely handle the guilt of her part in bringing down TH. It would destroy her if she ruined Kurt and Tina's marriage, on top of everything else.

Just being this close to her father filled Francesca with more joy than she thought possible. After all the lonely years in foster care, all the years of working every spare minute of every day to hone her craft, she'd settle for whatever scraps she could get. She refused to bemoan her current circumstances. While her connection to family would remain tenuous at best, as long as she worked at Timeless Heirlooms and it remained afloat, she could pursue a career she loved with all her heart and soul. Even better, she could remain in her father's orbit, even if she never became one of his inner circle.

And if that meant helping them beat Sev at his own game, so be it. "Is there anything I can do?" she asked. "Is there some way of convincing Juliet Bloom to go with TH?"

Kurt looked at her over Tina's head. "Put out some feelers among your associates. See if you can find out who this new designer is."

She froze. "I'm sorry. What new designer?"

Tina pulled free of Kurt's embrace. "That's right. We didn't tell her the best part. Wait until you hear this one." She planted her hands on her hips. "Dantes has convinced Bloom's people that they have some hot new designer on the hook who can give Dame Juliet exactly what she wants."

Oh, no. Oh, please don't let it be who she thought it was. "Who? Who's their new designer?"

"We have no idea. We haven't heard so much as a whisper of a rumor."

"That's where you come in," Kurt added. "We'd appreciate it if you'd keep your ear to the ground. See what some of the other designers are saying. It has to be someone they've acquired very recently, since this Bloom deal's only been around for the past few weeks."

"Maybe we should go downstairs and count heads," Tina muttered. "See if any of our designers are missing. It would be just like him to snitch one of them right from under our noses."

Francesca closed her eyes, her world tilting. Aware that the Fontaines waited for her response, she swallowed, struggling to speak around a throat gone bone-dry. "I'll see what I can find out."

Not that it would take much effort. In fact, it wouldn't take much more than a single visit. How many times had Sev offered her a job, each proposition more lucrative than the last? Suddenly, it all made sense.

Sev knew that TH was in hot negotiation with some big name. He'd been frank about that almost from the start. Chances were excellent he also knew which designer had piqued that person's interest, had undoubtedly known from the night they first met.

If he stole—*seduced*—her away from TH, he'd gain the ultimate prize. Now that he'd romanced the actress's name out of her, he'd land a highly lucrative account with Bloom *and* take away the Fontaines' best chance at revitalizing the company Dantes wanted to purchase. If she didn't miss her guess, Sev planned to use her to accomplish both those goals.

Overhead the storm clouds broke.

Francesca didn't give the assistant seated at a desk outside Sev's door a chance to stop her. She simply swept past the stunning blonde and barged straight into his office. Four men sat sprawled on couches and chairs in an informal sitting area at the far end of the enormous room. She recognized them from the photos that decorated the console in Sev's den, as well as the walls of his apartment.

The Dantes, all four glorious male specimens on display.

Sharp light, scrubbed clean from the recent storm, streamed from the floor-to-ceiling windows and haloed the twins, Marco and Lazz, who sat opposite each other like a pair of striking bookends. She pegged Marco by his wide grin and appreciative gaze, not to mention the sexual sizzle he gave off with every exhalation. Lazz regarded her with a cool, analytical stare, everything about him suggesting a man who kept his emotions under tight control. And then there was Nicolò, the youngest at twenty-nine, but according to Sev, the most dangerous of the bunch. Had he been the one to suggest her as a creative solution for taking over Timeless Heirlooms? Finally, her attention switched to Sev.

He knew why she'd come. She saw the knowledge settle across a face she'd covered with sweet kisses just a few hours earlier. He jerked his head toward the door and his brothers stood en masse. Before Nicolò left, he handed Sev a file folder with her name prominently displayed across the cover.

Sev lobbed the opening volley. "I have one question before you say anything. Have you signed a formal contract yet with Timeless Heirlooms, or are you still on probation?"

She couldn't believe his nerve. "That's none of your business," she retorted, stung.

"Answer me, Francesca." His quiet tone gentled the implacable demand. "Have you signed with them?"

"I intend to, just as soon as I tell you what I think of you."

He simply nodded, but she caught a hint of relief that came and went in his expression. "Would you care to sit?"

"I prefer to do this standing." Her hands curled into fists. "You used me. You used me to try and take over TH. I'm here to tell you that you've failed. And I'm also here to tell you that I think you're despicable."

"Let's set the record straight on several points." He stood, tossing the folder Nicolò had given him to one side. "When we first met—*hell,* when we first made love—I had no idea who you were. Maybe if I'd answered my cell when Marco phoned that night, I would have. But if you recall, I was a little preoccupied and he didn't get through to me until the next morning."

She folded her arms across her chest and shook her head. "I'm not buying it. You could have discovered my identity before you ever arrived at the showing."

"It would have been possible, I suppose. But the fact is, I didn't." He stalked closer. "Next point. The Fontaines and I were already negotiating the sale of Timeless Heirlooms before you and I ever met. Tina knew I intended to buy them out, either when she eventually sold out to me, or after she was forced to declare bankruptcy. That hasn't changed."

"But you hadn't counted on the success of the showing."

"No."

"Or that they might acquire Juliet Bloom as their spokeswoman. Or that she would use their collection in her next film."

"Correction. *Your* collection. And Juliet Bloom has postponed her decision." He paused a beat. "Indefinitely."

Undisguised fury ripped through Francesca. "Because you told her that you had a collection as good as TH's. That you had the perfect designer for her. Me." He didn't deny it and desolation battled with anger. "You thought you could hire me away from the Fontaines and steal the Bloom account so they'd be forced to sell to you."

"Yes."

The simple confirmation cut deep. "You're not even going to deny it?" *Please deny it!*

"Why should I? It's true. If you'd accepted my job offer that's exactly how it would have gone down." For the first time, she saw a businessman instead of her lover. "That's how it's still going down."

She shook her head, so angry she could barely see straight. So heartbroken she could barely feel past the pain. "Not a chance in hell. Do you think I'd ever agree to work for you after this? That I'll ever sleep with you again?"

"One has nothing to do with the other. One is business, the other personal." He shrugged. "The two are mutually exclusive."

Her chin wobbled precariously. Didn't he get it? "One has everything to do with the other. I've lived a lifetime of betrayal in one form or another. I can't . . ." She ground to a halt, correcting herself. "I *won't* be with a man I can't trust."

"Francesca, I didn't seduce you in order to tempt you away from Timeless."

Liar! "You actually expect me to believe that?"

"It's the truth. I made you a legitimate job offer for two reasons. First, you'd be an incredible asset to Dantes. You're the best designer I've ever seen, and that's saying a lot."

"And second?" Not that she needed him to spell it out. She already knew.

"Second, having you leave TH makes them more vulnerable to a Dantes' takeover."

Did he really think she'd find his reasoning appropriate? That A plus B equaled acceptable in her book? He had a lot to learn. "Maybe if you only wanted me because of my talent, I could somehow justify it. Somehow. But that's not the case. You want to take down Timeless Heirlooms and you want to use me to do it. I can't allow that. I can't allow you to do anything that threatens Tina and Kurt."

"Because Kurt's your father."

The breath escaped her lungs in a heady rush and her vision blurred. One minute she stood staring at Sev in utter betrayal and the next he pressed her into one of the nearby chairs. He disappeared from her line of sight for a moment, then returned with glass in hand.

"It's just water, though I have something stronger if you prefer."

She shook her head without speaking and downed the water in a desperate gulp. *"How?* How could you possibly know that?"

"Nicolò hired a private investigator." Sev cupped the curve of her cheek and for a brief, insane moment she relaxed into his touch. The instant she realized what she'd done, she jerked back and his hand fell away. "Before we met at Le Premier I arranged to have each designer investigated. Marco and I attended the showing in order to collect names. By the time Nicolò called the next morning, the PI had matters well underway."

"You're going to blackmail me now, aren't you?"

"Yes."

She closed her eyes. Oh, God. He made it seem so simple. So obvious and acceptable. "You're a total bastard, you know that?"

"When it comes to taking care of my family, you're right." She could literally feel the change come over him as he shifted from lover to adversary. "I'd rather you come to us of your own free will. But I'll do whatever necessary to restore Dantes."

She looked at him, searching his face for some sign of the man she'd taken to her bed. If he still existed—if he *ever* existed—he was lost to her now. "Don't do this," she pleaded. "You don't need TH. Dantes will still be a success without hurting Tina and Kurt."

"Their business is failing." She hated the compassion gleaming in his burnished gold eyes. Hated him all the more for being right. "Bloom might revitalize it for a short time, but Tina is too capricious to keep the business going for longer than a few years. She hired three designers, two of whom are worse than mediocre. The fact that she also hired you is more dumb luck than true discernment. The only reason the company hasn't gone under before this is thanks to Kurt's business acumen."

"So now you're the hero? You're going to rescue Timeless Heirlooms?"

He gathered himself, exuding an uncompromising determination that had long been a hallmark of the Dante legend. "Timeless Heirlooms belonged to us. Because of my father's own capriciousness, I had no choice but to sell it off. Now I'm in a position to right that wrong. Do you expect me to walk away without recovering what I lost?" Regret colored his words. "That isn't going to happen and you know it."

"Because you feel responsible for Dantes' fall from grace?"

"Because I *am* responsible. You know why I feel that way."

She remembered the night he'd explained it to her, and how sympathetic she'd felt. Not anymore. Not when he demonstrated such ruthless disregard in order to achieve his goal. "So, you'll do anything to return the company to its former glory. No matter who gets hurt. No matter who gets in your way or who you have to steamroll over." She wasn't asking, but acknowledging fact.

"No one has to get hurt. The Fontaines will be in a far better position if they sell out to us now than if I'm forced to collect the broken pieces after their fall."

"Very generous of you, I'm sure."

For the first time, a spark of anger flared to life in his eyes. "It's time to negotiate, Francesca. Will you come to work at Dantes of your own volition?"

"What happens if I refuse? Will you tell Tina that I'm Kurt's daughter?"

For the first time he didn't give her a straight answer. "I don't want to do it that way."

"But you will if you think there's no other option. You will because you know that the news will devastate Tina, since she and Kurt were married at the time of my conception. Knowing how volatile she is, she'll throw him out. And even if they eventually reconcile—which they will since they truly love each other—the damage will have been done. Their neglect will hand you TH."

"That's Nicolò's assessment of the situation, yes."

"It's a rotten thing to do, Sev."

Pain sliced across his face. "I've been forced to make far more difficult decisions, decisions that have had a disastrous impact on people's lives." His voice dropped, landed in some dark, desolate place that echoed through his words. "I've had no choice. There was no one else to make those decisions. And I don't doubt there'll be other occasions when I'm forced to make still more."

She could see the truth in his eyes, see that he'd made an uncomfortable home for himself between that proverbial rock and a hard place. She could also sympathize with him, up to a point. Because from now on she'd have to make difficult decisions as well, to stand on her own without Sev at her back. Well, she'd been there before, just as Sev had. She'd lived most of her life with no one beside her when times grew tough. She could do it again. She needed to be strong, to refortify the barriers she'd created years ago to hide her vulnerability and weakness. And she would. There wasn't any other choice.

"If I agree to work with you, I have one request." She didn't allow herself to consider that her statement as good as conceded defeat.

"Name it."

"The Fontaines are to receive full price for TH. I want it in my contract. I won't lift a finger to help Dantes otherwise."

He gave it a moment's reflection. "In that case I want an exclusive two-year contract with you with an additional two-year non-compete clause. If you walk away without meeting the terms of your contract, I won't allow you to work for anyone else in the industry in any capacity, whatsoever, for two full years."

Suddenly she found herself right there with him, a hard place boring into her back, a boulder slamming her from the front. "That seems a bit harsh."

"I have an investment to protect. I have no intention of buying out TH only to have you walk away from Dantes and help the Fontaines start up a competing business."

It hadn't occurred to her to do any such thing. But now that he mentioned it, it would serve him right if she'd planned to do precisely that. "Very well. I agree."

He held out his hand. "Welcome to Dantes."

Francesca realized her mistake the instant she put her hand in his. The Inferno reared its ugly head, darting from his hand to hers and setting her blood on fire. It didn't seep into her bones, but burned inward, branding her more deeply and completely than she thought possible.

She saw a similar kick of reaction from Sev, the sensation filling his expression with a predatory hunger. "Oh, and there's one more detail I forgot to mention."

She didn't have to ask. She knew precisely what detail he'd omitted. "Forget it."

"I can't forget, any more than you can." Sev's eyes turned to molten gold. "I still want you in my bed."

Chapter Seven

Sev deliberately kept his distance from Francesca over the next few days while she gave notice at TH and settled into her new home at Dantes, not wanting to throw any more fuel on a situation already on the verge of a messy explosion. He'd done enough by insisting she return to his bed, as well as come to work at Dantes.

Though she'd accepted the latter with dignified anger, when it came to his former demand, she'd told him in no uncertain terms which dark corner of his body to put his suggestion and precisely how to achieve such an impossibility. Though he regretted the means he'd used to force her compliance on the work front, at some point she'd face facts.

Timeless Heirlooms teetered on the edge of destruction, and not even Francesca's brilliant designs would save it. Not in the long run. He'd rather acquire TH while he and his brothers could still turn it around, rather than attempt to pick up pieces shattered beyond repair. Quite simply, the Dantes were in a position to fix problems. The Fontaines weren't. Unfortunately, he doubted he'd ever be able to convince Francesca of that simple fact.

He'd respected her preferences and kept his distance, missing her from both his life and his bed. But now Sev couldn't stand it another minute. Whatever existed between them, whether The Inferno or simple desire, the craving to have her close at hand threatened everything he'd worked the past decade to accomplish.

A nagging compulsion consumed him, as though an emergency signal lit up the connection between them. He couldn't recall ever being this distracted. After the sixth time he stood with the subconscious urge to track her down, he finally gave in and acted on the impulse.

He found her in the studio he'd arranged for her use, a huge, bright room with every possible amenity at her disposal, right down to a plush sitting area and tiny kitchenette. Giving her door a brief knock, he entered. And then he allowed his senses to consume him, the thumb of his left hand moving automatically to ply the palm of his right.

She sat at her desk, a drawing pad flipped open and a charcoal pencil in hand. He couldn't say whether the sketch she applied herself to with such assiduous attention had anything to do with her job. But whatever she worked on, he suspected she'd lost all awareness of time and place.

Sunlight streamed from nearby windows and swirled within her hair, spinning the honey-blond strands to pure gold. It also illuminated the creamy tone of her complexion, making her appear lit from within. Even from this distance, he picked up traces of her unique perfume, the scent light and crisp and uniquely hers.

The pressure that had been building over the past few days eased with his first glimpse of her, forcing him to concede just how tense he'd become without constant contact with her. Every instinct begged him to go to her and carry her off. To take her as far from Dantes and the Fontaines as possible.

"Is there something I can help you with, Mr. Dante?" she asked without looking up.

He lifted an eyebrow. "Mr. Dante?" He leaned against the door, forcing it shut.

"Don't."

Just that one word, but it contained a full measure of pain and disillusionment. She looked at him then, sparing him nothing. He knew he'd hurt her but refused to consider how badly. Until now. More than anything he wished he could go to her and find a way to ease her despair. But not only wouldn't she welcome it, he suspected she'd tear a strip off his hide if he came anywhere near her.

"Do you have any idea what it's like being here?" she continued. "The untenable position you've put me in?"

He cocked his head to one side. Okay . . . Maybe more was going on than his forcing her to work for him. Something had exacerbated the situation. "What's wrong?" he demanded.

She threw down her pencil and glared at him. "Why did you give me this office?"

He didn't hesitate. "Because it's the best one available."

"Great. Just great. Would you care to know the first question my coworkers asked me?" She didn't wait for his response. "Not my name. Not general questions about my background. Not where I attended school or who I studied with or where I last worked. They wanted to know who I'd slept with to get this studio."

Sev winced. "Hell."

"Oh, it gets better."

She swept a hand toward the pretty little sitting area tucked beneath the windows. "Guess what's now called the 'casting couch'? Of course, my coworkers treat it like a big joke, but I can see the speculation. They're wondering who I am and why I rate such consideration. As far as they're concerned, I'm brand-new to the industry. An apprentice in their eyes. But somehow, I've leapfrogged over them and they don't like it one little bit. In a single thoughtless move, you've made it impossible for me to associate effectively with the other Dante employees."

Damn. "I didn't realize."

"Fine. You didn't realize. But now that you do, you have to fix it."

He could guess where this was going. "What do you suggest?"

"Transfer me to one of the other Dante locations. New York. London. Paris. The way things are right now, I'd even take Timbuktu. Just send me someplace else where they don't know me. Where . . ." She snatched a shaky breath. "Where I don't have to anticipate seeing you around every corner."

Not see her for months on end? He couldn't do it. The mere suggestion threatened what little sanity he had remaining. "Forget it. Not for at least two years."

"Two years?" He hated the cynical light that pitched her eyes to a black both deep and diamond-hard. "Unless The Inferno burns down to ashes before then, right?"

Sev ignored the question. It hit uncomfortably close to home and he hated the thought that his actions could have so base a motivation. "Other than transfer you, what else can I do? Name it and if it's in my power I'll give it to you."

She laughed, the sound so filled with sorrow that he flinched. "You can give me my old life back. You can let me work for the Fontaines again. Live my life the way I choose. I want to work with—" Her voice broke. "With my father. Even if he didn't know about our relationship, at least I could see him every day. At least he didn't hate me."

Sev froze. "Hate you?"

She stared at him in disbelief. "Are you *really* so blind? Didn't it occur to you what would happen when I refused to sign with Kurt and Tina? What would happen when I turned my back on them after all they've done for me? How they'd react when I jumped to Dantes instead of honoring my promise to sign the contract they were on the verge of offering? I betrayed them, Sev. I betrayed them in the cruelest manner possible and they despise me for what I've done to them."

Dammit to hell. He should have anticipated this. His distraction had cost them both. "I'll talk to them."

"And tell them what?" She thrust back her chair and stood, the movement lacking her usual grace. "Don't you get it? I'll be the proximate cause for the Fontaines losing Timeless Heirlooms. I'm the one they'll blame when you take over. Talking to them isn't going to do a bit of good."

He hadn't considered that aspect of the situation for a very simple, yet vital reason. He'd been so focused on his family's business and restoring all he'd been forced to dismantle, that he hadn't fully explored how his decision would impact Francesca. And he could guess why. He didn't dare look too closely or he'd never be able to make the tough calls. Examining the problem from Francesca's side of the fence would also force him to take a long, hard look at his past choices, something he refused to contemplate.

He'd ruined so many lives when he'd sold off the bits and pieces of Dantes. Until then they'd been a premier business, marketing the most exclusive and magnificent jewelry, worldwide. When his father died, he'd been forced into the top position fresh out of college, with little preparation. And even though Primo had come out of retirement during those first difficult days, his grandfather's heart attack, just three short months after the death of his eldest son and daughter-in-law, had put a swift end to his involvement.

From that point on, Sev shouldered the full burden. He, and he alone, had made the tough choices, choices vital to Dantes' survival. He'd been merciless all those years ago. There'd been no other option. One by one, he'd shut down Dantes' subsidiaries, cutting a swath of destruction throughout the company with ruthless disregard for the lives his decisions destroyed. It had been the only way to save the core business. And now here was one more tough choice to add to the lengthy list he'd accepted as part of his "chain of shame."

"I'm sorry," he said, knowing the sentiment to be both inadequate and unwanted.

She turned her back on him. "Is there anything else I can do for you? I need to return to work."

An idea came to him, an idea so outrageous it might have been one of Nicolò's crazier schemes. He didn't give himself time to consider all the ramifications. To pull this off, he needed to act, and act fast. "Actually, there is something else. It's the reason I came here, as a matter of fact. There's a charity auction this Saturday night. Dantes has donated a few wedding rings to help raise money for the Susan G. Koman Breast Cancer Foundation. I need an escort."

Instantly she shook her head. "No, thank you."

"It isn't a request."

She spun to confront him. "You must be joking." One look at his expression and her mouth tightened. "Dating you is now part of my job description?"

"I don't recall referring to Saturday night as a date. It's a business function. And yes, on occasion you'll be expected to attend them, just as the Fontaines expected you to when you worked for TH."

He could see the frustration eating at her. "Why is my presence so important?"

"Because it aligns you with your new employer in a public setting."

She paled. "Will the Fontaines be there?"

"I assume so." Compassion filled him. "You're going to have to face them sometime," he added gently.

For a brief, heartrending moment, her chin trembled. Then she firmed it and squared her shoulders. "Fine. We might as well get it over with. Where is it, and what time should I arrive?"

"It's at Le Premier again." He sympathized with her slight flinch, understanding that she probably regarded the hotel as the scene of her downfall. Or at the very least, the point where her life took a sharp, painful ninety-degree turn. "I'll pick you up at your apartment at eight."

"Not a chance—"

"Don't." He cut her off without compunction. "You're not going to win, so don't waste your energy fighting me."

Her chin shot up. "It's your way or . . . what? You'll fire me?"

He didn't bother answering. She knew the terms of their contract without him reiterating them. He approached, drawn by a force beyond his ability to control. "Do you really want to turn our relationship into a war when there are so many better ways we could expend our time and energy?"

Passion exploded across her face. Unfortunately, anger drove it rather than desire. "I refuse to fall into your arms after you've forced me into this situation. How could you think I would?"

"Then don't fall." He caught her close and offered a teasing smile. "Trip a little and I'll catch you."

Her anger vied with a naked longing and she splayed her hands across his chest to hold him off. "Please don't do this, Sev. Either let me work for you or let me go. But if you keep forcing the issue, we'll end up despising each other."

He tucked a lock of hair behind her ear, the silken feel of her curls rivaling that of her skin. "I could never despise you." His smile tilted. "But maybe that's all you feel for me."

She closed her eyes. "I—I don't despise you."

He knew how hard her confession came. He leaned into her, basking in her feminine warmth. Somehow, someway, he'd find a way to fix this, while still protecting Dantes and all the people who depended on him.

Somehow.

Francesca dressed with more than her usual care. She tried to tell herself she did it for her own peace of mind, that the extra pains she took helped give her the strength and composure she needed to face the Fontaines, as well as others in the industry who felt she'd sold out. But that would be a lie. Everything she did to prepare for the night ahead was with one person in mind.

Sev.

She checked the mirror a final time. The sleek bronze-toned dress hugged her curves, while her hairstyle, a simple knot at the base of her neck, helped draw attention to the topaz chandelier earrings she'd designed before joining Timeless Heirlooms. In fact, it had been one of the pieces that convinced Kurt and Tina to hire her. Checking the mirror a final time, she nodded in satisfaction. Simple and understated, while subtly advertising why her talents were currently in such high demand. Or at least she hoped that would be the overall reaction.

Promptly at eight, Sev knocked at her door. His single sweeping look convinced Francesca she'd chosen the perfect ensemble. Hot molten hunger exploded in his gaze. She fell back a step before the wall of heat radiating off him. Heaven help her, when had her apartment grown so small? And when had Sev grown so large? Even worse, after everything he'd done, why did she still long to throw herself in his arms and surrender everything to him? It didn't make a bit of sense.

"Tesoro mio," he murmured. The lyricism she'd come to associate with him caressed the words. "You stagger me."

Good. She wanted him staggered. She wanted to knock him clean off his feet. It seemed only fair considering he'd done the same to her. Not that she'd allow any hint of that to show. Behind her, the bed called to her, whispering such innovative suggestions, it brought a blush to her cheeks. She gathered up her wrap and purse. Time to leave. She didn't dare stay another second in such close confines with Sev. Not with her bed misbehaving. Stupid bed.

She suffered the short drive to Le Premier in silence, reluctant to do or say anything that might put her mental and emotional state in jeopardy. The next few hours would prove incredibly difficult and she wanted a few minutes to prepare herself, to slam every barrier she possessed into place. She succeeded beautifully, right up until he helped her from the car.

Leaning down in a sweet, intimate move, he whispered in her ear, "Back to the scene of the crime."

"Yours or mine?" She managed to ask the question with barely a tremor to betray her agitation.

"Mine," he claimed without hesitation. "I accept full blame for what happened here."

"Considering how little resistance I offered, that's rather generous of you."

He gathered her hand in his and tucked it through the crook of his arm. "Not at all. Because if I had to do it over again, I would."

She stiffened in outrage. "You'd blackmail me into leaving the Fontaines?"

He looked down at her, his eyes burning with tarnished lights. "I'd steal you away and make love to you until morning broke." A teasing smile came and went. "And then I'd blackmail you, if only to keep you close."

Francesca didn't know how to respond to his provocative statement, so she remained silent. If he noticed her discomfort, he didn't let on, chatting casually with associates and taking pains to introduce her as "the most talented designer he'd ever met." To her relief, the first part of the evening passed without a hitch. She and Sev wandered through the ballroom, examining the various offerings available for bid. He paused to show her the three pieces Dantes' donated to the cause.

They were all wedding rings, of course. The first she saw featured a "fancy" yellow diamond in a vintage setting that whispered of romantic styles from the late nineteenth century. A Verdonia Royal amethyst complemented the diamond. The second ring appeared more sophisticated, the diamond solitaire a clear stone in a swirl of platinum with a round brilliant cut. But Francesca found it too cold for her taste. Moving on to the third ring, she froze, not even realizing she held her breath until she released it on a prolonged sigh. Never had she seen anything so beautiful.

"Is this a fire diamond?" she asked in amazement.

She'd heard of them, of course, but had never been fortunate enough to see one, let alone use them in any of the jewelry she designed. She'd read that the fire of its transformation from coal to diamond lingered at its very heart and gave the gemstone its name. Sure enough, she could see the flames that licked outward from the fiery depths. Mesmerized, she could only stare in awe.

"There's only one mine that produces them and Dantes owns it," he confirmed. "They're even more rare than pink diamonds."

The fire diamond was breathtaking in its simplicity, and yet the band lifted it from stunning to extraordinary. Woven together into a gorgeous setting that combined gold with white gold, it provided a perfect backdrop for the stone.

"Two disparate halves made one," he explained.

"Oh, Sev," she murmured. "I wish I'd designed this. It's magnificent."

He shot her a look of amusement intermingled with pride. "Primo will be delighted to hear you think so, since he created it. It's one of a kind."

"And you're auctioning it off?" She stared at him in dismay. "How can you bear for it to go out of the family?"

"It's for a good cause."

Over the next few hours Francesca forgot her animosity toward Sev. She had so much fun examining all the donated items, she didn't even remember the Fontaines and the strong possibility she'd run into them. When the time came for Primo's ring to go up on the block, she waited anxiously to see who would claim it. To her surprise, Sev put in the winning bid at the very last minute.

"Now I know why you weren't worried." She gave a wry grin. "I should have known."

He inclined his head. "Yes, you should. Primo would have killed me if I'd lost that final bid. Wait here for a minute while I retrieve it."

He left her side to go and claim the ring. No sooner had he disappeared from sight than she caught a glimpse of the Fontaines. Every other thought fled as she stood frozen in place, utterly vulnerable to the approaching storm. Before they reached her, Sev reappeared with a ring box bearing the distinctive Dantes logo.

Spotting the Fontaines, Sev dropped a hand to her shoulder. "Look at me, sweetheart," he murmured.

"I'm all right. Really. I'm fine." So why did her voice sound so thread and terrified?

"You will be." He gently turned her toward him. Lifting her hand, he slid Primo's ring onto her finger. "Trust me."

She glanced down, stunned. "What are you doing?"

"I'm trying to fix things. To protect you."

"I—I don't understand."

"I need you to go along with what's about to happen." He spoke low and urgently. "I owe you this much, sweetheart. Hell, I owe you far more."

Before she could demand a further explanation, the Fontaines descended. Sev greeted them with a broad smile. "You can be the first to congratulate us." He held up her left hand. The fire diamond caught the light and burst into flames. "Francesca just agreed to marry me."

"You must be kidding." Disbelief overrode Tina's anger. "This is a joke, right?"

Kurt studied Francesca with open concern. "This is sudden."

Did she look as dazed as she felt? Probably. She'd never handled surprises well. She'd learned long ago that surprises meant something unpleasant. Like losing a parent. Like being adopted and then returned. Like moving to a new foster home. "I—"

"She's still in shock," Sev said with an understanding smile. "She didn't see it coming."

"You think I believe this?" Tina demanded. "You think I believe you've actually fallen in love with her?"

Sev tucked Francesca close in a protective hold. "Why do you find it so difficult to believe?" A hard note underscored the question. "Do you consider her so unlovable?"

"Just the opposite," Tina snapped. She started to reach for Francesca before realizing what she'd almost done and snatched her hand back. "It's you I don't trust, Dante. She may be too inexperienced to figure out what you're up to, but I'm not. You've romanced her away from Timeless Heirlooms because she's our best designer. You know perfectly well that without her—" Her voice broke.

It was Kurt's turn to pull his wife into protective arms. "Don't, love. At least now we know what happened."

Tears flooded Francesca's eyes. "I'm sorry," she whispered. "You have no idea how badly I feel."

"Give it time," Tina shot back. "You're going to feel a lot worse before he's done with you. The only reason he's romancing you is to facilitate his takeover of TH. You realize that, don't you?"

Francesca couldn't bring herself to respond to the question. How could she when every word Tina spoke was the truth? Her fingers dug into Sev's arm as she struggled to keep from bursting into tears. She needed to get away. Now. "Excuse me, won't you?"

Spinning free of Sev's embrace, she pushed her way through the crowd of people. She needed air, needed time to regroup. She adored Tina and Kurt, had wanted to spend the bulk of her career working for them. At least, that had been her dream. But Sev changed all that, turning her life upside down.

She gazed down at the engagement ring gracing her finger. And now he'd tried to restore her relationship with the Fontaines. To put himself in the line of fire, instead of her. What he didn't realize was how difficult she found wearing this ring. To her an engagement ring symbolized a soul-deep love. A promise that she'd have someone at her side who cherished her and would be her lifelong partner. This gorgeous, incredible, breathtaking ring was nothing more than a sham. It wasn't real.

And more than ever, it left her feeling like an outsider.

Chapter Eight

Sev stood there, annoyed to discover himself acting the part of the stereotypical hapless male as Francesca disappeared into the crowd in one direction, and an infuriated Tina stormed off in the opposite. Sev stopped Kurt before he could charge after his wife. For Francesca's sake, he had to find a way to make this right.

"Francesca didn't have any choice," Sev stated. "You realize that, don't you?"

Kurt swung around with a snarl, shaking free of Sev's hold. "I realize you forced her to quit a promising job with us and go to work for you."

Sev fought for patience. "It wouldn't have worked, Kurt. It would have put her in an impossible position. Because of our relationship, she'd have been trapped between you and Tina, and the Dantes. She'd have had to watch every word she said, both at work and at home for fear of betraying one side or the other."

Kurt's anger hadn't diminished, but he still stood there, which counted for something. "So, you made her choose between us?"

"Yes. She doesn't deserve your anger. The only thing she's guilty of is falling in love. Her decision hurt you. Trust me when I say that same decision hurt her every bit as much. She adores you and Tina. You've been her mentors. Her friends. Her family. She owes you everything, and don't think she isn't aware of that fact."

Kurt's expression softened ever so slightly, right up until he looked at Sev. "And you?" he asked harshly. "Is Tina right? Is this your clever way of getting your hands on TH?"

"I don't need Francesca to do that. TH will be mine whether she's working for you, or for me."

"Not if I can help it."

"Kurt . . ." Sev grimaced. "Talk to Tina. The two of you are important to Francesca."

"Important enough to get you to back off?"

Sev couldn't prevent a smile. If circumstances had been different he might have formed a friendship with Kurt. He'd prefer that over their current contentious relationship. "Good try, Fontaine, but it isn't going to happen. Why don't you and Tina make it easy on yourselves and sell out? I'll give you an excellent price."

"Not interested."

Sev shrugged. "I didn't think so, but it was worth a try." He hesitated. "Will you talk to Tina?"

Kurt released his breath in a rough sigh. "Yeah, I'll talk to her. I don't expect it'll change anything. But I will encourage her not to take her anger out on Francesca."

"I'm the one at fault. Tell her to keep me in the crosshairs where I belong, and we'll all do just fine."

With an abrupt nod, Kurt turned and walked away. Sev had no idea whether his plan stood a chance in hell of success. For Francesca's sake, he had to try. She deserved an opportunity to get to know her father, but because he'd been so focused on Dantes and his plans for the business, he'd stolen that opportunity from her. No. Not just stolen. He'd effectively annihilated any chance of it ever happening. If he could restore that much, maybe, just maybe, he could live with the guilt he felt over the rest.

Sev went after Francesca, not in the least surprised to find she'd retreated to the balcony off the ballroom. It was where they'd first met and he struggled not to read anything into her choice. She stood by the railing, her back to him. He could tell she sensed him the instant he appeared in the doorway, her awareness betrayed by the mantle of stillness that settled over her.

He approached. "I'm sorry to spring that engagement ring on you, sweetheart."

"Have you lost your mind?" She threw the question over her shoulder without turning. "What in the world were you thinking?"

"That I was Nicolò, I guess."

That did prompt her to swing around. "This was Nicolò's idea?"

"Hell, no. I get all the credit for this one." Sev scrubbed his hand across his jaw. "Or should I say blame? I just meant, it's the sort of crazy scheme he'd have come up with."

"I don't understand. Why would you do such a thing?"

He shrugged. "I had to try and fix the problem somehow."

"Because that's your job. To fix things." It wasn't a question.

"It always has been," he answered simply. "Since the day my father died, I'm all that stood between Dantes succeeding or going under."

"Well, I'm not some business you have to rebuild. You don't have to fix things for me," she insisted. "I've been taking care of myself for a very long time now. I don't need you to step in and assume the job at this late date."

Strongly stated. Maybe a bit too strongly. "Just out of curiosity . . ." He cocked his head to one side. "Have you ever needed anyone since you turned eighteen?"

He caught the faintest of quivers before she stiffened her chin. "No."

He lowered his voice to a caress. "Or should I ask, have you ever wanted anyone?"

"Don't do this," she whispered. "It's not fair. I want permanence, not temporary."

"Not a string of foster homes."

She conceded the accuracy of his observation with a small nod. "Growing up I always felt I had to change who I was so I'd fit in, that being myself wasn't good enough. I refuse to do that any longer. I won't pretend to be something or someone I'm not, not any longer." She tugged at the ring he'd given her. "This doesn't belong on my finger. Not until it's the real thing."

He stopped her before she could remove it, closing his hand over hers. "Leave it there for the time being. I forced you to work for me. Caused dissension for you both at Timeless and at Dantes. The ring will help protect you. It may even right a few wrongs."

She hesitated. "What's the point? It has to come off sometime."

"But not yet." Not until he'd had time to come up with a resolution to their problems. "Listen to me, honey. There's a very good possibility that our engagement will give you the opportunity to reestablish a relationship with the Fontaines. They're less likely to blame you for leaving them if they believe I forced the issue. They could be part of your life again. You might not see your father as often as you would if you still worked for TH. But at least they won't be angry with you any longer."

"Do you really think so?"

Stark longing filled her expression, ripping him apart. "Give it a chance and see," he suggested roughly.

She teetered on the edge of temptation. "How long do you expect me to keep up this charade?"

"For as long as it takes."

"But it's a lie," Francesca protested.

"Is it?"

A single tug had their bodies colliding in the sweetest of impacts. Sev wrapped his arms around her. The mere touch of her body fomented a reaction unlike anything he'd ever felt with another woman. He'd assumed the acuteness of their passion would ease after a few weeks, that eventually they'd both become sated and the sexual intensity would diminish. It hadn't, and from his perspective, neither of them was close to sated.

A tremor swept through her, one so slight he'd have missed it if they hadn't been fused together from hip to shoulder. He recognized that shiver, felt it each time he pulled her into his arms, and it never failed to excite him. It betrayed a sensual helplessness, one reserved only for him. It whispered her secret to him, teased him with the knowledge that with one touch, her defenses would fall before his advance.

"Let me in, sweetheart."

She gripped his shoulders, pushing even as she yielded. "We're through. Whatever existed between us is over. It ended the minute you forced me into this devil's bargain with you. Putting a ring on my finger to protect me doesn't change that. You put business ahead of our relationship and that's the end of anything personal."

"You know that isn't true."

He swept a hand from the base of her spine to the nape of her neck. Her shiver became a shudder. The give of her body ripened into a heated abandonment, one that silently incited him to deepen their embrace. She wanted him. She might resist it, but nothing could stop the combustible reaction whenever they touched. Not personal preference. Not logic or intellect. Not even her hurt and anger at the hideous position in which he'd put her.

The dragon's breath of The Inferno incinerated both reason and intellect, and left behind a single urge. To mate. To step into the fire of that joining and allow the flames to consume them.

He lowered his head, his mouth hovering above hers so their breath became one. "I wish this weren't happening when it's clear you don't want it. I wish I could do what you ask and let you go. But I can't."

"You don't have any choice," she asserted. "Do you really think that after all you've done I could ever trust you again?"

"I'm not asking for your trust."

"Just me in your bed."

He didn't bother denying the truth. "Yes, I want you there. Or here. Or anywhere I can have you. Any way you'll allow it."

He closed the final gap between them and sank into her mouth. He heard her sigh of pleasure. Felt it. Drank it inward. Their lips molded, shaping themselves one to the other, before parting. Her breathing grew ragged. Or maybe it was his. More. The insistent demand sounded in his head, so clear and sharp he almost thought he'd said it aloud. And maybe he did, because she reared back, breaking the kiss almost as soon as it began.

She turned her head a fraction to avoid any risk of their lips colliding again. "Making love to you is too intimate. It leaves me too vulnerable," she told him with devastating frankness, the stark pain underscoring her words ripping through him. "I can't open myself to you if I don't trust you."

"We'll find a way to make this work," he insisted.

He'd said the wrong thing. Instantly, she ripped free of his embrace. "There's only one way that's possible. I can work for you or I can sleep with you. But I refuse to do both. It's your choice, Sev."

She gazed at him and he could see the burgeoning hope in the inky darkness, a hope he had no option but to crush. "I believe we've already had this conversation. You work for Dantes."

He forced himself not to flinch at the acrid disillusionment that shattered the last of her hope. Her chin shot up and she embraced her fury. God, she was even more gorgeous, if that were possible, filled with righteous indignation and feminine power.

"You're the consummate businessman to the bitter end, aren't you, Sev?" she said bitterly. "No matter who gets in your way or how many get hurt."

He opened the door a crack so she could see inside. "There's never been any other choice for me. My family has always depended on me to be the ruthless one."

"I'm not in your way, Sev."

He inclined his head. "Not anymore. You need to understand, sweetheart, that my family still depends on me to make the hard decisions. If I don't make them, if I'm too weak to make them, I put Dantes at risk again."

"Fine. Now you've made one more hard decision. You've chosen Dantes over our relationship." She stepped back. "Just don't expect me to reward you for that decision."

He dared to touch her a final time. He scraped his knuckles along the curve of her cheek and pretended not to see her flinch. "I'm sure that's your intention now. But you will be back in my bed. There won't be any other choice." He smiled, a painful pull of his mouth. "For either of us."

Francesca twisted the engagement ring she'd worn for the past ten days, the fire diamond flashing fiercely up at her. It still surprised to discover it decorating her finger. "Who all will be at your grandparents' house for dinner?" she asked Sev.

He shot her a quick glance of reassurance, which dashed any hopes that he hadn't picked up on her nervousness. "Just Nonna, Primo, and my brothers this time around. I'll save the rest of the family for another occasion."

"Oh." She started to twist her hands together again, but the fire diamond stopped her, flashing an additional message of reassurance. To her amusement, it worked and she found herself relaxing despite herself. "Does your family get together often?" she asked, honestly curious.

"Once a month without fail."

"Do they know our engagement isn't real?"

"It is real. For now. As far as my family's concerned, you and I are engaged," he warned. "I'd appreciate it if you wouldn't disabuse them of that notion."

Her brows pulled together. "And how did you explain the suddenness of it? Or the fact that I used to work at TH and now work for you?"

"Easy. I told them we had no choice. It was The Inferno." He shrugged. "I didn't need any other explanation after that."

She caught her bottom lip between her teeth. So much for relaxing. Whenever she'd been sent to a new foster home, that first meeting always proved the most difficult for her. Most of the time she walked into situations where the other foster children, or her foster parents' natural children, had already formed tight family units. Sure, they always welcomed her. At first. But she dreaded those early days of adjustment, hovering on the outside of their too jovial camaraderie as she tried to figure out how to best fit in. What hole she could fill, regardless of whether the fit felt comfortable.

This time around they all believed her madly in love with Sev. How could she possibly convince them of that? "I don't think I can pull this off."

"Don't worry about it," he told her softly. "We won't stay long if you're not enjoying yourself."

"I'll be fine." And she would. She could handle the situation. After all, she wasn't a lost child any longer. And if she'd learned nothing else during those formative years, she'd learned how to fake it.

To her delight, she discovered she didn't have to fake anything. From the moment she and Sev walked in the door, the Dantes welcomed her with open arms. Primo and Nonna both gave her exuberant hugs, exclaiming in pleasure over her choice of engagement ring.

"It's a stunning design," Francesca complimented Primo with utter sincerity. "I told Sev how envious I am that it isn't my own creation."

"I am honored," he said, clearly moved. "And I am even more honored that you have chosen this particular ring to wear for as many years as God blesses your marriage."

The breath caught in her lungs, the weight of his words pressing down on her. "Thank you," she managed to answer, shooting Sev a look of clear desperation.

He responded by lifting her left hand to his mouth in a move that should have come across as hackneyed. Instead, it struck her as unbelievably endearing. Her throat closed as his gaze linked with hers. And just like that, in front of all the Dantes, The Inferno struck and she totally melted.

Nonna dabbed at her eyes and smiled at Primo reminiscently. Then she clapped her hands together, scolding in Italian. As one, the Dante men shuffled toward the kitchen, where they switched from English to Italian. Sev left last.

He ran his thumb along the curve of her bottom lip. "You okay?" he asked quietly.

She blew out her breath in a sigh, murmuring in an undertone, "Well, I don't think we have to worry about whether or not they believe our engagement is real."

He bent and captured her mouth, no doubt because he knew she didn't dare protest. Not that protesting occurred to her until long after he'd released her. "No, we don't."

Nonna grinned as she watched their parting. "It is good, what you have. Special."

"I think complicated might be a more accurate description."

Nonna nodded in agreement. "With Dante men, it can be nothing less." She gathered Francesca's hand in hers. "He needs you, that one. Oh, you may look at him and wonder. He is so strong. So hard-nosed. He is quite capable of standing on his own. But he has had to be. He has had no choice but to take the one path open to him. Anything else would have meant disaster for his family."

"Because—" Francesca broke off, realizing it might not be politic to mention her son's poor business skills had almost destroyed the business her husband built.

Nonna nodded. "You are tactful. I appreciate that. But what you are thinking is true. Dominic almost destroyed Dantes." Lines of grief couldn't detract from a face still handsome despite the weight of her years. "If not for Severo, Dantes would be no more."

"It couldn't have been easy for him."

"It was more than difficult. The decisions he has made . . ." Nonna shook her head. "Any man would find them near to impossible. But at so young an age, so soon after the death of his mother and father?" She clicked her tongue in distress.

"You're saying he had to be ruthless." As he'd proven to her on more than one occasion these past weeks.

"Yes." Nonna closed her eyes and whispered a silent prayer. Then she looked at Francesca, joy replacing her sorrow. "But then he found you. He needs you, *ciccina*. You soften him. And after all that has been forced on him, all the horrible choices, you give him peace. Best of all, you give him The Inferno."

With a grateful smile, she linked arms with Francesca and urged her toward the kitchen. It troubled Francesca to see the situation from Sev's side of the fence. She didn't want to sympathize with all he'd been through.

Worse, rather than fading, her physical and emotional response toward him grew progressively stronger with each passing day. Considering all that stood between them, it would make life easier if it would just go away. She entered the kitchen and spared him a swift look, confirming those feelings weren't going anywhere anytime soon.

To her surprise, she spotted Primo at the stove, commandeering the burners like an admiral overseeing his fleet, while the Dante men moved in practiced synchronicity, taking care of all the domestic chores in preparation for the meal.

Her surprise must have shown because Nonna grinned. "This is my night off. It is a Dante tradition," she explained, gesturing toward her grandchildren. "They take care of me on family day."

"I like that." Francesca's eyes narrowed in suspicion. "They do dishes, too, right? You don't get stuck with those?"

"No, no." She gave a broad wink. "I am too clever for that. Here. You take Gianna's seat next to me. She's in *L'Italia*. Visiting *famiglia* with her parents and brothers. You will meet them next time."

Assuming there was a next time, Francesca almost said, before catching back the words at the last second. Fortunately, dinner came together just then and the Dante men descended on the table like they hadn't eaten in a month. After grace, conversation exploded, for the most part in English, occasionally in Italian, as a bewildering array of dishes passed back and forth.

The choices were endless. Marinated calamari vied with *panzanella*. Cannellini beans cooked with garlic, olive oil and sage competed with stuffed tomatoes. Then the main dishes marched around the table. Chicken Marsala with red peppers, tortellini, pasta with a variety of sauces.

"Save room for dessert," Sev warned as he piled her food high.

She shook her head at the overloaded plate. "I can serve myself, you know."

He gave her a look a shade too innocent. "I just wanted to make sure you try a bit of everything."

She knew him too well to buy into that one. "I think you want to stuff me full of carbs so my brain goes to sleep."

"Now why would I want to do that?" But his mouth twitched, giving him away.

"So I can't think fast enough to argue with you."

He grinned. "But, *cara*, I love arguing with you."

A liquid warmth swept through her again at the teeny-tiny accent that crept through his words. No doubt the setting contributed to it, and the fact that he constantly switched back and forth between English and Italian.

"Ho-ho. What a liar you are," Nonna corrected in Italian. "It is not the arguing you love. It is the making up afterward."

"Well . . ." Francesca offered judiciously. "He does excel at both."

Silence descended over the table. *"Parlate italiano?"* Nonna demanded in astonishment. "And why did you not tell us this?"

Francesca grinned. "How would I know what you were all saying about me if I admitted I spoke Italian?"

Delighted laughter rang out as they all bombarded her with questions in rapid-fire succession. Primo rapped his knuckles in an effort to regain control. Instantly, silence descended. "I will ask the questions at my own table, if you do not mind," he informed his grandsons. Eyes identical to Sev's fixed her with uncomfortable shrewdness. "You have Italian relatives? This is why you learned Italian?" he asked.

She shook her head. "As far as I'm aware I'm not of Italian descent." A shadow of regret came and went. "I'm afraid I don't know much about my ancestors, so anything's possible, I suppose."

She caught a hint of compassion in Primo's expression, though he didn't allow it to color his voice. "Then why?" he asked. "Why did you learn Italian?"

"Because it's always been my dream to work at Dantes," she admitted. "It made sense to learn the language." A subtle shift in attitude occurred after her confession, one that left her somewhat puzzled.

"Figured it out yet?" Sev asked softly.

Her gaze jerked up to meet his. "Figured what out?"

"You'll get there." He gave her a small wedge of *panforte*, a traditional Tuscan dessert filled with nuts, fruit and a hint of chocolate, serving her a cup of strong coffee to accompany it.

"Do you mean . . . ?" She glanced around the table, reassured to see that a heated discussion about the best time to expand Dantes raged on, preoccupying the rest of Sev's family. "Do you mean have I worked out the change in your family? The change in their attitude toward me?"

"Almost there," he murmured.

She shrugged. "That's easy enough. It's because they found out I speak Italian. I blend in better."

"Not even close."

Startled, she gave him her full attention. "What? They love me now because I told them I've always wanted to work at Dantes? So what? Lots of people would kill to work for you."

"Nope. Come on, honey. You know. You just refuse to accept the significance of it."

He saw too clearly and it left her far too vulnerable. She returned her fork to her plate, before confessing, "It's because I learned Italian in the hope I'd someday work for Dantes. That I took that extra step."

A slow smile built across his mouth. "I knew you'd get it."

She scanned the table again, realizing that with that simple, painfully honest statement she'd become one of the family, her acceptance into their inner circle absolute. Most important of all, she'd done it by being herself. Even so, the knowledge filled her with guilt. "But it's a lie."

He helped himself to a second slice of *panforte*. "You didn't learn Italian because you wanted to work for me?"

"Not you," she stressed. "Dantes. And not that." She shoved her left hand under his nose. "This. This is a—"

He leaned over and stopped her with a kiss. "We'll discuss that later," he murmured against her mouth. "In the meantime, don't worry. These things have a way of sorting themselves out."

They lingered over their coffee for another hour before Sev stood and told his family they needed to leave. Hugs were liberally dispensed before they made it out the door. The instant they slid into the car, she returned to the concern uppermost on her mind.

"Can't we tell your family the truth? I really like them, and I'd rather not lie to them."

"We're not lying to them. We are engaged."

"You know what I mean." Impatience edged her voice. "They think we're getting married."

"That might prove a problem at some point," he conceded. "But not today."

They both fell silent until he pulled up outside her apartment complex. After curbing the wheels to keep them from rolling downhill, he threw the car in

Park and shut off the engine. A gentle rain tapped against the windshield and blocked out everything but a watery blur of city lights.

"Have you really always wanted to work at Dantes?" he asked.

"Yes."

"Then you've achieved your dream. Is a temporary engagement to me so high a price to pay for that dream?"

"No." She touched her engagement ring in an increasingly familiar gesture. "But what I've done to the Fontaines is far too high a price for any dream."

"You need to trust me. It's all going to work out. It may not be a perfect solution. Compromise will be involved. But it's going to work out."

"Because you say so?"

"Because I intend to make it so."

He cupped her face and drew her close. At the first brush of his mouth against hers, every thought evaporated from her head. The Fontaines. The Dante clan. Work pressures. They all slipped away beneath the heat of his taking. He played with her mouth, offering light, teasing kisses. But it only took her tiny moan of pleasure for it to transform into something more. Something deep and sensual and unbearably desperate. Passion exploded, fogging the windows and ripping apart both intent and intention. It needed to stop before stopping became an impossibility.

"You don't play fair," she protested, struggling to draw breath.

"It doesn't pay to play fair." He eyed her in open amusement. "What it does is give me what I want most."

"And what's that?" she couldn't resist asking.

"You." He lifted an eyebrow. "Invite me in and put us both out of our misery."

Did he think it would be that easy to recover the ground they'd lost? She swallowed a groan. Maybe if their embrace had continued for another few minutes, though she'd never admit as much to Sev. But it hadn't, and she still found enough self-possession— *somewhere,* if she looked around hard enough—to stand firm in her resolve not to tumble back into his bed.

"No, I'm not inviting you in." She gave him her sweetest smile. "I don't play fair, either. As far as I'm concerned, you can sit here and suffer for your sins."

"But not for much longer," he said.

Or was it a warning?

Chapter Nine

Francesca flipped through her sketchpad and experienced a sense of accomplishment unlike anything she'd ever felt before. She'd worked on the creations contained on these pages for most of her life.

It hadn't been her first glimpse of the sparkle and glitter of gemstones that had drawn her to jewelry design. Sure, she loved the beauty of them. And she loved the endless ideas that danced through her imagination, ideas for how to combine the different gemstones into stunning patterns. But that hadn't been what snagged her heart.

From the moment she'd understood the true symbolism of a wedding ring and what it stood for . . . From the instant she realized what her mother never experienced, and no doubt longed to share with the man she loved, Francesca had been drawn to create the dream. And now she had.

She studied her designs one last time, thrilled that she'd completed what she'd set out to achieve all those years ago. She'd given birth to something beyond her wildest expectations and, ironically, she owed it all to Severo Dante. Somehow, at some point, he'd crept into her heart and given her the final spark of inspiration she'd needed to bring her designs to life.

Tears filled her eyes and she shook her head with a smile. How ridiculous to get all weepy over a bunch of drawings. She hadn't even completed a mockup of them, yet. Not that it mattered. She knew how the finished product would look. She even knew how they could market the collection. An entire campaign existed between the covers of her sketchpad, a campaign that would relaunch Dantes into a full line of women's jewelry, should that possibility interest them.

Flipping her pad closed, she locked it away just as her studio door banged open. Tina stood there, looking more devastated than Francesca had ever seen her.

"Tina? What's wrong?" Francesca asked, half-rising. "What's happened?"

"Is it true?" Tina slammed the door closed behind her, closeting them together in the room. "All this time I thought you were the innocent in all this. That Dante had you completely snowed.

I actually thought maybe we could work things out between us. But now I'm not so sure."

A sick suspicion clawed at Francesca's stomach. "What are you talking about?"

"I'm talking about my husband." Tina's mouth twisted. "Or should I say . . . your father."

Francesca felt every scrap of color drain from her face and she sank back into her chair. "You can't be serious. I'm not—"

Tina cut her off with a swipe of her hand. "Don't. At least have the decency not to lie to me." Her heels pounded out a succession of hard staccato raps as she crossed the room. "I have the evidence."

"How?"

"That's not important." She reached the edge of the desk and Francesca could see the wild pain lurking in the older woman's eyes. "You lied to me. To Kurt."

"Only about my connection to him. Only that, I swear."

A wild laugh ripped loose. "Only that? Only?"

How could she explain? "I just wanted to get to know him. From a distance," Francesca emphasized. "I never planned to tell either of you the truth."

Fury ignited. "What were you waiting for? To worm your way into our good graces and then spring it on us? Hope Kurt was smitten enough with the idea of having a daughter that he'd give you a piece of my business?" She slammed her palms on Francesca's desk. "*My* business. Not Kurt's. He may keep the production end of things afloat, but I'm the creative force behind Timeless Heirlooms."

Francesca shook her head. "You don't understand. I'd never do anything to cause trouble for you two." Guilt overwhelmed her. She never should have applied for a job at TH. Never should have put her own selfish needs ahead of respecting the sanctity of her father's marriage. "I just wanted to get to know my father," she confessed miserably. "I never planned to tell either of you who I was. Please, Tina. This isn't Kurt's fault."

"I'm well aware of whose fault this is." She stabbed a finger at Francesca. "*Yours.* You chose to come into our life. You chose to become involved with Severo Dante. You ruined my marriage."

"Ruined?" Francesca shot to her feet. "No, Tina. Don't walk out on Kurt. Not because of me."

"I can add. Better yet, I can subtract. According to our personnel records, you're twenty-six. That means Kurt and I were married three years when he—" She broke off, clearly softened the description she'd been about to use. "When he had an affair with your mother."

"It was a long time ago, Tina. All anyone has to do is look at him to know he's crazy in love with you." Francesca jettisoned every scrap of pride to plead on Kurt's behalf. "After thirty years of marriage, surely that counts for something?"

"Maybe it would have, if not for you. But every time I see you, every time I hear your name or see your designs, it's a slap in the face. Living proof of my husband's infidelity." Tina spun around and stalked to the door. Once there, she paused. "Oh, and by the way? You can thank your fiancé for clueing me in to your true identity. It would seem he'll do anything to get his hands on TH. Even destroy my marriage."

Sev sat behind his desk, papers strewn across the thick glass surface. Some were preliminary jewelry designs, others financial statements from the various international branches, still others proposals for expansion. All of the reports demanded his immediate attention.

A knock sounded at his door just as he reached for the first report. Before he could respond, Francesca entered the room. She shut the door behind her with a tad too much emphasis, warning of her less than stellar mood.

"How could you?" she demanded.

He stilled, studying her through narrowed eyes. "Clichéd, but intriguing nonetheless. Dare I ask, how could I what?"

"Tina knows. Tina knows I'm Kurt's daughter. There's only one person who could have told her."

"I gather that's where I come in." He leaned back in his chair, reaching for calm. For some reason that only served to push her anger to greater heights.

"Don't," she warned sharply. "Don't play with me."

"I'd love to play with you, though not about this." He gave her a level look. "Honey, I haven't broken my promise to you. The only contact I've had with Tina is to up my offer for Timeless Heirlooms."

Francesca shook her head. "You don't get it. You—or one of your brothers—are the only ones who could have told her. No one else knows."

He smiled at that, which might have been a mistake judging by the flash of fury that glittered in her dark eyes. "Someone must know, otherwise we wouldn't have uncovered the information in the first place."

She slowly shook her head. "I hired a private investigator four years ago to find my father. He couldn't. But he did find an old friend of my mother's and she's the one who revealed my father's identity. I never told anyone, not even the PI. So unless someone tracked this woman down and forced her to talk, I have trouble believing the leak came from her."

That caught him by surprise. Shoving back his chair, he stood and circled his desk. Cupping her elbow, he drew her over to the sitting area on the far side of the room. "Are you certain she didn't tell anyone else?"

"I can't be positive." She perched on the edge of the couch and he sat next to her, too close judging by the tide of awareness that washed through her. She struggled to hide her dismay by directing it toward anger. "But I find it highly unlikely she'd call Tina out of the blue and just hand over that information. It doesn't make any sense."

He analyzed what she'd said, looking for alternate explanations. "What about your foster parents? Is it possible they had that information?"

"Not a chance. They'd have turned Kurt's name over to the state to force him to pay child support." She leveled him with a censorious look. "How did you find out about Kurt? Who in your organization knows the truth?"

"We hired a private investigator to check you out," he admitted.

She couldn't prevent the accusation. "You've had me investigated?"

"We had all of TH's designers investigated as a matter of course." He held up a hand to ward off her indignation. "Listen, I'll contact the investigator and ascertain how he came across the information. All I can tell you is that I didn't betray your secret to Tina. Nor did any of my brothers."

She surged to her feet and paced across his office. "This is going to destroy the Fontaines' marriage."

"Maybe. Maybe not." Though, privately, he'd rate it closer to probable, edging toward definite.

"If it does, you'll be able to pick up TH for a song."

He absorbed the accusation. "Which automatically makes me guilty?"

She spun to face him. "Tina claimed you told her. And it makes sense. Who else profits from revealing the truth to her?"

He shrugged. "As far as I know, no one."

"You're not helping yourself." Frustration riddled her expression. "You realize that, don't you?"

"I realize that nothing I say will change your mind. I also realize you don't trust me."

"How could I? Why would I?" She thrust her fingers through her hair, tumbling the curls into delicious disarray. "Since the minute we met you've done nothing to inspire that trust."

That got to him, shaving some of the calm from his temper. "Our nights together didn't inspire trust? Our time together hasn't proven the sort of man I am?"

Tears welled in her eyes again. "Those nights meant everything to me, more than they could have meant to you or you'd never have blackmailed me. You'd never have forced me to betray the Fontaines and work for you."

He climbed to his feet to give weight to his words. "I intend to return Dantes to its position as an international powerhouse, no matter what sort of sacrifices that requires. I made that fact crystal clear to you right from the start. I will recover every last subsidiary I was forced to sell off when I assumed the reins of this company. And that includes TH."

She tugged off his engagement ring and held it out. "Take this. I refuse to wear it a minute longer."

He simply shook his head. "That's not happening. If we break our engagement so soon after we announce it, your life within the jewelry world will become unbearable." He held up his hand to stem her protest. "As my fiancée, you have the Dante name to protect you. No one will dare say a word about you, your talent, or where you choose to work. Nor will anyone dare say anything should Tina decide to be indiscreet."

Her mouth trembled. "You think she'll tell people I'm Kurt's daughter? You think she'll publicly blame me for TH's demise?"

"A woman that angry is capable of anything. There's no telling what she'll do."

Francesca made a swift recovery, one that impressed the hell out of him. "I don't care about any of that. Let people talk. Let Tina do her worst. Let the world assume whatever they want."

"Right. And maybe you could handle the public fallout. Damned if you don't seem determined to try. But I have Dantes to consider. Becoming engaged one day and ending it only weeks later is not the image I want to project to the general public, my suppliers, or my associates and competitors."

"Then you never should have come up with this scheme."

"Point taken, but it's a little late for that." He offered a wry smile. "When I came up with the idea, my only consideration was you and trying to salvage your relationship with the Fontaines. That's what I get for thinking like Nicolò."

For an endless moment she wavered between acceptance and rejection. To his profound relief, she released her breath in a sigh of reluctant agreement. "How long? How long do we have to keep up the pretense?"

"For as long as it takes." He ran his hands up and down her arms, picking up on the slight shiver she couldn't quite suppress. "Give it time, sweetheart. Is it really so bad being engaged to me? You liked my family, didn't you?"

Once again, he'd said the wrong thing. Her eyes darkened in distress. "I don't want to fall in love with them."

He could guess why. "Because it hurts too much when it ends and you're forced to walk away."

She didn't deny it. Instead she changed the subject. "What about the Fontaines? You have to promise me you won't take advantage of this latest wrinkle. You have to promise me you're still going to pay full price for TH, even if their marriage falls apart."

He refused to be anything other than straight with her. "If they offer me a good deal, I'm not going to turn it down."

Maybe he shouldn't have been quite that straight. She pulled back and glared. "We have a contract. You have to pay them full price for their business. And I intend to make sure you stick to that agreement."

"Our contract states I'm to pay fair market value. That's what I intend to pay and not a penny more."

"Even if the fair market value drops because Kurt and Tina divorce?"

"Fair. Market. Value," he repeated succinctly.

She stilled and something drifted across her expression, something that had the businessman in him going on red alert. Then she gave a careless shrug. "If that's the best you're willing to do, I guess I have no choice but to accept it, do I?"

He stared at her through narrowed eyes. "That's precisely what I expect you to do, since that's precisely what the contract calls for."

She turned to leave his office without further argument, which worried him all the more. Hell. No question about it. She was up to something, and he suspected he wouldn't like whatever scheme she was busily hatching.

Later that evening, Francesca stood outside Sev's apartment building, her head bent against the rain, soaked to the skin from an unexpected shower. Why had he demanded she come by tonight of all nights? she wondered in despair. Maybe if she hadn't gotten together with Kurt she wouldn't be finding this so difficult. But when she'd suggested waiting until morning to show Sev her latest designs, he'd insisted that he needed to see them tonight.

She shivered uncontrollably, wanting nothing more than to crawl into her bathtub at home and have a long, hot soak in conjunction with an even longer cry. Swiping the dampness from her cheeks—rain, she attempted to reassure herself, not tears—she rode the elevator to the top floor of Sev's apartment building and applied fist to door.

It opened almost immediately. "What the hell?" Sev took one look at her and swept her across the threshold and into his apartment, ignoring her disjointed protests about dripping all over his hardwood floors. "I don't give a flying f—" He tempered the expression. "A flying fig about the damn floors. I care about you. What the hell's happened? Are you all right?"

"I'm wet." She trembled and held out the packet of designs. "Maybe cold, too. I'm shaking so hard it's sort of tough to tell."

He snatched the designs from her hand and tossed them aside. The packet hit the floor and skidded under an antique coat closet. Then he unceremoniously swept her into his arms and carried her into the master bathroom. She couldn't rouse herself enough to fight him when he stripped first her, and then himself, and pulled them both into the glassed-in shower stall. He turned the jets on high and she stood docilely beneath the blazing-hot torrent and let the water wash away all emotion.

"What happened?" he asked again, more gently this time.

She didn't even realize she spoke until she heard her voice echoing against the tile. "He didn't want me, Sev. My father. He agreed to meet me tonight and then sent me away. He said he was sorry. Sorry!" She covered her face with her hands as she fought for control. "Sorry he had an affair with my mother. Sorry she became pregnant. Sorry Tina found out the truth. He said he couldn't see me ever again."

"He's a fool."

She dropped her hands and stared up at Sev. "What did I do? What did I do wrong?"

He hugged her fiercely. "You didn't do anything wrong. Not a damn thing. It's them, honey. Something's wrong with them. But you have me and you have the rest of the Dantes. And they flat-out adore you." A raw ferocity coated his words. "We'll be your family from now on."

"When they find out we're not really engaged, they won't want me, either," she felt obligated to point out, tears welling anew.

"They will. I promise." He continued to hold her close while the water poured down on them. "Easy, sweetheart. Let it all out. You'll feel better if you do."

Let what out? Didn't he understand? She felt dead inside. Her father rejected her. She couldn't say why she cared so much. After all, what did one more rejection matter after so many?

At long last, Sev shut off the water and left her dripping, naked and alone, in the middle of the tile floor. An instant later he reappeared with an armload of towels. He slung one around his waist and dropped another on her head, before swathing her from shoulders to knees in a third. Then he proceeded to rub her down with a briskness that caused her skin to glow.

"What are you doing?" she asked, emotional exhaustion leaving her only mildly curious.

"You're in shock. I need to get you warm."

She peered at him from beneath the towel. "I'm not shocked. I'm not even surprised. I knew what would happen if Kurt and Tina found out the truth about me."

He knelt at her feet, drying her with an impersonal touch that had her responding in far too personal a way. "You'd be rejected, just as you've been rejected so many times before."

She shrugged, admitting, "I'm sort of used to it."

"Yeah, I know. That's what kills me."

"Don't let it bother you. It doesn't bother me. Not anymore."

"I shouldn't ask. But I will." He rocked back on his heels and stared up at her, his face set in grim lines. "Why doesn't it bother you anymore?"

She spoke slowly, as though to a backward child. "Because I can't feel."

Sheesh. Didn't he get it? "When you can't feel, it doesn't hurt."

For some reason that made him swear. When he'd run out of invectives, he planted a hand low on her back and ushered her from the bathroom. "I don't know about you, but I could use a drink."

"Several, I think."

"Hmm. And something to eat."

Ten minutes later, she was curled up on the floor in front of a fire, dining on a selection of imported cheese and crackers while sipping the smoothest single-malt whiskey she'd ever tasted. Sev lounged beside her, a towel still knotted at his waist. She woke to her surroundings sufficiently to admire the miles of toned muscle rising above the soft white fleece.

Lord help her, but he was the most gorgeous man she'd ever seen. He hadn't bothered to brush his hair, simply slicked it back from his face so it clung damply to the back of his neck in heavy, dark waves. His features reminded her somewhat of Primo, with the same rugged handsomeness and noble bearing. And, of course, the same stunning eye color. But the rest . . . Oh, my. The rest was pure Severo Dante.

She buried her nose in the crystal tumbler and took a quick sip. Unable to help herself, she peeked at him from over the rim. Memories from their nights together came storming back. They'd made love right here in front of the fire at least a half-dozen times. Several more times on the couch behind them when they'd been too impatient to traverse the short distance from there to the bedroom. Most nights she shared with him, a pathway appeared, one strewn with clothes spreading from front door to bed.

How she enjoyed those moments, especially when she wrestled him free of that last article of clothing. He had the most incredible body, lean and graceful, yet powerful enough to lift her with ease, which he often did, then tip her onto silken sheets and cover her with that endless length of potent masculinity.

She drained the last of the whiskey and set the glass aside. "I need you to do me a favor," she informed him.

"If I can."

"Oh, you can." The only question was . . . Would he? "I want you to make love to me. I want to feel something again."

He studied her for a long, silent moment and she could see him preparing a list of excuses. She was too vulnerable. He didn't want to take advantage of her. There were still so many issues unresolved between them. But something in her gaze, or perhaps it was something buried deep in his heart, must have convinced him otherwise.

Instead of turning her down, he tugged the towel free of her hair and tossed it aside before pulling her onto his lap and thrusting his hands deep into her damp curls. Turning her to fully face him, her knees settling on either side of his hips, he closed his mouth over hers in a kiss hot enough to leave scorch marks. She opened for him, welcoming him home. The duel was short and sweet, a battle for supremacy that neither lost, yet both won.

"Do you feel that?" he asked.

The question slid from his mouth to hers and she laughed softly in response. "I'm not sure. I might have noticed a slight tingle."

His eyes narrowed. "Slight tingle? Slight?"

She blinked with patently false innocence and wiggled her bottom in a provocative motion against him. "Very slight."

"Let's see what we can do about that."

He flipped her off his lap and onto her back. Firelight lapped over his determined face and caught in his eyes, causing the gold to burn like wildfire. She missed this. Missed seeing his abandoned reaction whenever they touched. Missed the romantic soul that blunted the contours of his male sexuality. Missed opening to him—physically and emotionally—in the darkest hours of the night and sharing all she hid within her heart. And having him share what he kept locked away in his. But most of all, she missed this. The intimacy. The passion. Possessing and being possessed.

He kissed her again. Deeper. More thoroughly. He worshiped her with mouth and tongue until she went mindless with pleasure. "Tell me you feel that," he demanded.

She groaned. "A tickle. Barely a tickle."

"Right. That's it."

Uh-oh. Annoyed obstinance if ever she heard it. He kissed a path downward, mixing the gentle caresses with love nips that had her toes curling into knots. He ripped the towel open and bared her to a combination of firelight and heated gaze. He shot her one last lingering look before applying himself to his appointed task.

He glided his hands along the sides of her breasts, using just the very tips of his fingers so he barely connected with her skin. She shivered at the sensation, shocked that so light a touch could provoke such a strong reaction. She bit back a cry, forcing herself to remain silent, even though it just might kill her. No. *Definitely* would kill her.

Around he circled, edging ever closer to the pebbled tips of her breasts. She fought with every ounce of self-possession to keep from begging him to take her, almost shooting off the plush carpet when his teeth closed over her nipple and tugged.

If she'd ever questioned The Inferno before, she didn't now. It erupted, low in her belly, spilling over like molten lava. It liquefied everything in its path as it began an onslaught of hunger so deep and all-consuming, she literally shook with the effort to contain it.

He moved lower, touching her belly with his fingers and mouth. Lower. Brushing the nest of curls that protected her feminine core. Lower. Took the heart of her with his mouth. She went deaf and blind as her climax ripped her apart. She fought to draw air into lungs squeezed breathless, barely aware that Sev had left her side.

She still hadn't recovered when he returned, carefully protected, and settled between her thighs. "Do you feel alive now? Do you feel wanted?"

Sensations toppled one on top of another, so intense she couldn't process them all. *"Sev . . ."* His name escaped in a husky cry, half concession, half demand. "Pleaseohpleaseohplease."

He probed inward, a teasing, swirling movement. "Do you feel this?"

"Yes." She moaned as he slid deep, driving all the way home. "I'm definitely feeling something I never have before."

She wrapped her legs around his waist and held on. She'd never felt more alive. Never felt more wanted or cherished. Never belonged with anyone as she did with Sev in this moment. Her climax approached again, every bit as powerful as before. Only this time he joined her. To her amazement, it didn't rip or shred, but melded, uniting them together in something so different, so special, she couldn't at first find the word to name it. And then it came to her and in doing so, overwhelmed her with the devastating knowledge.

In that brief moment, she no longer stood on the outside looking in. Love opened the door and she flew inside.

Chapter Ten

Morning found Sev in bed wrapped around Francesca in a complicated tangle of arms and legs. He had a vague recollection of scraping her boneless body off the carpet and tossing her over his shoulder before staggering to the bedroom. Or maybe they'd just crawled here.

She stirred within his embrace and flopped onto her back with a groan. He smiled at the sight. She'd gone to bed with damp hair and now it surrounded her head like a fluffy halo. Something told him she wouldn't appreciate her appearance anywhere near as much as he did.

His smile faded as a new and unfamiliar realization took hold. Last night their relationship had changed, a change that went way beyond what it had been before, on either the work front or as former lovers. Somehow, it had shifted them into an entirely new realm, a realm neither of them anticipated.

"Who glued my eyes shut?" She forced one open. "Hey, we're in bed."

"Excellent observation."

"How'd we get here?"

"Beats the hell out of me."

"Maybe I carried you in before I had my wicked way with you. Again."

He grinned. "That's entirely possible."

"Is it just me?" She hesitated, an innate wariness flickering like a warning light. "Or did something peculiar happen to us last night? Even more peculiar than The Inferno, I mean. Although how that's even possible is beyond me."

He framed her face, tracing the delicate bone structure with his fingertips until the shape and texture became as familiar to him as his own. The need to remain in physical contact with her had become an urge he no longer bothered resisting. The Inferno had won.

"I believe we both realized the truth last night," he admitted.

She regarded him with some reservation. "Which is?"

"This isn't going away." He lifted her left hand and studied the engagement ring she wore. The inner fire seemed to erupt from the center of the diamond, fiercer than he'd ever seen it before. "Maybe we should consider making this permanent."

He absorbed her jerk of surprise, felt her heart rate kick up a notch. "Are you serious?"

"I think it's worth discussing, don't you?"

A small smile played at the corners of her mouth. It grew until her entire face radiated with it. "I wouldn't mind," she admitted softly.

On the nightstand table, his cell emitted a soft buzz and Sev swore beneath his breath. "I should have left the damn thing in the other room."

She jackknifed upward and snatched a swift kiss. "Go ahead and take it while I get cleaned up."

"You sure?"

"Positive."

She bounced off the bed and darted into the bathroom. Her muffled shriek of dismay put a grin on his face. Something told him she'd just discovered a mirror. He snagged the phone and took the call. "This better be good," he growled.

"It's Lazz. And it's not good. In fact, it's an effing mess. If you'd bothered to come to work this morning—"

"Get to the point," Sev interrupted.

"Seriously, bro, what the hell are you doing and why aren't you here?

There is a fan sitting on my desk cranked to high and you can't believe what just hit it."

"What's wrong?"

"It's Francesca."

Hell. He glanced toward the bathroom. Water ran in the sink and he could hear her humming, the sound light and happy and slightly off-key. "What's the problem?"

"Bloom's rep called. They've decided to go with Timeless."

"Not good, but we knew winning that account would be a long shot. What's it got to do with Francesca?"

At the sound of her name, she appeared in the doorway. She'd tamed her hair, much to his disappointment and, even more disappointing, slipped on one of his shirts. She shot him a questioning look as she rolled up the sleeves, an incandescent happiness pouring off her in waves. After the meeting with Kurt, he didn't think she'd ever find joy again. But she had, and it humbled him that she found it in his arms.

"Francesca's the one who convinced Bloom to go with TH," Lazz said.

Sev shot off the bed. "Not a chance."

"I'm dead serious. Sev, I spoke to the rep. Personally."

He bowed his head and stared at the floor. "She wouldn't have done that. I want you to double-check, Lazz. Triple-check, if that's what it takes. Find out why Bloom's rep would lie to you." And then he looked up, straight into Francesca's eyes. What hovered there in the shadowed darkness had him breaking off with a word he'd never normally use in her presence. He hit the disconnect button. "Lazz doesn't need to triple-check, does he? Bloom's rep told him the truth."

His shirt hung on her, making her appear small and fragile. Or maybe it was the barriers she slammed back in place. He never realized how utterly they enshrouded her until she emerged from their protective folds. Last night she'd bared herself in a way she never had before, not in all the time they'd been together.

Francesca shook her head. "There's no point in his checking again."

"You contacted Juliet Bloom's representative?" At her nod, he hit her with his accusation. "You advised her to go with Timeless."

"Yes. I guaranteed she wouldn't lose if she did so. That it would only benefit her."

He lifted an eyebrow. "Payback, Francesca?" he asked softly.

She tilted her chin to a combative angle and fixed him with a cool, remote gaze that shot his blood pressure straight through the roof. "I prefer to call it insurance."

"Explain," he rapped out.

"Timeless Heirlooms owns the designs that Juliet Bloom is so crazy about. The ones *I* created. She wants to wear them in her next film. Dantes plans to purchase TH, not put them out of business, so Timeless will endure regardless of ownership. Once the company is safely tucked back into the Dantes' fold, you'll receive the continued benefit from having someone of Bloom's caliber as your spokeswoman."

"If we tuck TH back into the Dantes' fold," he corrected tightly. "That's a big, fat effing *if!*"

"You've already assured me it's going to happen, regardless of me, or the Fontaines, or even Juliet Bloom." She lifted an eyebrow. "A lie, Sev?"

His back teeth clamped together. "It's no lie."

"Then what's the problem?" She stepped from the bathroom, wary enough to keep her distance. Smart woman. "All I've done is ensure that you honor the contract we signed and pay the Fontaines a fair price for TH. Now that Bloom's agreed to be the spokeswoman for them, Kurt and Tina will reunite. They'll have no other choice if they want that contract. Knowing Tina as I do, she won't let a little thing like an illegitimate daughter stand in the way of a deal of this magnitude."

"It will, however, make it more difficult for me to acquire TH."

She graciously conceded the point, which had him backing up a step so he wouldn't give in to temptation and throttle her. "But it will happen. And when that day comes, since I work for you, I'm also available to work with Ms. Bloom should she wish to expand the current collection I designed for her. Or I can create a whole new line for her at some point in the future. And if you don't buy out TH, Ms. Bloom will most likely jump ship and become Dantes' spokeswoman, since I now work for you. As far as I can tell, everyone comes out of this a winner."

"Except for you."

That stopped her. About damn time. "What are you talking about?" For the first time a hint of uncertainty crept into her voice.

"I'm talking about the fact that I have the option to either fire you, in which case I'll see to it that you don't work in the industry for the next two years. Or I can transfer you to another office. Either way, Bloom will no longer be your problem."

"Which do you intend to do?"

Francesca asked the question so calmly, if he didn't know better he'd have thought she didn't care. But if he'd learned nothing else about her, he had learned that designing jewelry was as much a part of her as her heart or soul. In fact, it was her soul. He couldn't take that away from her, no matter how badly her actions had hurt him.

And they *had* hurt him. This wasn't about business, anymore. In fact, she'd shown a ruthlessness he could almost admire. A ruthlessness he, himself, had been forced to employ on occasion. No, this had become personal. It felt personal. It felt as though he'd risked opening himself to her, only to have her use what she'd learned to hurt him.

"I believe there's a spot open for you in our New York office. I'll make your transfer effective immediately."

She jerked as though he'd struck her, staring at him for an endless moment with huge, wounded eyes. Without a word, she turned on her heel and moved through the apartment, gathering her possessions. Sev hardened himself as he waited for her to finish and leave.

Even so, it tore him apart watching her. One more rejection. One more door slammed in her face. Once more out in the proverbial cold. They made one hell of a pair.

He scoured his face with his hands. All the while, The Inferno consumed him, raging with the urge to go to her. To fix this. To take her back into his arms and make her his again. His jaw tightened. The hell with it. This was just one more roadblock. A huge one, granted. But surely they could—

The front door opened and quietly closed, locking behind her. Sev charged into the living room, but she was gone, leaving nothing behind but a cold gleam emanating from the fireplace. Sitting on the hearth he found the engagement ring he'd given her. He crossed the room and picked it up.

Maybe it was his imagination, but he could have sworn the fire deep within the heart of the diamond had dimmed.

Francesca sat at her drawing board in her New York office, an office not that dissimilar from the one she'd occupied in San Francisco. Exhaustion dogged her, thanks to an endless round of sleepless nights. She'd only been in New York for a month, but already it felt like a lifetime. She rubbed her eyes, struggling to get them to focus on designs that could only be described as mediocre, at best. For some reason, her heart wasn't in her work anymore.

But then, how could it be? The past few weeks had been some of the darkest and most difficult of her life, far worse than anything she'd gone through in foster care. Worse even than her father's rejection. She'd made a hideous mistake when she'd contacted Bloom's rep.

Why hadn't it occurred to her that by helping the Fontaines, she was betraying Dantes . . . and more specifically, the man she loved? She'd been so busy easing her own guilt over leaving TH, that she never gave a thought to how her decision would impact Sev. Or that thanks to their feelings for each other, he wouldn't see her actions from a business standpoint, but take her betrayal personally. She'd simply reacted to what she'd perceived as an unfair situation and taken matters into her own hands.

That still didn't explain why he hadn't acknowledged the designs she'd given him on their last night together. She'd hoped he'd understand what they meant. Hoped he'd realize that while she'd won the Bloom account for TH, she'd left him something far more valuable.

A familiar longing filled her as The Inferno gave her a small, petulant kick. Even after all this time the connection remained—stretched thin and taut, granted. Yet, it held with unbelievable tenacity.

The phone on her desk let out a shrill ring and she picked it up, surprised to have her greeting answered with a cheerful, *"Ciao, sorella.* It's Marco."

Pleasure mingled with disappointment at the sound of his voice. Pleasure to hear from a Dante. And disappointment that it wasn't the right Dante. "It's good to hear from you," she replied. "Though I'm surprised that any of you are willing to talk to me."

"You'd be even more surprised by how many of us are on your side." He hesitated. "I'm afraid I can't talk right now. I actually called to ask about some missing designs. Sev would like to know what happened to them. They're not in your old office. I don't suppose you took them with you to New York?"

She frowned. "I don't understand. I gave them to Sev."

"When, Francesca?"

"The night—" She broke off. The night they'd last made love. "The night before I transferred to New York. I brought them to Sev's apartment."

"He claims he doesn't have them."

Memory kicked in. "It had been raining the night I gave him the designs and I was soaked through. I vaguely recall he took them and tossed them onto the floor, out of the way." An image flashed through her mind. "I think they slid under that lovely old armoire he has in the entryway. You know the one I mean? He may not have noticed."

"Got it. Thanks, Francesca." He hesitated. "Are you . . . are you doing okay?"

No. Not even close to okay. "I'm fine."

"Right." She could hear the irony slipping through the line. "About as fine as Sev, I'd guess."

Francesca closed her eyes. "I have to be fine," she whispered. "We both do. There isn't any other choice."

"You didn't need to come with me," Sev informed Marco. "I'm perfectly capable of looking under my own coat closet."

"I came to try and make you see sense, as you damn well know."

"I always see sense. I'm the most sensible

of the lot of you."

"Not about this. Not when it comes to Francesca."

Sev shoved his key into the front door lock and twisted so hard it was a wonder the metal didn't snap off in his hand. "What's gotten into you, Marco? What part of *she betrayed us* don't you get?"

"And how many times did you betray her?" his brother shot back. "I know. I know. You had valid reasons. It was all about protecting Dantes. So, answer me this, hotshot. What makes that okay and what she did not okay? She was protecting her family the same as you."

That very question had been tearing Sev apart. How could he explain to his brother that it wasn't about business anymore? How could he explain the irrational belief that this betrayal felt personal? That this time he'd allowed his emotions to override his common sense? For the first time in his life, he, the Dante who prided himself on cool, emotionless deliberation, who used calm logic and rational thinking to govern all of his business decisions, hadn't been able to utilize any of his skills or abilities.

When it came to Francesca he was neither emotionless, nor logical, let alone cool and calm. The very thought of her caused a burning desire so overwhelming it didn't leave room for anything else.

Marco followed Sev into the apartment. Stooping, he reached under the coat closet and snagged a large, thick envelope. "Here it is. Right where she said it'd be." He sent the packet spinning in Sev's direction. "Happy now? Glad you didn't accuse her of selling her designs to the competition?"

Sev jerked as though punched. "She'd never—" he said automatically.

"You're right. She'd never." Marco glared at him. "Do you have any idea how lucky you are? Do you have any idea what the rest of us would give to feel The Inferno for a woman like Francesca? To know we could actually share a life with a woman like her, instead of longing for what we can never have? Instead of settling for second best? I never thought I'd say this to you, of all people, but you're an ass, Severo Dante."

Without a word, Sev ripped open the envelope and pulled out a sketchpad. He flipped it open and spared it a swift glance. And then he froze. "Marco . . ."

"What now?" He shifted to stand beside Sev and whistled softly. "If you needed proof how much she loves you, here it is."

Sev nodded. Page after page revealed some of the most incredible jewelry designs he'd ever seen. Designs ideal for the expansion Dantes' planned for some point in the future. It didn't take much thought to understand what she'd done.

Or why.

He understood all too well why she'd left these designs, designs she'd clearly been working on for years. She'd taken with one hand by giving the Bloom account to TH, and given with the other by presenting Dantes with these designs, dispensing a rough sort of justice. Only, she had more than compensated Dantes for what she'd given to Timeless Heirlooms.

She'd left him an incomparable gift, one that decimated the priorities he'd set in stone the day he'd first taken over from his father. A gift that made him realize there could only be one priority in his life from this point forward, and it wasn't Dantes.

The gift she'd given him wasn't the designs contained in her sketchpad. She'd left behind the gift of her heart.

Another month passed after Francesca's conversation with Marco. A month of pain and sorrow and regret. During those weeks, she'd come to the realization that Sev's feelings for her were truly dead, that The Inferno no longer burned for him the way it still burned for her.

Even when she received instructions to return to San Francisco on company business, she'd been unable to summon so much as a spark of hope. After all, miracles didn't exist. She'd learned that at the tender of age of eight when she'd been discarded by the people she'd hoped would one day be her adoptive parents. She knew better than to expect the door to open and for her to be welcomed in. She'd been disappointed too many times. And Sev had made himself abundantly clear before sending her to New York. She no longer belonged to the Dante inner circle.

She crossed to the mirror and examined her dress. She'd been specifically asked by Sev's assistant to wear red in order to fit in with the theme chosen for this evening's festivities. What theme, no one had bothered to explain. So, Francesca picked the brightest, most glorious shade of red she could find.

The fitted bodice glittered with Swarovski crystal beads, while the chiffon skirt drifted outward from her hips to the floor in layers of handkerchief veils that lifted and swirled on an invisible breeze. After some debate, she chose to leave her hair down and it fell in heavy curls to shoulders bared by the halter neckline of the gown.

Dantes had sent over jewelry to wear for the evening. She'd never seen the pieces before, but they were positively breathtaking. The necklace and earrings were simple confections, as romantic as they were elegant, featuring some of the most stunning fire diamonds she'd ever seen. Based on the design of the engagement ring she'd worn for far too brief a time, she would bet these latest items were Primo's creations, as well.

After checking the mirror a final time, she forced herself to leave the relative safety of the suite before Sev sent out a search party. Not giving herself a chance to reconsider, she took the elevator to the lobby and crossed to the steps leading to the ballroom. She hesitated at the threshold, searching for a friendly face. Instantly a hum of desire turned her insides molten. She didn't doubt the cause. Without any hesitation, she turned her head, keying in on Sev.

How could she ever have imagined The Inferno had finished with them, or her love would dwindle over time? The urge to go to him, to touch him, to have him possess her mouth, her body, her very soul, slammed through her. It grew so strong, she could do nothing more than obey the silent imperative. She took a half-dozen steps in Sev's direction before a sudden whisper of voices swelled, then faded, leaving behind a thunderous silence.

Her step faltered and she glanced around, only then realizing that while she wore flaming red, everyone else present was dressed in black and white. Only one other person also wore red, if only a scrap of the color. Sev's pocket handkerchief was a rich shade of ruby that stood out against his black suit and white dress shirt. Feeling painfully conspicuous, she held her head high and finished wending her way toward him.

She greeted him with a cool nod, while inside she thumbed with the hellish fires of desire. "Mr. Dante."

A small smile played about his mouth. "Ms. Sommers. If you'll come with me?"

He led the way to a small dais and approached the microphone. "I'd like to thank everyone for coming this evening to Dantes' launch of a brand-new collection. With me is the creator of that collection, its heart and soul, Francesca Sommers."

She froze in total shock. More than anything she wanted to grab Sev's hand for support, to demand an explanation. She turned to look at him, and every thought slid from her head, except one. She still loved this man. Utterly. Totally. Completely. From this day until the end of days.

"What's going on?" she pleaded.

"Smile, sweetheart," he murmured. "They're all here for you."

"But . . . why?"

He stepped toward the microphone again. "Please enjoy your evening, as well as our grand launch of—" He swept his arms wide. *"Dante's Heart."*

From either side of the ballroom, models appeared, each wearing a different one of the designs Francesca had left behind for Sev to use. Designs she'd envisioned as a teenager. Designs she'd worked on for a full decade and never quite brought to life, until she'd opened her heart to love. To Sev's love. Only then had she found the spark that turned her creative flame into a creative inferno.

She began to tremble in reaction. "You're using my designs to relaunch Dantes into a full line of jewelry?" Why had he done this? What did it mean?

"Jewelry for the contemporary woman." His hands settled on her shoulders and he gazed down at her with eyes more vivid than the sun. "You're Dante's Heart, my love. At least you're this Dante's heart."

Applause exploded around them and excited chatter swelled as the assembled guests got their first look at the new line. Tears filled Francesca's eyes. "I love you, Sev. More than you can possibly guess. I'm sorry, so sorry for everything—"

He stopped her words with a shake of his head. "Don't apologize. That's for me to do. I never should have put you in such an impossible position. It won't happen again. From now on you are, and always will be, first in my life." He inclined his head toward the gathering. "Do you hear them, sweetheart?"

She said the first thing that popped into her head. "They're clapping."

He grinned. "How could they not? They're witnessing something extraordinary." He laced his hand with hers and something deep inside gave way, a rending of barriers that had been erected when she'd been a frightened child of five. And in its place, the connection between them expanded and grew, rooting deep and permanent. "Come with me. We need to talk."

She glanced toward the doors leading onto the balcony. "I think I know the perfect location."

Together they left the dais, intent only on escape. Not that they were allowed such an easy out. Family came first, as Primo enveloped her in a huge bear hug, followed by a warm embrace from Nonna. Marco approached, sweeping her into a dizzying dip and laughing kiss full on the mouth. Then Lazz, who settled for a chaste peck on the cheek. And finally, Nicolò, who kissed the back of her hand with old-world gallantry.

Next, friends and associates impeded their progress, raving about the collection and using words that left Francesca choked with emotion. Words like "spectacular" and "unparalleled" and "generation defining." Mere feet from escape, Francesca came face-to-face with the Fontaines.

Instantly, Sev's arm wrapped around her, offering strength and protection. She gave his hand a reassuring squeeze, an unspoken message that even though she appreciated his support, she intended to handle this confrontation on her own terms.

"Tina, Kurt." She offered a smile. Not one of apology. Not one of nervousness or regret. But an open smile of genuine affection. A smile from the heart.

To her astonishment, they responded in kind. "Has Severo told you the news?" Tina asked.

Francesca glanced in bewilderment from Sev back to the Fontaines. "What news?"

Sev shook his head. "I was hoping we'd run into you, so you could tell her, yourself."

Tina grinned. "We reached a compromise. Timeless Heirlooms is now a subsidiary of Dantes. But Sev's agreed that we can continue to run it, with a few changes to assist the bottom line."

"Such as Dantes being in charge of acquiring new designers," Sev inserted. "And a few fiscal repairs that Kurt will oversee."

Tina waved that aside. "With Dantes' name behind us and our contract with Juliet Bloom, TH is guaranteed to skyrocket to the top." Ever the businesswoman, she added, "Anytime you want to contribute one of your designs, my dear, you're more than welcome."

Sev gave Tina a pointed look. "I believe there's something else you wanted to tell Francesca."

Tina squirmed. "Oh, right. That." She released a gusty sigh. "I owe you an apology. Sev didn't tell me about your connection to Kurt. His PI did. The man tried to double his profit by reselling the information."

"I've since taken care of the matter," Sev added.

The tone of his voice left little doubt in Francesca's mind that the PI was bitterly regretting his most recent business decision. "Thank you for clearing that up," she said.

A nervous light appeared in Kurt's soft-blue eyes. "We were wondering . . . That is, Tina and I were wondering . . . Perhaps you'd be available some evening for dinner. I'd like the opportunity to get to know my daughter. If you're willing, that is." He visibly braced himself. "After all we've put you through, I'll understand if you'd rather not."

Francesca could feel her face crumpling and knew she teetered on the edge of totally losing it. Only Sev's presence at her back gave her the necessary strength to respond. "I'd like that. I'd like that very much," she managed to get out, praying they didn't hear the tears sprinkled through the words.

Tina broke from her husband's side and gave Francesca a swift hug. "I never wanted children. It's a messy business, one that never suited me. But having a grown stepdaughter sort of appeals. We can, I don't know, do lunch, or something. Shop and have drinks. Or if you'd prefer a more traditional stepmother, I can have you sweep out the hearth and fix me tea and dress you in soot-covered rags."

Francesca grinned through her tears at the Cinderella reference. "Works for me. The first part, I mean. Not the rest."

"Well, then. Fine." Tina cleared her throat, more awkward than Francesca had ever seen her. "We're all good, right?"

Francesca laughed. "Very good."

The instant the Fontaines departed, Sev cupped her elbow and urged her through the double doors and onto the balcony. The night held an unseasonable warmth, soft and balmy. Together they wandered to the balustrade and leaned against it. From their Nob Hill perch they could stare out at the bright lights that glittered below them like a carpet of diamond shards.

"This is where I first saw you," Francesca murmured.

"This is where I first fell in love with you." He turned to face her. "I'm sorry, Francesca. I should have trusted my instincts from the beginning. Hell, I should have trusted you. For most of my adult life it's been my job to protect my family and our business from all threats."

"And you saw me as a threat." Not much question about that.

"The biggest threat, because you were the one person capable of tempting me to forget honor and duty and responsibility."

"I'd never ask that of you," she protested. "All I've ever wanted is for you to open your heart and let me in."

"It's wide open, love, and just waiting for you to step across the threshold."

"Is that The Inferno talking?"

"Maybe it is. Or maybe The Inferno knows what lies in our hearts and forces stubborn men to see the truth. Because the truth is you're my heart and soul, and always will be. But I'd also like you to be my wife."

All her life she believed herself on the outside, looking in. Now she realized it wasn't true. It had never been true. Fear kept her from taking that final step, from seeing the open doors. They'd always been there, she'd just been too busy protecting herself from hurt to take that leap of faith and walk inside.

She took the step now, hurtling herself against Sev. His arms closed around her, bringing her home. And then he kissed her, telling her without words just how much he loved her. Long minutes passed before they drew apart.

He reached into his pocket and removed a familiar looking jeweler's box, emblazoned with the Dantes' logo. He thumbed it open, revealing a set of rings. The first was the engagement ring Primo designed, the other the band that mated with it. Maybe it was his imagination, but the fire diamond no longer appeared dim. Now it seemed to rage with its own inner inferno.

He slipped the engagement ring on her finger. "Will you marry me, Francesca, for real this time?"

She positively glowed. "Yes, yes, *yes!*"

And then he kissed her again, soothing old hurts and offering a promise for the future. Much, much later Francesca rested her head against Sev's shoulder, her happiness a palpable presence. She gazed toward the ballroom, misty-eyed, and then stiffened within his arms. "Sev, look."

He glanced in the direction she pointed and shrugged. "It's Marco. So what?"

"Look what he's doing with his hands."

Sev stared, his eyes narrowing when he saw it. Marco was busy entertaining a guest with one of his stories, and as he talked he dug the fingers of his left hand into the palm of his right. It could only mean one thing. Sometime, someplace . . .

"My God," he murmured. "Marco's been struck by The Inferno."

Marco's Stolen Wife

*The Dante Dynasty Series:
Book #2*

by

Day Leclaire

USA Today Bestselling Author

Dedication

To Danielle Andre Skeen, who
knows all about chasing her dreams!

Chapter One

"I'm warning you, Marco. No more scandals. If your family continues to be featured in the gossip magazines, we will have no choice but to place our account elsewhere. The reports have carried all the way to Italy. I even caught Ariana reading them. My own daughter!"

Marco Dante inclined his head. "I understand, Vittorio. We don't know why *The Snitch* has embarked on this campaign against Dantes. But I promise you, I plan to put an end to it, no matter what it takes. You and my father were good friends. We appreciated your business when he ran our jewelry business, and now that we're moving back into the European market, we hope to have your patronage once again."

Vittorio gave a shrug to accompany his expression of vague regret. "I'd enjoy seeing the names of Dante and Romano mated once more. But we're extremely private people. We choose our associates with great care." He deliberately switched to Italian to add weight to his words. "If you wish to have our support for your European expansion, you must take care of this problem."

Marco nodded. Unfortunately, they'd lost the Romanos' backing years ago, shortly after his father's death. At that time, Dantes teetered on the brink of ruin, and would have gone under if not for Marco's brother, Severo, who'd assumed the reins of the family jewelry empire straight out of college. During his first year on the job, he'd been forced to scale back on the size of the business, stripping Dantes to the bone.

Little by little over the past decade, under Sev's brilliant direction, Dantes had made an impressive resurrection and now stood on the verge of regaining their place as the premier jewelers, worldwide. At least they would if they recovered the European trade they'd lost. And Marco planned to make certain that happened.

It was imperative to their success that they return the Romanos to the fold, something he'd worked tirelessly on for the past year. And it was all due to a single ancient expression, one that had floated around the most elite circles for countless generations—Where the Romanos lead, Europe follows. The Romanos were considered Italian royalty and Marco intended to have Europe follow Vittorio and Ariana straight to Dantes' front door. And now that possibility hovered within reach.

The Romanos craved the glorious designs Dantes offered, designs that featured only the finest stones available, including the fire diamonds found nowhere else in the world other than in one of Dantes' display cases. But the Romanos wanted them without any unsavory scandal attached. Thanks to the type of gossip *The Snitch* dished on a weekly basis—as well as their current focus on the four Dante brothers—Marco had reached an impasse with Vittorio Romano.

It was an impasse Marco planned to overcome, no matter what it took. He clapped Vittorio on the shoulder. "Consider it done. We'll deal with *The Snitch*, after which we look forward to providing for your every need." He held out his hand. "Thank you for coming all the way to San Francisco. I'm sorry Ariana didn't accompany you on this trip. My family would have enjoyed meeting her."

Vittorio grinned. "She is lovely, my Ariana, is she not?" He returned Marco's handshake. "Next time I am in San Francisco I will insist she come with me."

"We'll make it a family affair."

"*Eccellente*. I look forward to it. I understand Severo just became engaged to that new designer you recently acquired. Francesca Sommers?

Please offer the couple my warmest congratulations."

With that, Vittorio walked briskly toward the huge etched glass doors that graced the entryway of the Dantes San Francisco office and held one open for a woman entering the building. He offered her a courtly nod and a smile of pure masculine appreciation, before exiting. Not that Marco noticed Vittorio's departure. The instant he set eyes on the woman, he paused, riveted. Every thought vanished from his head, replaced by a whispered demand unlike any he'd ever experienced before.

Take this woman. Possess her. Make her yours.

Without hesitation, he approached, compelled to obey. She stood in the three-story entryway, absorbing the elegant decor. Sunlight streamed through the tinted windows, capturing her within its golden embrace. It plunged into hair so deep an ebony it rivaled the nighttime sky, while turning her complexion to pure cream. She tipped her head back to look at the glass sculpture hanging above the receptionist's desk, a sculpture that resembled leaping flames, and her hair sheeted down her back in heavy waves. It took every ounce of self-control Marco possessed to keep from sweeping her into his arms and carrying her off.

She crossed to the receptionist and he caught the murmur of her voice asking for information. The man behind the desk glanced at Marco, frowned in momentary confusion—no doubt trying to decide which twin he was, something that amused Marco no end—then pointed in his direction. With a nod of thanks, the woman approached and Marco smiled in open delight. At his smile, the receptionist made a frantic effort to catch the woman's attention, before giving up with a shrug.

Marco only had eyes for the woman. God help him, but he wanted her. It was as though someone had delved deep into his mind and plucked loose his personal image of perfection, then created this glorious example of femininity from that image. She stood at the exact right kissing height, not too short, nor too tall, with a full, smiling mouth he couldn't wait to explore. Her features were delicate and ivory pale, with a straight, no-nonsense nose, determined jawline and high, arching cheekbones that lifted her from elegant beauty to sheer poetry.

His gaze dipped lower and his forward momentum faltered. She was dressed for business, but no fabric existed capable of concealing a body created for the pleasures of the night. Full breasts strained against her crisp, tailored navy suit, and some kind soul had designed the jacket so that it nipped in at a waist he could have spanned with two hands before flirting with the curves below—tight round curves that were the devil's own temptation.

He must have made some sound—a groan, if he were a betting man—because she studied him curiously. Her eyes were a deep teal blue and made a striking contrast to her dark hair. Before he could introduce himself, she stuck out her hand.

"Ah, Mr. Dante," she said. "Just the man I was looking for. It's a pleasure to finally meet you. I'm Caitlyn Vaughn."

She said it as though he should recognize her name, but he couldn't recall ever having heard of her before, maybe because in the last sixty seconds every single one of his brain cells had leaked out of his ears. Not that he'd admit his foolishness.

"Of course," he said with his most charming smile. "It's a pleasure to meet you, as well."

He took the hand she offered, and that's when it happened. A hard jolt of electricity zapped him, sinking deep into muscle and bone. He'd never felt anything like it. It didn't hurt, precisely, just surprised and shocked. Based on Caitlyn's startled expression and the way she jerked free of his hold, she must have felt it, as well . . . and didn't like it.

"*Oh!* What was that?" she asked.

"I'm not certain."

But he suspected he knew. Based on his reaction toward Caitlyn, as well as what his eldest brother, Sev, had described, this must be The Inferno. Such an odd Dante blessing—or was it a curse?—that irrevocably bound the men in his family with their true soul mates, the one and only woman they would ever love.

Marco and his brothers had believed the story to be a charming family fairy tale. But ever since Sev had encountered the unremitting burn of its existence, Marco wondered if he would experience it. Wondered if he were *capable* of experiencing it.

He was a man who adored women. All women. He loved everything about them. The unending glorious shapes and sizes. The delightful palate of hues. The music of feminine voices. Their unique scent. As far as he was concerned, women were as beautiful as they were fascinating, and he delighted in each and every one. The idea of choosing one specific flower, instead of the bounty nature offered, struck him as unreasonable. And yet . . .

When he looked at Caitlyn, he saw a woman who was a bounty in and of herself, a bouquet of such depth and beauty that it would take the rest of his life to fully explore each and every aspect. Where hardheaded Sev fought, where the accountant soul in his twin brother Lazzaro questioned and analyzed, where problem-solver Nicolò flat-out denied, the romantic in Marco accepted. He'd take this gift from the gods.

"I've been waiting for you," he told her.

He'd been waiting for her?

Caitlyn stared at Lazzaro Dante as though hypnotized, struggling to get some part of her, any part of her, functioning again after that peculiar handshake and her even more peculiar reaction to it.

During her job interview to be the new CFO for the national branch of Dantes, Lazz had been pointed out to her. He was in charge of the international end of the finance business, a far larger, more complicated department. And though she wouldn't work directly with him, they would come into regular contact during the course of their workday. HR had informed her she'd be introduced to him directly after she arrived at Dantes. It never occurred to her he'd be waiting for her in the lobby, until the receptionist pointed him out.

During that first glimpse, he'd appeared attractive enough, though she'd gotten the impression of tight control and a cold, dark demeanor. Somehow that had changed, possibly because they stood so close. The impression of rigidness gave way to someone filled with lightness and warmth, his control more of a natural part of him rather than an unyielding suit of power.

Not that he lacked power. It came off him as innately as his breath. But it didn't stifle her. It simply . . . infected her the same way as everything else about him. He towered over her, his broad shoulders narrowing the scope of her view to him and little else. Dark brown hair fell in unruly waves across his forehead, escaping the ruthless discipline she'd thought more natural to him. He was sinfully attractive, with high, sweeping cheekbones, a straight masculine nose, squared jaw, and a mouth made for kissing.

Even more appealing, he exuded an irresistible charm that urged her to close the few feet—inches really—separating them and settle into his arms. To lift her mouth for his taking. To allow him to possess her and brand her with his kiss, his touch, with his very essence.

He gazed down at her with a slow, sensuous smile, as though sensing her need. His gaze held hers, his eyes a brilliant hazel, glittering with shards of gold and brown and green, and filling with a shocking desire.

"*Cara . . .*"

The word whispered between them, echoing his desire and causing the feminine core of her to fill with need. And it was that hint of desperate need that brought her tumbling back to reality.

What the *hell* had she been thinking? How could she forget every lesson learned at her grandmother's knee? She fought for some sense of normalcy and found it only when she took a swift step back and dragged air into her lungs. Air that didn't contain Essence of Lazz. Air that helped clear the fog of lust that held her enthralled.

She attempted a cool, polite, *professional* smile. And failed miserably. "It really is kind of you to meet me here on my first day, Mr. Dante, but—" The shock she experienced when they first shook hands continued to tickle her palm and she rubbed her thumb across it. To her totally inappropriate amusement he copied the gesture, distracting her. "Okay, I have to know. What was that?"

He eyed her sympathetically. "Did I hurt you, *cara?* I am sorry."

"Hurt me? Oh, no. Not really." That surprised her, given the intensity of the shock. "It was just . . ."

"Unexpected?"

"Exactly," she said with smile, relieved he understood. "Very unexpected."

Worse, though it seemed a ridiculous concept, the shock seemed to have intensified her awareness of him. When she'd first seen him last week after her final interview, she'd have described Lazz as incredibly attractive, almost too good-looking for a woman's peace of mind. But now . . . A slight panic stole over her. Somehow, with that single touch, she became keenly aware of him and the startling allure that formed between them. It felt as though a light switch had been flipped, igniting thoughts and emotions she'd never experienced before. She didn't understand it, didn't want to understand it.

In all her twenty-eight years, she'd never done anything to jeopardize her professional career. How many times had Gran warned her about that? How many times had her grandmother used her own life as a hard-won lesson? Caitlyn understood the cardinal rules, had learned them well.

One. Don't let a man charm you into ruining your career for a brief ride over the rainbow. Because all that waited on the other side was fool's gold. *Two.* Build a strong foundation with a serious-minded man capable of staying power. Someone who believed in the same things as you. *And three.* Charm and beauty are only skin deep and both are shallow as hell. Neither are capable of lasting past the first pothole in life's road.

Well, she'd listened and learned. She wouldn't allow any man to take her for a ride. And yet . . .

She shot Lazz a glance from beneath her lashes. Their surroundings seemed to melt away, and the noises faded to a soft murmur. The light appeared to dim until only the two of them were caught within the sun's halo. Every beat of her heart sent desire coursing deeper and more powerfully through her veins until the sheer want of him overrode every other thought and emotion.

"Caitlyn," he murmured.

Her name on his tongue made her think of wine and poetry, and though he didn't have an accent, his voice contained a noticeable Mediterranean lilt, deep and ripe and musical. He held out his hand and almost—*almost*—she took it, willing to follow along whatever path he led her down and tumble into bliss with him wherever and whenever he suggested, even right here and now.

Instead she utilized every scrap of common sense she still possessed and made a production of checking her watch. "I'm due in personnel in five minutes." Instinctively she moved to extend her hand again in a businesslike parting, but withdrew it quickly, and took several steps toward the elevator. Some irresistible compulsion had her turn and offer a final nod of farewell. "I'll see you soon, Mr. Dante. I believe we have an appointment scheduled for ten."

At that, a blinding smile lit his face. "I didn't realize. My assistant neglected to mention it." He advanced in her direction. "But, why wait? Why not move our appointment forward?"

The elevator doors opened just then and she didn't dare linger or she'd cave to his request. Heaven only knew what would happen between them if she did. Good Lord! On her first day of work, no less. "Ten o'clock," she repeated. "I look forward to seeing you."

She darted inside the car, fighting to maintain a calm expression while the doors whisked silently closed. To her relief Lazz didn't give chase but stood perfectly still, his features carved into lines of determination while he watched her retreat. Because that's what it was, a full-scale, tail-turning, white-flag-flying, unabashed retreat.

The instant the doors shut, she leaned against the back wall and closed her eyes. She hadn't been in the building a full thirty seconds and look at how much she'd already risked as a result of a single, casual handshake. What in the *world* had gotten into her? For that matter, what had gotten into Lazzaro Dante? Whatever had just happened between them, from this minute on, she needed to put such foolishness aside and focus on work.

Thirty minutes later, she realized that not only couldn't she forget, but it had become an absolute impossibility. Something about that single touch had changed her. Caitlyn struggled to concentrate on the reams of HR paperwork to be completed and the workaday tour of facilities, trying to convince herself that vital information was being given. But with every passing minute, she grew more and more tense, keenly aware she'd soon see Lazz and discover if she'd imagined her reaction to him.

When the moment finally arrived, she greeted him with a professional demeanor, meant to conceal her nervousness. "So, we meet again." She caught the faintest hitch in his step and a tiny frown formed between his hazel eyes before he offered his hand, a hand she eyed with undisguised apprehension. "That's brave of you, after what happened last time. But if you're game, so am I."

He paused a beat before inclining his head. "I'm willing."

To her relief she didn't receive a zap again. And then the relief faded to a vague disappointment. Maybe she'd imagined the surge of electricity. And though she felt an unmistakable warmth toward the man holding her hand, it bore little resemblance to the unrelenting desire she'd felt just a scant hour before. Not that she let on.

Lazz studied her with just as much interest as earlier, and the hungry spark in her eyes remained, as well. "Welcome to Dantes. I'm looking forward to getting to know you better," he said.

As before, she couldn't misinterpret the intent behind his comment. It was an invitation, Caitlyn realized in that instant. Right now, the two of them teetered on the verge of a relationship that went beyond business. The power it offered intrigued her. *Her move*, it said. She could either back away and put an end to it. Or she could take the next step—cautiously, of course—and see where it led. Time seemed to slow, giving her a moment to consider

She couldn't be certain what she'd experienced Dantes' lobby had anything to do with love, but she would never have gotten so far in business if she'd shied away from a challenge out of sheer timidity or contrariness. The opportunity in front of her represented a challenge, but she also spied all the pieces necessary to build the foundation her grandmother had so often talked about. He was sexy and successful, but most of all smart. Someone she could build a castle with. And the tingle they'd shared earlier? Lucky bonus.

She didn't hesitate another instant. She offered Lazz a brilliant smile and surrendered to whatever fate ordained. Maybe their current setting put a slight damper on that sizzle of attraction. She'd just have to wait and see what happened from here. The bottom line was, whatever had occurred in the lobby of Dantes, she wanted more.

"I'm really looking forward to getting to know you," she said.

Chapter Two

Six Weeks Later

Caitlyn took her customary seat around a generous-size smoked glass table, joining the two women with whom she'd formed a fast friendship over the six weeks she'd been working at Dantes. They always met for lunch at the same time and place thanks to Lazz, who'd been generous enough to offer the use of a small conference room connected to his office.

The minute they were seated, Britt preened for them, showing off a stunning pair of diamond earrings. "Check these out. They're a Dantes exclusive. Aren't they gorgeous?"

"Who gave those to you and how do I meet someone like that," Angie demanded.

"I bought them for myself," Britt confessed with a hint of bravado. "I figured it was the only way I'd ever get a pair."

"On whose salary?" When Britt simply made a face, Angie let it go and glanced at them with barely suppressed excitement. "Well, I have news. You won't believe what I heard." She spared a brief glance toward the door exiting onto the executive floor to confirm they'd shut it before staring uneasily at the open doorway leading to Lazz's office, a doorway only steps from their table. "Maybe I shouldn't say anything here."

"Lazz is out to lunch with his brother, Nicolò, if that's what you're worried about. I booked the reservation myself," Britt reassured. "No one can overhear us."

"Okay." Even so, she lowered her voice. "I heard something interesting at Dantes Exclusive."

Caitlyn understood that to mean Dantes' private retail operation, a select by-invitation-only showroom catering to the elite. Angie had started there as a saleswoman two full decades ago, before climbing steadily up the retail end of the corporate ladder.

"Who visited this time?" Caitlyn asked. She'd forgotten to leave her reading glasses in her office, an all-too-common occurrence, and shoved them into her hair on top of her head. "Show business, finance, or royalty?"

Britt offered a catlike grin. "I bet I know."

Angie laughed. "Since you're his personal assistant, I'll bet you do, too."

Caitlyn blinked in surprise. "Are you talking about Lazz?" At Angie's nod of confirmation, Caitlyn wrinkled her brow in confusion and asked, "Why is it odd he'd be at Exclusive?"

Angie paused, before dropping her next bombshell. "Maybe because he was looking at engagement rings."

Both women gazed at Caitlyn with broad smiles, while she sat for a long moment in stunned silence, rubbing her palm. "No. You can't really think . . ."

"Not only do I think, I'll bet dinner at Le Premier on it."

"Well, it makes perfect sense to me," Britt offered. "You two hit it off right from the start. Plus, you're so alike. You're both practical. Logical. Not to mention financial geniuses. It takes every bit of my ability to keep up with him. But the two of you . . ." She shook her head in wry amusement. "Whenever you're together, it's like you're talking in shorthand. It's almost as if you're already an old married couple."

Angie made a face. "You make it sound so dull. It isn't like that, is it, Caitlyn?" A frown of distress touched her brow. "I mean, there's romance, right?

Excitement? Give an old woman hope. Tell me there's romance and excitement, even if it's a lie."

Caitlyn felt herself blushing. "Of course, there's romance and excitement," she muttered. *Somewhere.*

"Now if it were Marco," Britt offered, "I guarantee there'd never be a dull moment. Have you crossed paths with him, yet?" Before Caitlyn could respond, she gave an impatient click of her tongue. "No, of course not. He just flew in from overseas today. I think he's only been home two other times. Once was about a month ago when Sev threw a bash for Francesca to publicize the release of the Dantes' Heart Collection."

"I was in New York at the time," Caitlyn reminded her.

"Oh, right. And then Marco showed up for Sev's wedding."

Caitlyn shook her head. "New York, again. I did meet Sev last week, though," she said. But for some reason, Lazz had shown a notable reluctance to introduce her to the various members of the Dante clan, something that filled her with a vague unease. "But he's the only other Dante so far."

Britt tilted her head to one side. "Hmm. Sounds to me like Lazz wants to keep you all to himself. He's probably afraid if he introduces you to his brothers, you'll decide you like one of them better, especially his tw—"

"Don't be ridiculous," Caitlyn interrupted, taking instant exception. "I was attracted to Lazz from the minute we first shook hands." Just because the weeks since had failed to lived up to that initial contact didn't mean a bone-deep attraction couldn't still exist. They just needed to add a bit more fuel to the flames. "As for his brothers, I expect I'll meet them at his grandparents' anniversary party tonight."

"Nothing against Lazz, but . . ." Britt leaned back in her chair, a dreamy expression slipping across her face. "Just once, don't you long to have Zorro come sweeping down and carry you off?"

"And have his wicked way with you?" added Angie.

"Instead of planning every move down to the last nanosecond?" Britt's gaze sharpened on Caitlyn, filled with open curiosity. "Is that how he makes love?" After an instant of stunned silence, she added with a mischievous smile, "Oh, come on, Angie. Back me up here. It's not like you haven't been wondering the same thing. I just want to know if Lazz makes love the same way he works. Is it by the numbers, or is he a bit more creative in the sack?"

"*Britt Jones!*" Angie reprimanded furiously.

She must have realized she'd gone too far. She mouthed a hasty apology to Caitlyn before deliberately changing the subject. "So, tell me how the Dante's Heart Collection is going. I realize five weeks isn't much time to determine its success, but considering Dantes' CEO and the designer of the collection married shortly after its big launch must have helped sales. Am I right?"

Caitlyn smiled reluctantly. "Sorry, Britt. I can't answer that. It's confidential, I'm afraid."

She changed the subject, all the while uneasily studying her friends while they chatted about the whirlwind marriage of the eldest of the four Dante brothers. To tell the truth, she couldn't have answered Britt's earlier question even if she'd been so inclined. She didn't have a clue how Lazz made love, since matters hadn't progressed quite that far. Though now that she thought about it, why hadn't they had sex?

Because they were busy putting all the pieces together, that's why. Well, clearly not all the pieces. She wanted to be sure they were standing on firm ground before taking the next step. And although that sounded good in theory, it still didn't resolve the issue to her satisfaction.

She pretended to give her full attention to her lunch. It seemed that after the sizzle and heat of her first meeting with Lazz in the lobby of Dantes, the sexual tension between them had eased to a pleasant, comfortable warmth. Since that first shocking handshake, she'd never again experienced the spark and burn, no matter how many times they touched or kissed, nor how often she longed for it to happen just once more, if only so she'd know she hadn't imagined it.

Their dates had been enjoyable. No. That struck her as too bland a description for her time with Lazz. They felt passion. Sure they did. Lazz left no doubt about his feelings for her. He'd made it crystal clear how much he wanted her and expressed his interest in taking their relationship to the next step. If anything, she had slowed the pace, something he'd reluctantly allowed. She picked at her salad. And why had she done that?

She released her breath in a slow sigh. Because she'd been waiting. Waiting to feel that amazing rush of emotion again. To be swept away exactly the way Angie described. But with each passing day, it became clearer and clearer she and Lazz were as alike as two peas in a pod, both far too practical for their own good.

It looked as if all the pieces for a proper foundation were there, just the way Gran had instructed, but the longer she and Lazz worked at putting those pieces in place, the more she realized some vital parts were missing. Such a shame since she really, truly liked Lazz. And too bad that whatever spark had first ignited between them had died in the weeks since to no more than a warm glow.

She set her fork down and slipped her glasses onto the tip of her nose, her "getting down to business" mode. It was time to face facts. She wanted more than a warm glow. She wanted what she'd felt when she and Lazz had first met. Tonight she intended to confront Lazz, to take their relationship to the next step and discover once and for all whether the spark still existed, waiting to be fanned to life, or if it had been extinguished before it ever had a chance to catch fire.

"Caitlyn?"

Her head jerked upward and she realized her friends were standing by the door exiting the conference room, staring at her in concern. "You okay?" Britt prompted.

"What are you waiting for?" Angie added.

Caitlyn knew what she was waiting for, what she wanted and who she intended to have. "Zorro," she murmured in reply. "I'm waiting for Zorro."

"No, Marco." His grandmother's whispered order stopped him in his tracks, preventing him from bursting from Lazz's office into the conference room and confronting the women they'd just overheard. "You cannot go in there. You would embarrass them."

He hesitated, driven by a compulsion so strong he shook with the effort to control it. "Don't try and stop me, Nonna. I'm going to put an end to this. I've waited so long to return home again, to have an opportunity to finally approach Caitlyn. These past few weeks have nearly driven me insane. And now . . ." He shook his head. "I can't let Lazz propose to her. She doesn't belong to him."

His grandmother crossed to his side and slid a gentle hand along the clenched muscles of his arm. "He claims otherwise, *nipote*. You have been gone much of this past month and a half. A lot has happened in that short period of time. Lazzaro and Caitlyn Vaughn have experienced The Inferno."

He spoke between clenched teeth. "That's not possible."

"Of course it is. Just because you are attracted to this woman—"

"No. You don't understand." Marco swiveled to face his grandmother, barely able to restrain himself.

"Caitlyn and I experienced The Inferno, not Lazz. And he knew it. That's why he sent me away, Nonna. Deliberately. He found crisis after crisis in the foreign offices that required my personal attention. The few times I've been home, Caitlyn has conveniently been sent off on Dantes' business. And it was all done to keep me away from her so Lazz could take her for himself. Something his assistant, Britt, said to me on the phone the other day finally clued me in on what he's been up to."

Nonna stared at him, shocked. "Do you realize what you are suggesting?"

He held out his right hand, palm up, and dug his thumb into the center where the bond had first formed. He softened his voice so they wouldn't be overheard. "I felt the burn the day Caitlyn arrived at Dantes. From the moment I saw her, I suspected. But when we touched, I knew. It was her first day at work, her first few minutes under our roof. We met in the lobby and shook hands and ever since that moment the need for her has grown. Grown to unbearable levels. I realize now she mistook me for Lazz." His expression darkened. "And when my dear brother discovered that fact, he took great care not to correct her error."

"She does not know you are twins?"

"Apparently not."

Nonna sank into the chair in front of Lazz's desk and made the sign of the cross. "You came here to confront him over this, to demand he give her up, didn't you?"

"I landed an hour ago and came to find him," he confirmed. "I want to know why he's trying to take my woman."

"From what Lazz said, we all thought—" She broke off with a look of confusion. "We assumed he'd felt The Inferno for Caitlyn."

"You assumed wrong." Marco hesitated, a sudden thought occurring to him. "Or did you? Is it possible twins can feel The Inferno for the same woman?"

To his relief, she didn't hesitate. "No, Marco. That much I do know." She made a helpless gesture. "What I do not understand is why he would claim her if she is not his. How could he make such a mistake?"

"I haven't made a mistake," Lazz announced from the doorway. He stepped inside his office and crossed to where his grandmother sat. Leaning down, he gave her a kiss on each of her cheeks. "Did you bring the ring?"

She nodded unhappily. "Lazzaro . . . Are you sure? Marco claims—"

"You took Caitlyn Vaughn from me," Marco interrupted, fury ripping through him in the face of Lazz's absolute calm. "You had to know something had happened between us or you'd never have gone to such lengths."

Lazz gave a careless shrug. "You're right. Based on how Caitlyn greeted me, I knew immediately you'd been up to your usual tricks. Fortunately for me, she has no idea we're twins or that I wasn't the one in the lobby that morning."

Marco took a step closer to his brother and balled his hands into fists. "Maybe I should rearrange your face a bit so she has an easier time telling us apart from now on."

Bull's-eye. More than a hint of irritation slid from behind Lazz's impervious facade. "Last time we fought over a woman, I ended up with a scar. One from you is plenty, thanks."

"Has she seen it?" He'd have given anything to call back the words the instant they'd been uttered, especially when Lazz offered a lazy smile of confirmation in response. "You son of a—"

"Marco!" Nonna interrupted sharply.

Lazz's voice cut across the reprimand, aimed straight at his brother. "Let me explain something to you. You have this insane notion that I've somehow taken Caitlyn from you.

For your information she's not mine to take, any more than she's yours. She's her own person and will make her own decision about who she will or won't date." He paused deliberately. "Or who she will or won't marry."

Marco fought to maintain control. Where he preferred action, Lazz chose reason. Long, hard experience had taught Marco one simple fact. When it came to a war of logic, his only chance at winning required he keep his temper in check. And when that failed, beat his brother to a bloody pulp. Right now, a thorough beating struck him as the most satisfying option. If he could find a way to maneuver Nonna out of the room, he might just give it a shot. Until then, words were all he had available.

"You told the family you'd experienced The Inferno with her," Marco accused. "You and I both know that's a lie."

"As is The Inferno."

"Lazzaro!" Nonna lifted a trembling hand to her throat. "How can you say such a thing?"

He stooped beside her chair. "I'm sorry to hurt you, Nonna, but I don't believe in The Inferno. I think it's a very sweet, very romantic fairy tale to rationalize allowing a passionate nature to overcome common sense. Sev used it to justify blackmailing a top jewelry designer into leaving our main competitor. Marco wants to use it in order to coax a Dantes employee into his bed. And Primo used it as an excuse to steal his best friend's fiancée. The Inferno doesn't exis—"

To Marco's shock, Nonna did something he'd never seen her do before. She slapped Lazzaro, stopping his words. Tears flooded her eyes. "Not another word," she ordered in Italian, before drawing a shaky breath. "Marco is right. This woman is not your soul mate. If you had felt The Inferno for her, you could not say the things you have here today. You mock and dismiss what you have never experienced. How dare you assume you know more about what happened between your grandparents and brothers than those of us involved. How dare you accuse us of lying."

Lazz's jaw tightened. "Not lying. Merely attempting to rationalize irrational emotion."

"Is what you feel for Caitlyn rational?" Marco demanded.

Lazz slowly rose to face his brother. Nonna's slap had left its mark. A light streak of red kissed the curve of his jaw. "Of course it is. Emotional attraction is quite rational. And I'm attracted to Caitlyn physically and intellectually, as well as emotionally. But I'm not going to try and pretend what I feel for her is due to some family curse."

"Blessing," Marco and Nonna corrected in unison.

He dismissed the word with a wave of his hand. "What I'm feeling are the normal sensations men and women have experienced toward one another since Adam and Eve first bumped into each other in the Garden of Eden."

"You're in love with Caitlyn Vaughn?" Marco questioned tightly.

"Are you?" Lazz shot back. "You met her once. Spoke to her for all of five minutes. And now you're trying to tell me that she's . . . What? Your Inferno bride?"

Anger flared anew. "Not trying. I *am* telling you. You've deliberately kept us apart. You had no business doing that."

Lazz waved that aside. "Oh, please. You go through women faster than Nonna's *pan forte*. All I did was save her from heartache."

"While taking her for yourself."

To Marco's fury, his brother simply smiled. "Now that Nonna's brought me the ring I requested, I plan to propose to Caitlyn tonight. It's up to her whether or not she accepts. Considering how alike she and I are, I think we'll suit very well. Oh, she probably won't accept right away. It's much too soon and much too fast. But if nothing else, it will cement our relationship until she does agree to my proposal."

"Please, Lazzaro," Nonna interrupted. "If you persist in following this path, you will regret it the rest of your life."

"And I'll make sure of it," Marco added.

Lazz lifted an eyebrow. "What do you plan to do? Tell Caitlyn I have a twin? I'm sure she'll find that very interesting, but hardly life altering. Tell her it was you in the lobby on her first day of work? She and I have been dating for six weeks. Do you really think she'll care after all this time?" He shook his head. "It's too little, too late. She's committed to me now. Go find someone else to charm."

"Caitlyn is meant for me and you know it. Why else would you have worked so hard to keep us apart?"

For the first time a hint of temper sparked to life in Lazz's eyes, belying his legendary control. "You think all women are meant for you, Marco. You always have, which explains the scar I carry. Don't you remember? It's because of that day, we created a 'no poaching' rule."

"I haven't forgotten, even if you have."

"There wasn't anything between you and Caitlyn, therefore I can't be guilty of poaching." Lazz folded his arms across his chest, his stance hard and firm. "Face facts, Marco. This is the one woman you can't have, which is probably why you want her. Well, you're too late. You're just going to have to find a way to deal with losing. Caitlyn and I suit each other and you're on official notice to back off. Besides, considering how vindictive *The Snitch* has gotten these past six weeks, chances are excellent they'll get hold of this story. If you don't back off, I guarantee they'll run with it. I don't think the Romanos would be happy reading about another Dante scandal. Do you?"

Far from backing off, Marco chose to approach, determined to take on anyone and anything threatening the bond he and Caitlyn had experienced in the lobby that long-ago morning. It didn't matter he'd only spoken to Caitlyn for five short minutes. It could have been five seconds. The instant they'd touched, their fates were sealed. He couldn't explain it. Before it had happened to him, he'd have called it insane, just as Lazz did. But their distinct connection compelled him to find Caitlyn. To take her for his own. To make her his in every way possible.

And he would.

Marco went toe-to-toe with his brother. "You let me worry about the Romanos and *The Snitch*. As for Caitlyn . . . Would you care to put your faith in her affection to a small test? Why don't you give me a clear field tonight and we'll see which of us ends up going home with the lady."

If Nonna hadn't stepped between the two of them, Marco didn't doubt Lazz would have hit him. "Don't mess with her, Marco. Final warning. *Back off.*"

"And I'm warning you, Lazz. The Inferno is real. And I won't let *any* man take my woman from me." He leaned in past his grandmother to give weight to his words. "Not even my own brother."

"*Late, late, late!*"

Caitlyn flew to the mirror for a final check, throwing a swift, desperate glance toward the clock. Five minutes. The car arrived in five minutes. Why, oh, why had Lazz chosen tonight of all nights to change the time they were to meet?

She perched her reading glasses on the end of her nose and checked the note he'd sent a final time. He must have been in a hurry when he wrote it because she barely recognized his handwriting. It seemed bolder and less precise. More passionate. And how amusing was that after her conversation with the girls? Now, where were they to meet? On the balcony of Le Premier for moonlight drinks. She shoved her glasses into her hair with a smile. How romantic.

Pausing in front of the mirror, she examined her reflection a final time. She'd dressed with extra care for the Dantes' anniversary party, choosing a floor-length gown in teal, several shades lighter than her eyes. She'd also applied a touch more makeup than usual. She stared at the mirror, slightly stunned at how different she looked when she wore something other than her more mundane business attire. The makeup added a hint of glamour and sophistication, while the halter top drew attention to her shoulders and bustline. Even the sweeping skirt gave an illusion of magic and romance, floating around her like wisps of fog. Then she grinned. Her reading glasses, however, were another story.

She carefully removed them from her upswept hair and tossed them onto her bed beside her purse. She'd have to remember to grab them before she left or she'd be depending on Lazz to read anything put in front of her tonight.

Thinking of Lazz caused her smile to falter a shade. She knew Britt and Angie believed he planned to propose sometime this evening, but they couldn't be more wrong. Her friends weren't aware matters between her and Lazz simply hadn't progressed to that point. Her chin firmed. Until now.

Thanks to her lunchtime conversation she'd decided the time had come for a change. She wanted Lazz to make love to her, something she'd hesitated to agree to up to this point. But after some long, hard consideration, she needed to know, once and for all, whether their connection went deeper than the lighthearted romance they currently shared.

She needed to know if Lazz had any Zorro in his soul.

Turning away from the mirror, she checked the clock once more and gave in to panic. She hated, hated, *hated* being late. Thanks to a last-minute change in Lazz's plans for the evening, she'd have to run to avoid that horror.

Thank goodness for the car he told her he'd send or she wouldn't have had a hope of making it to the hotel on time. And she wanted to make it on time, to wallow in every minute of the promised romantic rendezvous before the start of his grandparents' anniversary party. Snatching up her purse, she hurried outside to the waiting car and a night she hoped would change her entire future.

The instant she entered the hotel lobby, a uniformed employee approached. After confirming her identity, he escorted her along a corridor running parallel to the ballroom. A single gesture brought her through an archway opening onto the starlit darkness of a large balcony that overlooked downtown San Francisco.

She paused for a moment, giving her eyes time to adjust. She instantly realized she didn't need her eyesight. Another sense kicked in, a keen awareness of someone's presence just off to her left. An odd fever began to sizzle through her veins, flaring to life in a way that caught her by surprise. She hadn't experienced anything like this since . . .

Caitlyn inhaled sharply.

Since the morning she'd stepped through the front doors of Dantes and first met Lazz. A smile built across her mouth.

"I can feel you," she whispered into the darkness. "I can't see you, but I can feel you." She slowly turned until she faced him, or faced where she'd have bet a month's salary he stood. "Well? Aren't you going to say anything?"

"I've been waiting for you," he simply replied.

Chapter Three

Just that one comment and Caitlyn's nerve endings fired to life with a stunning fierceness. She shivered in reaction. They were the same words Lazz had used when she'd first met him in the lobby of Dantes. How many times had they spoken since? How many times had they been together in other settings, if not one quite this ripe with romance? And yet, just that one sentence succeeded in knocking her totally off-kilter.

Perhaps it had to do with his voice. It sounded deeper than all those other times. Huskier. More passionate than she'd ever heard it and fused with blatant desire. Every feminine instinct she possessed responded to his unspoken command, urging her to go to him. To surrender. To give herself as completely and fully as only a woman can.

She took an impulsive step in his direction. This was the man she'd met all those weeks ago. The man who'd roused her from sleep and ignited emotions she never even realized she possessed.

"Where have you been?" she asked.

He stepped from the shadows and approached. If he found her question peculiar, he didn't let on. If anything, she suspected he understood precisely what she asked.

"Does it matter? I'm here now." He held out his hand. "And I have a question to ask."

She didn't hesitate, but slipped her hand into his. A small voice whispered inside her head, acknowledging the rightness of his touch. *Yes!* Even more remarkable, she felt a surge of desire so strong and overwhelming she couldn't think straight. Elation filled her. Here was the perfect man for her, a man who mirrored her own ideals. Practical. Safe. Successful. And powerfully alluring. All the building blocks for a successful relationship.

"What question did you want to ask?" she managed to say.

"Do you trust me?"

If he hadn't spoken with such intensity, she would have laughed. "Of course, I trust you."

"Then kiss me."

She resisted the seductive lure, curiosity getting the better of her. "I don't understand. What in the world's gotten into you?"

"I'm trying to make a point. To prove what we felt when we first touched was real. That the fantasy can become reality. That you're a woman who deserves to be swept off her feet, not just tonight, but every night."

She felt the color drain from her face. "You heard. You were in your office at lunchtime. You overheard what Britt and Angie said." Oh, God. What she'd said—that she was waiting for Zorro. "You heard us, didn't you?"

He inclined his head. "I did."

"I'm so sorry. I—"

He offered a tender smile. "Don't apologize. It was important for me to know."

Lazz closed the distance between them and stopped the words hovering on her lips in one easy move. Lowering his head, he cupped her face between his hands and kissed her. And with that kiss he sent her tumbling to a place she'd never been before.

He'd kissed her any number of times over the past six weeks, but it had never been anything like this. The first taste came slow and delicious, a slide of lips mingling with a whisper of tongue, combined with a bone-melting sensuality that Lazz had kept hidden from her until now. It had all the newness of a first kiss, which she found as strange and bewildering as it was utterly enchanting.

She sank into the embrace, opening to him, engaging in an escalating thrust and parry that caused a delicious friction to thrum through her veins. Why had she hesitated all these weeks? Why had she held him at arm's length? This is what she wanted. This is what she needed. If Lazz had kissed her with such sweet aggression right from the start—as she'd half anticipated after their first meeting—she would have tumbled into his bed on their first date.

He drew back ever so slightly. "Better?"

"Like night and day," she confessed. Her brows drew together. "But I don't understand. Why didn't you kiss me like this sooner?"

"I'm kissing you like this now."

His hands swept along her jaw before tracing the length of her neck and tripping across her bared shoulders. She shivered beneath the teasing caress, and he smiled knowingly, his expression containing a suggestive, blatantly male quality. The air hitched in her lungs and then escaped in a small gasp as his hands continued their descent, exploring her curves with undisguised enjoyment. He gazed down at her as he drew her close once again, joining them together in seamless perfection.

His face eased into a slight blur thanks to her farsightedness, but she could still tell that his eyes never left hers as he held her, consuming her with their intensity. And then the color changed, burnished with brilliant sparks of amber and brown and a hint of green. In all the weeks they'd been together, she'd never seen the expression they currently displayed, a heady combination of passion, longing, and determination. Nor had she ever reacted this way when he held her, as though she'd been lost and had finally found her way home.

The discrepancy bewildered her. She didn't understand it, any more than she understood what had gotten into Lazz. But whatever had transformed him, she hoped it never went away. If she had any doubts about their relationship before tonight, they dissipated beneath that one single kiss.

"All of this is because you overheard my conversation at lunch?" she asked, dazed.

He didn't deny it. "You want Zorro? I can give him to you. You want to be swept away? I can do that, too."

"Oh, Lazz." For some reason he flinched, possibly from the compassion in her voice. "I don't want you to change who you are. I just want you to be yourself." In truth, his extravagant promises shook her. Men who sold fairy tales went the way of Cinderella's carriage at midnight. Poof. She had no desire to be stuck holding a pumpkin like her grandmother.

"Believe it or not, I am being myself."

Her mouth curved into a slight smile. "You're Zorro at heart?"

"More than you can possibly imagine."

She didn't bother arguing. She'd spent enough time with Lazz to know he wasn't Zorro. Zorro's brother, perhaps, but he struck her as too dispassionate and analytical to embody the mysterious swashbuckler, no matter how much she might wish it otherwise.

"I can live without Zorro," she reassured him. "At least I can if I have you." She tightened her arms around his neck. "Like this."

"You can, on one condition."

"Name it."

"That you come away with me. Right now. Tonight." He stopped her automatic refusal with a single shake of his head. "Listen to me, Caitlyn. I know you, the real you. You may cling to facts and figures, and charts and graphs because they seem safe and familiar and logical. But you don't want safe or familiar or—God forbid—logical in a lover. You long for a man who sees beneath the surface, who realizes that you have the soul of a romantic and fulfills all your most passionate fantasies."

She stared at him, stunned. It was as though he'd looked inside her heart and read her deepest secrets. She'd spent a lifetime doing the "right" thing. Following the rules and toeing every one of the lines her grandmother had laid down for her. Just once she wanted to smudge the line. To step over it. Hell, to leap over it. To take a risk. And now here was Lazz, a man she was wildly attracted to, offering the chance to do just that.

"Where do you want to go?" she asked, inching closer to that line.

"Forever, Nevada."

She blinked. "You want to go to Nevada. Tonight." At his silent nod, she stared at him in confusion. "But why? If you want to spend the night together—"

He stiffened. "Go on."

For some reason she reddened. "I know we haven't." Her color darkened further as she confessed, "Yet. But we don't have to go all the way to Nevada for that."

He relaxed enough to laugh. "There are other reasons to go there."

She lifted an eyebrow. "You want to see a show? Gamble?"

"No, *cara*. I want to marry you."

Marco could see he'd shocked her. She stared at him, her eyes huge and dark with disbelief. *"Marry me!"*

He spoke from the heart. "From the moment I saw you, I wanted you. I knew you were the one."

"But these past six weeks—"

He'd anticipated that question when he'd planned the evening. "What would you have done if I'd tried to sweep you away that first day?"

"Run like hell."

"And now, after six weeks?"

"I'm not running," she conceded. "But I am stunned. This isn't something we should leap into blindly."

"You want me." He didn't phrase it as a question.

"I can't deny that." She sank against him and pressed her cheek to his shoulder. The silken strands of her hair brushed against the line of his jaw, and he inhaled the heady fragrance. "But marriage? So soon?"

"Waiting isn't going to change my feelings for you."

"But it will give us time to get to know each other better." She pulled back a few inches. "Be practical, Lazz." Then she laughed. "What am I saying? Other than myself, you're the most practical person I've ever met."

Every time she used his brother's name, he longed to correct her, to demand that she see *him,* not Lazz. Soon she would. But first he had to get her to Nevada. All the arrangements he'd set into motion tonight hinged on that single point. The note he'd sent asking her to meet him a full hour ahead of the time she'd originally arranged to meet Lazz, the timetable of car and plane, the excuses Nonna would offer his brother regarding Caitlyn's failure to appear at the party—they all depended on his ability to charm one simple agreement from the woman before him.

"You had practical," he argued, "and it didn't make you any happier than it made me. It's not what I want and it sure as hell isn't what you want, either."

"Okay, I admit it," she confessed with a sigh. "I'd like more than practical."

"Then, come with me."

She teetered on the brink of surrender. "What about your grandparents' anniversary party?" She shook her head. "Let's not rush this. We can go to Nevada another time. We should be here for their special night."

"I already told Nonna about my plans in case you agreed, and we have her and Primo's complete approval. She'll make our excuses to the rest of the family." And with luck, keep Lazz running in circles until far too late. "Say yes, Caitlyn," he coaxed. "You want to be swept away and that's what I'm offering to do."

Before she could marshal any further arguments, he kissed her again. There was nothing new or tentative about this one. This kiss was a taking, powerful and physical. A demand. A seduction. A union. Never again would she mistake him for another man. Even if Lazz were to walk out onto the balcony this very moment and gather her into his arms and kiss her, he'd leave her wanting. Leave her with a bone-deep dissatisfaction coupled with an awareness that she belonged to another.

"Trust me, Caitlyn. Take a chance."

She stared at him in a total daze and he barely managed to suppress a smile. She looked like he felt. If he'd had any doubt at all about his plans for the next twenty-four hours, they'd vanished the minute she'd joined him on the balcony. From the instant they'd touched, a certainty took hold. They belonged together. He'd never been more positive of anything in his life.

"I'd like to go to Forever with you." She shook her head as though clearing it, and her hair slipped from its elegant knot to swirl about her shoulders. "But not to marry you," she hastened to add, fumbling with the pins she'd used to anchor the weighty length.

"We'll see."

"I'm serious, Lazz. No marriage."

"So am I, Caitlyn." He took the pins from her and dropped them into his pocket before stealing another kiss and practically inhaling her soft moan. "I want you for my wife."

He didn't give her an opportunity to argue, but escorted her from the balcony and out of the hotel. He'd ordered the car that had brought her to Le Premier to wait for them right outside the door so they'd have it instantly available to convey them to the airport. He'd also arranged for the corporate jet to be standing by for their trip to Nevada.

He didn't want to risk any delays that might give Caitlyn an opportunity to have second thoughts. Once they were married, he'd deal with the inevitable fallout when she discovered his true identity. But right now, he'd bind her to him with the most sacred commitment of all.

The instant they were airborne, he handed her a flute of a particularly fine sparkling wine from the Franciacorta territory in Italy. The lights in the cabin were dim and the seats wide and plush. They'd lifted the armrest separating them and sat joined at the hip with

Caitlyn closest to the window. Outside the aircraft, the moon and the stars peeked in at them. He leaned toward her and kissed the dampness from her lips, all the while struggling to keep his hands to himself until a more appropriate time and place.

"Comfortable?"

"Mmm. I can't remember the last time I felt this good."

"I think I can improve on that."

"Not possible."

Without a word, he slipped an arm under her knees and swiveled her so her spine rested against the wall of the cabin and her feet were cushioned in his lap. He slipped off her high heels and let them drop to the floor. Then he wrapped his hands around the arch of her foot and began to massage her feet. He watched in amusement as she tightened her grip around her champagne flute and closed her eyes on a breathless sigh.

"I think I'd like to revisit your previous offer," she said.

His laugh rumbled softly. "I assume you'd like to make a counteroffer?"

"Absolutely." She peeked at him from beneath her lashes. "If we get married, will this be part of our evening ritual?"

"Anything you want, *cara.*"

"Why didn't you explain this particular advantage before now? All these weeks of working together and you never— Oh, that reminds me."

She switched to business mode with such ease he figured it had to come from long practice. Slipping her feet from his lap, she set aside her champagne and rifled through her purse for her tablet. "And where did I stick my reading glasses?" she muttered. "Oh, damn. I left them on the bed, after all. Listen, I nearly forgot to tell you. The Reed account called about setting up a meeting for Thursday. Could I borrow Lassiter—"

She broke off when he took the tablet from her hands and dropped it back into her purse. "Not tonight, Caitlyn. No cell phones. No tablets. Tonight is for romance. Not another word of business. Instead, I want to hear about your version of happily-ever-after. What does it look like, feel like? I want to know the woman, not the exec. What are your dreams?"

She blinked at him in frank astonishment. "Excuse me? How many romantic evenings have we talked shop over a bottle of Chianti? I thought that was what you preferred."

Tension filled him. "Do you want to spend your life with a business partner or with a lover? When the sun sets on our day, does it set with us discussing the Reed account, or will we be exchanging the sort of intimate details about ourselves that only lovers can share?"

Her eyes grew dark with an emotion he couldn't quite put his finger on. Something between nervousness and hope. "You're serious about this, aren't you?"

"Very serious. In fact, I want to ask you a question. A serious question."

"You can ask me anything. You know that."

"Do you believe in love at first sight . . . at first touch?"

"At first touch?" Her expression gentled and she slipped her hand into his. "Are you aware you're massaging your palm the same way I do?"

"I . . ." He glanced down with a frown. "What?"

"Your palm. Ever since we first shook hands and felt that odd spark. I catch myself massaging it. I didn't think you ever did, but you've done it twice so far tonight."

"You're right." He could have told her it was a reaction to The Inferno, one he didn't realize any of the women shared. Did Sev's wife, Francesca? He'd have to ask. He returned his attention to Caitlyn. She wouldn't understand the significance of the burn they shared. Not yet. But she would. He'd see to it. "Do you ever wonder about the day we first met?"

"All the time," she confessed softly. "I thought I'd imagined it."

He tried to curb the intensity behind his question so he wouldn't alarm her. "Why?"

She shrugged uneasily. "You know."

He'd made her uncomfortable, no doubt because she didn't want to hurt his feelings. "Because I changed after that."

"I understood," she hastened to reassure. "I'm an employee in your family's business. It wouldn't have been appropriate that day to—" She broke off with another shrug.

"To take what we'd started in the lobby to its inevitable conclusion?"

To his amusement, she avoided his gaze. "Discreetly phrased, but yes. We both know where matters were headed that morning."

"What do you think would have happened if instead of walking on to that elevator and pushing the button for personnel, you'd gone with me?"

Her head shot up and this time she gave him a direct look. "Neither of us would have reported for work that day. I'd probably have been fired and you'd have . . ." She broke off with a shrug.

"Have what?" he prompted.

"You would have found my behavior totally inappropriate. We'd have had an interesting day and I'd be working elsewhere." Her smile wavered. "And we wouldn't be sitting here discussing it."

"I have another scenario." He forked his fingers deep into her hair and tilted her face up toward his. "I think we would have slipped away and allowed what we felt for each other to reach its natural conclusion. And then I would have called personnel and explained that I'd misappropriated you on official Dantes' business and that you would begin work the next day."

"That's a nice fantasy."

He shook his head. "It's what should have happened. Instead I almost lost you. What happened in the lobby became nothing more than a dream, one that faded with each passing day until you began to think you'd imagined the connection we forged that morning."

"But it's back now," she reminded him with a misty smile. "So it's all good."

"And it's going to stay good. Because this time we're listening to our instincts, instead of running from them."

"And when reality intrudes?"

"I want you to promise you'll keep listening to those instincts. That you'll follow your heart instead of your head."

She laughed again, louder and more freely than before, which pleased him no end. "I can't believe you of all people are telling me that, Lazzaro Dante."

He stiffened at the name. "And why is that?"

"Oh, please. Just yesterday you were explaining that emotion and instinct weren't to be trusted. That the reason we get along so well is because we're both rational, logical people." A frown creased her brow. "What's changed your mind since then?"

"I'm surprised you bought into that load of horse manure," he replied, attempting to turn it into a joke.

She persisted, her eyes narrowing. "You're the one who said it. Don't you believe it?"

"Not even a little."

"Well, I do. Did," she corrected. A hint of tension underscored the word. "Now I'm really confused. What's going on, Lazz?"

"Caitlyn . . ." He needed to find a way to put them on a different footing than the one she shared with his brother. "I'd like to start over. Right here and right now. For the rest of this trip, let's pretend it's that first morning again and we've just met. Do you think you can do that?"

"I suppose." The tension seeped away little by little. "Actually, it sounds like fun."

To Marco's relief, Caitlyn took his suggestion to heart and accepted, where before she'd questioned. The attendant approached just then to inform them they were about to land. Once again, he'd arranged for a car to take them to their hotel, a gorgeous rambling structure beside a small, sparkling lake. They were immediately escorted to a private suite on the top floor, one with acres of bed, a sunken bathtub, a whirlpool that could have doubled as a swimming pool, and a private balcony complete with hot tub.

He turned to her and grinned. "Which one do you want to get naked in first?"

Chapter Four

Caitlyn simply stood and stared at the amenities in utter disbelief. "My entire apartment could fit into that bathtub."

"Hmm. Sounds like you need a larger apartment. Maybe we can do something about that when we return. My place is at least as large as that bed. What do you say, *cara?* Interested in swapping a tub for a bed?"

She spun around to face him. "You know, that's the third time tonight you've called me by that endearment, which is really strange considering you haven't used it since the morning we first met. In fact, I've heard you use more Italian in the past couple hours than in the past couple weeks."

"Get used to it. Passion brings it out in me." He looked around with almost boyish enthusiasm and rubbed his hands together. "Let's try out everything. Where do you want to start? A long, romantic soak with candles and chocolates? A spin in the hot tub?" His voice deepened. "Or should we play hide-and-seek on that football-field-size bed?"

"Lazz—"

He couldn't help it. His brother's name on Caitlyn's lips sent him straight over the edge. He needed to find a way of separating the two of them in her mind, to put an indelible mark on her that could never be erased.

"The bed it is."

He reached her side in two easy strides and scooped her up in his arms. She shivered within his hold, trepidation warring with desire. He saw the instant desire won. It leaked into her eyes and tinted her cheeks a gentle rose. It trembled on her lips and rippled endlessly through her, turning her soft and pliant. With the quietest of sighs, she wrapped her arms around his neck and buried her face in the crook of his shoulder.

"I don't want to be a high-powered business exec anymore," she informed him in a muffled voice.

He felt unbearably tender toward the woman in his arms. "Who would you like to be?"

"Me. Right now. With you." She lifted her head to look at him with an endearingly solemn expression.

"What could be more perfect?"

"Nothing that I can think of."

He stripped back the plush comforter and blanket before easing her onto the mattress. Her hair spilled like black ink across sheets of baby-soft ivory cotton, the ebony strands as soft as spun silk. He came down beside her, in no hurry now that he had her where he most wanted her.

"We could make this trip even more special, if you want," he offered gently. "When we return tomorrow, it could be as Mr. and Mrs. Dante."

For a split instant he thought he'd pushed an inch too far. Staring up at him, she moistened her lips. "You know," she admitted hesitantly. "I'd planned how I'd answer you tonight, just in case Britt and Angie were right about your intentions."

"And what did you decide?"

"To tell you how much I appreciated our friendship and hoped over time it could become more than that. More intimate than that." The explanation sounded more like a confession. "That I was willing to take the next step if you were, but that we'd have to take it slowly."

"And now?"

Tears sparkled like diamonds in her eyes. "And now all I can think about is how lucky I am to have found you again and how afraid I am that I'll wake up tomorrow and it'll just be a lovely dream. That our relationship will go back to the way it was and I'll lose all this."

"This isn't a dream and you're not going to lose me."

The apprehension lingered, a shadow that darkened the clear blue of her eyes. "What happens if everything changes again? What happens if we revert to how we were before?"

"That won't happen, I promise." He feathered a kiss across her mouth. "Marry me, Caitlyn, and I'll fill your days and nights with more romance and adventure than your wildest dreams."

"Considering some of my dreams, that's a pretty tall order."

"Try me."

Joy welled upward and she nodded. "I do believe you just won yourself a bride, Mr. Dante."

"Are you sure?"

"Very sure."

"Then, what do you say we do this right?" He checked his watch. "The marriage bureau doesn't close until midnight—"

Her arms tightened around his neck. "And how do you know that?"

"Cara," he admonished, laying on a thick Italian accent. "It's my great pleasure to anticipate your every need."

"Which you're doing brilliantly."

"Which I'll soon do even more brilliantly. Let me make a quick phone call and then we'll go for our license."

"Perfect. That'll give me time to freshen up."

She didn't shift from her position, but simply gazed at him with such yearning that Marco knew that if he didn't get them off the bed and fast, they wouldn't leave it anytime soon. He risked another kiss, sliding across the lushness of her mouth before dipping inward. Just a gentle give and take, a lazy teasing duel that teetered on the edge of flaming out of control.

She broke off the kiss with a strangled moan. "I don't understand any of this. It's like kissing an entirely different person."

That had him levering off the bed. He softened his desertion by holding out his hand with a warm smile. "Come on. Now that you've said yes, I want to turn my brand-new bride-to-be into my brand-new wife."

She sat up, delightfully appealing in her rumpled state. He'd done that to her. He'd upended her neat little columns and smudged all her meticulous rows. And she'd let him. More, she'd encouraged him to yank her outside her box and into his world, a world without order or logic. It did, however, have a plan, one he'd executed with all the care and precision of his twin brother.

"A bride-to-be and a wife, all in one night." She wrinkled her nose. "I'm not sure it gets much crazier than that."

"Give it time," he said, hoping she missed the irony underscoring his comment.

While Caitlyn freshened up, Marco placed a phone call to confirm the arrangements for their wedding, arrangements that would, he hoped, make the night as special as possible. The trip to and from the marriage bureau took hardly any time at all, though filling out the necessary forms gave Marco a moment's worry. Fortunately, since Caitlyn had forgotten her reading glasses in her rush to meet him, the forms were a total blur.

Draping an arm across her shoulder, he helped her without making it too obvious. And all the while he wondered how they'd get through the wedding ceremony. He had a sneaking suspicion that when she was asked if she took Marco Dante for her husband, she might take serious exception to marrying the wrong name, even if he were the right man.

Returning to the hotel, Marco found his requests had not just been met but exceeded. The small chapel overflowed with flowers of every shape, color and variety, while pure white candles gave the room a soft glow. A string quartet played in the background, filling the room with soft, romantic music. He'd asked for a priest to officiate, preferably in the Latin he'd grown up with, and discovered that even that had been arranged. And the "attendants" he'd hired to help with any special touches Caitlyn wished to make to her gown, hair, or makeup were waiting to usher her to a small anteroom, while he paced nervously in front of the altar.

The minute the priest arrived, he explained the changes he wished to make to the ceremony. Come tomorrow there'd be hell to pay for this night. He'd have to deal with his wife's shock and anger when she discovered his duplicity. With his brother's fury. With his family's disapproval at the method he'd chosen to circumvent Lazz. None of that mattered. All he cared about was Caitlyn's instinctive reaction whenever he took her in his arms. Her head might not know him but every other part of her did, and responded with loving abandon. The rest would come in time.

Assuming he could convince her to give him that time.

She appeared in the doorway of the chapel just then, and he could have sworn his heart froze in his chest. He'd never seen anyone more beautiful in his life. With a shy smile she came to him, floating down the short aisle, her gown drifting around her as though spun from cobwebs. A wispy lace veil framed the elegant contours of her face, and she clutched a bouquet of simple white roses.

The ceremony proceeded as though part of a dream. The one time the priest used Marco's name, he leaned forward an instant beforehand and whispered a teasing comment in her ear so that the discrepancy went unnoticed. Toward the end of the ceremony, he put his ring on her finger, pleased at the sharp little gasp she uttered when she saw it.

He'd chosen an exquisite fire diamond solitaire in an antique platinum setting from a selection of rings Nonna had obtained, along with matching wedding bands. "You planned this from the start, didn't you?" she asked in a shaken undertone.

"Let's just say I'd hoped that when I asked, you'd agree."

Color blossomed in her cheeks. "Thank you. I don't think I've ever been happier."

He shot her a smoldering look. "Give it time. I intend to make you a lot happier in a little while."

Her color deepened, but she didn't look away. If anything, her eyes held a promise he hoped would last the rest of their lives. On the dot of midnight, they were pronounced husband and wife, and Marco swept Caitlyn into his arms and kissed his wife for the first time.

Afterward they returned to their suite. "Would you like another glass of wine?" he asked, stripping off his suit jacket.

She gently set her bouquet on a side table and ran her fingertip across the velvety blossoms. "I don't want the wine blurring my memory." She lifted her gaze to his. "You do want me to remember everything, don't you?"

He could feel his body clench in anticipation. "Every minute," he confirmed.

Heat fired in her eyes. "Then I'll pass on the champagne."

For his own peace of mind, he had to be certain. "Does it bother you that we've rushed things? That we didn't have our family here?"

She shook her head. "Not really. Gran is gone now, and I haven't a clue where my mother is these days."

"Why not?" he asked without thinking.

She stilled, staring at him strangely. "You know why, Lazz."

"Right. Sorry." He snagged his jacket from where he'd discarded it, and crossed to the far side of the suite to hang it in the closet, using that as an excuse to conceal his expression. "I'm afraid there's going to be hell to pay from my side of the family," he offered from the depths of the closet.

To his relief the dangerous moment passed and she focused on this latest concern. "They'll be upset they weren't invited, won't they?"

"We're not the first in the family to elope. But they won't be pleased, no."

"Especially since it wasn't necessary."

He took instant exception. "On the contrary. I think it was very necessary. I think we needed to get away from work and family and just trust what we feel for each other." He cocked his head to one side. "Don't you?"

She gave it a moment's serious consideration before nodding. "I'm beginning to suspect it wouldn't have worked out between us otherwise." A swift smile came and went. "Too much brick and not enough mortar."

"The mortar being the romance?"

She nodded and satisfaction filled Marco. His brother had been so wrong about her, as were Britt and Angie. Caitlyn and Lazz were nothing alike. Granted, they both shared an accountant mentality. But that was about as far as it went. Inside, where it counted, she epitomized all that was most female. The monumental spirit, the softness covering indomitable strength, the brilliance tempered by compassion and creativity. They were qualities that had gotten lost at Dantes. Qualities his brother had neither noticed nor understood.

But Marco understood them. Savored them. Intended to revel in them from this moment forward. He took his time, determined to make this night the most special possible. He slowly approached, ripping free his tie and unbuttoning his shirt as he came.

"Tell me what you're feeling, Caitlyn."

"Happy. Nervous." Her gaze dropped to his bared chest. "Hungry."

He continued to close the distance between them. "The first I intend to feed. The second I can appease. And the third I plan to fully satisfy. On every level."

He reached her side and cradled her against him, kissing away any lingering doubts until she shuddered helplessly, the want in her so huge, it couldn't be contained. "Wait," he murmured. "First things first." He removed the veil, using more than his usual care, and draped it across the back of a nearby chair.

Caitlyn stood silently, waiting for him. And then she wasn't waiting. She slid into his embrace and slanted her mouth over his in a hot, greedy kiss, one that told him in no uncertain terms how much she wanted him. He found the fastening for her gown at the nape of her neck and flicked it open. The edges of the halter top fluttered to her waist, baring her to his gaze. Without a word, she reached behind her and unzipped the gown, allowing it to drift to the floor before she stepped clear of it.

She wore nothing but a minuscule triangle of lace that barely concealed the heart of her femininity. She should have appeared provocative. Instead she struck him as proud and elegant, and more desirable than any woman he'd ever known. He took his time, looking his fill until he realized that beneath her calm facade, his lovely wife trembled with nerves. Maybe he'd have caught on sooner if he'd known her a little longer, if they'd shared some of those bricks she'd referred to. The reminder had a frown cutting across his face.

"I can fix that for you," he offered.

Bewilderment momentarily eclipsed her apprehension. "Fix what?"

He captured her hand in his and opened her bunched fingers one by one. "This."

She shut her eyes in chagrin and blew out a sigh. "Gave myself away, didn't I?"

"Just a bit." He drew her against him, allowing the heat from his body to sooth the tautness from hers. Slow and easy, he reminded himself. "Tell me what you're worried about."

"It's a long list," she confessed.

He shrugged. "We have all night." He sent his fingers on a dance of exploration, one along the smooth length of her spine, the other across the fragile bones of her shoulder blades. "First problem?"

She shuddered beneath his touch, and to his amusement it took her a moment to gather her thoughts. If he didn't miss his guess, that was a novel experience for his new bride. "I . . . It's just the speed of all this, I suppose," she explained with a shrug. "Just a couple hours ago we were in San Francisco on the balcony—"

"And I promised you a moonlit drink that we never quite got around to." He skated his mouth along the path his hand had taken, kissing his way from the curve of her shoulder to the base of her throat. There he paused.

"Well, that's not quite true. We did have a drink on the plane. And there was a moon peering in on us. Did you notice?"

"The moonlight was perfect and I had my drink," she managed to reply. As though unable to help herself, her head dipped to one side to offer him better access. "But how did we end up here?

We were just supposed to share a romantic interlude before the anniversary party."

"Which is what we're doing right now. Unless you want to stop interluding?" He nuzzled her ear, catching the lobe between his teeth. Slowly he tugged. "Yes? No?"

The breath hissed from her lungs in reaction. "No, don't stop. Just explain to me how we went from there to here."

"Ah. You want logic." He smiled against her heated skin at her attempt to bring order to disorder. Since when was romance and passion logical? "Let me guess . . . . You want a map of points and coordinates so you can trace your path from point A to point Z."

His teasing eased something within her. He sensed the slight loosening as humor defeated tension. "Something like that."

He slanted his mouth over hers until nothing existed for either of them but the play of their lips and tongue. "I can do that for you." He lifted her hand and brushed a kiss in its center. "For your information, this is point A, the place we first touched."

She gasped for air. "Oh, right. I remember now. That's where this all started."

He didn't give her time to recover her breath. He swung her into his arms and carried her to the bed. "And right here is point Z." He followed her down onto the mattress. "There are a few other miscellaneous points in between." He dismissed them with a wave of his hand. "But you get the general idea."

"Lazz—"

He nearly swore out loud at her use of his brother's name, knowing full well he had no one to blame for that but himself. Aware of her watchful gaze, he managed a teasing smile. "Would you like to go back to point A, or is Z good enough for you."

She pretended to consider. "Z, please. With a few Gs, Rs and Ws thrown in for good measure."

"Excellent suggestion, *cara*. I'm particularly good at W."

"I know I had a long list of other worries, but right now I can't think of a single one." Her hand feathered across the planes of his face. "All I want is for you to prove how well you do W."

"My pleasure."

She lay beneath him, a veritable palette of subtle colors. The flush of palest rose against a sweeping canvas of ivory curves. Lips a shade just shy of coral. The tips of her breasts a shade deeper than her lips. Against all that flowed the black of darkest night, the rippling waves of her hair striking a sharp contrast to the expanse of pastel. And finally there shone the brilliant teal blue of her eyes, staring at him as though the sun rose and set at his command.

Would she still feel that way about him tomorrow? If not, that only gave him tonight, a night he intended to make as perfect as possible. He gathered her hands in his and guided them to his chest, and where she explored his body, so he explored hers, mirroring each and every move.

A smile of delight appeared the instant she caught on to his game. She deliberately ran her fingers along the sculpted muscles of his chest, circling the flat discs of his nipples. Her eyes widened when he did the same to her, eliciting a choked gasp.

"Is this how you want to play?" she demanded when she'd recovered sufficiently to speak.

"We'll see who caves first."

She lifted an eyebrow. "So, the loser is the one who cries uncle first?"

"Trust me. There are no losers in this game." He flashed her a swift grin. "Unless you count losing out on bragging rights."

But he could tell he'd intrigued her and he could see the determination build in her, the desire to have him be the first to put an end to this novel form of foreplay. "We'll see who's bragging come morning," she muttered.

He didn't want to think about tomorrow. Only tonight mattered. He lowered his head to her breast and captured her nipple between his teeth, tugging gently. Her soft cry was all he could have asked for and more. When she didn't immediately reciprocate, he asked, "Giving up, already?"

Then it was his turn to shudder, his turn to struggle to master his self-control. She played the game better than he'd anticipated, proving more creative than logical, which only confirmed his suspicions about her. Even so, he didn't think what was happening between them had to do with creativity, alone. He'd never been touched with such attentiveness or such open curiosity before. And he suddenly realized she was having fun, almost as though such playfulness were a rare treat for her. Almost as though her life had been all work, with far too little play.

"You're laughing," he accused at one point.

She struggled to control herself, failing miserably.

"Do you mind? I swear it's not at you. I've just never tried this game before."

"And you're enjoying it."

"I really am."

The bed became their playground. At some point, his trousers and boxers vanished. He used the opportunity to switch off all but one of the lights, a lamp that bathed the room in soft shadows. He returned to the bed and rolled with her to the darkest section of the bed, where the light couldn't betray that he lacked the scar his brother carried. And then the game turned serious.

He started the chase again, intent on pushing her over the edge. As though picking up on the change, her laughter faded, replaced by an escalating passion. Where before his hands tripped across her skin, now they sought out the areas he'd discovered to be the most sensitive. The back of her knees. The inside of her thigh just below the panty line. The silken slope of her belly. The dimpled hollow above her backside. And along her side where taut skin became soft breast. He gave each and every section of her body his full attention. Gave to her, pleasure after pleasure.

"You win." The breath sobbed from her lungs. "Please, make love to me.

I can't wait any longer. Make love to me now."

"I only win if you win."

She fisted her hands in his hair and drew him down to her, in a long open-mouthed kiss. He'd removed her panties at some point during their game and she opened herself for his possession, encouraging him without words to give completion to the escalating passion that had been building between them.

He threaded his fingers with hers, locking them together palm to palm. This is where The Inferno had first burned, and he could feel it there still, uniting them just as he planned to unite their bodies. He whispered her name as he slid inward. Taking, giving, melding.

Gently, he possessed her. Then not so gently. She reared up to meet him, incandescent in her passion. The urgency grew, bit hard. She called to him, urging him on. Pleading. Demanding. Laughing and crying. He'd never experienced with another woman anything close to what he did in that moment with Caitlyn. Not like this. Never like this.

He could feel the building. Feel the ending approach. He wanted to snatch it back. To live in this moment forever, until the pleasure ripped them both apart. And then it did. She fisted around him, her climax careening through her, surging in wild, crashing waves. Unable to help himself, he crashed with her.

Together they tumbled into an aftermath of weak, tangled limbs and quiet bits of love speak that made no sense but somehow maintained the emotional connection. Marco wound his arms around his bride, his wife, this soul mate The Inferno had given him, and rolled them into a warm ball that wedded soft with hard in a timeless blending of opposites.

He couldn't remember how long they slept. He woke once more during the night and they made love again, this time long and languid. The game they'd played gave them a greater awareness of each other's wants and needs and added a depth and power to their lovemaking.

The second time he woke, he felt the advent of morning. Slipping from the bed, he crossed first to the coffeemaker and turned it on and then to the bathroom where he opened the faucet full force. He picked up a jar of bath salts and removed the lid, sniffed, then upended a goodly portion into the water. Foam erupted. Satisfied, he padded to the sitting area to pour the coffee and transport the two steaming mugs to the tiled platform around the tub. Then he went in search of his wife, finding her, much to his pleasure, right where he'd left her.

Not a morning person, he realized the instant he lifted her from her warm cocoon. "I'm shocked you even know that word, let alone would use it to describe your husband," he said with a husky laugh.

"I know a lot more swear words and I'm going to use them if you don't take me straight back to bed."

"I have something better in mind." He maneuvered down the three short steps into the sunken tub and eased her into the water. Her shriek of surprise turned to a groan of pleasure. He chuckled. "Ah, there's the woman I married. You had me worried for a moment there."

"This feels amazing." She leaned against the sloping edge opposite him and rubbed her foot along the length of his leg. "What do you say we start every morning this way."

"I'll see what I can arrange." He handed her one of the mugs. "I wonder if we can order breakfast in here. They've been so accommodating about everything else."

"There's a phone on the wall by the tub," she said, burying her nose in the mug. "See if you can reach it."

"I'm game, if you are." He levered himself upward, his fingers just glancing off the receiver. He half rose and tried again. Behind him, he heard her coffee mug clatter into the bathtub.

"Oh. God."

At first he thought she'd scalded herself and whipped around to help. And then he knew.

Time was up.

Chapter Five

"Who the hell are you?" Caitlyn demanded.

"Your husband."

"Don't treat me like a fool. You're not Lazz."

She forced down the surge of hysteria battering to escape. But she couldn't keep herself from folding in on herself in an attempt to hide her nudity beneath the scant covering of rapidly dissipating bubbles. Though why she bothered after what the two of them had done last night, she couldn't say.

"Lazz has a scar on his hip. I saw it when we went swimming. You don't have a scar."

"No, I don't. And no, I'm not Lazz." He slowly rose, water sheeting off him as he stepped from the tub and snagged a towel. "That doesn't change the fact that I'm your husband."

It took every ounce of self-control to keep from totally losing it, tremors of fear ripping through her. She felt hideously exposed, and more than a little frightened. She'd married this man—a complete stranger—and didn't even know his name. She'd made love to him all through the night. Frolicked like a child in a bubble-filled bathtub. But she didn't have a clue who he was, other than a dead ringer for Lazz.

She fought to apply reason to insanity, to use what little logic and common sense remained at her disposal, while all around her bricks and mortar crumbled. "Since you look exactly like Lazz, I'm assuming you're related. His brother?" Her brain gave a kick-start. "His *twin* brother?"

"Yes."

"Lazz never mentioned a twin," she stated tightly. "Is this your idea of a joke? Is he in on whatever amusing little scam you're trying to pull? Or is this all your own idea?"

"This isn't a joke or a scam. And if you'll look closely, you'll see I'm not the least amused. Here." He ripped another towel off the glass-and-wrought-iron rack and held it out to her. "I suspect you'll be more comfortable having this conversation if you aren't naked."

She struggled to hold tears at bay. "I can't believe I'm having his conversation at all. I want to know who the hell you are and what sort of hideous game you're playing."

Clutching the towel to her breasts, she stood and wrapped the thick length of cotton around herself. Lazz—no, *not* Lazz—cupped her elbow to steady her as she climbed out of the water. She almost thanked him before catching it back at the last instant.

"Cara—"

She yanked free of his hold. "Don't. Don't you dare call me that. Now, who are you?"

"Marco Dante."

"Marco." She recognized the name. Hadn't she heard Britt rhapsodize endlessly over the past six weeks about the "charming" one of the Dante brothers? Why, in the name of everything holy, had her friend neglected to mention that Marco and Lazz were twins? "How did this happen? Why did it happen? Does Lazz know what you've pulled?"

He removed a terry cloth robe from the back of the door without answering and handed it over. She didn't want to appreciate his thoughtfulness. She didn't want him doing or saying anything that would make her feel kindly disposed toward him. She shrugged on the robe and belted it tightly around her waist before allowing the towel to drop to the floor at her feet.

Lazz—*Marco*—didn't bother with a robe but exited into the bedroom with the towel slung carelessly around his waist. She desperately wanted him to cover up, to hide the impressive chest she'd peppered with kisses. To conceal those amazing arms that had held her with such tender strength. To turn from mind-blowing lover back into a normal, average man, despite the fact that there wasn't, and never would be, anything normal or average about him.

To her relief, once they'd reached the sitting room, Marco gave her some much-needed breathing space. "First, this is no game," he began. "And it happened because Lazz gave me no other choice. At least none, given the limited amount of time I had to work with."

She held up a hand to silence him, wishing she'd chugged that coffee instead of losing it in the bathwater. Spying the coffeemaker and—*hallelujah*—a half pot of coffee remaining, she crossed the room and poured herself a cup. Then a second. Satisfied that her brain was firing on at least half its cylinders, she faced the man she'd married only hours earlier.

"I need you to explain things, but I need them explained in a way I can understand. So, I'm going to ask the questions and you're going to answer them, simply and concisely. Got it?"

He lifted a sooty eyebrow. "Logic, Caitlyn?"

She resented the knowing look in his eyes, a look accompanied by a familiar flash of humor. She lifted her chin to a combative angle. "It's what I do best. Or did, until recently," she corrected.

She struggled to come up with a logical first question, but for some reason it hovered just beyond her reach. All she could think of was that she'd been tricked into a bogus marriage by this man so that he could . . . Could *what?* Get her into bed? That didn't make a bit of sense. He didn't have to go through this sham of a wedding in order to accomplish that. Hit out at Lazz? Possibly. But, why?

She rubbed at the tension headache forming behind her temples, wishing with all her heart that she wore a business suit, had her reading glasses to hide behind, and a pad of paper and pen to help organize her thoughts.

"Okay, first question. Is there a rational beginning to all this? Someplace we can start from?"

"You'd like a point A?"

The poignancy of the question ripped into her, making it almost impossible to keep her voice steady enough to answer. "Yes. Point A would be an excellent place to start."

"That's easy enough." His hazel eyes grew watchful and intent, while the color darkened to autumnal flashes of gold and brown. "You and I met the morning you started at Dantes," he surprised her by saying. "In the lobby near the reception desk."

She blinked in surprise. "That was you?"

"Yes." He kept his voice even, though she sensed it cost him. "I didn't realize it at the time, but apparently you thought I was Lazz."

"The receptionist," Caitlyn explained. "He told me you were Lazz. And since the head of personnel had already pointed out your brother to me during my interview. I assumed . . ." She trailed off with a tired shrug.

"A natural mistake."

She inclined her head. "There's no reason why I'd think there might be two of you, especially since no one's mentioned anything about a twin in the interim. Maybe they thought I already knew."

"If I'd realized that, I'd have corrected the misunderstanding right then and there and it would have saved us—" he swept a negligent hand through the air "—all this."

He couldn't be more wrong. She'd heard stories about Marco, stories that ensured she'd have given short shrift to any advances coming from the sort of man cut from her grandfather's cloth. "Just to be clear? I would never get involved with a man like you."

"But we are involved, *cara*. More than involved," he replied gently. He didn't give her time to argue his statement. "I think I know the next part of the story. Lazz didn't bother straightening out the mix-up in the lobby. And I was sent off on a sudden emergency. A very convenient sudden emergency."

She caught the ripple of tension whenever he mentioned his brother's name. Something had happened there, and somehow she'd been put in the middle of it. Before this ended she'd find a way to change that. "You believe Lazz is responsible for your change in job assignment? Why?" She read the answer in his gaze and shook her head in disbelief. "Because of me? You must be joking."

Marco leaned against the archway between the bedroom and sitting area and folded his arms across his chest. "He wanted you," he said with a shrug. "He didn't realize you were already taken."

"Taken!" Her temper flashed like wildfire. "Let me clarify something for you, Mr. Dante. Despite current evidence to the contrary, I'm not some brainless object to be picked up or discarded or, even worse, fought over by

a pair of schoolboys. I make my own choices. I always have and I always will."

"I'm relieved to hear that, since it means you won't give in to whatever demands Lazz makes when he hears about our marriage. I won't have him coming between us again."

She sucked in a breath and felt her face go white with shock. "Dear God. Are you saying that the events of the past twenty-four hours are your way of retaliating against your brother?" Her voice rose despite her best attempts to control it. "Are you kidding me? Just because he succeeded in dating someone you'd chosen for yourself? You did this to me so you could hit out at Lazz?"

He straightened, a wash of color sweeping along his elegant cheekbones. "You chose Lazz because you didn't realize we were the ones who connected that morning in the lobby. Who bonded."

"We shook hands, Marco! That was it."

"And experienced The Inferno."

She stared at him, nonplussed. "I know I'm going to regret asking this, but what's The Inferno?"

"It's a connection all Dante males experience when they first touch their soul mate." He sank his thumb into the itch centered in his palm. "A burning that never goes away. We experienced the first time we touched."

So it had a name, came her first thought, before she downed the last of her coffee, praying it would help her make sense of what had to be total nonsense. "And you actually believe in this superstition or fantasy or whatever?"

He took instant exception. "It's not superstition or fantasy. All the Dantes believe in it. Well, except for Lazz." He considered for an instant. "And possibly Nicolò. The jury's still out on my cousins, only because they haven't had it happen to them, yet. But that's not the point, damn it. It's real. It happened to us. And before long you'll believe, as well."

She glared at him. She didn't want to accept a single word he said, even though it helped explain how she'd ended up here, married to a complete stranger. For some bizarre reason—other than The Inferno—she'd decided to chase after Zorro and gotten herself in this mess, all in the name of a little excitement. This was why steady and predictable won the race every time. Still . . .

She shook her head, more for her own benefit than his. "I don't believe you. Not that it matters, because after today I'm never going to see you again."

He simply smiled. "And why would you want to do that? We're married. Did last night mean so little to you?"

To her embarrassment, the tears she'd managed to hold at bay earlier escaped. "It meant everything to me." The words escaped in tight rush, emotion threatening to close her throat. "Or it would have if you hadn't lied to me. You committed fraud. You knew full well that if you'd introduced yourself as Marco, I'd have had nothing to do with you. So you pretended to be Lazz in order to trick me into marriage. To trick me into bed. I guarantee a good lawyer will put a fast end to our marriage."

To her dismay, he approached, rousing emotions she had no business experiencing. "Yesterday your friends warned you Lazz planned to propose at Primo and Nonna's anniversary party. Tell me, Caitlyn. What answer would you have given him if he had?"

She couldn't quite bring herself to meet his intense gaze. "I don't see what that has to do—"

"You would have refused him, wouldn't you?" he pressed. "At the very least you would have asked for time. You told me as much last night."

"Okay, fine," she conceded. "That's what I would have done. So?"

He hooked her chin and forced her to look at him. Passion vied with angry frustration. "Why did you change your mind? Why did you agree to marry me?"

She jerked free of his touch. "Temporary insanity combined with too much champagne," she blatantly fibbed.

"Ah, *cara,*" he murmured with a laugh. "You can't lie to me. Last night had nothing to do with too much wine and you know it. You left the party with me, married me, made love to me, because you recognized on a visceral level that I'm the man with whom you belong. And you planned to refuse Lazz for the same reason. Just as you sensed the connection between us, you felt the lack with him."

"Why didn't you simply explain about the mix-up?" It was a cry from the heart. "Why resort to subterfuge?"

"I ran out of time," he said simply. "Lazz planned to propose and even if you'd refused him, you would have refused any advances on my part, as well. Don't you understand? He doesn't love you, sweetheart."

"And you do?"

"I'm not going to answer that because you won't believe anything I say at this point. Only time will convince you whether or not we're meant to be together. Lazz has decided that you two have enough in common to make marriage a logical choice, but that's not reasonable grounds for marriage."

"It's more reasonable than the way you went about it," she retorted. "Until last night, we'd been in each other's company for a whole five minutes. And now you've locked us into this bogus marriage."

"It's not bogus," he corrected calmly. "My legal name is on the marriage license. The priest used it during the ceremony."

She stared in dismay. "He did?"

He hesitated. "I might have distracted you about then. It's possible you weren't paying strict attention."

"Oh, Marco." Satisfaction flared to life in his eyes, brought on, she suspected, by her use of his real name. "This isn't going to work. You realize that, don't you?"

"You're right."

She opened her mouth to argue, then closed it again when his comment sank in. "I am?" she asked, a tad shocked that he'd given so easily. Or was it disappointment?

"It's not going to work if you're unwilling to take a chance."

He wrapped his arms around her. She shuddered at the familiar feel of his arms, at the scent of the oils from their bath that still clung to his bare chest. More than anything she wanted to close her eyes and return to those magical hours they'd shared the previous night. To tumble into bed with this man and sleep, secure in the certainty that all was right with her world.

Only it wasn't. Not any longer.

"I can't stay married to you. I don't know you."

"Yes, you do." He settled a hand over her heart. "In here you know me better than anyone. Or do you think that's not enough? That what we shared last night won't last?"

"It can't. We're strangers, Marco."

"We're lovers, Caitlyn. And in time we'll be friends and companions as well as lovers. In time we'll learn each other's secrets. We'll fight on occasion and adjust to accommodate each other. We'll talk and laugh. And all the while this bond we share, this Inferno, will bind us together until we think and feel as one. All you have to do is give our marriage a chance."

"You're asking me to build a life with you based on fairy tales and wishful thinking. There's no foundation here," she said desperately. "Sex isn't enough."

"We'll create that foundation together over time."

"What about Lazz?"

A change swept over him. Where before he'd been the ultimate charmer, now a toughness tautened muscle and sinew and struck like flint in his voice. "I'll deal with Lazz."

"He didn't do anything wrong," she urged. "He was attracted to me, just as you were."

"Don't." He moderated his tone slightly. "Don't defend him to me. What he did was carefully calculated. He knew I wanted you and deliberately intervened to keep us apart."

She rested her palms against the warmth of his chest, a small plea entering her voice. "I can't believe it was deliberate, Marco."

"I won't discuss this with you, Caitlyn. I just want your promise to keep your distance from now on."

"Because I'm yours now?" His silence said it all, and she fought free of his embrace. "You realize that's going to be difficult since both Lazz and I work in finance? Our paths cross on a regular basis."

"I'll take care of it."

That didn't sound good. "You'll take care of it *how?*"

But he simply shook his head. "He's my brother, Caitlyn. My *twin* brother. He's my problem from now on."

If she were smart, she'd put an end to things right now. Walk—hell, *run*—in the opposite direction. But memories of their hours together intruded. Of the picture-perfect wedding and a night unlike anything she'd ever experienced before. As much as logic and reason warned her to end things, irrational desire drew Caitlyn to Marco.

As though sensing her weakness, he captured her hand in his and gave a gentle tug. "Kiss me, Caitlyn. Just once. Kiss me. Marco. And not my brother."

She could read between the lines. He was asking for what amounted to a first kiss, because in a way that's what it would be. Hurt and anger warred with a desire she couldn't suppress, no matter how she might long to. The connection he'd referred to, a connection she wanted to deny, continued to link them. Not that she believed his superstitious nonsense about The Inferno. All it did was gave a name to the uncontrollable emotions she'd experienced in the lobby. It was a pretty bow used to dress up a battered box. This was lust, not love, no matter how bright and shiny the ribbon.

Caitlyn stared at Marco, determined to turn away. But it was almost as though her body divorced itself from her brain. Without a word she wrapped her arms around his neck. She watched him closely, waiting for a glint of satisfaction or triumph. But the only emotion that came through was a stoic longing and a barely banked heat. Slowly she pulled his head down to hers and gave him the kiss he'd requested.

She'd planned to make it fast and passionless. To prove that whatever had existed between them had been destroyed by his duplicity. And she would have, except for one small problem. The instant her mouth touched his, she lost total control.

Hot, heavy desire ripped her apart while images flashed through her mind. A voice, deep with passion asking her to trust him. Soft, shared laughter. A priest blessing their union. The tenderness with which he touched her. The fun he'd somehow incorporated into the short time they spent together. The joy. The romance.

The passion.

She turned her head sharply away and shoved against his shoulders, fighting back tears. "I can't. I can't do this."

Before he could argue, his cell phone rang. "Time to face the music," he murmured. Releasing her, he picked up his trousers and rummaged through the pockets for his phone. He flipped it open and listened for a second, then winced. "Sorry, Sev. I completely forgot I'd promised to meet with the Romanos. It'll take me a couple hours to get there. Can you postpone the meeting until after lunch?" He thrust a hand through his hair, rumpling it into appealing disarray. "Never mind where I am. You can tell Lazz— No, forget it. I'll tell him myself.

I'll explain everything when I get there." He ended the call and pocketed his cell. "We need to return to San Francisco."

"And then?"

Determination settled over his features. "You're my wife, Caitlyn. That hasn't changed. Since we can't go back, there's only one way to go from here." His determination solidified. "And that's forward."

It took the entire flight home for Marco to convince Caitlyn to give their marriage a chance instead of ending it precipitously. And it took the entire drive from the airport into the city to gain her promise to say nothing to Lazz until after his meeting with the Romanos.

She argued, long and determinedly, that she should break the news to Lazz. Heaven protect him from a logical wife. Though Marco didn't say it—he wasn't *that* stupid—he had no intention of allowing her anywhere near his brother without being glued to her side.

They used up precious time returning to their respective apartments to change, before driving into Dantes together. "If you'd stay in my office during my meeting with the Romanos,

I'd appreciate it," he said as he worked his way through noontime traffic.

"That's okay. I'll just go to my office and—"

He released his breath in a frustrated sigh. "That wasn't a request, *cara,* despite how it may have sounded."

She stiffened. "Please tell me you're joking."

"I'm afraid not. As soon as we announce our marriage to the family, you'll be free to return to work. Until then, it would be better to keep a low profile."

"I see," she said, though he could tell that she didn't. Not even a little. "And what am I permitted to do during your meeting? Is twiddling my thumbs acceptable?"

"Perfectly acceptable. Though if you'd rather, you can phone your secretary and ask her to bring you messages or work files." Unable to resist, he leaned in and snatched a quick kiss. It relieved his mind no end when she responded to it. "Just warn her not to alert anyone to your presence."

"Like Lazz."

"Exactly."

He took them in through the back entrance, in the hopes of attracting as little attention as possible. They arrived at his office only moments before the

Romanos and, after reluctantly parting from his wife, he escorted Vittorio and his daughter, Ariana, into the conference room. The meeting didn't go as well as he'd hoped. A new article had appeared just that morning in *The Snitch*, detailing how Sev had blackmailed his wife into marriage. Not quite accurate, but damning enough.

"What do you want me to do, Vittorio?" Marco finally asked. "I can't prevent them from publishing these stories. No one can. Look at the royal families in Europe. There are constant, scurrilous articles about them in the various rags. If the Royals can't put a stop to it, how can I?"

"He has a point, Papa," Ariana said.

Vittorio folded his arms across his chest and his face fell into stubborn lines. "All I hear is excuses. Maybe if you and your brothers were more circumspect, your antics wouldn't attract the attention of this rag."

Before Marco could reply, he heard Lazz's voice raised in anger from the general direction of his office. Then the door slammed open and his brother burst into the room, Caitlyn hot on his heels.

"You son of a bitch," Lazz snarled, and launched himself at Marco.

Chapter Six

Marco absorbed the impact and they hit the ground with a thud. Lazz landed several hard punches before realizing that his brother, while protecting himself, wasn't striking back.

"Fight, you bastard," Lazz shouted. "Give me an excuse to tear you apart for stealing what was mine."

Before Marco could respond, Sev and Nicolò descended on the conference room, dragging the two combatants apart. A babble of voices erupted, some in English, more in Italian. Through the mass of bodies, Marco saw Caitlyn standing off to one side, looking horrified. But even as he watched, her chin set and he could practically read her thoughts. She intended to face the ramifications of her actions, just as Marco would.

"Did you touch her?" Lazz demanded. "Did you put your hands on her?"

"Touching was unavoidable, all things considered." Marco fingered his split lip and winced. "Caitlyn and I are married."

Stunned disbelief held everyone silent for a second before all hell broke loose again. Across the room Vittorio Romano shot to his feet. Ariana began a heated argument with him but Marco could tell it wouldn't do any good. He could kiss that account goodbye. Something Ariana said must have made an impact because Vittorio hesitated and then with great reluctance pointed in Lazz's direction.

And then something very strange happened. Ariana turned to look at Lazz, whose focus remained fixed on Marco. A strange smile tilted her mouth and she nodded. "Yes, he's the one," he heard her voice in a brief lull in the shouting.

Vittorio waded through the herd of arguing Dantes to Marco's side. "Fix this," he warned. "Then call me."

Marco didn't have a clue what had just happened, but he'd take whatever fortune the gods cared to bestow and run with it. "You have my word. This will sort itself out in time."

"Make it soon," Vittorio advised.

The minute the Romanos left, Lazz swiveled in Caitlyn's direction and Marco read the determination in his brother's eyes. He leaped to his feet to put himself between the two. Sev and Nicolò moved in to block him, grabbing hold when he would have fought his way to his wife's side.

"You owe him this much," Nicolò growled.

"I don't owe him a damn thing. You don't know what he did." Unable to break free, Marco swore long and virulently. "I'm warning you, Lazz," he roared in Italian. "Stay away from my wife."

Lazz simply shot a mocking glance over his shoulder and crossed to Caitlyn's side. Marco began to fight in earnest, suspecting he knew what was to come.

"I'm sorry," he heard Caitlyn say. "I swear what happened wasn't planned."

"Not by you," Lazz agreed. "Just out of curiosity, who did you marry last night?"

She frowned in confusion. "Marco."

"Marco? Or Marco posing as me?"

Her breath hitched in sudden understanding and the sight of tears glittering in her eyes nearly tore Marco apart. "Does it matter?" she asked softly. "It's done."

He hesitated a moment before nodding. "Fair enough. But, I'd still like to know. When did you know it was Marco, and not me?"

Marco stilled as his eyes locked with Caitlyn's. The fight drained from him as he waited for her to tell them all what he'd done. To betray his lies and deceit. For something fragile and unique to die before it ever had the change to gain in strength and power. He'd messed up. Badly. Broken something precious while risking the bonds of his family. And he didn't know if he could fix it. If he'd have the time to fix it.

"I knew it was Marco the instant I first set eyes on him. I immediately realized that he was the one I'd met in the lobby on my first day at Dantes." She focused on Lazz, the expression in her eyes calm and unflinching. "Why didn't you set me straight my first day here? Why did you pretend it was you I met in the lobby?"

"I—"

She released a laugh of amused exasperation, but Marco could hear the heartache behind it. "I know. I know. You two have been competing for women since you were schoolboys."

"I'm sorry," Lazz said stiffly. "It was wrong of me. I should have told you."

A sharpness crept into her voice. "You had six weeks to correct my error. The fact that you couldn't find an appropriate occasion in all that time can only mean you deliberately kept silent in order to keep me in the dark. You also made damn certain I didn't discover you had a twin because you worried that I might question who I'd really been attracted to that day." She waved the topic aside as though it held no further importance. "Never mind. Marco and I worked it out between us. We'll consider the rest water under the bridge."

Lazz frowned. "Caitlyn, I kept silent because I didn't trust Marco to respect our relationship."

"We didn't have a relationship that first day," she said with devastating logic. "You saw an opportunity to cut your brother out of the picture and have spent weeks keeping Marco and me apart so we wouldn't catch on. Well, sorry. The game's over and you lose."

"You have every reason to be upset." He hesitated. "But Marco's joking about the two of you getting married, isn't he?"

She shook her head and summoned a brilliant smile, one that succeeded in fooling Lazz, but it didn't fool Marco in the least. She held out her left hand where her wedding rings flashed. "He wasn't kidding."

Lazz stared, stunned. "My God, Caitlyn."

"Don't." A hint of strain bled into her voice. "When it's right, it's right. That's why I was so confused while we were dating. Something happened during that first meeting with Marco, something that didn't happen in all the times you and I were together since. As soon as I met Marco, everything became clear. Just because you don't understand what my . . ." Her voice almost broke before she gathered it up again. "My husband and I feel for each other, doesn't mean it doesn't exist."

Marco could see she'd reached the breaking point. This time when he fought off his brothers' hold, they released him. He crossed to Caitlyn's side and dropped an arm around her shoulders and held her close.

"Hang in there just another minute," he murmured for her ears alone. Then louder, "Caitlyn's answered all the questions she's going to. The two of us will be out for the rest of the day. Don't call unless it's urgent. And just so you know, urgent isn't on the schedule for the next twenty-four hours."

Without another word, Lazz stepped back. Sev gave an agreeable nod. "Congratulations on your marriage. Take the rest of the week if you want. We'll make sure your jobs are covered."

"Thanks." Marco answered for himself as well as Caitlyn. "We'll take it into consideration." He didn't waste another minute but escorted his wife from the building and to his car before she broke down. "We'll go to my place," he told her.

She shook her head. "I just want to go home."

"My place is your home," he reminded her gently. "Living apart now will make it too easy to continue living apart. That's not my idea of marriage."

"Neither is this," she whispered.

He shot her a concerned look. "Give it time. It'll get better, I promise."

She closed her eyes and leaned her head back against the seat. "You make a lot of promises, Mr. Dante."

"And I keep each and every one of them." They drew to a halt at a stoplight. "Why did you do it, Caitlyn?"

She didn't pretend to misunderstand the question. "Lazz wasn't an innocent in all this, either. In fact, a large portion of our situation can be placed squarely at his door. If he'd told me it was you in the lobby that day or warned me that he had a twin brother, last night wouldn't have happened."

Marco shrugged. "It would simply have delayed the inevitable."

She opened her eyes, eyes gone dark with painful memories. "I would never have agreed to date you."

"You're wrong."

She considered for a moment before conceding the truth. "Okay, fine. I would have gone out with you. But as soon as I'd realized that you were—what did Britt call you?—sinfully charming, I'd have put an end to our relationship. I don't date charming."

"You married charming," he reminded her. "Besides, by the time you'd discovered just how charming I am, it would have been far too late." He put the car in gear and cruised through the intersection. "I would have won you over, just as I did last night."

When they arrived at his apartment, he took her on a brief tour. "We can shop for a new place, if you want, though this should be big enough for two. I'll let you decide."

"It's at least four times the size of my place." Impressed, she ran a hand along the back of his couch and paused to study the collage of photos on the wall, most of which were family pictures. She focused on Nonna and Primo's wedding photo. "I never did get to meet your grandparents."

"You will. Did you know they also eloped?" She shook her head and he added, "Nonna was engaged to Primo's best friend. Once The Inferno struck, that was that. There was no turning back for them, either."

Caitlyn stilled. "Is that the only reason you married me? Because of this Inferno you believe you felt?"

"We both felt The Inferno, *cara.*"

Was he serious? She turned from the wall of photos to fully confront him. "Let me get this straight. The reason we're together is because of The Inferno. It has nothing to do with me? With who I am, with what type of person I am? You felt this reaction and therefore that's it. End of story. You'll marry me simply based on some family legend."

"It goes deeper than that."

"You're wrong, Marco. There isn't anything more. Nothing deeper. We felt something when we first shook hands and you assumed it was this Dante legend come to life. And all because of that, you interfered in my relationship with Lazz. You tricked me into going with you to Nevada." She fought to keep the pain and tears from her voice with only limited success. "You married me, even though you knew I thought you were your brother. And all because of a fantasy. A family superstition."

"It's not superstition. It's fact."

Anger rose to the fore. "I live by facts and figures, Marco," she informed him sharply. "The Inferno is far from fact. You may believe in it. Your grandparents may believe in it. Even Sev may give it some credence, though how a man so intelligent could, is beyond me. But that doesn't make it real. That doesn't make it factual. And it's sure as hell not enough of a foundation for marriage."

"In time you'll understand."

"No, I won't, because our marriage won't last that long."

He approached with an easy, unhurried stride and slid his arms around her waist. "Let's see if I can't convince you to change your mind about that."

"What are you going to do?"

She didn't know why she bothered to ask the question. She knew precisely what he planned. It was there in his heated gaze and in his slow smile and in the tender manner in which he held her. He moved against her in a way that instantly brought their wedding night to mind, then lowered his head to coax her mouth with a single kiss.

She could feel the slight puffiness from his encounter with Lazz's fist and kept the kiss as gentle as possible, though why she felt the need for such consideration she couldn't explain. To her surprise, he didn't demand. Didn't insist. He simply seduced with lips and teeth and tongue.

How was it possible that she surrendered with such ease after all he'd done over the past twenty-four hours? Was she so desperate to return to his bed that nothing else mattered? Where was the logic in that? How could she reconcile heart with head when every time he kissed her, her heart went wild and her head lost all ability to reason?

"Give us a chance, Caitlyn. We can make this work."

"That's not possible."

"I'll make it possible."

He swept her into his arms and shouldered his way into the bedroom. She had a brief glimpse of bright colors and gleaming woodwork before falling into the sumptuous embrace of raw silk and velvet. The handcrafted comforter cushioned her, cradling her in softness, while Marco covered her in all that was hard and male.

"This is wrong." Her hands settled on his shoulders to push, but clung instead. "I don't want you to make love to me again."

"This is even more right than last night." Urgency blazed within his eyes, sparking with green and gold lights. "When you make love to me this time, it won't just be with your husband. You'll make love to me knowing I'm Marco, not Lazz."

"So you can put your mark on me." She couldn't decide if that fact annoyed or amused her.

A hint of a smile cut through the hard edge of passion. "That happened long ago."

"You can't truly believe in this Inferno," she argued desperately. "That it's responsible for the attraction between us."

He hesitated, his hand tracing the curve of cheek and throat as though he was unwilling—or unable—to keep his hands off her. "I've been attracted to many women." His voice held a hint of apology. "But it's never been like this. I can look at you objectively and see a beautiful woman, a woman I'd want in my life and my bed."

She couldn't help stiffening against him. "And you've succeeded."

"Let me finish. I've never once wanted more from those women than a casual affair. I've never been tempted to extend our relationship beyond its temporary boundaries. But with you . . ." His breath exploded from him and he caught her hand in his and drew it to his chest, pressed it tight to the solid beat of his heart. "With you it's as though those women were mere shadows of possibility. Shades of gray without color or substance. I don't want shadows. I want light and color. I want a woman of depth. And that's you."

"This is too much, too soon. We need time to get to know each other."

He laughed, the sound soft and deep and oddly arousing. "We have all the time in the world, *cara*. Decades to get to know every intimate detail."

"That's not what I mean—"

"I know what you mean. It's just not something I can offer you."

So compassionate, and yet so absolute. He didn't give her time to argue any further. His mouth drifted across hers, nibbling a lazy path. The casualness of the kiss should have allowed her to turn away. Instead it incited a desire to deepen it, to drive it from temperate to ardent. To feel the burn that happened only with Marco.

She whispered his name and felt him practically inhale the sound of it, felt his need as though it were her own. She expected him to exhibit some sign of victory or complacency. But he didn't. He simply gave to her, allowing her demand to set the pace.

"If I ask you to stop, will you?" she asked.

"Yes. Reluctantly. But, yes."

He needed to stop. Now. "Don't stop. Not yet. Soon—" She groaned as the buttons of her blouse gave, one by one, and he stroked his finger from the dip at the base of her throat to the scalloped edge of her bra. *"Marco!"*

Then his mouth followed the same path, his tongue tracing the lacy contours while he found the back fastening and released it with a flick of clever fingers. Cool air sliced across her bared skin before Marco warmed it with a single touch. He palmed her breasts and laved each tip into tight peaks, catching first one and then the other with his teeth until she could barely contain her response to the pleasure.

Her hands moved of their own accord, tearing at his shirt. She heard the cotton rip, heard the muted ping of buttons popping before she finally, finally, *finally* hit hot, bare flesh. Satisfaction bubbled through her like warm syrup as her hands plied the sculpted muscles, tripping across them with her fingertips. He groaned his encouragement.

She wanted more. Needed it. She cruised across rippled abs until she found the belt anchoring trousers to hips. Two deft tugs and she had it open and her hands plunging downward, cupping and stroking. Harsh Italian exploded from him, an endless stream of what sounded like a combination of demand, curse, and plea.

"Panties," she managed, praying he understood her shorthand. "Off."

Rending silk competed with the sound of their desperate breathing. And then came the pause, that long moment of sweet hesitation before temptation tipped over into inevitability. She stared up at Marco, wishing she didn't see Lazz mirrored in her husband's face and eyes, wishing that with one glance or touch or word, she could tell the difference between them. But she wasn't sure she could. Not unless she demanded he show her his hip each time they came together.

"I'm not him," Marco bit out.

"I know you're not," she attempted to soothe.

"Not yet, you don't. But you will." He fumbled behind him. She heard a drawer being yanked open and the distinctive crinkle of foil. The instant he'd protected himself, he measured her length with his eyes. "Maybe this will help."

He swept his hands from her knees to her thighs, dragging her skirt upward as he went, baring her to the waist. She'd never been taken like this, simply flipped onto a bed and driven so insane with want that removing their clothes proved beyond them. She shuddered as he palmed the back of her thighs, lifting and opening her for his possession. A rush of cool air competed with the scalding heat of him as he came down on her, drove inward with a single, powerful thrust. She thought she screamed, but if she did, he caught the helpless sound in a desperate kiss.

She locked her legs around his hips and surged upward to meet his next stroke, the need in her so huge and overwhelming, nothing else mattered but having this man inside her. The past didn't count any more than the future. All she cared about was right here and right now.

Marco loosened another barrage of Italian, and she answered as though she understood, inciting him to go higher and harder and further than they'd gone before. It was her turn to plead. To demand. To pray that she survived the encounter if only so she could do this again and again.

Her climax hit with unexpected suddenness, careening through her in chaotic, unmanageable waves. No order. No logic or reason. She could only hang on and give in to something beyond her ability to control. To surrender utterly. Endless minutes passed while they fought to regain their breath.

"*Cara,* please." Concern lashed the words. "Don't cry."

"Am I?" She lifted a boneless hand to her cheek. "I didn't realize."

"Does it seem so wrong to you?"

No, that was the scary part. It seemed all too right.

"It's just . . ." Damp hair curled across his brow, framing a face still carved with the remnants of desire. She itched to brush it from his eyes, and with a sigh of impatience, caved to the impulse. "It has to be more than this. More than just good sex."

He lifted an eyebrow. "Is that how you'd describe what just happened here? What happened between us last night?"

She refused to consider it might be anything else. That would give it too much importance. "There's more to a relationship than great sex," she argued doggedly. "Far more to a marriage."

"So now it's *great* sex," he said. "At least that's an improvement."

She slammed the heel of her palm against his shoulder, hurting herself more than him. "Would you be serious? At least with Lazz—" She broke off at the expression on his face, eyeing him apprehensively.

"Do not," he said in a low voice, "do *not* put my brother in bed with us. Not ever."

"It's just—"

"Am I not clear on this point?"

"Fine. You're clear." She shoved at his shoulders. "I'd like to get up, please."

He rolled to one side, allowing her to escape. It annoyed her that he remained so comfortable with his partial nudity, while she needed desperately to cover herself while they talked. She tugged at her wrinkled skirt, attempting to restore it to some semblance of order. Next, she tackled the buttons of her blouse, only to realize she hadn't a hope of hooking her bra unless she removed her blouse first. Turning her back on him, she did just that. A small, choking sound emanated from the direction of the bed and sounded suspiciously like a smothered laugh, though when she turned back around he regarded her with such a sober expression, it stretched the bounds of credulity.

She decided to give him the benefit of the doubt. "I'm a logical person, Marco," she finally said. "And though I enjoy sex as much as the next person—"

"Great sex," he reminded her.

"Fine. *Great* sex." He'd thrown her off track and it took a split second to find her stride again. "Marriage is more than sex. Even great sex," she hastened to add before he could correct her again.

"True," he surprised her by saying. "Since we have that part down pat, we can spend the next fifty or so years working on the rest." He lifted an eyebrow. "Does that alleviate your concerns, *moglie mia?"*

Caitlyn planted her hands on her hips. "Why do you use so much Italian? Lazz never—" She broke off and rubbed the exhaustion from her eyes. He was right, Lazz didn't belong in the room with them. "I'm sorry. I meant to say that you use a lot of Italian and I don't understand a word of it. What does mog-whatever mean?"

Marco left the bed. *"Moglie* means wife." After stripping off the remains of his tattered shirt, he disappeared into the adjoining bathroom. When he reappeared, he paused in front of her and dropped a swift kiss on her brow. "Thank you for trying."

She didn't dare admit that Lazz might as well not have existed right then, despite her reference to him. Not while Marco stood in front of her, shirtless, his trousers gaping at the waist where a thin line of dark hair darted downward along a path she'd just recently followed. She struggled to keep her gaze fixed on his face. He must have known how difficult she found it not to peek, because a slow grin built across his mouth.

"I'm your husband, remember?" he said. "We have a piece of paper that says it's not rude to look."

Her lips twitched, "I must have missed that particular line on our marriage license."

"Ah. That's because you forgot your reading glasses."

She lifted an eyebrow. "And if I'd remembered them?"

He shrugged those magnificent shoulders of his. "Fate and chance give life interesting twists and turns, wouldn't you agree?"

"Since I'm currently in a twist over one of those wrong turns, I'm not sure interesting is the word I'd use."

He fell silent for a moment. "I don't consider our marriage a wrong turn," he informed her quietly. "In time I hope you won't, either."

She'd been inconsiderate, and hurt him without meaning to. It occurred to her that in the short time they'd been together, he'd used great care with her. Despite some of his more outrageous actions, everything he'd said, as well as his overall treatment of her, had been not just careful but downright tender. The least she could do was follow his example.

"Where are we supposed to go from here?" she asked.

"I was thinking the kitchen might be a good direction."

She stared at him in patent disbelief. "You want me to cook for you?"

Lord help her, but Marco liked to laugh. "Actually, I thought I'd cook for you."

After snagging a shirt, he ushered her into the kitchen and seated her at a tiny table tucked within the sunny embrace of a bay window. Opening a drawer, he removed an apron, which he tied around his waist with such familiarity and efficiency, she realized this was far from his first foray into the kitchen. Coffee came first, freshly ground. And then he proceeded to cook. Really cook. In less than thirty minutes he placed two steaming plates of shrimp fettuccini on the table. After whipping off his apron, he joined her.

"If this is meant to impress me—"

"Has it succeeded?"

"And then some." She sampled the dish and groaned.

"Do you cook like this all the time?"

"When I'm not out of the country or entertaining potential clients. I got lucky and found a woman to shop for me who appreciates fine food as much as I do. I email her when I want something to appear in my refrigerator." He shrugged. "And it appears. She also takes care of general housekeeping and various other chores that don't appeal to me as much as cooking."

For some reason, that had Caitlyn returning her fork to her plate. "Maybe this would be a good time to discuss our marriage."

He picked up her fork and speared a succulent piece of shrimp and held it to her mouth. "Fine. What, in particular, would you like to discuss?"

"Marco . . ." She couldn't resist. She ate the shrimp, took the fork from him and dug in again. "What do you want from our marriage?"

"Ah. You'd like rules. Order."

"I'd like some idea of your expectations."

"Scintillating conversation and companionship. Incredible sex—we'll have to work to nudge it up from great. And with God's blessing, more laughter than tears." He lifted an eyebrow. "I can go on. Do you want me to fetch your tablet so you can jot down some notes?"

"I need you to be serious. Marriage is a serious business." Her fork clattered to her plate. An empty plate, she realized to her amazement. "I'm sorry. I just can't do this. None of this is real and it's pointless to pretend otherwise."

"Marriage is not a business and I refuse to turn it into one." He reached across the table and caught her hand. "Relax, *cara*. You need to give our relationship time and stop applying an agenda to it. Do flowers bloom on command? Does spring arrive simply because the calendar says it must? If it makes you more comfortable to create some sense of order, then let's call this moment in our marriage point A. In a few weeks we can reassess and see if we haven't moved to B or C."

For some reason his comment had her eyes filling. "This is crazy, you know that, don't you?"

"Tears," he said with a frown. "Now that I will keep track of. Because for every tear, I'm going to make certain you have reason to laugh at least a hundred times."

"At this rate I'm going to spend all day laughing."

"See how easy that was? We already have our first marital rule. A hundred laughs for every tear." The humor in his gaze eased, replaced by undisguised warmth. "I know you planned to tell me today that you're leaving and putting an end to our marriage. But will you agree to stay and give it a try? We can set a time frame if that makes you more comfortable."

"A negotiation, Marco?"

"I could, if I considered marriage a business deal. I could use *The Snitch* as an excuse or the Romano account."

She stirred uneasily. "Will our marriage have an adverse impact on that?"

"No. But our divorce would." He let that settle for a minute before continuing. "I could explain how much more beneficial it would be to your career to remain with me, or how it would look if we divorced after a single day of marriage. But this isn't about business, as I've already explained. There's only one real reason to stay together."

"Which is what?" She hazarded a guess. "To get to point Z?"

He smiled, a gorgeous, sexy smile that she'd never, ever seen on Lazz Dante's face. Only Marco could smile like that. "Why would I want to jump straight to Z when there are so many fun points to explore in between? The point of a dance is not to rush to the end, but to enjoy each step along the way." He pulled her up from her chair and swung her into his arms, causing her to melt helplessly against him. "Come, my beautiful wife. What do you say? Let's dance."

Chapter Seven

Over the next few days, Caitlyn discovered Marco meant just what he said. He didn't seem to care about the business ramifications should she walk out on him. He only cared about her. For some reason, that realization left her shaken. All the while a small voice whispered insistently in her ear that it had to be a lie. How could she possibly be more important than winning an account that would guarantee the meteoric success of Dantes in the European market?

Marriage should be more complicated than Marco made it out to be. It certainly had been for her grandmother. Thanks to her disastrous union, there'd been exhaustive instructions on how to build a proper foundation and which qualities to look for in a husband, an endless list to be detailed, considered, and checked off long before marriage should ever be contemplated. She and Marco hadn't done any of that, and Caitlyn couldn't help but believe that lack would bring a fast end to a short marriage.

Fortunately, she didn't have long to dwell on her worries. The minute she returned to work, she was assigned a huge, complex project to oversee that involved transferring decades worth of old financial records from paper to computer.

"With the expansion into the international market, we need to have this information available at the touch of a button," Caitlyn's supervisor explained. "And we need someone with your background in finance and attention to detail to sort the wheat from the chaff. Determine what's important to computerize and what can be safely discarded."

"But what about my current duties?"

"We're assigning you temporary help with that while you concentrate on getting this other project in hand. I'll be honest with you, Caitlyn. We're hoping you can succeed where every other person who's attempted this assignment has failed."

It was like waving a red flag in front of a bull, Caitlyn realized with a touch of Marco's sense of humor. The idea that she could accomplish what no one else could, appealed immensely and she threw herself into the project with unfettered enthusiasm. Unfortunately, it meant a temporary move from the

Dantes main office to their warehouse where most of the records were stored.

Toward the end of the week, Britt tracked Caitlyn to her new location and tossed a folder onto her desk. "Here. Lazz said you needed this. I could have emailed it to you, but it gave me an excuse to come for a visit. Just so you know, you're missed."

"Thanks. I miss you and Angie, too." She checked her watch. "I wish I'd known you were coming. I'm actually scheduled to have lunch with Francesca in about five minutes."

"Sev's wife, right?" Britt grimaced. "Makes sense. I guess she's been assigned to explain what the family will expect from the latest Dante bride."

Caitlyn's brows drew together. "Expect? What are you talking about?"

Britt snapped her fingers. "Oh, come on, girl. Get with it. You're in the public eye now. *The Snitch* will be all over you when news of your whirlwind marriage to Marco breaks. I suspect Primo or Nonna assigned Francesca as your handler, to guide you through the various family dos and don'ts so you don't accidentally make matters worse for them than you already have."

It took an instant before Caitlyn could gather herself enough to reply. "I'm sure that's not the case at all."

Britt shrugged. "If you say so." She shoved a pile of papers to one side and levered herself onto the desktop. Lifting Caitlyn's left hand, she let out a low whistle. "That's one hell of a rock, sweetie. Even more impressive than the one Lazz was planning to give you."

Caitlyn tugged her hand free, annoyed at the hint of color she felt creeping into her cheeks, and even more annoyed at Britt. "You and Angie made a bigger deal of my relationship with Lazz than it warranted."

"Apparently. Poor Lazz. I guess you fell for Marco's charm just like every other woman working at Dantes." She leaned in, lowering her voice. "So? Is it true?"

"Is what true?" But Caitlyn could guess, given the various rumors flying around the office about the events that had transpired the night she and Marco had eloped.

A wicked light gleamed in her friend's eyes. "Did you realize it was Marco before he made love to you, or did he wait until afterward to tell you the truth?"

Even though Caitlyn had seen the question coming, she still winced. "I should have expected something like that from you, but you must realize I'm not going to answer it."

Britt blew out a sigh. "Or which of the two is the better lover?" She paused a beat, but when Caitlyn remained stony-silent, added, "It's gotta be Marco. I mean, why else would you marry him, especially considering that jealous streak of his?"

"Caitlyn?" Francesca's voice came from a short distance away.

"Oops. That's my cue to scoot." Britt jumped off Caitlyn's desk and waggled her fingers. "We'll catch up again later."

Francesca, tall, blond, and as elegant as she was beautiful, appeared in the doorway. She waited with ill-disguised disapproval while Britt made good her escape. "Come on, let's get out of here," she said to Caitlyn. "I don't know about you, but I could use some fresh air."

"Where are we going?"

"To Nonna's so she can explain how you're expected to behave now that you're a Dante bride." She waved the comment aside with a broad grin. "Sorry. I couldn't resist. We are going to Nonna's for lunch, but I assure you if there's a Dante bride how-to instruction booklet somewhere, Britt will have to show it to me. To be honest, there are times I could really use one."

On the way to Francesca's car, Caitlyn attempted to defend her friend, though why she bothered, she couldn't say. "Britt's just a bit outspoken."

"Is that what you call it? I call it pea green with envy." Slipping the car in gear, Francesca pulled out of the parking lot and jumped on the 101 toward the Golden Gate Bridge. "She's always had a thing for Marco. But he and his brothers made an agreement years ago that they wouldn't date in the workplace. Of course, that agreement fell apart when I came onboard."

"Did that count? I thought you were dating Sev before you joined Dantes."

"Was blackmailed into joining Dantes. Don't you read *The Snitch?* I guess Britt saw my relationship with Sev as a loosening of the rule and made a concerted effort to catch Marco's eye. Then when both Lazz and Marco went after you . . ." Francesca shrugged. "I'm sure it felt like a slap in the face to poor Britt."

Caitlyn considered the situation. Sunlight poured down across the red spans of the bridge and bounced off the whitecaps far below. If Francesca's comments were accurate, it explained many of the barbed remarks Britt claimed were jokes. "Thanks, Francesca. I appreciate you clueing me in."

Sympathy gleamed in Francesca's dark eyes. "Anytime. I'm just sorry I had to trash someone you consider a friend."

Caitlyn leaned back against her seat and studied her sister-in-law for a long minute. How odd that with one simple "I do" she'd gone from having almost no family to having one so sizeable that she didn't even know all their names or faces yet.

A few minutes later they climbed the hillside above Sausalito and pulled into the drive of a large, rambling gated home. Francesca led the way through the dusky interior and out into a huge, meticulously tended garden, overrun with flowers, shrubs and shade trees. A wrought iron table had been placed beneath the widespread arms of a mush oak and set for lunch. Seated at the table was a woman who could only be Nonna.

Caitlyn returned the older woman's stare, fascinated by Marco's grandmother. She must be well into her seventies, considering she and Primo just celebrated their fifty-sixth anniversary. Yet she looked a full decade younger, her face one of radiant beauty despite the lines life had carved there. Or maybe because of them.

"Marco has your eyes," Caitlyn observed.

Laughter danced within the hazel depths, revealing that Marco had inherited a second characteristic from his grandmother. "So does Lazzaro," she said, her voice carrying the lilting strains of her Italian heritage. "Or did you not notice?"

Caitlyn blinked in surprise. "I guess I never did. Of course they would since they're identical twins."

Nonna lifted a shoulder. "Ah. Once you have been touched by The Inferno, you see only one man clearly." She kissed Caitlyn on both cheeks, followed by Francesca, then gestured to the two empty chairs. "Come. Sit. You will call me Nonna as Francesca does, and we will break bread together and talk as women have talked since the day we were formed from Adam's rib. About men, life, children, and then, inevitably, about men again."

Francesca grinned. "Sounds good to me. Especially the men part."

"Hah. With you I suspect children are more on your thoughts, yes?"

"Not quite yet, Nonna."

"Time will tell. I am rarely wrong about these matters. But since that is not yet an issue, we will have a lovely glass of wine with our lunch." A mischievous expression twinkled in her eyes. "Maybe two."

"I'm sorry, Nonna," Caitlyn began. "I can't—"

"Because you are not finished with your workday." Nonna waved that aside and poured the wine. "If it makes you more comfortable, consider keeping me happy for the rest of the day one of your duties. One of your primary duties since I have arranged for you to have the afternoon off. And keeping me happy right now involves drinking some Dante wine while we get to know each other."

Caitlyn gave in gracefully. "A dangerous proposition. Last time I had a glass of your Dante wine, I ended up married to Marco."

The other two women dissolved into laughter. "Such is The Inferno," Nonna said. "It turns sane, rational women into creatures of instinct."

The comment roused Caitlyn's curiosity. "Would you mind if I asked you both a personal question?"

"Hit me," Francesca said.

Nonna looked momentarily disconcerted at the response but nodded energetically, anyway. "Yes, yes. You may hit me, too. But I am old, so do it very gently."

"It's more of a verbal hit," Caitlyn explained with a smile. "I know you believe in The Inferno, Nonna. Marco told me how it changed your life and forced you to make a difficult choice."

"Not so difficult. More sad and unpleasant."

Caitlyn glanced at her sister-in-law. "But you, Francesca. Do you believe in it?"

Francesca relaxed in her chair and took a sip of the crisp, golden Frascati. "I gather you don't?"

Caitlyn shook her head. "I think it must be legend or fantasy," she said, shooting Nonna an apologetic look.

"Yes, so did I. At first. It's only natural, all things considered."

"You said *at first*. That implies that at some point you bought in to the story."

Instead of laughing, an odd expression settled over Francesca's face. "Give me an honest answer, Caitlyn. Was there an electric current when you and Marco first touched? I mean, an honest-to-goodness spark?"

"There was something like that," she admitted.

"And do you feel him, even when you don't see him? If I lined up Lazz and Marco in identical suits. If I mixed them up and turned them so their backs were to you. Could you tell which was your husband and which your brother-in-law?"

"I'm not sure." Perhaps if she could look directly at them, catch some clue as to expression or attitude. Or would it take that much effort? The mere idea of

Lazz putting his hands on her struck her as downright distasteful. She closed her eyes. "I honestly don't know. Maybe."

"Does Marco rub his palm, like this?" Francesca demonstrated, digging the fingers of her left hand into the center of her right. "Look familiar?"

"Yes," Caitlyn whispered. "I've caught him doing it on occasion. I catch myself doing it, too."

"It happens with all the Dante men once they have been struck by The Inferno, and it would seem, with some of the Dante brides," Nonna explained. "Primo. Our two sons. And now Sev and Marco. So it has been since the beginning of the Dante line."

"It's up to you whether or not you choose to believe that it's The Inferno." Francesca shrugged. "I happen to believe."

Before Caitlyn could ask more questions, Primo delivered their lunch, one he'd prepared himself. Clearly, Marco had inherited Primo's ability in the kitchen, despite there being more of a physical resemblance between the older man and Sev. Though Primo's countenance reflected an almost harsh nobility, only warmth showed in his expression. After welcoming her with a warm bear hug and a smacking kiss on each cheek, he checked to see whether they had everything they needed, then made himself scarce.

The hours raced by after that, brimming with sweet, tart laughter and rich, full-bodied feminine conversation. Caitlyn couldn't remember ever having a more enjoyable time in the company of women. At one point she attempted to compare Nonna with her own grandmother, but aside from a certain strength of character, the two couldn't be more dissimilar.

Early evening had just crept into the garden, pinching shut colorful day blooms and coaxing open their heavy-scented nocturnal sisters, when the Dante boys descended. Sev took one look at his wife and shook his head in mock dismay. "I see Nonna's been a bit heavy-handed with the wine," he addressed his grandfather. "I'm going to need your wheelbarrow to get this one home."

"You know where I stash it," Primo said with a chuckle. He pulled a chair up beside Nonna and gathered her hand in his. Heads bent toward each other like a pair of sleepy white daffodils and they murmured softly in Italian.

Caitlyn sensed Marco's approach and knew that Francesca and Nonna would claim it was The Inferno at work. Whatever caused the awareness, it mitigated her surprise when he simply picked her up in his arms, stole her seat, then sat down again with her on his lap.

"How was your day?" he asked.

"Perfect." Her head dropped of its own accord to his shoulder. "Better than perfect."

"I'm glad. Nonna is . . ." He offered a very Latin shrugged.

"There's no describing her, is there?" Caitlyn agreed.

They continued to sit, the six of them, and talk for another hour before Marco called it a night. They made their farewells and exited through the garden gate to the circular drive, maintaining a comfortable silence on the drive from Sausalito to Marco's apartment.

"Nonna's different from my grandmother," Caitlyn commented on their way inside.

"You know, I think that's the first time you've mentioned your family since our wedding night." He inclined his head toward the rear of the apartment. "Fill me in while we change. How's your grandmother different from mine?"

She followed him into the bedroom and stripped off her suit jacket. "They're both strong women," she said, heading for the closet. "But Gran was rigid. Nonna, not so much."

He reached around her for a wooden hanger. "Let me guess. Your grandmother came from the school of thought that teaches seeing is believing." He nudged her with his elbow. "Passed that right on to you, did she?"

A smile flirted with Caitlyn's mouth, then faded. "She didn't have much choice. She raised me, you know. Or maybe you don't know." She shot him an uneasy glance. "Sorry. I guess it was Lazz I told."

To her relief, he didn't take offense. "Tell me now," he encouraged. He unzipped her skirt for her, before ripping free his tie with a sigh of relief.

She stepped out of her skirt and clipped it to the hanger holding her suit jacket. It never ceased to amaze her how comfortable she felt performing these little domestic chores in front of him. Relishing the sizzle of awareness combined with the gentle bite of sexual tension. Wondering if the sight of her half-undressed would tempt him to pick her up and toss her to the bed behind them. If his nudity would tempt her to entice him there. She suddenly realized he was waiting for her response.

"Oh, it's an old, sad story," she hastened to explain. "One told by countless women over the years. My grandfather was a charmer."

She broke off when Marco lassoed her with his tie and yanked her up against him. "Excuse me?" he rumbled.

She couldn't help but grin. "Oh, stop glaring at me. I don't mean *your* kind of charmer."

"What other kind is there?" he asked, genuinely bewildered.

Her amusement evaporated. "The sort who makes pie-in-the-sky promises and neglects to keep them." She strained against the confines of the tie, regarding him with amused exasperation. "Do you mind?"

"Another time, perhaps." He reluctantly released her and continued to undress. "That explains why my promises worry you so much. You don't know me well enough to believe I'll keep them."

"Something like that," she confessed. "Gramps encouraged Gran to give up a high-powered budding career, which in those days, very few women managed to achieve. But she did it because he sold her on the dream."

He leaned against the closet doorjamb, shirtless, his only covering a black pair of boxer briefs. "Which was?" he prompted.

She tore her gaze away and scrambled to remember where she'd left off in her story. "He wanted the dream. A two-story home and white picket fence, dinner on the table at six, where a freckle-faced son with a slingshot tucked in his back pocket would be waiting for him, along with a sweet little daddy's girl dressed in a frilly dress and pigtails."

"What did he end up with?"

"A ramshackle house in dire need of repair with a fence falling into splinters, a dinner of mac and cheese because the budget didn't stretch to more than that, and a squalling daughter suffering from colic. Somehow it managed to escape his attention that in order to have the dream, someone had to earn a living. Not long after my mother was born, he took off. He'd found a new dream that appealed far more than the realities of the old one."

"What happened to your grandmother and mother?"

She turned to face him. "Gran raised my mother the best she could. Worked whatever menial jobs she managed to pick up, since by then the possibility of a career had passed her by. My mother took off at sixteen with the first man who looked twice at her. I landed on Gran's doorstep nine months later."

"Hell, sweetheart." He wrapped her up in a hug. "Saying I'm sorry sounds so inadequate. But I am."

Caitlyn shrugged, inhaling the unique scent of him. God, he smelled good and felt even better—strength and warmth and comfort all rolled into one. "I had Gran. And my mother showed up periodically, whenever she found herself between boyfriends. Then the next rainbow would appear in the sky and she'd go dashing after it, certain that this time she'd luck into that pot of gold. Took after my grandfather, Gran always said. It's been years since I last saw her."

"And your grandmother?"

"She died of Alzheimer's a few years ago. She'd talk about him sometimes. Gramps. She didn't have a clue who I was, but she'd talk about when Jimmy came back, how they'd have the dream. Maybe it's good that her disease offered her some happiness at the end. I don't think she experienced much all the years I knew her."

He pulled back an inch to gaze down at her. "You have the Dantes now, *cara*." Emotion gave his voice a musical lilt. "You know that, right? No matter what anyone says about our marriage, we look after our own."

His comment reminded her of her run-in with Britt. "Would you mind if I asked you a question about your past?" she said hesitantly. "You don't have to answer. It's just . . ."

He winced. "Uh-oh. Busted. Who, what, when, and why?"

"Britt stopped by my office today right before Francesca arrived to take me to lunch."

His expression gave nothing away. "And?"

"Francesca mentioned that Britt once hit on you." Caitlyn struggled to keep her voice casual. Not that she succeeded in fooling him. "Did she? Hit on you, I mean?"

He released a rough sigh. "I'd call it more of a tap than an actual hit, one I politely ignored."

A swift smile came and went. "Mr. Irresistible," she managed to tease.

He gave a short, ironic laugh. "I'll take your word for it. Some women hit on me, though whether it's because I'm irresistible or not, I can't say. More irresistible for most women is that I'm a Dante and they want the sparkle a Dante husband can bring to a marriage. After all these years, I can tell the difference. Britt likes the sparkle."

"While I prefer the spark."

"So I've noticed." He slid a hand around the nape of Caitlyn's neck and lifted her for a lingering kiss. "My turn to ask a question."

She wrinkled her nose. "Who, what, when, and why?"

"Why did Francesca feel the need to tell you about Britt?"

Once again Caitlyn tried for casual and once again came up short. "Britt demonstrated a bit too much curiosity about how I ended up with you instead of Lazz."

"It was more than that, wasn't it?" When she didn't respond, he let it go. "You're a loyal friend, Caitlyn. But you have nothing to worry about when it comes to other women. Once The Inferno strikes, that's it. No one else exists as far as I'm concerned."

"Prove it."

The words slipped out before she could stop them, and his response came in a flash. Determination hardened his features and he kissed her with a passion that instantly sent her spinning out of control. Over the past several days he'd gained a familiarity with how to arouse her, how to drive her soaring to the highest peaks. Of course, it didn't take much. A kiss. A touch. Even a look seemed to ignite the flame between them.

Their remaining few clothes slid away with soft sighs, forming a path of cotton and silk from closet to bed. Where had her anger gone these past days? Her indignation over his deception? They'd both vanished in the face of a far more powerful emotion, one that left her mindless with need, a need only one man could fulfill.

Gran would have called her every kind of fool for putting fantasy ahead of reality. But in that moment Caitlyn didn't care. Winding her arms around her husband, she surrendered, soaring over rainbows and floating away on clouds of pleasure. Tomorrow would have to take care of itself.

Tonight she'd take the dream.

Chapter Eight

She was gone.

Marco came instantly awake. He didn't try to explain this new awareness of Caitlyn's presence or absence, but simply tossed back the covers to go in search of his wife. He tracked her down raiding the refrigerator. To his amusement, she'd prepared a snack for two.

"I see by all those sandwiches that you knew I'd come," he said with a yawn.

"Yes." He caught a hint of resignation in her voice. "No doubt you'll say it's The Inferno."

He took the plate from her and set it aside. Wrapping his arms around her, he rested his forehead against hers. "It still bothers you, doesn't it?"

"Yes."

Simple and concise and down-to-the-bones honest. He appreciated that about her. "Do you think The Inferno makes what we feel for each other less real?" he asked.

Despite the lack of light, he could see her gaze grow troubled. "If our relationship is all at the whim of this Inferno, then it isn't because of who I am as a person. Or who you are, for that matter. We're just mated to each other without anything in common other than sexual attraction. How long do you think that's going to last?"

"Got it." He cut straight to the heart of the matter. "You want security. You want assurances. You want to know that we're still going to be together fifty years from now."

She choked on a laugh that contained more than a hint of tears. "I'll take a year, for now. Even a week. But I keep waiting for the other shoe to drop. For it to all go horribly wrong. If what we feel is due to The Inferno, then it's fantasy, not reality."

"It's more than that, Caitlyn, and you know it." He leaned back against the kitchen counter and cushioned her against his chest. "Either The Inferno is real or it's fantasy. If it's fantasy, it'll end and you'll get hurt. But if it's real, you're afraid your ability to make your own choices in life will be taken out of your control."

Caitlyn nodded. "What if we decide we don't like each other? What if we aren't able to build a lasting foundation together? What if we discover that our goals in life are entirely different?

According to you, we're trapped together forever."

Okay, that hurt. "Do you feel trapped, *cara?*"

"Sometimes," she confessed.

He cupped her face and kissed her, imbuing it with as much tenderness and reassurance as he could. "I suspect that's true of all love, not just with The Inferno. You haven't lost a piece of yourself. You've gained something you didn't have before. At least, I have."

Instead of relaxing, her frown deepened. "But when The Inferno happened, didn't you feel as though you'd lost all control?"

"Of course. And I understand you feel the need to direct your own life." He shrugged. "I have no intention of interfering with that."

"You already have," she pointed out softly.

A hint of impatience colored his words. "Honey, no one has total control over their lives and most have only limited self-direction. Control is the illusion, self-direction the fantasy."

"It's my illusion and my fantasy, just as The Inferno is yours," she insisted stubbornly.

"You refuse to believe it might exist because of your grandmother." He could see he was treading on dangerous ground, but no longer cared. "Your bedtime story may have been a cautionary one of lost dreams. Mine was more along the lines of 'The Big Bad Wolf.' You know, the one with all those annoying little pigs."

A brief smile flirted with her mouth, a mouth he'd practically ravaged only hours earlier. "I believe that was 'The Three Little Pigs.'"

"Yeah, well, at the tender age of three, I was a blood-thirsty little savage and cheering for the wolf. The point is, I'm well aware that if we build our foundation with straw that it will get blown away. Or we can build it with stone so it withstands the fiercest storms. We choose the tools and materials. We also choose our dreams. Together."

"You make it sound so simple." She hesitated and he could practically see her organizing her little list of ifs, ands, and buts. "This obsession of yours isn't logical, Marco. I don't understand why you're so dead set on believing in a fairy tale. So set that you'd marry a woman you only knew for five minutes."

His mouth tightened and a hint of old pain came and went in his eyes. "My parents were excellent examples of the worst a marriage can be, just as Primo and Nonna were excellent examples of the best. My grandparents heeded The Inferno when it struck, and their marriage is fast approaching six decades. My father ignored it, and he never knew a happy day in all his married life."

Her eyes widened in shock. "You're kidding. I assumed . . . Your mother wasn't—"

He shook his head. "Dad's Inferno bride, no. She was a business transaction. Despite Primo's warnings, my father married my mother for the good of Dantes, though even that didn't turn out the way either of my parents planned." He had to make her understand. "You may think it's superstition or fantasy. But I lived with the reality. I'll take anything else over that."

"Oh, Marco. I'm so sorry."

He could see the lingering doubt, could tell that she thought his actions in marrying her were an overreaction. "Listen to me, *cara*. If I hadn't made the choice I did, if I hadn't swept you off to Nevada and married you, Lazz would have eventually found a rational argument to convince you to marry him. The only person I've ever met more logical than you is him." She started to interrupt and he cut her off. "If you hadn't married me, if you'd married my brother instead, it wouldn't have just been the two of us who'd have suffered, but Lazz and his future wife, as well. He may not thank me for what I did right now, but that will change when he experiences The Inferno for himself."

She shook her head in wonder. "You really believe this."

"I do." He held her gaze. "And before long, so will you. I don't care how long it takes, or what I have to do to convince you, eventually you'll believe in The Inferno."

For the first time since they'd been married, Caitlyn arrived at the apartment without Marco. He had a meeting with Nicolò that he'd warned might run late, and sure enough, it had. She changed into jeans and a tee, then wandered restlessly through the apartment. It had an uncomfortably empty feel. She'd never realized how much her husband filled it up with his personality until he wasn't there.

There were signs of her presence around the place now, bits and pieces that Marco had plucked from her apartment and scattered about his. He hadn't pressured her to give up her old lease. At least, not yet. And she appreciated his patience. But little by little her apartment became emptier and emptier while his became fuller and more complete.

Most interesting of all, her personal treasures had found places here, places where they fit and meshed. Her grandmother's silver tea service gleamed proudly atop Marco's chiffonier in the dining room. Her collection of blown glass knickknacks glittered softly along the fireplace mantel. Her mysteries competed with his science fiction books. And their clothes, which had started out rigidly organized into proper his-and-hers sides of the closet had somehow met in the middle and mated into a colorful collection of "theirs."

She glanced at the box of files she'd brought home and stretched out on the couch with a sigh. Might as well get to work. Maneuvering the box onto the endmost couch cushion by her feet, she perched her reading glasses on the tip of her nose and pulled out the first stack of files.

She'd found a number of confusing records buried among the personal papers and wanted to take her time and sort through them in order to determine how best to handle the information they contained. Before she could do more than flip open the first folder, she heard Marco's key in the lock.

There was a confusingly long pause. Then, *"Cara?"*

She couldn't stop a smile from spreading across her face. "In here."

He appeared in the archway between the living room and hallway, a briefcase in one hand, a newspaper in the other. She could tell from his face that something was wrong and sat up.

"What's happened?"

"Damn rag. I found it shoved under our door." He tossed it to her. "Let me warn you, you're not going to like it."

That explained what had slowed him at the door. She adjusted her glasses and the newsprint swam into focus. *Marital mix-up . . . Marco or Lazz? Confused bride is tricked at the altar.* With an exclamation of fury, she ripped through the pages to the article the front teaser had alluded to. "My God, Marco, they know. It's all here. That I was dating Lazz first. That I met you and you pretended to be your brother. How we ran off to Nevada for a spur-of-the-moment marriage. The fight. They've chronicled every last detail."

"Not every detail, I hope."

Delicate color washed across her cheekbones, though whether from anger or embarrassment, she couldn't have said for certain. "No, not every detail. But close enough. When did this come out? I wonder if it's what set Britt off. It would certainly explain a lot."

"It's possible, though I doubt Britt needs anything specific to set her off." He joined Caitlyn on the couch and unceremoniously dumped the box of files onto the floor. Stretching out his legs in front of him, he leaned against the back cushion and loosened his tie. "Something's bothering me about these articles and I haven't quite put my finger on what it is."

"You mean something more than the articles themselves?"

"Yeah." He scooped up her legs and pulled them across his lap. His large hands closed over her sock-covered feet and began to absentmindedly knead the narrow arch.

"This last month or so they've changed in tenor."

Ever since that night on the plane he'd continued his habit of massaging her feet, something that never failed to drive her straight up the wall. She stretched like a cat, sending the stack of files cascading off her lap and scattering across the hardwood floor. Marco started to get up to rescue them and she planted her toes against his rock-hard abs and pushed him back down. No way was he going anywhere anytime soon.

"Forget the files. I'll get them later. Tell me how the articles have changed. What's different about them?"

He subsided against the cushions. "They've gotten personal. Vindictive. Yes, I think that's it." His brow creased in thought. "I mean, before, they'd write up some chatty little piece about a party we'd attended, who we were dating. Every once in a while, there'd be a slight hiss or meow behind the captions. But nothing damaging."

"It's sure damaging now. It's gotten downright personal."

"That's exactly what's bothering me. It is personal. And damn specific." His frown deepened. "Too specific, now that I think about it. Whoever's writing these articles must have a mole working at Dantes. It's the only explanation."

"You must be kidding."

Marco shook his head, smiling a bit at her shock. "It's not unheard of. And it's not like we have our employees sign a confidentiality agreement regarding the family's personal life."

"Maybe you should start."

"I'll mention it to Sev. Get legal on it. In the meantime, if we can find the person passing on the information, we can cut off *The Snitch*'s source and salvage the Romano account."

Oh, dear. "Have we lost it?"

"I like the way you say 'we.'" He reached out a long arm and snagged the neckline of her tee, pulling her in for a lingering kiss. "And no, we haven't lost the account. Yet. I warned them this would come out. Too many people overheard the commotion when we returned to Dantes the morning after our wedding for it not to have hit *The Snitch*. But the very fact that the fight is detailed so precisely in the article is evidence that the rag has an internal source of information."

"What I don't understand is why it's such a big deal for the Romanos if the Dantes are featured in this thing." She balled up the newspaper and tossed it toward the fireplace. "I'm serious, Marco. Why does it matter what a stateside rag prints about you and your family? It can't have that serious an impact on the Romanos."

Marco shrugged. "They have a reputation to protect. According to Vittorio, scandal doesn't touch the Romanos. Nor does it touch the Romanos' associates, or they're no longer associated."

"Huh. That seems a bit over the top." She lifted an eyebrow. "Doesn't his reaction strike you as excessive?"

"That's Vittorio for you. He's ferocious when it comes to guarding the Romano name and I gather he doesn't want *The Snitch* turning its investigative light on him."

"Makes sense." She gave it a moment's consideration. "I guess a family that old must have a lot of skeletons they'd rather not have uncovered, especially if they're publicity shy."

"Let's just hope to God they don't find out about The Inferno. We consider the Inferno intensely private. No one knows about it, except family, and we intend to keep it that way." Marco rolled onto his hip to face her.

"Let's forget about the Romanos. And *The Snitch*'s snitch. And everything Dantes. There's only one thing I care about right now."

She couldn't help grinning. "And what would that be, Mr. Dante?" she asked, all wide-eyed innocence.

He maneuvered on top of her and plastered every foot of hard male body over every inch of hers, pressing her deep into the soft cushions. He plucked her glasses off the end of her nose and carefully set them aside. "I'm sure we'll come up with something."

It wasn't until hours later that they drifted from couch to bed. Their clothes had long since disappeared into the jumble of files and documents papering the floor. And Caitlyn simply left them there, something that would have been unheard of a few short weeks ago.

The next morning was a different story and she zipped around, gathering up the papers while Marco rescued their clothing. She didn't bother sorting or organizing—something else unheard of only weeks before—but dumped everything haphazardly into the box. She reached for a final stapled document when Lazz's name, coupled with the Romanos', practically jumped off the page. She scanned swiftly, aware that if they didn't leave soon they'd both be late for work. But what she read had her rocking back on her heels.

"What is it?" Marco asked. "What's the holdup?"

"Nothing." She shoved the document into the box and tamped down the lid. "Let's go."

"Seriously, what is it?"

She avoided his gaze and retrieved her purse and briefcase. "Just a document I need to read more carefully. I can do that when we get to work." All business now, she gestured toward the box. "Would you mind carrying it out to the car for me?"

To her relief, the moment passed. The instant Marco dropped her off at the warehouse, she made a beeline for her temporary office and ripped off the lid of the box. She snatched up the document and read it three times before she could convince herself that it was authentic. A second document followed the first, this one in Italian. But she suspected it said the exact same thing as the English version.

She didn't waste any further time. After concealing the document within the protective cover of a file folder, she called for a cab to take her to Dantes' corporate building and, once there, waited impatiently for the elevator to sweep her up to the finance department. Britt sat in the small reception area just outside Lazz's office, and Caitlyn hesitated. She'd forgotten she'd have to go through Britt to get to Lazz.

Caitlyn clutched the file against her chest. "Is he free?" she asked, striving for casual and breezy.

"Change your mind already?" Britt asked with a laugh. "Poor Marco."

"Seriously, Britt. It's important and I'm short on time."

Her friend's expression cooled. "I'm sorry, Mrs. Dante. I didn't mean to keep you waiting. I'll see if Lazz is available." She picked up the phone and hit a button.

"Your sister-in-law is here to see you. No, Marco's wife. She claims it's urgent. Certainly. I'll send her right in."

The second she hung up the phone, Caitlyn tried again. "Look, I'm sorry. It's just that this is rather urgent. I didn't mean to be rude."

"That's okay." Britt offered a smile that did nothing to hide the anger in her eyes and warned the interaction between them was far from okay. "I'd be equally as unpleasant, if I'd just figured out what Marco was pulling on the job front. I wondered how long it would take you."

Caitlyn released her breath in a sigh. She shouldn't ask. Shouldn't play into Britt's game. "Found out what?" she asked wearily.

The other woman took her time, savoring each word. "That this project they've dumped in your lap is a put on. I mean, doesn't it just bug you right down to the bones that you're stuck working in that dump of a warehouse all because Marco wants to keep you away from Lazz?" She smiled knowingly. "Not that it's worked, because here you are."

It took every ounce of self-control not to react, not to hit out and cause any further talk that might find its way into *The Snitch*. "Excuse me, won't you?" she said, and swept past Britt's desk and into Lazz's office.

Caitlyn closed the door behind her and leaned against it, struggling to calm down. So much for friendship. Francesca had warned her, but she'd hoped against hope to prove her sister-in-law wrong. That Britt would work through whatever lingering issues stood between them. But maybe there was no working through them. Caitlyn found it a hard fact to accept.

"Caitlyn?" Lazz shot to his feet. "What's happened? You look like hell."

She almost confided in Lazz and explained the issues between her and Britt. But she hesitated to involve him. She and Britt might not be friends any longer, but she didn't want to cost the other woman her job. Suddenly aware of the file she clutched, she used that as an excuse to explain her distress.

"There are some documents you need to see." She crossed the room and offered him the file. "I came across this when I was going through a bunch of family records stored at the warehouse."

Lazz took the folder and flipped it open. Waving her toward the chair across from his desk, he took a seat and began reading. "Holy hell," he muttered. "What was the old man thinking?"

"Did you know about this contract?"

"Not even a little."

Interesting. "Do you think Primo knew?" she asked.

"Are you kidding? He'd have killed my father if he'd found out."

He glanced at her with eyes the exact same shade of hazel as Marco's. And yet they were nothing like her husband's. Where Marco's held all the warmth and passion of a Mediterranean summer, his twin brother's struck her as cool and remote as a mountain lake. The realization left her momentarily stunned. Why had she never noticed the difference before?

"Have you told anyone?" he asked.

She struggled to focus her attention on Lazz and answer his question. "About the document? No, not a soul. I brought it straight to you."

"What about Marco?"

"I haven't said a word," she told him, more sharply this time. "And you have no idea how guilty that makes me feel."

"This has nothing to do with him and I want it to stay that way." His voice reflected the same sharpness as hers. "I'd like your promise on that. I need time to decide how to handle the situation."

"You have it."

"I'd also like you to hold on to this contract while I consider my options. I'd rather not keep this file in my office where someone might stumble across it."

"No problem. I'll put it back in the box where I found it."

After handing her the folder, he didn't speak but studied her in silence while he made up his mind about something. The moment stretched long enough to put her on edge. She saw the instant he'd reached his decision.

"I felt something that morning, you know," he surprised her by saying.

She shook her head in genuine bewilderment. "I have no idea what you're talking about."

"In the conference room. The morning after you married Marco." He came out from behind his desk to join her and edged his hip on the corner nearest her chair. "I don't believe in The Inferno. At least, I never have. But that morning . . ."

She could guess where he was going with this and dismissed it with a shake of her head. "The only thing you felt that morning was anger and perhaps a touch of jealousy."

"True. But I also felt a tingle." He rubbed his thumb across his palm and frowned. "Right here."

"I don't know who's set off your little Inferno detector," she replied, gesturing toward his palm. "But it wasn't me. It's not possible." Or was it that she didn't want it to be possible? Because if Lazz felt it, too, it would be proof that The Inferno didn't work.

His brow creased in genuine bewilderment. "Well, there wasn't anyone else there who could have set it off."

"You Dantes and your itchy palms. Do you feel it now?" She put more than a hint of exasperation into the question.

"Maybe." His brows drew together. "A little."

"Well, Marco doesn't feel it a little. If he's not careful, he's going to rub himself raw."

Lazz's mouth tilted upward at the corner. "You sound like a mother hen." Then his amusement faded, replaced by an emotion she didn't want to see in any man's eyes but one. And it wasn't the man lounging in front of her. "I was going to propose that night, you know."

"I know," she whispered.

"It should have been us in front of a priest."

"No, it shouldn't have."

She'd never been more certain of anything in her life. The insight came in a bittersweet rush, and she shut her eyes, accepting what she'd been steadfastly denying for weeks now. It didn't matter whether or not The Inferno was real, or whether or not she believed in it. It didn't matter that she hadn't followed Gran's directives before marrying. Or that she'd chosen a charmer instead of someone more logical and down-to-earth like Lazz. None of it mattered, but one simple fact. Her breath caught, stumbled.

She loved Marco.

"Caitlyn?"

"Oh, God." Tears filled her eyes and leaked into her voice as she shot to her feet. "I am such a fool."

He straightened. "It's okay. Don't cry." He wrapped his arms around her shoulders and patted awkwardly. "We can fix this. I'll find you a lawyer. It'll all work out."

"No. You don't understand." She lifted her head and looked at him. Truly looked at him. How could she have ever thought she couldn't tell one brother from the other? They were nothing alike. Felt nothing the same.

"I love him, Lazz."

"Aw, hell. That's not good."

"No. What's not good is you having your hands on my wife." The door banged closed behind Marco. "I suggest you remove them before I remove them for you."

Chapter Nine

Marco fought against a blinding rage. Fought to keep his hands off his brother so he didn't do something one of them would barely live to regret. Caitlyn was his wife. His. Lazz had no business touching her, and he'd explain that fact in language his brother couldn't mistake.

"You're being ridiculous," Caitlyn said.

He spared her a brief glance. "Don't. Don't act like I'm the one at fault when I walk in and discover you in my brother's arms." He transferred his attention to his twin. "For some truly annoying reason, you're still touching my wife."

Swearing, Lazz held up his hands and took a step back. "Satisfied now?"

"I won't be satisfied until I've pounded less identical into your face."

"So Caitlyn can tell the difference between us?" Lazz bit off a laugh. "Trust me. She's not the least confused on that front."

Marco formed his hands into fists. "I think I'll just make sure of that fact."

Caitlyn stepped between the two brothers, the one place she least belonged. "Could we please bring the testosterone level down a notch? Lazz, you're not helping a bit. Marco, there's a very simple explanation for all this."

"Which is?"

"Well . . ."

She lifted an eyebrow at Lazz, who shook his head. A flash of annoyance flitted across her face, though it was nothing compared to Marco's annoyance that she needed his brother's approval before explaining the situation.

"I can't tell you," Caitlyn said, a statement that succeeded in shooting Marco's temper straight through the roof. "But I assure you, it's strictly business."

"Lazz with his arms around you was strictly business?" He struggled to rein in his fury. "'Strictly business' made you cry?"

"That was . . ." She faltered. "That was something else."

"I think it's time I clarified matters," Marco said. "Just in case there are any lingering questions."

"Marco—"

He cut her off with a sweep of his hand. "No, this needs to be said. The wound can't heal until the poison's been drawn out." He turned on his brother.

"In case you missed the announcement, Caitlyn and I are married now, Lazz. We're in the process of building a life together. And I won't let anyone, particularly not my own brother, dismantle so much as a single brick of what Caitlyn and I have struggled to cement in place. You are not to interfere in our marriage again. Am I clear on this point?"

Marco watched the war waging across his brother's face. Even though he understood why Lazz found it so difficult to let go, this needed to end, here and now. In the past his family had always had his back, just as he'd always had theirs. He never had to question their unconditional loyalty and support. He wanted that assurance again, to trust implicitly instead of constantly checking behind him to see whether someone had stuck a knife between his shoulder blades.

He waited for Lazz's response, waited for the poison to well up, a poison that had been left to fester for far too long. Finally, it erupted, spilled over in messy waves.

"You took her from me. You lied to her!" Lazz accused. "You went after her like some thief in the night and tricked her into marrying you. She should have the choice to leave, if she wants."

Marco inclined his head. "I agree. But what you don't understand, what you continue to ignore, is that she has always had the choice to leave. And yet she stays with me. There's a reason for that, Lazz. And that reason is why you need to step aside." He let his comments sink in before adding, "She was never yours. You tried to convince yourself she was, tried to bind her to you. But from the moment you first saw her, it was already too late."

"I planned to marry her!"

Didn't Lazz get it? "Even if she left me now, she would still never be yours. Not in the way you want, not the way a wife should be. I would always stand between you. And if not me, then the ghost of our relationship."

"Isn't that what I'm doing?" Lazz hit back. "Standing between the two of you? Isn't that why you're so jealous, because I had a relationship with her?"

Marco shook his head. "You know it wasn't a true relationship. Caitlyn and I settled that issue long ago. You're not part of our marriage, Lazz. What you had with her was merely an illusion."

Stubbornness clung to Lazz's face. "Only because you interfered."

Marco tried again to get through to his brother. "If you'd taken the relationship further than those first few steps, it would have eventually fallen apart. The woman you are meant to have hasn't come into your life yet. But,

I swear to you, Lazz. You will know her when she does. And when that happens you'll realize that what you feel for Caitlyn is a pale imitation of the real thing."

"That's enough, Marco. You've made your point." Once again Caitlyn placed herself between the two men.

"Lazz, I realize this is your office, but could you give Marco and me a minute, please?"

He hesitated just long enough to nudge Marco's temper back into the hot zone, before nodding. "Sure."

The minute they were alone, Caitlyn caught Marco's hand in hers. "Listen to me. I promise you, the information I relayed to Lazz was confidential and absolutely business related. If you want to know more, you'll have to discuss it with him, since it's his information to share."

"Why were you crying?" He could still see lingering traces of her tears. That troubled him more than anything, and he could only think of one explanation. He steeled himself against that possibility. "Was it because of us? Because of our marriage?"

She hesitated just long enough to make him doubt her eventual response. "I was happy crying."

She was holding something back. He could tell. Just as he could tell that her tears weren't ones of pure joy.

"Then answer me this, cara. Why were you happy crying with your brother-in-law instead of with your husband?"

"It just sort of hit me while I was in here." This time when she looked at him, he couldn't mistake the unwavering certainty in her gaze. "In case there's still any question in your mind, I don't regret our marriage. And I don't wish I'd married Lazz instead of you. But there is an issue we need to clarify."

"Which is?"

"It's this project I've been assigned, and how it came about."

She caught him off guard with the change in subject. He could guess the direction she was headed with this, and it wasn't a place he cared to go. "And?"

She hesitated, no doubt organizing her thoughts. He'd always found it one of her more endearing characteristics. Until now. "You should know that my career gives me security and independence, and I have a serious problem being kept in the dark about decisions that affect my job."

"I thought you were happy with your new assignment," he offered cautiously.

A hint of fire sparked in her blue eyes. "You're missing the point—deliberately, I think. I love my job, both old and new. But I've worked hard to get where I am and I refuse to be sidetracked. My career ensures that I don't have to depend on anyone for anything. I'll always know that if something should happen at some point down the road, like it did with Gran, I can take care of myself."

His mouth tightened. "In other words, if some charmer—*me*, for instance—sweeps in and tries to sell you a ticket for the next ride over the rainbow, you'll have a pot of gold stashed away to fall back on." He cocked his head to one side. "Close?"

"Dead on."

"Just where the hell did you get the idea I'm trying to interfere with your job security?"

She released his hand and turned toward Lazz's desk. A folder rested on the edge, and she played with the cover. "Tell me something, Marco. Who arranged for me to head this new project, a project supposedly no one else on the face of the planet is capable of successfully completing but me?" She shoved the folder to one side and shot him a keen look. "It was you, wasn't it? You asked my supervisor to use me on this job."

Over the past several days he'd begun to pick up on his wife's moods. Her eyes gleamed the most brilliant shade of teal whenever something satisfied her. And they darkened to indigo whenever heartache threatened. Worry caused her to nibble at her lower lip, something he was quick to stop with a kiss. He had personal designs on that lip, as he took pains to show her on a regular basis. But most telling of all were the danger signals that flashed, warning of her anger. And holy hell, they might as well be flashing bright red right now.

"Yes, I asked that you be assigned this new project," he informed her.

"In order to keep me away from Lazz?"

"Huh." He pretended to give it some thought. "If that was my goal, it doesn't seem to be working, does it? Because here you are."

His flippancy didn't go over well. "This is serious, Marco. The morning after we were married you told me you wanted me to keep my distance from Lazz and that you'd make certain it happened. Is this your way of making certain? So much for trust."

He answered truthfully. "It's not you I don't trust. It's my brother. In case you didn't notice, he's feeling a bit raw right now. I don't want you in the middle, despite how often you feel the need to put yourself there. This project should only take you a month or two to organize, and to be honest, I can't think of anyone more qualified to head it up. By the time you have it under control—and it is a critical project, by the way, not crayons and busy work—the family dynamics will have settled down and returned to normal. Especially after our little talk here today. At that point, you're free to resume your old job."

"Funny. I don't remember being in on that discussion when it happened."

"Yeah." He thrust a hand through his hair. "It's possible you didn't get the memo. I'm sorry, *cara*. I should have told you."

"Discussed it with me," she corrected sharply. "Allowed me to have a say in the final decision."

"It wouldn't have changed anything," he informed her gently. "You would have argued. I would have argued. But in the end, I would have won."

She stiffened. "Is that how all the decisions will be made in our marriage?"

"I'm just trying to protect you."

"That didn't answer my question, and I don't need your protection," she protested.

"Yes, you do. You married a Dante, Caitlyn. You may not have realized which one at the time you said 'I do,' but you were well aware when you took your vows that your life would change because of my family. The stories in *The Snitch*, alone, should have warned you of that."

Temper flashed to the boiling point. "And part of marrying a Dante is having my decisions made for me? Thanks, but no thanks."

"Enough, Caitlyn. I promised to consult you in the future. And I will. Just as you're going to promise me that you won't use my brother's shoulder for anymore happy tears."

"No one's shoulder but yours?"

"I'll try and bear up under the strain." He hesitated. Since they were clearing the air, this struck him as a good time to warn her about his own job change. "There's some other news I should tell you about."

"Tell me?" She lifted an eyebrow. "Or warn me?"

"A little of both, I suppose. I consider it good news, though knowing *The Snitch*, they'll find a way to put a negative spin on it." He watched her closely, hoping to gauge her reaction to the news. "I've decided to turn my international duties over to Lazz. Since he's already put in extensive time dealing with our foreign offices, it made the most sense."

A hint of worry edged into her eyes. "But, why? I thought you loved your job."

"I do. Unfortunately, it means I'm out of the country more often than I'm home. I didn't mind before we met, but I don't like being away from you so often or for so long. It's not healthy for a marriage."

Caitlyn removed the folder from Lazz's desk and tucked it under her arm. "Does this have anything to do with keeping Lazz and me apart?"

"Let's consider that an added bonus."

She closed her eyes for a brief instant. "Oh, Marco." She looked at him then, gazing with such sorrow that he flinched. "After everything that's been said here today, this still isn't over, is it?"

"You and Lazz? Over and done. Some of our issues?" He couldn't lie. "Let's just say we have a way to go yet."

Over the next several days it became clear to Caitlyn that a rift had formed between her and Marco, one they found difficult to bridge. When they came together each night, she sensed a desperation behind their lovemaking as each of them struggled to find a way to repair the damaged connection. To make matters worse, Marco announced that he and Lazz would be flying to Europe for a few days to help smooth over the transition of duties.

"I'll be back next Friday night." Experience had him making short work of packing his bags. "When I return, we settle this once and for all."

Before he left, he took her in his arms and kissed her in a way that knocked down barriers and left her hoping that maybe, just maybe, their marriage would work out. And then he was gone.

The week passed at a crawl, and Caitlyn used the opportunity to make significant strides with the warehouse project. She set aside the personal files she'd unearthed, including the contract she'd shown Lazz, and focused instead on reorganizing her team. By midweek, she'd gotten the transfer from paper to digital moving along at a record pace. In a few days she would have the time and focus necessary to go through the box of personal files more carefully in order to decide what to do with the contents.

Friday morning she headed into work feeling more cheerful than she had in days. Marco was due home that evening and she couldn't wait. The time had come to face facts. She loved Marco, loved him with all her heart. It didn't matter anymore how their marriage had come about. What mattered was where they took it from here.

Entering her office, she picked up the box of files she'd sidelined over the past week and set it on her desk. And that's when she saw it. Someone had gotten to her office ahead of her and left an early edition of *The Snitch* on her desk. She almost trashed it, unread. But the headlines caught her eye and she sat down to read. Twenty minutes later she jumped up and went flying out the door. With Marco in Europe, she had his car at her disposal and she headed straight over to the main office building. Once there, she hastened to Britt's desk, a desk occupied by Angie.

"Where's Britt?" Caitlyn demanded.

Angie stared at her in confusion. "I thought she was with you. She asked if I'd cover her desk while she went over to the warehouse."

Caitlyn inhaled sharply. The warehouse. The warehouse where sitting on her desk were files that were a literal goldmine of information for *The Snitch*'s snitch. She fought to stay calm and think. First off, she needed help. Marco and Lazz were out of the country. Sev was in New York with Francesca. That left Nicolò.

A single phone call confirmed that he hadn't arrived at work yet, which left her on her own. She thought fast and then headed for the legal department, hoping against hope that Marco had gotten them working on that confidentiality agreement. She could have kissed the man when he handed it over without a qualm. Next, she requested that a notary be located and sent to the warehouse. And then she made a beeline for the exit, struggling not to panic as she went tearing back to her office.

She already knew what she'd find, despite praying she'd be proven wrong. Sure enough, Britt sat in Caitlyn's chair, her feet resting on the desktop, one of the personal files Caitlyn had protected with such care open in her lap.

"Put it down," she snapped out the order.

Britt simply grinned. "Wow. You look a bit peeved. Bad morning?"

"I'm not going to ask you again, Britt."

"Funny. I don't remember you asking me the first time." She dropped her feet to the floor but didn't close the file. "This makes for fascinating reading."

Caitlyn retrieved the document she'd picked up from legal and slapped it in front of Britt. "I've called for a notary. She'll be here in the next few minutes. When she arrives, you're going to sign this."

"Let me guess. It's a confidentiality agreement." Britt shook her head. "Too little, too late, I'm afraid."

"We'll see."

"You know, something's been bugging me."

Caitlyn lifted an eyebrow. "Bugging you down to the bones? Isn't that one of the lines you used in your latest article for *The Snitch?* As soon as I read it, I knew it had to be you. You used that expression when we last spoke."

"Caught that, did you?" Britt lifted a shoulder. "I wondered when I wrote it if you would."

"What did you do? Listen at the door when Lazz, Marco, and I had our disagreement? There are too many accurate quotes in that article for it to have happened any other way."

"You all made it so easy for me. Why shouldn't I take advantage of the opportunity?" She waved that aside. "You know, I've been curious for some time why everyone's in such an uproar over my stories. I mean who cares what *The Snitch* prints about the Dantes? It's free publicity. It sure as hell hasn't hurt sales from what I've seen and heard."

"It's affecting Dantes' expansion into the European market."

"Yes, Lazz was kind enough to explain that part to me. But what I didn't get for the longest time is why the Romanos care about what *The Snitch* prints. What's it to them, anyway?"

"They're protecting their reputation."

Britt snapped her fingers. "Truer words have never been spoken. And would you like to know precisely what they're protecting?" She leaned across the desk and whispered, "The Romanos are broke."

"You're making that up."

Britt shook her head. "No, I'm not. Ironic, isn't it?" She leaned back in Caitlyn's chair and folded her arms behind her head. "Marco's spent all this time and money to win their patronage and the Romanos can't even afford a nickel-plated nose ring, let alone a Dantes original."

"How in the world could you possibly know anything about the state of the Romanos' finances, Britt? You write for a penny-ante scandal sheet."

"Oh, I have a few European contacts. According to them, rumors about Vittorio Romano have been floating around for quite a while now. But the Romanos still have an amazing amount of influence over there." Her hand fluttered through the air. "Italian royalty and all that. They've managed to squelch any negative talk. But that won't last much longer." She tapped the file she held. "Unless, of course, they decide to force Lazz to honor his father's little business contract. Won't *The Snitch* readers find that a fascinating little tidbit."

An idea came to Caitlyn, as though a gift from on high. Not just how to stop Britt, but how to use her as she'd been using Dantes. She just needed a few minutes to think. To organize the various pieces into a logical whole.

"I don't think your readers will find your next story interesting at all," Caitlyn said with exquisite calm. "Because you're not going to print it. In fact, your days writing about the Dantes are about to end."

Britt's eyebrows shot upward. "And you're going to somehow end them?"

"Well, the way I figure it, the Romanos—those same Romanos who have such an amazing amount of influence—will have a bit more sway over here than you might think. And I'm guessing they're not going to be too happy when I tell them what you're about to do. I'm also willing to bet that you're going to find yourself in an even more uncomfortable position now that you're outed as *The Snitch*'s snitch. What use will you be to the tabloid when Dantes fires you? Or sues you for defamation? The Romanos might not have the money to pursue legal action, but I assure you that the Dantes can afford it, and then some."

Britt gave a careless shrug, but a hint of worry flickered behind her eyes. "I still have plenty of ammunition to sell to *The Snitch*."

"It's going to run out eventually," Caitlin pointed out. "And then where will you be? I doubt *The Snitch* is going to keep you around when you can't deliver the goods any longer."

Britt's expression turned shrewd. "I gather this is leading somewhere? Maybe a deal of some sort?"

Caitlyn nodded. "You leave the Romanos alone, as well as forget all about that contract you found, and I'll give you a huge final story. A really special one."

"I don't know . . ." Britt caressed the folder she held. "The story I just found is pretty darn special. Why would I give it up?"

"That contract is twenty years old. It isn't worth the paper it's written on. Plus, although the Romanos might get big play in Europe, the average American reader doesn't know them. Why would *Snitch* readers care whether some aristocratic European family is struggling financially? Your editor isn't going to pay much for that story. Trust me, Britt. The one I have in mind is far better."

Avarice gleamed in Britt's eyes. "How much better?"

"A dream come true."

Suspicion tempered her greed. "If your story is so much better, why are you willing to trade it for the Romanos? I must be missing something."

"For one reason and one reason only. It will salvage Marco's deal, and I'll do anything to help my husband."

She didn't say anything more, but waited to see if the other woman would take the bait. For a minute Caitlyn didn't think it would happen. Then greed won out.

"This had better be good, or it's all going in."

Caitlyn shook her head. "You're going to sign that confidentiality agreement. After this story, you're done writing about the Dantes and their associates." She almost laughed at the sly expression in Britt's eyes. "Don't bother looking for a loophole. Marco had Legal create a nice, airtight document. Knowing them, you probably can't even speak the Dante name without serious repercussions."

Britt moistened her lips. "Is your story that good?" At Caitlyn's nod, she pressed. "First, I need a hint."

"Fair enough. Ever heard of Dantes' Inferno?"

Britt's eyes widened. "Once. When I asked Lazz about it, he clammed up and I couldn't pry another word out of him."

Caitlyn raised an eyebrow. "I take it we have a deal?"

"Absolutely."

"Just one other question while we wait for the notary."

Britt grimaced. "I can guess. You want to know why. Why would I betray the darling Dantes after all they've done for me?" She rolled her eyes. "Would you like me to make up some sob story about a poor, sick mother? How about a desperately ill child? Would that satisfy you?"

"The truth will do."

"Oh, come on, Caitlyn. Why do you think?" She caressed the earrings she wore, earrings she'd bragged about during lunch that fateful day Marco had swept her off to Nevada. The fire diamonds licked coldly across Britt's earlobes. "I got ticked off when Marco and Lazz wouldn't give me the time of day but were all over you. Seemed to me selling my stories to *The Snitch* was the only way I was going to get my hands on the Dante jewels, even if they weren't the ones I'd originally had in mind." Then she had the nerve to wink.

The notary arrived a short time later and Britt signed the confidentiality agreement. The minute they were alone again, she leaned forward. "Just so you know, I'm going to quote you, word for word. Your name's going to be all over this article so that everyone knows it was you who betrayed Marco and the Dante family. You may be Mrs. High-and-Mighty Dante now. But how long do you think your marriage will last once your husband finds out what you've done?"

Caitlyn didn't have any doubt about that. It would last about as long as Britt's future at Dantes.

Chapter Ten

Caitlyn had planned to tell Marco what happened with Britt the instant he walked through the door. To explain what she'd done and why. But the longer it took for him to return home, the less she wanted to confess her sins. Pacing through the empty apartment, she faced some hard, cold facts.

Her actions today, even though she'd tried to base them on the better good of Dantes, would damage her relationship with Marco, perhaps irreparably. She could explain that she'd attempted to choose the lesser of two evils, but in all honesty, she'd made some huge mistakes along the way. For one thing she'd confronted Britt on her own without consulting the Dantes first. Granted, there hadn't been anyone to consult when she'd reached her decision. But that didn't change the fact that it wasn't her decision to make.

Worse, she'd told Britt about The Inferno. Would Marco understand that she'd revealed the information with the best of intentions? Would he understand that she'd thought it would protect the

Romanos, in addition to the Dantes European expansion? That she had a plan in mind when she'd made the revelation?

Or would he believe she'd put a friend before family loyalty? That her doubts about The Inferno had led her to be indiscreet? Because if there was one thing that she and Marco agreed to disagree about, it was The Inferno.

Still, that didn't mean she had to tell him what she'd done the minute he walked in the door, she suddenly realized. This night could still be theirs. All she had to do was remain silent until morning.

His key sounded in the lock and the next instant he was there, filling the apartment with body and spirit. Filling her heart to overflowing. "Why are you standing here in the dark?" He dropped his bags just inside the door and kicked it closed behind him. *"Cara?* Is something wrong?"

"No." She couldn't do it. She couldn't hide what she'd done from him. "Yes."

He was by her side before the words had even left her lips. His arms closed around her and she simply melted. Everything about him ripped her to pieces, shredded her emotions and then put them back together again. With one touch he turned her world upside down and sent everything safe and rational spinning into chaos. And with the next touch he made that world right again, made her realize that this was where she belonged. In his arms, tucked close to his heart.

She inhaled the crisp, delicious scent of him, filling her lungs until she was dizzy with it. She'd missed him, been empty without him. And more than anything, she needed his hands on her. Needed to feel him moving over her, the sweet dichotomy of male in life-affirming opposition to female. To hear desperate Italian endearments ripping through that deep, lyrical voice. To watch those beautiful angled features harden with passion, while the burn of want swept into his eyes and set them afire with sparks of gold and amber and jade.

She forced herself to ignore the yearning and tell him what she'd done. "Something happened today that I need to discuss with you."

"Stop." He covered her mouth with his fingers. "I've been gone a week. First things first."

He cupped her face and lifted her for his kiss. With a soft moan she opened to him, welcoming him home. He swept inward with lazy intent, nipping playfully, and she tumbled headlong into the embrace. Thrusting her fingers deep into his thick hair, she angled her head for better access and whispered her encouragement. His playfulness faded, replaced with blatant hunger.

At least here, when they came together like this, they were perfectly attuned. She only wished it could be enough. With a sigh of regret, she turned her head aside. "We need to talk first. We can have sex afterward." Assuming he still wanted to.

"No."

Surprise had her looking at him. "No?"

"No, damn it." Frustration ate through his words.

"It's not just sex and you know it. From the moment we first touched it's always been something more than that."

"The Inferno."

"Is that so hard to accept?"

"Funny you should mention that. I—"

He took her hand in his and locked it, palm to palm, with his. "Tell me you don't feel that."

She closed her eyes, shivering. Heat warmed the center of her hand, sinking deep inward and sending desire screaming through her body. "It's you. Just you."

"Someday you'll admit the truth." He stopped her before she could argue. "I know, I know. Fairy tales aren't truth."

"Marco—"

"Later. Right now I'm going to give you a taste of happily-ever-after. And if that's not enough to convince you, we'll start over again with once-upon-a-time. And I will tell you the tale again and again until you're convinced it's real, no matter how long it takes."

With that he swept her up and carried her through to the bedroom. They tumbled to the mattress together, locked in each other's arms. He found her mouth again and worried at her bottom lip before seducing her with slow, drugging kisses.

She fumbled with the knot of his tie and loosened it, stripping away the length of silk before tackling the buttons of his shirt. He moved to help and she chased his hands away, rolling until she was on top. "No. It's my turn. Let me do this for you."

One by one, she slipped button through hole, pushing aside the soft cotton. Heaven help her, but he was a beautiful man. She never tired of looking at him, of touching the delicious male contours that were so different from her own. She traced a path over his smooth chest, easing the shirt from his shoulders. He lifted onto his elbows so she could sweep it aside.

He remained silently watchful, his expression giving nothing away. Not that he'd remain impassive for long. She'd see to that. She lowered her head to trail kisses down the center of his chest. Then lower still. Without a word she unbelted his trousers and stripped him. And then she gave him the most intimate kiss of all.

She heard the harsh groan, the choked sound he made when he attempted to push out her name. His fingers forked into her hair. She resisted their tug, intent on giving him as much pleasure as he had given her over the past weeks. His voice filled the air, the Italian poetic in its expressiveness, ripe with power. She didn't have to understand the words to hear the desperate plea behind them. And then the tenor changed, became demand, a demand she found impossible to resist.

He dragged her upward, making short work of the few garments she wore. She expected him to take her then, fast and frantic. He must have read her thoughts because he simply shook his head.

"I can't," he told her. "This is too important to rush. Don't you understand? I want these times we spend together to last, so I can relish every moment of them. They're beautiful and intimate. These are the times I feel closest to you. Why would I rush that? That's not how I want you. It never has been."

He watched as confusion came, then eased. "We're dancing again, aren't we?" she asked in sudden understanding. "The goal isn't getting to point Z."

He caught the reference from one of their discussions early in their marriage and smiled in response. "No, it's not. It's all the points in between that are most important."

Mischief sparkled within her eyes. "Are you sure about that?"

He nuzzled the soft curve of her breast. "Point Z is inevitable in all things, not just making love. But to fully enjoy the culmination you have to savor each step in between. And that's what I plan for tonight. To savor you, *cara.*"

"Oh, Marco."

Tears sparkled in her eyes and he saw something there he'd waited a long time to see. Did she even realize she loved him? Or did fear keep her from acknowledging that, the way it kept her from acknowledging the truth of The Inferno?

If she couldn't see it for herself, he'd have to show her in every possible way. Time slipped softly by, an unnoticed tempo to the points along the way as

Marco lingered over each step of their lovemaking. He adored kissing her silken skin, worshiping it with lips, tongue and teeth. Loved the contrast of fine-boned strength that lay just beneath the lush roundness of feminine curves.

She called so sweetly to him as her climax approached, and that night the song she sang as she went over was unlike anything he'd ever heard before. He wanted to spend a lifetime drawing that song from her. Moving to it. Making love to it. Creating endless harmonies to accompany it.

Night filled the room when they exchanged a long, leisurely kiss and drifted into an exhausted slumber, arms and legs entwined. Marco smoothed his hand down his wife's spine and tucked her close. She wiggled against him, pillowing her head in the crook of his arm.

She murmured something in her sleep, something remarkably like, "I love you, Marco."

"I love you, too, *cara,*" he whispered. And then he slept.

Marco woke not long after dawn, the soft burr of his cell phone pulling him from a deep, peaceful sleep. Swearing beneath his breath, he carefully eased himself from his wife's embrace and snatched up the phone. Then he padded naked into the living room.

"This better be important," he growled.

"Where's Caitlyn?" Nicolò asked in abrupt Italian.

Marco glanced over his shoulder. The bedroom remained shrouded in silence. "The same place I should be." He answered in Italian, as well. "In our bed. Asleep."

"Listen, you need to come down to Dantes. We've got a problem."

"What's it got to do with Caitlyn?"

"How do you know—"

"You asked where she was. You'd only have done that if whatever's going on somehow involves her." At his brother's continued silence, Marco snapped, "Does it?"

"We'll explain when you get here."

Jet lag ate at the frayed edges of his temper. "You'll explain now."

"I can't do that. Won't," he corrected. "There's something you need to see. To read."

"And whatever this something is has to do with Caitlyn?"

"Yes." Nicolò paused. "And Marco? We'd appreciate it if you didn't mention this meeting to your wife."

Marco didn't know what the hell was going on, but he suspected he wasn't going to like whatever his brothers had to say to him. In fact, he knew he wouldn't. After quietly dressing he scribbled a quick note to Caitlyn, in case she woke before he returned, informing her he'd be back in an hour or so. Then he drove to Dantes.

His three brothers were all waiting for him when he arrived, grouped around the smoked-glass conference table off Lazz's office. He examined them one by one. Sev appeared troubled, and sat silent and tense. Lazz looked equally concerned, and that worried Marco since he suspected his twin still had feelings for Caitlyn, even if they now leaned toward a more brotherly regard. If Lazz had aligned himself with Sev and Nicolò, that didn't bode well for Caitlyn. Worst of all, Nicolò, the family troubleshooter, quietly steamed, his eyes black with anger.

Nicolò took the lead, spinning a well-thumbed copy of *The Snitch* across the length of the table toward Marco. "That edition came out yesterday, before you and Lazz returned home. Read it."

Taking his time, Marco gave the article his full attention. Fury boiled through him with each successive word.

"What the hell is this?" he demanded. "How could they know what happened that day in Lazz's office? There were only three—"

"Exactly," Nicolò pronounced.

Marco's head jerked up. "You can't think . . ." They did think. Every last one of them. "No way. No damn way did Caitlyn hand this information over to *The Snitch*. She wouldn't do it."

Next Nicolò shot several typed pages stapled together in a thin packet down the table toward Marco. "Now read this. I don't think you were meant to find it until Monday. But I came into work today to leave some papers in your office and found it sitting on your desk."

Reluctantly Marco picked up the papers. *Dantes' Inferno,* screamed the title. *Marco's bride tells all.* He read every last word. The innuendos. The endless quotes. The underlying mockery that clung like slime to every sentence. Through it all he looked for key phrases. Phrases like "fantasy" or "superstition" or "fairy tale." But they weren't there. He sucked in a slow, calming breath before lifting his gaze to his brothers'.

"So?" he said with a shrug. "She didn't do this, if that's what you're asking."

Nicolò shoved back his chair. "How can you say that?" he challenged in disgust. "Because she's your Inferno bride? Because once she's been struck by the family curse, she wouldn't dream of betraying us?"

"Blessing," Marco and Sev said in unison.

Nicolò swore. "This is serious. There were only three of you in Lazz's office the day you had that argument. Lazz says that most of what *The Snitch* has quoted is accurate."

"It is," Marco reluctantly confirmed.

"Now we have advance copy on the next article and once again Caitlyn is quoted."

"That doesn't mean—"

"I called the paper, Marco! I asked them about it and they've admitted this is the exact same article their reporter turned in to them, although they refused to identify her. *Her,"* he repeated. "They're planning to run this story in their next edition. Now, are you still going to tell me Caitlyn's innocent in all this?"

"Ah, guys—" Lazz began.

Marco waved him silent and shot to his feet. "You want me to explain how I know she isn't involved?"

"Oh, please." Nicolò folded his arms across his chest.

"This I've got to hear."

"Fine. I'll tell you." Marco planted his hands on the table and leaned in, speaking with absolute conviction. "I know Caitlyn didn't do this because I know my wife. Not because of The Inferno. But because I've lived with her. Worked with her. Spent time with her. And she's as honest and decent and honorable as the day is long. Nothing you can say will convince me that she betrayed us."

"Marco—"

"Stay out of this Lazz." He locked gazes with Nicolò.

"Now are we through here?"

Nicolò's smile was harder than Marco had ever seen it before. "I'm not sure. Why don't we ask your wife?"

Marco froze. Caitlyn was here? Why hadn't he felt her? Why hadn't he sensed her presence? The Inferno had always worked as a warning system before this. He spun around and found her standing there. Just standing there, looking more devastated than he'd thought possible.

He shook his head in confusion. *Cara?* What are you doing here?"

"Marco," she whispered.

And then he knew.

He'd believed her.

It was everything Caitlyn could do to keep from crying. During all the weeks of their marriage, she'd longed for proof that what he felt for her emanated from more than The Inferno. And now, at long last, he'd done just that. How bitterly ironic that he'd been wrong.

"I can explain," she said. "Britt Jones is the snitch."

"And you told Britt about The Inferno."

"Yes. She'd gotten into some files I had. Personal documents of your father's." She spared Lazz a swift glance and saw horrified comprehension dawn on his face. "I . . . I traded her the information."

"You gave her The Inferno?" Nicolò interrupted, furiously. "Why the hell would you do that? What could possibly have been in those files that made it more advantageous to tell her about private Dante business?"

"It was some rather damning information about the Romanos and your father." Lazz began to explain, but Caitlyn overrode him.

The details of the contract weren't what mattered. She needed Marco to understand the impossible situation she'd been in, and how and why she'd made her decision.

"When I read the latest copy of *The Snitch*, I realized Britt was responsible for the leaks. It couldn't have been anyone else. I swear I didn't know it was her before then. When I confronted her, she admitted it."

"Why the hell didn't you tell one of us?" Marco asked.

"I tried. None of you were there. Not even Nicolò. Britt had information about the Romanos. About the current state of their finances. Marco . . ." She caught her lower lip between her teeth. "Marco, they're broke."

"We already knew that," he replied. She'd never heard him speak in such a stony, remote fashion. "What we're after is their goodwill. We want their endorsement, their contacts. Their lineage."

Sev held up his hands. "Marco, you have to fly out and talk to Vittorio. Now. Fill him in about The Inferno before he reads about it."

"I'll leave immediately."

"Marco—"

He simply shook his head. Without a word, he left the conference room. Caitlyn followed him, desperate to try again. "Marco, please. Tell Mr. Romano that this will be the final story. I got Britt to sign a confidentiality agreement."

He turned to confront her. "Why didn't you tell me about all this before? Last night, for instance?"

"I was going to tell you." She spared a swift glance over her shoulder to confirm that they were alone. "We got distracted."

"I don't have time for this. We'll settle it when I return."

She couldn't let him walk away. Not now. Not like this. If he did, she might never have another chance to fix things. Because if he walked away this time, she didn't think the rift between them would ever be bridged. "Listen to me. I have an idea for how we can spin this. How we can use it as a marketing tool."

He stiffened, his eyes darkening to hard amber nuggets. "The Inferno isn't something you spin, Caitlyn. It isn't some marketing ploy to sell Dantes jewelry. I'd have thought by now you'd realize that."

For the first time she sensed how flat-out furious he was. She swallowed. "I do know that."

He stalked closer, practically scorching the air with his wrath. "No, clearly you don't. And that's the whole problem. You seem to think this is an amusing little story we recount over cocktails. It isn't. The Inferno goes to the very heart of who and what we are. It's part of our heritage."

He wrapped his fingers around her wrist and dragged her hand to his chest. Each beat of his heart sank into her palm, the very palm where The Inferno had first blazed. She tried to hold back her tears and failed. "Marco, I'm so sorry. I had to make a fast decision. I realize now it was the wrong one."

He simply shook his head. "Right from the start you've treated The Inferno as though it were a foolish fairy tale. No matter what I've said to you, no matter how many times I've explained it, you refuse to understand its true meaning."

"I understand that it's important to you. I do."

"You still don't get it, Caitlyn." Not *cara*, she noticed. Maybe never again if she couldn't find a way to fix this.

"The Inferno is part of me. You can't pluck it free, like a weed that displeases you. When you deny that part of me, you deny me."

"No, I—"

He spoke across her protest. "The time for discussion is over. You have refused to accept The Inferno from the very start. I thought given time you'd finally understand. That you'd see it was as much a part of you as it is me." Weariness cut across his expression. "But it isn't, is it? You don't believe. You indulge me as though I were a foolish child. Well, no more." He released her, cutting off her incipient response with a slicing motion of his hand. "No more."

She watched as he spun on his heel and walked away. Watched as he left her without a backward glance. And all the while she kneaded the palm of her right hand with the thumb of her left.

Chapter Eleven

The next three days were sheer hell for Caitlyn, filled with endless hours in which she combed over every decision, every word of every conversation, as well as those final heartbreaking minutes with Marco. She considered all the alternative choices she could have made and all the possible scenarios that would have resulted from those changes. But no matter which path she chose, she couldn't think of a single one that would have improved the end result.

Except if she'd told Marco she loved him.

She closed her eyes in distress. Maybe that would have made a difference. Maybe that would have made him less furious. Maybe then The Inferno wouldn't have been like an unscalable mountain between them. But she hadn't and he'd left, and she hadn't heard a word from him since. Only time would tell if they'd be able to find a way over that mountain. But with each passing day, the doubts piled up as hope faded.

"Caitlyn?" Nicolò paused in the doorway of her office and leaned a shoulder against the jamb. "Lazz says I need to come and talk to you. That it's urgent."

Caitlyn didn't bother to conceal her relief, though it didn't escape her notice that her brother-in-law didn't actually step foot into her office. "No one's been willing to listen, and there's not a lot of time."

"Yeah, well." He shrugged, gazing at her with eyes so dark a brown they appeared black. She'd never realized before just how disconcerting they were until he trained them on her. "Some of us aren't too happy with your efforts to save us from the Jones woman."

"Really?" Maybe if she hadn't been so tired or worried or downright ticked off, she wouldn't have let her temper get out of control. But it had been a rough few days and the expression on Nicolò's face set her off. Big time. She stalked across the room toward him.

"Isn't it interesting that none of you managed to uncover the mole and deal with her. None of you were forced to come up with a plan to derail Britt on the spur of the moment the way I was. Yet, you're all too happy to point out every last one of my mistakes. After the fact, of course." She planted her hands on her hips. "Well, I don't think I made a mistake. What do you think of that?

Now, do you want to come in and find out what I have in mind to salvage this mess? Or are you going to let *The Snitch* win?"

A slight smile eased the sternness of Nicolò's tough-hewn features. "Okay, little sister." He walked into the room and sprawled in the seat in front of her desk. "I'm always interested in hearing creative solutions to impossible problems. Tell me your idea."

Instead of returning to her desk, Caitlyn took the chair next to him and leaned forward. "It's quite simple. The day *The Snitch* is released, the very day, we release a press statement."

"We?"

She waved that aside. "Dantes, of course. We agree with everything *The Snitch* says. Yes, there really is an Inferno. Yes, when it strikes, Dantes mate for life. Yes, it's a connection between soul mates."

"I'm curious." He tilted his head to one side and fixed those unnerving eyes on her. "Have you lost your mind?"

Enough was enough. "Just wait for it, Nicolò," she snapped. To her surprise, he did just that. "And then we say that The Inferno's part of what makes Dantes' jewelry so spectacular and so special. We tell all those women out there, all those women who would give their eyeteeth to experience The Inferno, that not only is it real, but everything the Dantes touch is imbued with the passion from The Inferno—from the bracelet and necklace that grace a woman's arms and throat, right down to the fire diamond wedding rings that a man places on his bride's finger."

Nicolò straightened in his chair, his gaze sharpening. "Damn."

"Exactly."

"No, seriously. *Damn*. That just might work." He thought it through, before nodding. "You came up with all that during your negotiation with the Jones woman? On the fly?" he asked.

"Yes."

"You know what I think?"

"Not a clue."

His smile grew. "I think your talents are totally wasted in the Finance Department."

Marco arrived back in San Francisco so tired he couldn't see straight. In the week he'd been gone, his anger had cooled, if not the pain caused by Caitlyn's decision to tell Britt about The Inferno. He'd endured countless phone calls from each of his brothers, as well as Francesca, Primo, and Nonna. Every last one of them had been clear that Britt had acted on her own until that final story, when Caitlyn had taken desperate measures to protect Dantes. And every last one of them supported his wife's decision.

And so did he, he finally admitted to himself. When all was said and done, he loved Caitlyn and he was determined to find a way to make their marriage work. To his relief, Lazz met him outside baggage claim, though his relief turned to annoyance when his brother started in on him about Caitlyn the instant they climbed in the car.

"What you don't seem to understand, Marco, is that she had a plan to turn whatever Britt printed about The Inferno to our advantage." Lazz pulled a face. "Well, that's Caitlyn. She always has a plan."

"And how many times do I have to tell you," Marco responded coldly, "that The Inferno isn't a marketing ploy?"

"You haven't even heard her idea, yet."

Marco scrubbed his hand across his face, striving to push aside his jet lag and focus. "No, you're right. I haven't. So, tell me. What did she come up with?" Lazz gave him the details, and Marco leaned back against his seat, his eyes narrowed against the midday sunshine as he absorbed the details. "That's not half-bad," he conceded at last.

"Not half-bad? Are you kidding me? It'll send women flocking to the stores." Enthusiasm riddled Lazz's voice. "They'll all want their small piece of The Inferno. *The Snitch* is going to be furious at how we've turned this around."

"Even so . . ." Marco shook his head. "You know how I feel about profiting from The Inferno. And I guarantee Primo feels the same way."

Lazz studied his brother for a long, silent moment. "I've thought about this. Seriously, I have. Caitlyn's idea isn't some loud, brash ploy. It's softer than you're making out. Gentler. It's almost . . ."

"Almost what?"

"It's almost like she believes in The Inferno."

"We are talking about Caitlyn here, right?"

"That's what makes it so amazing," Lazz said. "This isn't a hard-sell campaign. It's sweet and romantic. And honest."

Marco cocked his head to one side, intrigued. "Honest, how?"

"Well, for one thing, if you truly believe in The Inferno—"

"I do."

"Then, you must believe that our jewelry is imbued with a hint of The

Inferno's passion. I mean, think about it, Marco. Didn't Francesca create her most spectacular designs after she fell in love with Sev? Doesn't Primo credit Nonna with the inspiration for his greatest achievements? Don't you think The Inferno influenced them, brought some of that passion to their work?"

Marco couldn't deny it. "You really think that's what inspired her to come up with the marketing campaign?"

Lazz shrugged. "Do you have a better explanation?"

"No."

A sudden idea struck Marco, one so out there that it could only have been a jet-lag-induced flight of whimsy. But the more he considered the possibility, the more viable it became. It offered him the best of all worlds, an avenue for fixing their problem as well as a way to convince his wife that not only did he love her with all his heart and soul, but that she loved him, too. He just needed a few minutes to wrap his poor, tired brain around all the various details and organize them into a semblance of a plan. Unfortunately, details and organization were his wife's specialty, not his.

As soon as he'd thought it through, shuffled some of the pieces around and thought it through some more, he turned to Lazz. "There's something we need to arrange, a small addendum to Caitlyn's idea."

Lazz glanced in his direction. "Aw, hell, Marco. I know that look. Nicolò gets it every time he comes up with one of his crazier schemes. Whatever you're thinking, forget it."

"Not a chance. If it works, it won't only guarantee Dantes' success, but it may prove to my darling, stubborn, pragmatic wife—hell, to all of you unbelievers—that The Inferno really does exist."

Lazz sighed. "I'm not going to like this idea, am I?"

"Not even a little." But this was important, perhaps the most important scheme he'd ever put together, with one exception—the night he'd convinced Caitlyn to marry him. "The timing on this is vital."

"That's what your wife said."

"No, I mean we need to time our call to Britt Jones very carefully."

"What call to Britt Jones?" Lazz asked in alarm.

"The one where I give her a heads-up about our new marketing plan."

Lazz's jaw dropped. "You're going to what?"

"If Britt responds the way I expect her to, not only will our sales double, but

more importantly, my wife will realize
The Inferno is no fantasy."

Events transpired just as Caitlyn
predicted. Britt's final article came out in
The Snitch to mixed reaction. Some
thought it sweet, but most treated The
Inferno claims with amused disdain.
Dantes' press release broke only hours
later and changed all that. To her
delight, the story piqued media attention
and received impressive coverage under
the banner of a light human-interest
story.

Women in particular found The
Inferno claims quite intriguing, and
traffic in and out of the various Dantes
stores picked up significantly. Thanks to
the extensive media coverage, Marketing
and PR arranged for a press conference
featuring all of the Dantes, and Caitlyn
decided that she had no choice but to
join the family on the dais, since she'd
been so extensively quoted in Britt's
article. No doubt she'd have to field her
fair share of questions.

The one thing she hadn't anticipated
was seeing Britt among the milling
press, a *Snitch* photographer at her side.
Her ex-friend made a point of catching
Caitlyn's attention in order to offer a
cheeky wave, and seemed delighted by

the surprise and dismay her appearance engendered.

"Ignore her," Francesca recommended. "She's just living off her five minutes of fame. She doesn't even warrant the usual fifteen."

"After the way she spun The Inferno story, I'd have thought this would be the last place she'd want to show her face." Caitlyn glanced down the row of Dantes. "Lazz looks on the verge of killing her. I think he felt her betrayal as much as I did."

"Probably because she was his personal assistant. That had to hurt."

Caitlyn caught her lip between her teeth. "When does Marco get back from Italy, do you know? I was hoping he'd be here for this."

Francesca gave her an odd look. "Sev said he got back last night. Didn't he—" She broke off at her sister-in-law's expression. "Oh, no. He didn't come home? Caitlyn, I'm *so* sorry."

As though their conversation summoned him, he appeared on the far end of the dais. He didn't even look her way and Caitlyn's breath hitched in reaction. She blinked hard against a rush of tears. She needed to calm down, to shove her emotions to one side. She didn't dare betray her distress. Not here. Not now. Not in front of all these witnesses.

The next several minutes passed in a haze. She heard various Dantes speak, heard questions being lobbed in, caught and spun back out again. It wasn't until Britt stepped forward that Caitlyn's focus sharpened to pinpoint intensity.

"Hello, Marco," she practically purred. "I just wanted to thank you for your call yesterday."

Caitlyn's head jerked in his direction. "Did you know about that?" she whispered to Francesca.

"No," her sister-in-law murmured in return. "Sev never said a word. And judging by the expression on my dear husband's face, he didn't know, either."

Britt continued to address Marco. "One of the things you said during our conversation was that there wasn't any way to prove or disprove The Inferno. Let's see. How did you phrase it? Something along the lines of 'that was the beauty of your family's scam.'" She laughed. "Oops. I mean, your family legend."

"I believe I said that you couldn't disprove it. You really should strive for accuracy when you quote people. I've noticed it's an ongoing problem of yours."

Caitlyn shut her eyes. Oh, Marco. Why did he feel the need to tweak her tail? Hadn't he learned yet how vindictive Britt was?

As though reading Caitlyn's mind, Britt bared her teeth. "Well, surprise, surprise. I have come up with a way to disprove it. Your marketing department claims that a bit of this Inferno is imbued in every piece of jewelry you sell." She touched her earrings. "Not that you could prove it by me—"

"I suppose there are some people even The Inferno can't help," he offered.

Britt's smile vanished. "Well, I'd like you to prove The Inferno, right here and now."

Marco folded his arms across his chest. "Don't be ridiculous, Britt. How are we supposed to do that?"

"No, no, no," Caitlyn whispered beneath her breath. "He's playing right into her hands."

To her surprise, Francesca began to smile. "Don't be so sure. I have the impression your husband has that woman's number better than you do."

Britt climbed onto the dais, looking thoroughly pleased with herself. "I happen to have the answer to that right here." She opened a voluminous bag she had slung over her shoulder. "I suggest we put it to a little test. You and Lazz are twins. I'd like to see if your wife can pick out which one of you is which, using only The Inferno."

Caitlyn stilled. "I can do that," she told Francesca. "That's simple."

As though Britt had heard, she pulled out a hood and a pair of earplugs. "Without the use of her eyes or ears, of course." Interest rippled through the gathering, and she played to the crowd. "Now, I've tested these myself. She's not going to be able to see or hear anything. Then I want Marco and Lazz to line up in front of her and if she can pick out the right brother, I'll take back every last word I ever said about the Dantes. Even the positive stuff."

"Interesting, but . . ." He shook his head. "It's not a sweet enough deal. I'm thinking we should go for broke."

"Oh?" Curiosity sparked, along with a hint of amusement. "You want to up the stakes?"

"Absolutely. How about this. You lose, I want every last piece of Dante jewelry you own. I'll even reimburse you for whatever you paid for them." He covered the microphone and his playfulness faded, replaced by a dangerous edge. "You see, Britt, I don't want you wearing anything we've ever crafted. Furthermore, you're banned from ever entering a Dantes store from this day forward."

Humiliation sent hot color streaking across her cheekbones. "And if I win, I want all of you to admit that this whole

Inferno business is nothing but a publicity stunt," she announced in ringing tones. "And I want you to tear up my confidentiality agreement. I've decided there are a few more articles I'd like to write about you Dantes."

Before Caitlyn had time to beg Marco to turn the offer down, he nodded in agreement. "Done."

Marco turned toward Caitlyn, but Britt stepped between them. "Oh, no, lover boy." An almost vicious note crept into her voice, one that didn't go unnoticed. "I'm not giving you an opportunity to speak to her and arrange for some way of signaling her. We do this my way."

"I have no problem with that," Marco said with an easy shrug.

He glanced over Britt's shoulders toward Caitlyn. She met his look, waiting to see the anger and disillusionment from when they'd parted earlier in the week. But not a trace of it remained. In its place was something that had tears flooding her eyes again. She saw a calm certainty. There was no doubt in her mind that he believed in her, without hesitation or exception. Before she could do more than stare in bewilderment, Britt crossed to her side.

"I'm going to put Lazz and your husband in front of you. When I tap your shoulder, you point either left or right toward your husband." She leaned in and spoke quietly enough that they couldn't be overheard. "When you lose, my expression of triumph is going to be the first thing you see and my laughter the first thing you hear. And, honey, I flat-out can't wait."

With that, she oversaw the placement of both earplugs and hood, before maneuvering Caitlyn to the center of the dais. There was an endless delay during which she sensed movement around her. And that entire time, she stood frozen in panic.

If Lazz and Marco had been lined up in front of her, even with their backs turned as Francesca had suggested all those weeks ago, Caitlyn no longer questioned her ability to tell one twin from the other. But blindfolded? How was she supposed to pull this off?

And what would happen if she chose wrong? Not much question about that. If she didn't succeed, they'd lose the Romano account for good. The campaign she'd come up with would flop because The Inferno would be disproved. But worst of all, Marco would realize she wasn't really his Inferno bride.

Why had he done this? Why had he looked at her with such confidence, with such . . . Such *love*. She stiffened. Dear God, that's what she saw in his eyes when he looked at her. He didn't just believe in her and trust her. He *loved* her. And because of that love, the crazy man was convinced she could feel him through the hood, through the earplugs, through everything that separated them. *Had he lost his mind?*

She could only think of one way—and a darned slim one at that—this might work. Her only hope was to trust in herself and believe that she could sense her husband, as she had the day she'd lunched with Francesca and Nonna. Pray The Inferno would miraculously help her separate him from Lazz. And with that thought came the realization she was putting her faith in something she'd always insisted didn't exist.

Somehow, at some point during their marriage, she'd started to believe in the existence of The Inferno. To accept it as fact instead of fiction, truth instead of fairy tale. The breath hitched in her throat. Whatever The Inferno was, she could feel it warming her, connecting her to Marco like a living conduit.

Britt shuffled her into position and tapped her on the shoulder. Caitlyn hadn't a clue why it had taken so long. Not that it mattered. She closed her eyes, despite the blanket of darkness provided by the hood, and focused on Marco. As she did, memories swept through her.

Marco offering his hand in the lobby of Dantes and the two of them experiencing that initial, startling electric shock. Marco on the balcony of Le Premier, kissing her for the very first time while pretending to be Lazz. Their wedding, where he'd gazed down at her with such passion she shivered just recalling it. Their wedding night, a night so beautiful it would be an integral part of her until the day she died. All the intensely passionate nights since, when the two of them had become one. And finally, Marco staring at her before Britt had placed the hood over her head, staring with absolute faith.

With love.

She opened herself to her husband, pausing in confusion when she didn't sense him in either of the two men standing before her. And then she felt the tickle of awareness, not in front, but off to her right. She turned. Hesitated. Felt the distinct throb in her palm. And then she didn't hesitate at all. She made a beeline for her husband.

His arms closed around her, lifted her. And then he stripped off the hood and gently pulled free the earplugs. "Any more questions about whether or not The Inferno exists?" he asked with a broad grin.

"Not a one." Caitlyn wrapped her arms around Marco's neck and kissed him, while cheers erupted all around them. "I love you, Marco."

"I love you, too, *cara*, from the minute we first touched. For the rest of our lives you are my Inferno wife."

"I wouldn't want to be anything else." She dropped her head to his shoulder. "I just have two questions."

"Name them."

"Why didn't you come home last night?"

"Because I would have wanted to prove to you once and for all that I love you, and that The Inferno exists. But I realized it was more important you discover that for yourself. I needed you to trust me without the words. To trust your feelings for me."

"To trust in The Inferno."

"Yes." He smoothed her hair back from her face.

"What's your second question?"

"What took so long?" she asked with a sigh.

He chuckled, the sound low and intimate. "I believe that's my question for you. What took you so long to trust in The Inferno?"

She answered readily enough. "The Inferno wasn't logical. It still isn't. But—" she blew out her breath "—you can't argue with facts."

He blinked in surprise, then gave a shout of laughter. "Do you realize you just called The Inferno fact?"

She wrinkled her nose. "Scary, isn't it? But that wasn't actually my second question. What I want to know is, why did it take so long to start Britt's experiment?"

"Oh, that. My brothers weren't happy about Britt changing the rules at the last minute. When she stuck Lazz and Nicolò in front of you, we almost had a riot on our hands. Even the crowd booed."

"But not you," she guessed shrewdly.

"I knew you'd find me."

Her arms tightened around him. "And now that I have, I'm never going to let you go."

Epilogue

A full week later Caitlyn remembered something else she'd found in that cursed box of personal files. The instant she did, she tracked down her husband, barging straight into his office. "Marco, there's something you need to know. Something important." She offered an apologetic look. "I would have told you sooner, but—"

He lifted an eyebrow, amusement gleaming in his eyes. "You've been a little distracted?"

How could she not after the blissful week they'd shared? "Yes." She worried at her bottom lip until he put a stop to it with a lingering kiss.

"First, before we deal with any more business, I have a present for you." He held out a box that he'd personally wrapped and tied with a slightly lopsided bow. "Fair warning. It sparkles."

"Oh, Marco. You know you don't have to buy me jewelry."

"I will be buying you jewelry," he told her quite definitely. "In fact, I intend to shower you in fire diamonds. But this is something a little different."

Without another word, she took the box. The weight of it surprised her and she opened it, lifting out the velvet inner box. After she removed the lid, she stared at the contents and then began to laugh. He'd bought her a gorgeous glass paperweight. And floating inside the glass, like glittering diamond bubbles, was every last piece of Dante jewelry Britt Jones had owned. She threw her arms around her husband and kissed him. How had she gotten so fortunate? A man who could make her laugh and shower her with diamonds.

She didn't want this moment to end. And even though she knew she had endless moments like this ahead of her, soon she'd have to put romance aside and get down to business. Marco must have sensed her thoughts. He pulled back and cupped her face.

"What's wrong?" he asked.

He didn't give her a chance to respond, but took her mouth in a series of deep, penetrating kisses. It was just as well. She really didn't want to tell him that she'd found evidence in the "box from hell" that the Dantes might not be the only legal owners of the fire diamond mine.

Later. She'd tell him later about the O'Dell brothers, who were the original owners of the mine. And she'd tell him about the possibility that Cameron O'Dell's granddaughter, Kiley, could have a legitimate claim to half the mine. Or maybe she'd put Nicolò on the case. After all, he was the Dante family troubleshooter, not Marco.

Her husband pulled back again, his smile one of wicked promise. "Well? What's up?"

"Nothing important." Caitlyn tightened her arms around Marco's neck and lifted her face for another of his drugging kisses. "At least, nothing as important as this."

His expression softened and he captured her mouth once again, his words the last thing she heard before she tumbled into the golden future stretching before her. "Nothing will ever be as important as how much we love each other."

Nicolò's Wedding Deception

The Dante Dynasty Series:
Book #3

by

Day Leclaire

USA Today Bestselling Author

Dedication

To Donna Totton, for being the best sister-in-law in the world . . . and for your constant support and assistance.

Thank you!

Prologue

Nicolò Dante anticipated trouble the same way he anticipated marriage—one part dread, and two parts determination to find a way out of the whole unfortunate mess.

Some men found a certain inevitability to the sorry state of "wedded amiss." His two brothers, Sev and Marco, had eventually succumbed to the entire process like the not-quite-proverbial rams to the slaughter. Well, not him. He had enough trouble in his life without looking for more.

And right now, that trouble took the form of Kiley O'Dell.

"We need you to look into this," his eldest brother, Sev, instructed. "According to the documents Caitlyn uncovered, there's a distinct possibility that this woman may own a substantial interest in Dantes' fire diamond mine."

Such a simple statement, yet the implications were dire, and could cause endless problems for Dantes' jewelry empire, an empire whose fame was built on the lure of fire diamonds. They could be found nowhere else in the world, except deep within the bowels of a Dante mine, and they were coveted by everyone from royalty to heads of state to the local shopkeeper around the corner.

Nicolò's expression darkened. "Our dear sister-in-law should have kept her nose out of those old papers. They've brought us nothing but grief." He lifted an eyebrow in question. "Does Marco have no control over Caitlyn?"

Sev shook his head in disgust. "You really don't have a clue, do you?"

"I'm probably the only one who does." Nicolò leaned a hip against his older brother's desk. "What's the point of being so damn charming, if he can't use some of it on his own wife? He tricked her into marriage, didn't he? Now that he's got her, the least he can do is keep her out of trouble."

Sev crossed his arms across his chest, his burnished gold eyes brilliant with laughter. "Keep digging that hole, bro. Your Inferno bride will be delighted to bury you in it when you eventually come across her."

"Forget it." Nicolò made a brisk slicing movement with his hand. "As far as I'm concerned the family curse—"

"Blessing," Sev corrected mildly.

"Blessing? Hell, it's more like an infection."

Sev tilted his head to one side and considered the description. "That's an interesting analogy, although I'd say The Inferno is closer to a melding."

Nicolò allowed a hint of curiosity to show. "What was it like when you first felt The Inferno for Francesca?"

"Are you finally admitting it exists?"

"I'm willing to admit you and Marco believe it does," Nicolò conceded grudgingly.

"And Primo."

Nicolò dismissed that with a swift shake of his head. "Our grandfather is the one who has perpetuated the legend all these years. It offers a convenient excuse to explain lust, no more and no less."

"Now you sound like Lazz," Sev said. "But if that were true, Caitlyn never would have been able to distinguish between Marco and Lazz, considering how difficult it is to tell the two apart. And yet, she picked out her husband without any doubt or hesitation. And she did it under the most extreme circumstances. Wasn't that enough to convince you?"

Nicolò couldn't deny fact. Nor could he rationalize what he'd seen that day. But that didn't mean he'd allow Sev to draw him into a discussion about the veracity of The Inferno. "You still haven't explained what it's like."

An odd smile drifted across Sev's mouth and his eyes seemed lit from within, filled with an unsettling combination of pleasure and satisfaction. "When I first saw Francesca, I felt a physical pull, as though we were somehow connected by a thin tenuous wire. The closer we moved in proximity, the stronger the connection between us. It kept growing until it became so powerful, I couldn't resist it."

"That's it? You felt physically attracted?"

"Shut up, Nicolò." There wasn't any heat behind the demand, just amused impatience. "Do you want to know, or don't you?"

"I asked, didn't I?" Though why he bothered, he couldn't say. Horrified fascination, perhaps. Or perhaps forewarned was forearmed. The instant he felt anything similar, he'd get the hell out. Get out long before he did something as outrageous as Sev—like blackmail his future wife into first leaving their competitor and working for Dantes, and later still agreeing to a pretend engagement. Clearly The Inferno did strange things to the men and women it mated. "Something happens when you touch, doesn't it?"

"A shock."

At the reminder, Sev kneaded the palm of his right hand with the fingers of his left. It was a habitual gesture, one Nicolò had seen both his grandfather Primo and his brother Marco imitate. They all claimed it occurred as a result of The Inferno, a lingering residual from that first touch. Even Caitlyn rubbed her palm periodically.

"A shock like static electricity?" Nicolò prompted.

"Yes. No." Sev grimaced. "It's a shock, yes. But it doesn't really hurt. It surprises. Then it seems to meld us. Complete the connection. After that, it's done. There's no going back. You've been matched with your soul mate and you're permanently joined for the rest of your lives."

Damn. Nicolò didn't like the sound of that. He preferred having his options open, to have a variety of choices. In his position as Dantes' troubleshooter, he required the freedom to jump from one creative opportunity to another should the need arise. Experiencing such a total loss of control didn't appeal to him at all. The Inferno stole that control, forcing its will on unwilling subjects. And though he didn't mind bending on occasion, so long as it happened to be in the general direction he was headed anyway, he resented like hell the concept of being broken, stripped of power, and forced along a path not of his choosing.

"Well, with luck The Inferno will be clever enough to leave me alone," Nicolò said lightly. "Now tell me what you've discovered about Kiley O'Dell."

"Nothing."

Nicolò's brows tugged together. "What do you mean nothing?"

"I mean that since the question of who actually owns the fire diamond mine broke in *The Snitch*—"

"Damn interfering gossip rag."

Momentary amusement flashed across Sev's face. "Now you sound like Marco. Not that it matters. Apparently, the O'Dell woman reads *The Snitch*." His amusement faded. "She's come forward demanding a meeting to discuss the situation. A meeting you're going to set up. Unfortunately, we haven't been able to get any substantive background info on her. At least, not yet."

Nicolò stared, appalled. "You expect me to go in blind?"

"I don't see what choice we have." Sev waved that aside as though an unimportant consideration. That's what he got for making his job seem so easy. "Listen, just hear her out. Primo bought that mine fair and square. Find out why she thinks her family might still have a legitimate claim after all these years.

Then stall while we put some P.s on this." A fierceness settled over Sev's face. "I don't have to tell you how much we stand to lose if Kiley O'Dell's claims prove genuine."

"Dantes will go under." Nicolò didn't phrase it as a question.

Sev nodded. "Everything we've worked to rebuild over the past decade will have been for nothing. We need to find out what proof the O'Dell woman has that she's a legitimate owner in the mine and then keep her happily oblivious while we find a way to take her down."

Nicolò's expression hardened. "Then that's what I'll do."

"Nic—"

"I understand how important this is." It was probably the most delicate job he'd ever handled, as well as the most difficult. "I'll find a way to keep her off balance."

"Tread lightly." At Nicolò's questioning look, Sev elaborated. "Her claim could be genuine. We don't want to do anything to set her against us. We want an amicable resolution, not a pitched battle."

Nicolò shook his head. "Then she shouldn't have started this war. Because one way or another I intend to finish it."

Chapter One

Kiley O'Dell wasn't at all what Nicolò expected.

But then, neither did he expect the tidal wave of desire that slammed through him, rendering him deaf and blind to everything but the woman standing in the doorway of her suite at Le Premier. He saw her mouth move, but the sound refused to penetrate the roaring that filled his ears, a roaring that demanded he take this woman and make her his. To put his mark on her in every way possible. To possess her and bind her to him until neither of them could escape.

No. He dropped his head and fought the sensation, fought for all he was worth. He flat-out refused to accept this feeling, flinching from the very real possibility that it might signify the start of The Inferno.

No. Way. In. *Hell.*

This woman spelled trouble from the top of her dainty red head to the tips of her tiny red-coated toenails. And he refused to allow trouble into his life, his bed, or his heart. No matter what it took, he'd put an end to this sensation. It couldn't possibly be that difficult. It only required a single, simple solution. All he had to do was figure out what that solution was and The Inferno would pass him by.

Lifting his head, he took a second to study Kiley O'Dell, using every scrap of creative skill at his disposal to search for a way out of his latest predicament. But nothing came to him and he simply stood and stared at her.

Her name suited her. She stood no taller than a minute, with a taut, lithe figure that packed just enough curves in just the right places to tempt a man to explore every inch of that creamy white skin. She wore her hair long and it fell in heavy strawberry-blond curls to the middle of her back. She also possessed the most stunning pair of pale green eyes he'd ever seen, eyes that dominated her triangular-shaped face.

"Mr. Dante?" she asked, clearly repeating herself. Her cultured voice contained a low, musical quality that fell easily on the ears. "Is there something wrong?"

"Nicolò."

He shoved the single word from between clenched teeth. Did she have any idea how hard he struggled to act with a modicum of propriety while instinct clawed at him, urging him to snatch her up in his arms and carry her off to the nearest bedroom?

Possibly, since a hint of wariness crept into her regard and a pulse kicked to life in the hollow of her throat, betraying her instinctive response to him. A response not all that unlike his own, if he didn't miss his guess. A streak of color highlighted her arching cheekbones and he could almost smell the whiff of desire that perfumed the air between them. Oh, yeah, this wasn't good.

She recovered far swifter than he. "I'm Kiley O'Dell. Thank you for taking the time to see me."

Everything about her appeared quick and decisive, from the sharp once-over she gave him to the way her gaze leapt from him, to the hallway, and then over her shoulder to the spacious hotel room. He couldn't help but wonder if that last glance was a final check to make sure she'd properly set the scene for their encounter.

"Come on in," she said, stepping to one side.

She didn't bother offering her hand, which suited him just fine. Considering the overwhelming hunger her appearance aroused it would be downright foolhardy to touch this woman. Not with The Inferno currently on the rampage, cutting a swathe of destruction through the Dante males.

Not that he believed in The Inferno. Hell, no. He hadn't when Primo first told the tale. Nor when Sev and Marco tried to convince him they'd both experienced it the first time they'd touched their future wives. And he damn sure didn't intend to start believing in The Inferno now. Not even with this desperate need filling every empty space inside him with a want so huge he could barely contain it all.

"Would you like something to drink?" Kiley tossed the question over her shoulder while she crossed the plush carpet. She moved with a hip-swinging stride that drew his gaze to her pert, rounded backside lovingly outlined by a pair of trim black slacks. He caught back a groan. Was it deliberate, or another aspect of the stage she'd set for their meeting? "I have sodas," she continued. "Or something stronger if you feel the need."

Whiskey. He'd kill for a double shot of single-malt. "I'm fine, thanks."

"Do you want to talk first or get straight down to business?"

"What's there to talk about?"

That had her turning around. A crooked smile tilted her mouth, giving her an almost gamine appearance. "We could take a stab at making this a friendly get-together. You know, exchange the usual pleasantries people do when they first meet."

Okay, he'd play along. "Like?"

"Like . . . Tell me what you do at Dantes, Nicolò."

"I solve problems."

Laughter gleamed in those odd green eyes, turning them spring-leaf bright. "And I'm your current problem?"

"I don't know." He lifted an eyebrow. "Are you?"

She shrugged. "Time will tell."

She folded her arms across her chest and leaned her hip against the back of a richly upholstered divan. She took her time, studying him at her leisure. Searching for a weakness? he couldn't help but wonder. If so, she'd have a long, fruitless time of it. The moment stretched, thin and sharp as razor wire. She broke first.

"It's your turn," she prompted gently.

"My turn . . . what?"

"To ask a question." She released a tiny sigh. "That's how this works, you see. When you're getting to know someone, you exchange pleasant chitchat in order to ease the tension."

"Are you tense?"

"You're kidding, right? You don't feel it?" She punctuated her questions with her hands, their movement through the air as brisk as everything else about her, yet graceful for all that. "Hell, Dante, it's thick enough to scoop out of the air and dish up for dessert."

So she felt it, too. It wasn't just his imagination. "Is that what you suggest? That we move straight to dessert?"

"Is that your way of resolving our problems?" she countered. Heat and awareness broke from her in splashy waves, building on his own. "Do you really think you can seduce my share of the mine out from under me? Is that your creative solution to this particular problem?"

Yes. "No."

"Good. I'm relieved to hear it."

"Because you don't have a share of the mine." He took a step closer to her, just to gauge her reaction. She didn't move, but he could see the slight tautening of the muscles across her shoulders and the momentary widening of her eyes before she forced herself to relax. *Gotcha*. She was good at this little game she played, but he was better. "Since you don't own any part of the mine, getting you into bed won't make any difference to the eventual disposition of your claim."

To his surprise, she laughed, the sound light and unfettered. "I'm so glad we have that out of the way."

"Funny. It still feels like it's right here between us."

It was her turn to take a step closer, to push at the electrical current sizzling between them like a live wire. "Shall we get it out of the way, Dante?" she dared. "It would be easy enough."

She reached for the first button of her blouse and thumbed it through the hole. Then a second. And a third. The deep V of her neckline revealed an intricate heart-shaped locket on a thin silver chain. Then he caught a flash of vibrant red, a sharp note of color trapped between the milky whiteness of her skin and the unrelenting blackness of her blouse. Before he could stop himself his attention dropped from her breasts to her low-riding slacks. Did she wear a matching bra and panties set? Did she conceal hellfire and brimstone beneath the pitch-black of her clothes?

He slowly looked up, his gaze clashing with hers. How long would it take him to find out? Judging by the hungry expression on her face, not long at all. Her fingers hovered above the final two buttons.

"Finish it."

His voice sounded as though it had been put through a shredder. He deliberately took the final step that separated them. Only the merest breath of space held them apart, that space awash with turmoil. Desire roiled there, along with mistrust and suspicion. It was a desire he intended to destroy, while nurturing the mistrust and suspicion.

"Finish it," he repeated. "And show me your true colors."

She jerked back. Where before her movements flowed, now they stuttered. Color stained her face and turned her eyes evergreen dark with horrified disbelief. She fumbled in her effort to rebutton her blouse, jamming the wrong buttons into the wrong holes.

"What the hell was I thinking?" she muttered. The question seemed aimed at herself rather than at him. She shook her head as though to clear it before demanding, "What are you doing to me, Dante?"

"You're the one doing the striptease, lady. Don't blame me if I expect you to put up or shut up. Now do you have proof to back up your claim that you own part of Dantes' mine, or is that what you were in the process of showing me?"

He'd rattled her, something he suspected didn't often happen with the self-possessed Ms. O'Dell. "You feel it, too," she insisted quietly. "Don't try and tell me I'm imagining things."

"And yet, I'm not the one taking off my clothes."

To his surprise, amusement rippled past the heat and turmoil and gentled the flames. "Too true, Dante. I'll have to watch my step with you. It would appear you bring out the wanton in me, though who knew there was any wanton in there to begin with." She shook her head in disgust. "Live and learn."

Taking a deep breath, she circumvented the divan she'd been leaning against earlier and gestured toward the coffee table in front of it, one littered with papers. She waved him toward a second divan, situated opposite the first.

"So, let's get down to business. You want proof. Here's my proof." She picked up her first batch of papers and shoved them across the table toward him. "My grandfather was Cameron O'Dell. He and his brother, Seamus, were the original owners of the fire diamond mine that your grandfather, Primo Dante, eventually purchased. I've just given you copies of my grandfather's birth certificate, his death certificate and a deed showing that he was a legitimate half-owner of the mine."

Nicolò leafed through the papers. "My understanding is he died before the sale to Primo was finalized."

"True. But that would have merely transferred his share of ownership to any surviving children—my father, to be specific." Kiley tossed another document in his direction. "Here's a copy of Grandfather's will confirming that fact."

"Do you have your father's birth certificate proving he was born before Cameron died?"

Another piece of paper came sailing across the table. "Right here." She rested her elbows on her knees and leaned forward. Her locket swung out from beneath her misbuttoned blouse. It was a curious piece of jewelry, thick and chunky, consisting of fragments of silver that had been laced together to form the heart. "Your grandfather may have paid off Seamus, but my great-uncle didn't have the right to sell my father's share of the fire diamond mine, despite what he may have claimed at the time."

Nicolò took his time studying the documentation even though he suspected he'd find everything in perfect order. A con artist would have made certain of that. What he hoped to uncover while he pretended to read was the slip in logic. It didn't take much thought to key in on it.

"Why has your family waited so long to bring this matter to our attention?" he finally asked. "Why didn't you file a lawsuit decades ago in order to get your fair share?"

"I didn't know I might be an owner. As for my father . . ." A hint of some painful memory came and went in her eyes. "I can't ask him that question since he died when I was little more than a baby."

Nicolò allowed a hint of sympathy to show. "You were raised by your mother?"

"What difference does that make?" she asked in sharp retort.

He lifted an eyebrow. For some reason what he intended as a throwaway question had provoked an unguarded response, and clearly a defensive one, which made it all the more interesting. It told him a lot. Without even intending to, he'd hit a hot button with her. It showed him how tight a control she kept over her words and emotional responses. Until now.

"You were the one who suggested we get to know each other better. That's what I'm doing." He pushed a little harder. "Tell me about her. What's her name? How did she make ends meet after your father died?"

Kiley's mouth tightened. "I think you're stalling."

He shrugged. "Believe what you want. I'm just trying to figure out whether she's in on this little scam or if you came up with it all by yourself."

"It's no scam."

"So you say. But I suspect Seamus will tell a far different story."

Her movements slowed, fluttering to stillness like a bird settling to its nest. It was a "tell," an unconscious look or movement—or lack thereof—that betrayed a lie. He'd always had an innate ability to pick up on them, a prime reason his brothers refused to play poker with him. He could always tell when they were bluffing, just as he could with Kiley.

She moistened her lips with the tip of her tongue, a second, more obvious "tell." "Seamus?" she repeated.

Nicolò took a stab in the dark. "According to Primo, he's still alive." He offered an expansive smile. "Tell you what. Why don't you sit tight for the next few days and enjoy the amenities Le Premier has to offer, while I track him down? I'm sure he can clear up this confusion in no time."

"Give me my papers." The words escaped, raw and harsh.

Without a word he gathered them and passed them across the width of the coffee table to her. Their fingertips touched during the exchange, just the merest glancing brush of skin against skin. A brief flash of electricity burst between them, sizzling for an instant, but not quite catching. Nicolò shot to his feet.

"What the *hell* are you trying to pull?" he demanded.

She shrank back against the divan, her eyes huge and vivid in a pale face. "I don't know what you're talking about."

For the first time in his entire life, Nicolò ignored instinct and went with pure suspicion. "Sure you do. You read *The Snitch,* didn't you, Ms. O'Dell? You read about the diamond mine, no question there, since it's what prompted you to contact us. But you also read all about the Dantes and their little Inferno problem. And it gave you the most brilliant idea. Let's gather up these old family papers, you tell yourself, and see if you can't fake a case for partial ownership in the fire diamond mine. And if that doesn't work, let's see if you can fake The Inferno."

She shot to her feet. "You are hands-down certifiable."

"Then how do you explain that little pop of electricity?"

"How the hell should I know? Maybe your brain short-circuited." She hugged the documents to her chest. Giving him a wide berth, she skirted the coffee table and crossed to the door of her suite. "I think you should leave."

Nicolò followed her to the door. "I'm not going anywhere. Not until we have this out. Because, we're not done here. We're not even close to done."

"Yes, we are. First thing in the morning I intend to contact my lawyer. Until then, get the hell out of my room."

He leaned in close, so close he could feel the tiny charges of electricity skipping off her and latching onto him. Pulling and tugging him toward that ultimate commitment, attempting to sear him with that final fateful touch. "This isn't over, you know."

Her breathing grew jagged and he could see his want reflected in her eyes, a mate to his own, just as he could sense their heartbeats thundering as one. He almost sealed her mouth with his, the temptation nearly overwhelming. It took every ounce of self-control to pull back at the last second. Without another word, he opened the door and stepped into the hallway. The door slammed closed behind him.

Nicolò stood there for a moment. He could still feel her, right through the damn door. She was leaning against it, fighting the same attraction he fought, telling herself, just as he did, that what she felt was insane. Impossible. And to be avoided at all costs. He shook his head in disgust. Right there with you, Gorgeous.

Nicolò headed for the bank of elevators and took a car to the main floor. Once there, he hesitated. The lobby offered a spacious sitting area, with groups of chairs arranged in cozy settings. Large, carefully tended ferns, bushes, and even a few ornamental trees created oases of privacy.

He eyed a set of chairs that were discreetly screened, while still offering a prime view of the elevators. Instinct kicked in again, growing too loud to ignore. In his thirty years of existence, he'd learned not to question that gut-deep demand. It always signaled something his subconscious had picked up on that his conscious mind hadn't caught up with quite yet.

Giving in, he took a seat and waited. It didn't take long.

No more than five minutes later Kiley came barreling out of one of the elevators with that brisk, hip-swinging stride he now realized was her natural way of walking. She wore her hair up and had thrown on a black jacket to match her slacks. Very businesslike. She made a beeline for the concierge, her foot tapping impatiently as she waited for him to answer her question.

Nicolò sensed a purpose behind her actions. She had a destination in mind and he intended to find out where . . . and with whom. It would be interesting to see if she had a partner in crime. The concierge must have given Kiley the answer she needed, for she rewarded him with a broad smile that seemed to cause the man's brain to short-circuit the same way Nicolò's had earlier. Then she spun around and started toward the lobby doors. And that's when disaster struck.

Even though there was absolutely no reason for her to notice him or glance his way, even though he was practically buried in a jungle of shrubbery, the instant she came level with his position, she stiffened and her step faltered. Whatever connection had been forged in those few minutes they'd spent together crackled to life, sending out tendrils of awareness.

Time slowed and stretched. The chatter of voices and clatter of humanity grew muffled and distant. Even the light seemed to dim, leaving just the two of them within its brilliant embrace. With unerring accuracy, Kiley's head swiveled in his direction and her gaze locked with Nicolò's. The instant she spotted him, her eyes widened in shock. Acute distress followed on the heels of her shock.

Her distress caused an unexpected stab of concern that threw him off stride. He didn't want to feel anything for this woman. Unfortunately, he couldn't deny fact. During their brief time together, something had sparked to life, and it was more powerful than anything he'd ever experienced before.

Time resumed its normal pace and Kiley shot toward the entryway and whisked through the glass doors embossed with Le Premier's name and logo. Nicolò followed, instinct urging him to run, the hunter giving chase to his prey. He hit the sidewalk outside the hotel just as she reached the corner intersection. People were still crossing, though the crossing light blinked a bright red hand of warning. She threw a quick glance over her shoulder. Spotting him, she darted into the crosswalk just as the light changed.

He saw it coming before it happened. A cab broke around a slow car, accelerating directly toward the intersection. Clearly, the driver didn't realize Kiley was there. Nicolò thought he shouted a warning. He knew he broke into a run. The driver didn't spot her until the very last instant. He hit the brakes at the same instant she tried to leap out of the way, but it was too late. The cab's bumper clipped her with just enough force to send her somersaulting into the air before connecting with the pavement. Even as Nicolò pelted toward her, he reached for his phone. He hit the emergency link without even looking and barked the information at the operator the moment the call went through.

He reached her side and knelt down. She didn't move. Didn't even seem to breathe. From what he'd seen of her fall, she'd been sent flying toward the opposite sidewalk and hit her head on the curb. Vibrant blush-red hair flowed around her, still shimmering with life, while her pallor warned of something far different. Her locket rested against her cheek like a kiss.

"Kiley!" He didn't dare touch her, though he wanted to. And then he saw it, the slow, steady rise and fall of her chest, and he almost lost it.

"I didn't see her." The driver of the cab appeared, staring down at Kiley and wringing his hands. Unabashed tears rolled down his bearded face. "She came out of nowhere."

"I saw what happened. It wasn't your fault." Nicolò's mouth tightened. The blame was all his, not the cab driver's.

"Is she—" The cabbie broke off, swallowing hard. "Is she . . . ?"

"No. I've called for an ambulance."

As though in response, sirens wailed in the distance. A small crowd gathered around them and Nicolò kept them back with a single terse command, followed by a look so black that it sent most of the onlookers scurrying on their way.

The police arrived minutes later, the ambulance shortly after that. Nicolò watched helplessly as they secured the area and tended to Kiley. He vaguely remembered giving his identification. Vaguely recalled claiming Kiley as his own, because on some visceral level he knew that she was. Her well-being had now become his responsibility.

All through the hideous ordeal, he watched the EMTs stabilize her, watched them attach endless medical equipment to her, watched them fit her head and neck with protective devices. And the only thing he could think about was that if he hadn't followed her, she'd never have run. She'd never have been hit by the cab. Never would have been injured.

He'd been so caught up in proving her a con artist, he'd put her life in danger. Based on the grim glances he saw the emergency personnel exchange, he may very well have killed her. He closed his eyes, forcing himself to face facts.

There was a connection between them whether he wanted it or not. That spark of electricity they'd experienced earlier hadn't been part of her con. She'd been as surprised by their physical reaction to one another as he had. The truth was this woman could be his Inferno mate. Since they'd never fully touched, he couldn't be one hundred percent positive. But he doubted they needed complete contact. Deep inside he sensed the truth, sensed it with every fiber of his being.

The Inferno had sent him his soul mate. Granted, she wasn't the one he'd have selected for himself. But by driving her to act so impetuously, he could very well have destroyed their future "might have been" before he ever got to know her. He'd claimed he didn't want an Inferno bride.

It looked like fate had given him exactly what he wanted.

Chapter Two

*"**Have you lost** your mind?"*

Nicolò glanced over his shoulder toward the hospital waiting room to make certain they couldn't be overheard. Spying a few curious looks, he addressed his brother Lazzaro in Italian. "No, I haven't lost my mind. It's my fault she's in here. If I hadn't been running after her, she would never have—"

Lazz waved that aside with a sweep of his hand. "You told me that already," he replied in the same language. "So now, in addition to having a claim on our fire diamond mines, Kiley O'Dell can sue you for chasing her in front of a cab. Is that what you're telling me?"

"Yes. No." *Damn it.* Why did Sev have to send the logical Dante? "You don't understand."

"Then explain it so I will. And while you're at it, explain to me why they're calling you Mr. O'Dell."

Nicolò folded his arms across his chest. "I need regular updates about Kiley's condition. And since they only discuss a patient's condition if you're a relative, the hospital staff may be operating under the misunderstanding that I'm her husband."

"They what?" Lazz shoved a hand through his hair while he fought a perceptible battle for control. "Don't tell me this is another one of your creative solutions."

"You never complained when my 'creative solutions' worked to Dantes' advantage."

"Damn it, Nicolò!"

"Look, it just happened, okay? They needed information about her and since I had her purse with her identification and medical cards, they leapt to a conclusion I didn't bother correcting, especially since it works to our advantage."

"It works to our advantage right up until someone recognizes you. It isn't like the Dantes are exactly low profile here in San Francisco. Our faces have been plastered all over the gossip magazines in recent months, or have you forgotten that minor detail?"

"Sev, you, and Marco, may have been prominently featured in *The Snitch,* but I've been maintaining a low profile. As for Kiley, I plan to play the part of Mr. O'Dell for the time being. Eventually, I'll straighten everything out. Until then—" Nicolò handed his brother

Kiley's purse "—get her information and give it to our head of security. Tell Juice that I need anything and everything he can discover about her as quickly as possible."

"I'm already ahead of you. I put him on it yesterday."

Nicolò nodded. "Perfect. Also, send someone over to Le Premier. Considering the amount of business we throw their way I don't think the hotel will give you too hard a time about packing up her belongings and checking her out. I want regular updates on this, Lazz. And once Juice's done gathering any surface info on her, I want him to dig for more. Tell him to dig deep. I want to know everything from what size clothes and shoes she wears right down to what brand of makeup she uses. Everything," he stressed. "Got it?"

"Why? What are you planning?"

Nicolò didn't dare answer that one. "It's still fluid."

Lazz shot a hand through his hair. "Aw, hell."

"Look, when I have all the details figured out, I'll let you know. Also, stop by my place and feed and walk Brutus, will you? I don't know how long I'm going to be hung up here."

"You've pulled some wild stunts in your time, but this . . ." Lazz shook his head. "This one makes all the others seem almost normal."

"This stunt won't last long. As soon as she wakes, the jig'll be up and I'll have to finagle some new plan."

"Like a way to get us out from under a massive lawsuit?"

Nicolò's expression fell into grim lines. "That's only a possibility if she ends up blaming me for the accident as much as I blame myself."

"You better hope like hell she doesn't."

The sudden appearance of a nurse saved Nicolò from having to reply. "Excuse me, Mr. O'Dell?"

"How's Kiley?" Nicolò immediately asked, turning his back on his brother.

Compassion darkened the nurse's eyes. "All I can say for certain is that she's stable. The doctor would like to see you and I'm sure he'll fill you in on the particulars." She inclined her head toward a nearby hallway. "If you'll follow me?"

He instantly fell in step with the nurse, only realizing afterward that from the moment she showed up he'd completely forgotten his brother even existed. Turning a corner, the nurse opened the door to a small conference room barely larger than a cubicle.

A doctor sat at a table, making notes in a tight, rapid scribble.

Flipping the chart closed, the man rose and offered Nicolò his hand. "I'm Dr. Ruiz."

"Just give it to me straight. She's alive, right?" Nicolò demanded tightly.

"Alive and stable," Ruiz confirmed. "But she took quite a hit. It was miraculous, given the circumstances, that she didn't break anything. She has various lacerations that we've stitched up and a deep hematoma to her left hip. It's going to be quite painful and make it difficult for her to get around comfortably for a while."

"And the bad news?"

"As you're aware, she experienced a head trauma. A concussion. There's been some minor swelling to her brain, but she's responding to the medications we're giving her to reduce it and all the scans are clear."

"Is she awake?"

The doctor shook his head. "She woke briefly and seemed highly agitated and disoriented. Since then she's been unconscious."

One of the skills that made Nicolò so good at his job was an innate ability to read people. "What aren't you telling me?" he asked.

Ruiz's mouth compressed. "I'm sorry, Mr. O'Dell. Head traumas can be tricky. Until she wakes, we won't know the full extent of her injury. She may be perfectly fine, with perhaps a slight loss of memory from around the time of her accident. Or it could be far more extensive. You should prepare yourself for the worst, and hope for the best."

"When can I see her?"

"She's in intensive care. You can peek in for a minute or two right now. Then I suggest you go home and get some rest. We'll call if there's any change."

Ten minutes later, an ICU nurse escorted him into one of the dozen three-sided rooms that comprised the unit. Kiley appeared small and frail in the bed, with various wires and tubes connected to her, while a dirge of machines beeped softly in the background. He wished she would open her eyes so he could see the vivid color brimming with that unsettling combination of hot awareness and keen intelligence, so he'd know she'd fully recover from her injuries.

He felt the kick that urged him to go to her, to link their hands and complete the bond he felt between them. But he couldn't. Wouldn't. As though sensing a similar awareness despite the drugs sedating her, she stirred restlessly. Clearly, The Inferno—if that's what it was—called to her, as well, for she muttered in whatever twilight land she occupied. Within moments a nurse appeared in response.

"She senses you," she said, before offering a sympathetic smile. "You'll need to go now. If you'll leave a phone number we'll call with any updates."

He did as instructed, but found he couldn't wait for them to contact him, and returned to the hospital first thing the next morning. The ICU nurses all turned to watch him with broad grins that gave him a second's warning before he stepped into Kiley's room and heard her attending doctor say, "Here's your husband now."

Both Nicolò and Kiley froze, staring for an endless moment at each other. Then she shook her head in wild-eyed disbelief. "That's not possible," she denied in no uncertain terms. "There's no way he's my husband."

Nicolò bit back a curse. "Dr. Ruiz—"

"Don't panic, Mr. O'Dell." The doctor tossed a reassuring glance over his shoulder. "We warned you she might have memory issues."

"No. I'd remember if I'd married him," Kiley argued.

"It's all right, Mrs. O'Dell," the doctor said in a soothing voice. "Your loss of memory is a result of your accident."

Nicolò shut his eyes. Time to 'fess up. "She's not—"

The doctor spoke at the same time, his voice rumbling over top of Nicolò's confession. "Kiley, you don't even remember your own name," he said gently. "It's perfectly natural you wouldn't remember you have a husband. I suggest we take this slow and easy. Your memory could come back at any point. Hours. Days. Possibly weeks. In the meantime, we can move you out of ICU and into a regular room while we run a few more tests."

"Why won't you listen to me?" Kiley's gaze landed on Nicolò before flinching away. Tears filled her eyes and her voice rose with each word, growing steadily more shrill and hysterical. "I'm telling you this isn't my husband. He can't be. I'd know if he were."

Ruiz signaled to one of the nurses, who began to prepare an injection. "Mr. O'Dell, I'm afraid I'm going to have to ask you to leave. Once she's had time to calm down and get accustomed to what's happened, you can come back."

Nicolò inclined his head. "Of course. If you'd just give me a second."

He acted without thought, running on sheer instinct, responding to a call no one heard but him. Crossing to Kiley's side, he reached down to take her hand in his. Behind him, Ruiz voiced an objection, while Kiley hissed in dismay as she drew back in a vain attempt to avoid his touch. He ignored everything but the demand screaming through him, one that insisted he finally act on the urge that had been clawing at him since the moment he'd met this woman.

He forcibly took Kiley's hand in his.

The Inferno struck with more ferocity than Nicolò believed possible. Even the machines trilled in momentary alarm before subsiding again into a steady rhythm. Never before had he experienced such a powerful connection. It felt as though every emotion he possessed flowed from his hand into hers before slamming him with a backwash that left him drowning in desire.

He responded without thought. Without giving her time to protest, he bent down and took her mouth in a kiss of utter possession, hard against soft, determination overwhelming uncertainty. She tasted even sweeter than he'd imagined, soft and warm and—after a momentary hesitation—receptive. No. More than receptive. Eager.

He couldn't resist. He swept inward, taking advantage of her unstinting welcome. Never had he felt such a reaction when he'd kissed a woman, as though every aspect of the touch and taste of her had branded him.

A certainty filled him, a certainty that no other woman would ever be quite right for him, except this one. The softest of moans, hungry and eager, slipped from her mouth to his, welcoming him home. And in that moment, he could no longer escape the simple truth.

This woman belonged to him.

Kiley froze at the first touch of her husband's hand, overcome by a sensation so all-consuming, it rendered her speechless. Fiery heat shot from palm to palm, almost painful in its intensity, before settling into a warm, steady connection that soaked deep into that point of melding. Second by second, with each beat of her heart, desire pierced straight through flesh and sinew and bone, until it invaded every part of her. It seemed to lap through her veins, filling her to overflowing with a heavy, irresistible want.

And then he kissed her.

It was a first kiss, worthy of fairy-tale legends. It was also impossible to compare to any that might have come before, since fate had veiled any such occurrences. Even so, she found it the most incredible experience in her very short memory. His mouth ate at hers, his hunger unmistakable, threatening to consume her with that single, unbelievably delectable kiss. Every instinct she possessed screamed to life, telling her this was her man. That he belonged to her and no one else. Her response came without thought or reason. She opened to him, unfurling like a flower beneath the blazing heat of the sun.

He possessed her mouth and she gave back to him with unstinting generosity. In that instant she didn't care who she was, or who this man claimed to be. All that mattered was that this moment never end. Where before all felt alien and unfamiliar, this she recognized. This she knew. Slowly, he pulled back, his breath escaping in a heated rush, his eyes burning with black fire. She could read in his expression all that she felt, a mating of tumultuous emotions.

She sensed on an instinctive level that she and this man had become permanently entangled, heart, body and soul. But how was that possible? How could something as basic as joining hands, or exchanging a single kiss, cause such an undeniable reaction? How could this simple contact bind her to a complete stranger with such relentless power?

Her reaction to his touch told her she knew this man, regardless of what she'd claimed only moments before. Slowly she lifted her gaze to her husband's. Or at least, the man who claimed her for his wife.

Her opinion of him hadn't changed in the few moments since he'd first stepped into her room. He remained fiercely handsome, a god of war, with hair and eyes of the deepest ink and a stare that silenced with a stony glare. He wore his hair longer than convention dictated and it fell to his neck in heavy waves. Maybe they would have tightened into actual curls if he hadn't subdued them, no doubt with a single forbidding look, the kind he currently had trained on the nurses and doctors surrounding them.

"Who are you?" she demanded. She waved away his response before it could even form. "I know you claim you're my husband. I mean, what's your name?"

"Nicolò. You call me Nicolò." A smile warmed the stark coldness of his features, touching a mouth that had left an indelible stamp on her own. "Except when you're angry with me. Then you choose a few more colorful terms of endearment."

"And how often does that happen?"

His smile grew, stunning in its beauty. "Often enough. We both have rather tempestuous personalities."

His gaze lifted to the medical personnel gathered around her bedside and he jerked his head toward the curtain that screened the cubicle. Without a word they filed from the room. It didn't come as any surprise they acquiesced. She had a strong suspicion few dared to argue with Nicolò, and those few who tried, didn't hold out against him for long.

"I'd also like to set one fact straight," he said the moment they were alone. "My name isn't O'Dell, it's Dante. Nicolò Dante. When you were first brought in, everything happened in such a confusing rush I didn't bother to correct the error."

He watched her closely as he gave her this latest piece of information, his penetrating look making it almost impossible to think rationally. "I don't understand," she replied. "If we're married, why do we have different last names?"

He shrugged. "We haven't been married long. And you haven't decided whether or not you want to take on all the baggage associated with mine."

She had questions, so many they spun, jumbled, around in the dark fog of her mind. She seized one at random.

"You said we haven't been married long. How long is 'not long'?"

"Only a few days. It was a whirlwind affair."

For some reason that upset her, possibly because she'd hoped for more. Proof of a lengthy, established history that he could document in word and picture. A connection stretching back across the empty recesses of her mind. Something that would anchor her in this confusing world in which she'd awoken. Instead, he could only offer a mere snippet to sum up the whole of her life.

"A whirlwind affair," she repeated. Her eyes narrowed in thought. "Somehow, Nicolò Dante, you don't strike me as the impulsive sort. I'd have pegged you as a very deliberate sort of guy. Someone who gets what he wants when he wants it, no matter who or what stands in his way. Am I wrong?"

At the question, a mask dropped over his face, sharpening the harshly beautiful features into diamond-hardness. "That's quite an interesting observation after only a minute or two of contact. Or have you remembered something about me?"

Dear Lord, how could she have been so foolish as to wed a man like this? The strength of his personality threatened to overwhelm her, something she wasn't certain she could prevent even if she weren't injured and in a hospital bed. She must have been out of her mind to marry this man, to believe for even one tiny second that she could cage herself with a hungry panther and emerge unscathed. Maybe—in that other forgotten life—she liked challenges. Or maybe she was simply crazy. Time would tell.

"To answer your question, I don't remember you at all," she confessed. "I wish I did, because then I'd understand how I came to be in this predicament." She plucked at the sheet covering her. "And in response to your other comment, I'm basing my assumptions about you on how you managed to clear the room with a single look."

He studied her in silence before conceding her point. "You're right. I do whatever it takes to accomplish my goals. My family will tell you I'm the most impulsive of all of them, since sometimes that's what it takes to succeed. Split-second decisions. Thinking outside the box. Finding a creative solution to an impossible problem."

"And us?" she couldn't help asking, lifting her gaze to clash with his. "How does our relationship fit into that dynamic?"

A hint of rueful amusement drifted through the darkness. "Even if I weren't the impulsive sort, you can tell by your reaction to my touch, there were other considerations."

She could make a fairly accurate guess about one of those considerations. "You mean we were attracted physically." She didn't bother to phrase her observation as a question. There wasn't any question about her reaction to him. Or his to her, for that matter.

He studied her in silence for a long, uncomfortable moment. "Apparently, it's far more than a simple physical attraction, Kiley. It goes deeper than that. If it didn't, my touch wouldn't affect you this way. When you lost your memory, it should have severed all of the connections between us." He held up their linked hands. "And yet, it hasn't."

She blinked in surprise to discover their hands were still joined. Despite the warning signals screaming through her system, she accepted the contact between them. More, she clung to it. "You think I recognize you on a subconscious level?" she asked slowly. "Is that even possible with amnesia?"

Again that hesitation, as though he used great care in choosing his words. Apprehension gathered like a hard, tight ball in the pit of her stomach, and she couldn't help but wonder what he wasn't telling her. Endless bits and pieces she had no way of guessing at, let alone verifying. Everything about her life, about his, about their past and present, even any plans they may have made for the future—the details were his to select, to shade if he so chose, and she'd be forced to accept them at face value. Only one person held the key to all the information comprising her former life, a man she had no choice but to trust. Heaven help her!

"Dr. Ruiz said your memory might return, given time," Nicolò said.

He hadn't answered her question, she noticed. Hadn't explained how or why she recognized him on an unconscious level. But his comment roused a far greater concern. "What if my memory doesn't return?"

He didn't sugarcoat it. "Then you'll have from this moment forward." That gorgeous smile flashed again, completely altering his appearance. "I suspect you'll start to regain bits and pieces of your past before too long, especially considering your reaction to me."

"Which reaction?" she asked with a hint of dry humor. "The part where I became hysterical, or the part where I melted into a heap of lust?"

Her question caught him off guard and a laugh escaped his control, the low rumbling sound like distant thunder. "A heap of lust?"

Her cheeks warmed, but she continued to meet his gaze. "Well, what would you call it?"

"The Inferno."

He spoke so quietly, she almost didn't catch his response. She tasted his words on her tongue, repeating them softly. "The Inferno. That's the perfect description for what I'm feeling." Then she made the connection. "Dante's Inferno? Clever."

"I can't claim the description as my own."

"A family joke?" she said, hazarding a guess.

Again, stillness settled over him and the gaze he fixed on her, so dark and damning, almost made her flinch. "A memory, Kiley?" he asked gently. "Or just a good guess?"

Understanding hit and she inhaled sharply. "My God, you suspect I'm faking amnesia, don't you?"

His expression never eased. Nor did the manner in which he stared at her. "Why would you do that?"

"I don't know. I'm the one with the memory loss, remember? So, you tell me. Let's start with how I was injured," she requested.

Much to her relief, he didn't weigh his words this time. "You were hit by a cab while crossing the street. I came out of the hotel just in time to see it happen."

Now he did pause, but she suspected it had nothing to do with choosing what to say and how to say it. She could tell how badly the accident had affected him, could glimpse the horror and helplessness he'd experienced in those final few seconds before she'd been hit. She wasn't the only one damaged when she'd been struck by that cab. His life had also been irreparably changed.

It took a moment for him to gather his self-control before continuing. "As I said, what possible reason could you have for faking amnesia? It was a stupid, regrettable accident."

"But there's something more. I can see it in your expression. What aren't you telling me?"

"We had a fight right beforehand." The admission came hard. "You left the hotel in a hurry. If I'd stopped you from leaving, or if I hadn't delayed going after you, I might have prevented the accident from happening."

She couldn't mistake his sincerity and something loosened inside of her. Apparently, even hard, powerful men suffered from vulnerabilities. It would seem she was his. "You blame yourself, don't you? For the accident, I mean."

His fingers tightened around hers. "Yes."

"What good would it have done if you'd been with me?" She offered a reassuring smile. "Chances are we'd both have been hit by that cab."

Again, that bleak expression. "Doubtful. It's far more likely I would have prevented the incident from ever occurring."

The absolute certainty in his voice amused her. "I see I've married an arrogant man."

"That isn't arrogance, but fact."

She laughed, the sound a bit rusty, but it felt good, nonetheless. "I believe you just proved my point," she said.

Kiley couldn't say when she accepted Nicolò as her husband. Not at first touch, despite the undeniable connection between them. She'd still been too traumatized by her loss of memory at that point to accept much of anything. Granted, the unmistakable surge of lust had convinced her she and Nicolò were two parts of a whole, clearly connected to each other physically. But that hadn't been enough to convince her they were husband and wife.

Perhaps she'd begun to accept their marriage because of the way she'd clung to him throughout their conversation. Or the scorching pain she'd glimpsed when her husband had described her accident. Or maybe it had been something as silly as his admitting she hadn't decided whether or not to take the Dante name as her own. Whatever the cause, the result was she accepted one undeniable fact. They belonged together.

"What are you thinking?" he asked quietly.

"I'm trying to remember, but . . ."

"But, what?" he prompted.

"I'm afraid." It amazed her she confided in him after only knowing him for mere minutes. Maybe it had been like that when they'd first met. In fact, she was certain it must have been. She could practically see their affair unfold as though part of some romantic dream, where they met and connected and established an instant rapport, both emotional as well as physical. It would explain so much about her current feelings for him. "I'm afraid of what I'll find when I do remember."

"Or not find?"

His perception unnerved her. "That, too."

"Now it's my turn to ask," Nicolò pressed. "There's something else. What aren't you telling me?"

For some odd reason tears gathered in her eyes. "I'm afraid if I go to sleep again, I'll lose more of myself, if that's even possible." She whispered the confession, almost afraid of speaking it aloud in case it gave form and substance to the nightmare. "That it'll be like that movie. You know the one? Where she wakes up each day having to start over again?"

"You mean 50 First Dates?"

"Yes, that's it." Kiley stirred restlessly, an intense throbbing in her hip making her catch her breath before she could go on. "Isn't it ridiculous? I can remember that movie but I can't remember when or where I saw it or who I was with." She shot him a hopeful look. "I don't suppose it was you?"

To her disappointment, he shook his head. "I should warn you we don't know each other all that well. Our relationship really is a whirlwind affair."

She offered a crooked smile, attempting to put the merest hint of shine on a bleak situation. "Then it shouldn't take us long to catch up, should it?"

That won her another grin, one that caused her heartbeat to kick up, a fact duly noted by the surrounding monitors. "Not long at all."

A wave of exhaustion hit her and her eyes began to drift closed. "I'm getting so sleepy. It must be that shot the nurse gave me." Her fingers tightened on his. "Will you still be here when I wake again?"

"I'll be right here. I'm not going anywhere."

So adamant. So solid and reassuring. "Will I remember you?" she managed to ask.

"If you forget, I'll remind you. And if that doesn't work . . ." He lifted her hand to his mouth and pressed a kiss in the center of her palm. "This is one thing you'll never forget."

"You're right. I'll never be able to forget that," she whispered. "Thank you, Nicolò. I'm so glad you're my husband."

And then darkness captured her again.

Chapter Three

"Have you lost your mind?"

Nicolò released his breath in a deep sigh. "I believe that's the same question you asked me last time we had this conversation."

"It bears repeating," Lazz proclaimed. He turned to the oldest Dante brother, Sev, for confirmation. "You can't possibly condone what he's doing?"

"Not even a little," Sev assured. He hesitated for a split second before adding, "Although—"

Lazz shut his eyes. "Oh, no. *Hell,* no. Do not in any way, shape, or form encourage him in this madness."

"It'll give us time to figure out what she's up to," Sev offered. "If she does get her memory back, we'll be prepared. Nicolò will have gathered enough information to put a plan in place."

"Is that straight from legal?" Lazz shot back.

Nicolò fought to keep from massaging his palm. Ever since he'd joined hands with Kiley, he'd been driven by the overwhelming urge to rub the spot where her touch had branded him. It had happened to Sev and Marco after they'd been bonded with their Inferno matches. And now it was happening to him, though he didn't dare let on just yet.

"In case it's escaped your collective notice," he announced, "I'm not asking for anyone's advice or opinion. I'm simply informing you of the latest developments."

"Which includes you continuing to pose as her husband," Lazz barked. "Just what the hell do you suppose will happen when she gets her memory back?"

Nicolò lifted a shoulder in a negligent shrug. "I'll deal with it."

Lazz's twin brother, Marco, spoke up for the first time. "I think the more intriguing question is, what do you intend to do with her if she never regains her memory?" He stared at Nicolò, seeing far too much. "How long do you plan to keep up the pretense? And what do you do with her once you're convinced of her guilt?"

"Or innocence," Nicolò inserted without thought.

Marco's gaze sharpened. "You think that's at all possible?"

Nicolò considered the possibility before reluctantly dismissing it. "No. When we met at Le Premier, I'm positive she was running a con of some sort. With luck, Juice can uncover the truth. In addition to checking into her background, I had him collect her possessions from Le Premier."

"What did he discover?" Sev asked.

"Nothing helpful." Which only made Nicolò's suspicions all the stronger. "We didn't find anything to indicate where she came from immediately preceding our meeting, or whether she has an accomplice. We haven't found an address book, tablet, or so much as a business card. Her cell phone is a disposable. And her driver's license lists an old residence. She moved from that location—Phoenix, to be exact—eighteen months ago and left no forwarding address."

Sev frowned. "That alone should give us pause," he said. "No one maintains that low a profile unless it's for a reason. I assume you told Juice to continue digging?"

"I did. He has instructions to call me with regular updates I can incorporate into what I tell Kiley about our history together. Until then, I intend to keep her close."

Lazz straightened. "I don't like the sound of that. What history? And just how close are you planning to keep her?"

Nicolò spared his brother an impatient look. "Try applying some of that logic you're so fond of. She's supposed to be my wife, remember? When she's released tomorrow, I'm bringing her home with me. I've already transferred her possessions to my house and have created an entire history of how, when, where, and why the two of us hooked up." All three of Nicolò's brothers shot to their feet, arguing at once. He waited until they ran out of steam before speaking again. "She's still recovering from a serious accident. She has no memory and no one to help her—except her husband."

"What if she's faking amnesia?" Lazz asked.

"Or is running part two of her con?" Marco added.

Nicolò's expression hardened. Then he'd see she regretted playing him for a fool for a long time to come. "All the more reason to have her where I can keep an eye on her. She believes I'm her husband. I intend to play the part to the hilt until I have a damn good reason not to. So far, none of you have offered me one. Once Juice has figured out the truth, we'll decide how to proceed from there."

"Do you have any idea the sort of trouble this could cause?" Lazz demanded.

Nicolò released a laugh, the sound ripe with irony. "It's going to cause more trouble than you can possibly imagine. Unfortunately, I don't have a choice."

The Inferno had seen to that.

"This is where you live?"

"We," Nicolò corrected gently. "This is where *we* live."

"Oh, right." Kiley stared up at the elegant turn-of-the-century Victorian. From deep inside the recesses of Nicolò's—*their*—home came a thundering bass woof that succeeded in rattling the stained-glass windowpanes bookending the front door. She swallowed. "What was that?"

"Ah." A brief smile came and went. "That would be a who. Brutus, to be specific."

"Brutus," she repeated faintly. "And what sort of creature is a Brutus?"

"Dog."

"Huh. It sounds more like a cross between a moose and a lion."

"That would be about right." He waited until she swiveled to face him in wide-eyed dismay before relenting. "He's a St. Bernard. Very gentle."

Time would tell. She took a deep breath and faced the front door once again. She slanted her husband a final glance. "I don't suppose you know whether I like dogs?"

"You love dogs," he stated categorically. "And you're crazy about Brutus. Everyone's crazy about Brutus."

"If you say so."

Nicolò slid his key into the lock and opened the door. A series of thuds drummed through the soles of her shoes as Brutus approached at a dead run. He reached the parquet flooring in the foyer and the speed of his forward momentum sent him skidding across the glossy wood. He slid to a stop inches from where she and Nicolò stood.

Kiley remained frozen in place, utterly petrified by the mammoth animal who probably topped her by a solid hundred pounds and appeared capable of swallowing her whole in a single gulp. The top of his head hovered at shoulder height and every inch of his massive body rippled with hard, lean muscle, while his rich, multicolored coat gleamed with health. He was a gorgeous animal, though right now she found it difficult to summon much appreciation for that fact in the face of overwhelming terror.

Nicolò dropped to his knees and performed some sort of ritualistic man/dog bonding game that had her backpedaling as fast as her aching hip would allow until her spine hit the front door. If she could have melted into the wood and out the other side, she would have.

"Nicolò," she whispered.

He glanced over his shoulder and frowned. "What's wrong?"

She fought to speak around a bone-dry throat. "I think the amnesia may have screwed up my dog appeal."

Nicolò came to his feet, creating a solid barrier between her and his dog. "Don't be afraid. I swear, Brutus is the gentlest animal in the world."

"It's just . . ." She swallowed. "He's so big."

"Yeah, he is," Nicolò agreed. He made a hand signal and in response Brutus dropped instantly to the floor in a sphinxlike pose. "So, we'll take this nice and slow. I'm right here beside you, and I won't let anything bad happen."

"Thanks." He held out his hand and Kiley took it without a second thought. She even allowed herself to be drawn toward the dog, who didn't so much as twitch a muscle. "Why isn't he moving?" It was downright unnerving.

"I've trained him not to." Nicolò offered a reassuring smile. "You're not the first person to be intimidated by his size. So I taught him certain behaviors that make him more approachable and less overwhelming."

"You're going to try and get us to be friends now, aren't you?" she asked with a marked lack of enthusiasm.

"Yup." He sent the dog another hand gesture and Brutus dropped his head onto his enormous front paws. Huge melting brown eyes peered up at Kiley. "Kiley, this is Brutus. Close your hand in a fist and just put it in front of his nose so he can smell you. Don't worry, he'll recognize your scent."

It took every ounce of nerve to do as Nicolò instructed and stoop in front of the huge animal. Closing her eyes and praying she wasn't about to lose half her arm, she lowered her fist to within a few feet of Brutus's snout. The dog's nose twitched and he sniffed her hand. His tail thumped in recognition and he squirmed close enough to lick her. It was as though someone had flicked a light switch. The fear didn't completely disappear, but how could she resist the sweetness exuding from Brutus?

She gave in to temptation and scratched behind his ears. After a few short minutes, her sore hip forced her to her feet and she gingerly stood with an assist from Nicolò. "His coat is so soft," she marveled. "Especially around his ears."

"Don't let him fool you. He's a cagey beast."

"Cagey?"

"It's all about food with this one. Be careful when you're eating because he'll find a way to distract you so he can snitch your meal off your plate." Nicolò interlaced his hand with hers. "Come on. Why don't I take you on the grand tour?"

"I'd love to see the place."

With Brutus leading the way, Nicolò escorted her through the lower rooms, featuring a generous-sized kitchen with a small table set in a bow window, a formal dining room off the kitchen, as well as a beautifully decorated living area. Deeper in, he showed her what was clearly his favorite room, a large den with built-in bookcases, a mile-wide plasma TV and a couch with cushions as soft and comfortable as down.

His cell phone rang right before they headed upstairs and, with a word of apology, he took the call. "What have you found out, Juice?" He listened for a long minute. "Any family other than . . . ? Got it. No, that's quite helpful, thanks. Just what I needed." He disconnected the call and offered Kiley one of the smiles that never failed to ignite a flame of intense awareness. "Sorry. Business update I've been waiting for."

"No problem."

Nicolò paused in the doorway of a large bedroom gilded by late afternoon sunlight. Leaning against the doorjamb, he waited while she circled the room. "This one's yours. I thought you'd be more comfortable having a room to yourself. At least for the time being."

Surprise held Kiley frozen for a split second. "That's very thoughtful of you," she murmured.

She didn't dare tell him it didn't feel comfortable at all. Instead, it made her feel all the more alone. On the other hand, did she really want to spend the night in his bed? Despite her instinctive reaction to him—an all-consuming passion that defied understanding—they'd only known each other for a few days, at least to the best of her current recollection. Her husband was being incredibly sensitive by not forcing them into an intimate relationship until she'd had time to adjust to their marriage. This situation must be every bit as difficult for him as it was for her.

Nicolò crossed to the closet and opened the double doors. "Your clothes are in here, as well as in the dresser."

Curiosity filled Kiley and she joined him, eager to see what sort of clothing she normally wore, hoping it might help her pick up clues to her personality. The wardrobe was stuffed full, with something for every occasion, though most of the items still had tags dangling from them.

"Why is everything brand new?" she asked.

"You're a Dante now. You needed clothing to match."

She examined the outfits a second time and inhaled sharply. "Nicolò, these are all designer labels. They must have cost the earth."

He shrugged. "That's what you wear. Take back whatever you don't like. You also warned me some of them would need to be altered before they could be worn." He gave her an odd look. "I thought you'd be delighted by a brand-new wardrobe."

Did she sound ungrateful? She bit down on her lip, struggling for something appropriate to say. "Thank you," she managed. "These are all gorgeous."

"And yet . . ." He tilted his head to one side, fixing those unnerving dark eyes on her, eyes that seemed to see straight down into her soul. "I can tell you're less than thrilled."

"It's just a little overwhelming." She spared the closet an uncomfortable glance. "I'll adjust in time," she said, before adding beneath her breath, "Maybe."

So, why the knee-jerk reaction to the unexpected riches? Why did she shrink from the beauty and luxury of what he'd shown her? She couldn't explain it. It just felt wrong, as if she'd fallen into someone else's life and didn't have a clue how to get back to her own.

Nicolò caught her left hand in his and she stilled, overcome by the burn of The Inferno. This she understood. This grounded and centered her. His touch. Her reaction to his touch. That remarkable kiss they'd shared. The need that clawed at her, insisting they complete what they'd started. More than anything she wanted to walk out of this room and into the bedroom she'd once shared with him. Where she belonged.

Before she could put thought to action, he said, "There's one other thing missing."

You, she wanted to say. His mouth on hers. His skin against her skin. Taking her and making her his. "What's missing?"

He lifted her hand. "Your wedding rings."

Her eyes widened in alarm. "Did I lose them in the accident?"

"As I mentioned, our wedding was a spur-of-the-moment affair. We were supposed to buy our rings the day you were injured."

Her brows drew together. "Oh, how sad."

"Don't worry. We'll get it taken care of as soon as you've recovered." He offered a crooked smile. "We'll make a special day of it. How about that?"

She hesitated. "Are you sure you don't want to wait until I get my memory back?"

"I hadn't considered that." Again came his penetrating look. "Do you think you'll change your mind about the style between now and then?"

She spared an uneasy glance toward the closet. "It's possible. Maybe our tastes are formed by our past experiences. I wouldn't want to make any decisions I'll regret later."

"If you change your mind later, we'll simply replace the rings."

"Just like that?" she marveled, before confronting him. "As though they had no meaning? As though one ring is as good as another? Tell me something, Nicolò, is that what you believe? More to the point, is that what I believed?"

He shook his head. "We never discussed it."

"No, of course not. Why would we?" Who could have imagined something like this happening? Or made contingency plans in the event it did. "I'll tell you what, let's stick with something simple. Something along the line of a plain pair of bands. If we change our mind later on, we can choose rings that strike us as more meaningful."

"You don't have to make a decision right now. You never know. You might see something you fall in love with when we go to the shop." He opened the top dresser door and removed a small square box. "Here. This is yours. You were wearing it the day of your accident."

She took the box from him, surprised by the weight of it. Removing the top, she found an intricate silver locket on a matching chain. "It's beautiful." She shot him a hopeful glance. "Did you give this to me?"

"I can't take credit for that, I'm afraid. It's your favorite piece of jewelry. A family heirloom, I believe."

"It does appear old." She turned it over, searching for a hinge. "It looks like it should open, but I don't see how. Do you know?"

He shook his head. "If it opens, you never showed me the secret. If you're curious, we can take it to a jeweler and see if they can figure it out."

"That's a good idea." She held the locket out to him. "Would you mind putting it on?"

He took the necklace and she turned, sweeping her hair aside so he could fasten the chain around her neck. She caught a brief glimpse of herself in the huge antique mirror hanging above the dresser and it gave her a start. From the moment she'd first seen her reflection in the hospital, it never failed to surprise her.

"What is it?" Nicolò asked as he fastened the locket in place.

The instant he finished, she turned her back on her image. "Nothing." She offered a bright smile. "Everything's terrific."

She could tell he didn't buy it. He dropped his hands to her shoulders and forced her to face her reflection once again. "Why do you have so much difficulty looking at yourself?"

"I guess because I see the sort of woman I wish I were." She released a frustrated laugh. "That sounds bizarre, doesn't it?"

"A little." He eased her hair back from her face so it poured down her back. "You don't have to wish to be the woman you see. You are her."

"You don't understand."

His hands tightened on her shoulders, giving them a gentle squeeze. "Then explain it to me."

"This is so frustrating. I don't even remember what I look like. The first time I saw myself in a mirror—"

"It was like looking at a complete stranger?"

"Yes!" She started to swivel around again, but he wouldn't let her. Instead, she met his gaze in the mirror, his midnight black, hers springtime green. "I keep staring at myself, trying to discover some clue to my personality. And the best I can come up with is that I seem . . . nice."

"I'd call you beautiful." He tilted his head. "Part pixie and part angel."

The color deepened in her cheeks, betraying her reaction to his words. "I meant character, as well as appearance. I'm pretty. Maybe even more than pretty. But I look . . ." She stared at herself.

For some reason his expression went blank. "Nice."

She couldn't help grinning. "Yes. Don't misunderstand. That's a good thing. I want to be a nice person. I feel nice." She touched a spot just above her heart, close to where her locket nestled. "Inside."

"Then you must be," he informed her lightly. "Otherwise I wouldn't have married you."

She relaxed within his embrace. "I'm relieved to hear you say it." Then she stiffened as another thought occurred to her. "But what if I've changed because of the amnesia? What if I'm not the same person I was before? What if I turn into a class A bitch or start throwing temper tantrums or pilfering the silver?"

In the mirror, she saw his eyes narrow and it caused her heart to give a small jump. "Are you feeling any larcenous urges?" he asked.

"Not even a little, but—"

"Not a little niggle to stick a silver fork in your back pocket?"

Her lips quivered. "None," she confessed.

"Any urge to throw things or call me foul names?"

The smile forming on her mouth grew. "Not yet."

He dropped a kiss on the top of her head. "Good. Then you don't have anything to worry about."

She turned and this time he didn't try and stop her. Her smile faded. "But, aren't our personalities formed by the events and circumstances of our past?

Since I don't have any background notes to draw from—"

"Then you'll have to rely on your instincts and allow yourself to live your life the way that feels right."

Frustration ate at her. "You make it sound so simple."

"It is that simple. Do what feels right inside." He brushed the back of his hand along the curve of her cheek. "Why don't you rest and I'll order up some dinner."

For some reason, that amused her, which helped break the tension. "I gather you don't cook?"

"I can manage toast, if forced. I leave the kitchen to experts like Marco and my grandfather."

"Marco's a brother?" she guessed.

"One of three older brothers." He ticked off on his fingers. "Sev, the eldest. Then there's Marco and Lazz, who are twins. We were raised by my grandparents, Primo and Nonna. Then there's a slew of cousins and the odd sister-in-law or two."

A sudden thought struck and she couldn't believe it hadn't occurred to her before this. "What about me?" she asked eagerly. "Do I have any relatives?"

He shook his head. "You don't have any brothers or sisters, and your father died when you were a baby. Your mother's still around, but I haven't been able to locate her. Don't panic," he added, when she started to do just that. "According to what you've told me, it's not unusual for her to take off for weeks at a time. You said she travels a lot."

Her excitement dimmed, replaced by dismay. So she really did have no one. Or next to no one. "It doesn't sound as though I have a very close relationship with my mother, if I lose track of her for weeks on end."

Imagine if she'd never met Nicolò. If they'd never fallen in love and married. She'd have been utterly alone dealing with the aftermath of her accident, with no memory and no family to help her. She shivered in distress. He must have read her thoughts, or maybe they were mirrored on her face.

"You have my family," he told her gruffly, "even if I haven't had an opportunity to introduce you to everyone."

"Our relationship developed that fast?" she asked uneasily.

"You're looking worried again. Don't be. There'll be plenty of time to meet them once you've had a chance to recover."

"And if I don't recover?" she asked, tension underscoring the question.

He smiled. "Since you never met any of them before, it'll be a new experience for both old and new Kiley."

"Huh." The concept intrigued her. "Old and new. That's an interesting way to look at it."

Nicolò frowned in concern. "You're exhausted, aren't you? And I can tell just looking at you that your headache has started up again. Probably from all the worrying." He nudged her in the direction of the bed. "Get some sleep. I'll be close by if you need me."

Without thought, Kiley lifted her mouth for his kiss, only a split second later realizing what she'd done. She caught a momentary glimpse of something dart through his gaze, a hint of surprise mingling with an intense desire. And then his head dipped downward.

Before, in the hospital, he'd consumed her, his need a hard, driven thing. This time the kiss came softly, leisurely, but no less powerful for all that. She shuddered within his hold, reveling in the hot spice of his kiss, as swept away this time as she'd been the first.

He tugged her closer, exploring the curves of her body as he deepened their kiss. He cupped her breasts through the knit material of her shirt, thumbing the tips until they tightened into hard, rigid peaks. Before she could do more than gasp in reaction, he slipped beneath her knit shirt to investigate further.

His hands spread across the narrow expanse of her waist and the inch of sensitive skin between the gap of shirt and jeans before finding her breasts again. He teased them through her bra, the slide of the thin silk across the aching peaks almost more than she could stand. He must have realized as much because he dragged his fingertips in a torturous path to her hips, his fingers just curving around her flanks.

She could feel his erection surging against her belly and his mouth grew more determined, driving instead of teasing. His hands began to move again, restlessly exploring the curve of her backside, lightly tracing the flare of her hips before sliding to cup her where her need burned hottest. She wanted him. Heaven help her, but she wanted him to rip away her clothes and spread her on the bed behind them and give her the relief her body wept for.

She sensed he hovered on the very edge of control. They teetered there for an endless moment, locked together, on the verge of taking that final, irrevocable step. At the last instant, he released her and stepped back. But it cost him, his expression drawn into taut lines of pain.

"Sleep," he told her, the single word shredded almost beyond recognition. "You need sleep far more than this."

Kiley would have argued, but exhaustion fell over her like a blanket and she did as he suggested, curling up on top of the bed. If she'd had any doubts about their relationship, Nicolò had put them to rest in the past few minutes. How was it possible that it only took one touch from the man? A single touch and she melted in mindless desire. No way would she do that unless on some level she recognized and trusted him.

She smiled sleepily. He had a knack for easing her fears, helping her to deal with her memory loss. She doubted she'd have been able to get through this if she'd been on her own. But with her husband by her side, she felt she could tackle just about any adversity. She yawned.

How had she gotten so lucky?

The sound of gunshots woke Nicolò and sent him leaping from the bed and racing into the hallway. It was only then he realized the noise came from the downstairs TV. After checking Kiley's room and finding it empty, he headed for the steps, surprised to discover every light in the house ablaze. He followed the trail of lights to the kitchen, turning them off as he progressed through the house.

Earlier, he'd planned to wake Kiley when their dinner arrived. But he'd found her sleeping so soundly, he didn't have the heart to disturb her. Leaving a note seemed the best option, and it had worked, since a quick check of the refrigerator told him that she'd polished off the Chinese leftovers. He was less pleased to discover Brutus had cleaned out everything else. Greedy mutt. It would seem this new version of Kiley was an easy touch, and Brutus sensed as much.

Next, he turned off the trail of lights leading through the dining room, into the living room and finally to the den. And that's where he found her. She and Brutus were curled up together on his couch, both sound asleep and utterly oblivious to the raging gunfight from a 40s gangster movie playing on the television.

She'd donned one of the nightgowns and robes he'd bought during her hospital stay, the robin's egg-blue setting off the vividness of her hair and the creamy paleness of her skin. She'd forked her fingers deep into Brutus's coat, her hand fine-boned and delicate against the huge, muscular dog. Brutus lay curled protectively around her, his breath escaping in deep, rumbling snores.

The desire Nicolò had felt earlier came storming back, just as messy and uncontrollable and incomprehensible as before. He hesitated, no more than an inch away from ripping off her nightgown and covering her body with his own. She wouldn't resist. Hell, based on her reaction a few scant hours ago, she'd open to him as sweetly now as she'd done then. He took a single step in her direction before he caught the violent purple bruising along the back of her shoulder.

He sucked in a shuddering breath and crossed to turn off the television, which instantly woke Kiley. Or maybe it was his lifting her in his arms that disturbed her slumber. He carried her from the room, much to the annoyance of a disgruntled Brutus.

"Where are we going?" she asked, wrapping her arms around Nicolò's neck and yawning broadly.

Her scent drifted to him, light and feminine and unmistakably her own. "Back to bed," he answered her question.

"Oh." She wrinkled her nose. "I'd really rather not."

That gave him pause. "You prefer sleeping with my dog?"

She hesitated, a heart-wrenching vulnerability sweeping across her face and shadowing her eyes. Nicolò found it difficult to believe she could fake the expression, especially straight out of a sound sleep. But perhaps he wasn't the best judge. At least, not right here and now.

"I'd rather not sleep alone," she confessed. "It's not that I'm afraid. Not exactly. It's just I don't like being by myself. I'm not used to it."

"I can solve that problem for you."

It was inevitable. It had been from the minute he'd first seen her. First touched her. First claimed her as his own. One way or another she was destined to end up in his bed. Better sooner than later.

"Are you taking me to our bedroom?"

"Yes."

"Will you sleep with me?"

"Without question." Even if it meant an eternity of hellfire and damnation.

She snuggled deeper into his hold. "That's okay then."

Nicolò shouldered through the door to his bedroom suite and crossed to the bed. He deposited her there, struck by how small and fragile she appeared curled up on his king-sized mattress. Maybe that's how she succeeded with her cons, by looking so utterly innocent. She blinked sleepily up at him and smiled.

"Aren't you coming back to bed?" she asked.

"I am. Although, now that I have you here . . ." He tilted his head to one side and studied her. "What will I do with you?"

Chapter Four

"I can tell you exactly what you should do with me," Kiley replied.

Desire flashed through Nicolò. "And what's that?"

Unable to resist, he joined her in the bed and scooped her close, cushioning her head against his shoulder. There was something different about her, he realized. A quality that hadn't been there when they'd first met, as well as a quality that had vanished as completely as her memory. And then it hit him.

The cunning he'd seen in that other version of Kiley was missing. And in its place sparkled kindness and generosity and an openness he suspected would have been utterly foreign to her nature only a few short days ago.

Of course, it could all be an act, a brilliant charade to keep him off balance. But if she were faking amnesia, he was absolutely certain he'd have caught her "tell," just as he had in the hotel room during their first confrontation. He'd have noticed some small indication of subterfuge. So far there had been none.

She curled into his embrace, fitting her curves to his angles as though it were the most natural thing in the world. As though they'd slept like this a thousand times before. For an instant they both stilled, and Nicolò became intensely aware of the intimacy of their position. He could hear her slow, shallow breathing and feel the slide of silk against his side, along with the pressure of her small, rounded breasts. Cautiously, her hand crept across his chest settling just above his heart.

More than anything, he wanted to flip her onto her back and fill her to overflowing, to take her with mouth and body. To join with her in that ultimate dance of pleasure. Nothing mattered except that he have her here and now, in his arms. He'd worry about the ramifications of his actions later. When Juice turned in his report proving Kiley's guilt. When Kiley regained her memory. When all his outrageous mistakes hit the fan, he'd find a way around it. Because that's what he did. That's what he'd always done. In the meantime, why shouldn't they enjoy what fate had so generously provided? He should take the offering and enjoy it to the fullest, and to hell with the consequences.

But he couldn't. She'd only been released from the hospital mere hours ago, he reminded himself. She had bruises on top of bruises. And most damning of all . . .

She was a con artist.

It didn't matter that The Inferno shrieked through him, clawing at him to take that final step of possession. It didn't matter that Kiley seemed equally inclined to make the ultimate commitment. He couldn't trust this woman, didn't dare believe that any of this was real. He'd put his family's well-being at risk if he fell for her game. Though right this minute he almost— *almost*— didn't give a damn.

She stroked her fingertips across his chest in tiny, tantalizing circles. "I know exactly what you should do with me," she repeated. "It occurred to me while I was downstairs." The softest laugh escaped her, her breath caressing his chin and neck and wreaking havoc with his self-control. "I'd like to start over."

Okay, not quite what he'd expected. He caught her hand in his before he lost it completely. "Start over," he repeated.

She nodded, eagerness brightening her eyes. "It occurred to me when I was getting reacquainted with Brutus. You see, I don't remember any of my previous interactions with him."

Maybe because there hadn't been any. The only reason Brutus had recognized her scent when he'd first introduced them was because he'd allowed the dog to sniff some of her possessions after he'd had them transferred into his house. "When your memory returns, all that will be resolved," Nicolò offered. Of course, when her memory returned, he'd be the one in the doghouse.

"No. I can't wait for that. I have to live my life now." She regarded him in all seriousness. "I don't remember any of my interactions with Brutus, any more than I remember our interactions. I can't ask Brutus what happened."

He found himself giving her back a sympathetic stroke. "But you can ask me."

Determination filled her expression, and perhaps a hint of desperation, as well. "I want to do more than ask. And that's where my idea comes in."

He needed to stop touching her and soon. But even as the thought dawned, Nicolò found himself tucking a strand of her hair behind her ear, his fingers lingering on the silky curve of her cheek. "Tell me your idea."

"You said ours was a whirlwind affair." She waited for his nod of confirmation before continuing. "So that means it wouldn't be too difficult to reenact, right?"

Aw, hell. "Reenact, as in create all over again?" he asked.

She smiled and he suddenly realized that her smile was a tiny bit crooked, her lips tugging ever so slightly to the right. For some odd reason, he found the imperfection all too appealing. "Exactly. We can recreate our first meeting, and each of our subsequent dates. Best of all, maybe it'll help me remember."

Actually, it was a very clever idea, one that would provide her with endless amusement if she were faking amnesia. Considering they didn't have a history, other than that one disastrous meeting at Le Premier, he'd find it impossible to come up with anything real, which left creating some ridiculous fantasy.

Everything within him flinched from the idea. He'd been dishonest enough by claiming her as his wife. Granted, The Inferno had united him with this woman, and perhaps if circumstances had been different he might have pursued a serious relationship in order to see where it might take them. But no way in hell would he permanently connect himself with a con artist.

The reminder of who and what she was stiffened his resolve. He'd put this game in motion for a reason. A very simple, extremely vital reason. If Kiley O'Dell succeeded with her scam, she could conceivably claim half the value of the fire diamond mine and the Dante family jewelry empire would go under.

He had to play out this game until he had proof of her true nature. Unfortunately, his physical reaction to her complicated matters.

"Nicolò?" She looked far less excited than moments before. "What's wrong? Don't you like my idea?"

"I love your idea."

"Then will you do it?"

He was digging himself deeper and deeper into an inescapable hole. How would he justify his actions if Juice proved her innocence? He couldn't. And when she recovered her memory, those actions would cause her unfathomable pain.

But then, he didn't believe for one minute she was an innocent in all this, not based on her actions and attitude that day at Le Premier. That woman and the one currently in his arms bore no relationship to each other. Until the two melded together once again, he'd follow the course he'd set for himself. For both of them. In fact, if he played this the way she requested, he might be able to prove what she was, as well as the truth behind her claim of amnesia.

"Yes, I'll do it," he agreed. "We'll start all over again."

He could feel her relief. "Where did we first meet?"

"In the park," he answered promptly, following the history he'd scripted in anticipation of this conversation. "I was walking Brutus."

"And what was I doing there?"

"Sitting. You'd just moved to the city in order to begin a new job. Unfortunately, the company folded the week after you started."

"You took pity on me, didn't you?"

The fantasy she'd created to fill in the holes in her memory showed an impressive ingenuity and amazed the hell out of him. Unfortunately, the warmth with which she regarded him left him stirring in discomfort.

"Brutus and I both did," he said, forcing out the lie. "We cheered you up with a rousing game of Frisbee."

"Then tomorrow that's what we'll do. We'll go to the park and play Frisbee."

"Actually, we won't."

"But—"

He shook his head. "You're less than a day out of the hospital. We're not doing anything that risks putting you back there again. Frisbee is out." When she would have argued further, he added, "It was just a brief encounter, Kiley. I have an alternate suggestion, if you're willing."

"Which is?"

"I'll recreate our times together, if that's how you want to play the game." And this very well could be a game for her, he reminded himself. "In return, you don't ask any questions beforehand. Let events unfold naturally."

"I don't understand. Why?"

"Because this way you don't have any preconceived expectations. You can just be yourself and enjoy the occasion. There won't be any 'did I do this' or 'did I say that?' You can just take it as it happens and respond naturally."

"But I don't know what's natural for me," she argued.

"Then go with what feels right."

She hesitated, considering, before giving a reluctant nod. "I guess I can do that. Are you sure we can't start tomorrow?"

He shook his head. "We wait until the doctor clears you for normal activity."

She grinned, her mouth taking on that lopsided slant again. "In that case, I'll call Ruiz first thing tomorrow."

Nicolò considered for a moment, then shrugged. "If he gives you the okay, I'm fine with it. But I'll need a little time to set everything up."

And the first thing he'd set up would be a few "dates" that would help him determine whether or not she truly had amnesia, while giving Juice additional time to complete his background check. Dates that would prove she was a woman who craved the good life and all the expensive accessories that went with it. Until then . . .

He stretched out his arm and flicked off the light. "Try and sleep." Because heaven knew, he wouldn't. Not with her in his bed, wrapped around him, while he couldn't do more than plant a chaste kiss on her brow.

She stirred against him, threatening to shred his ability for any sort of chaste embrace. Or so he thought until she said, "I—I don't like it this dark."

"I'm right here," he said, reassuring her. "I won't let anything happen to you. But if you'd be more comfortable with the light on . . ." He reached for the lamp again. "Better?"

"Do you mind?" Her eyes turned so shadowed they were almost as black as his own. "Ever since the accident—"

"What?" He threaded his fingers through her hair, careful to avoid the stitches from her injury. "Do you remember something?"

"No, it's not that." She moistened her lips. "As long as I can remember— which, granted, isn't long—it's never been this dark or so quiet. Hospitals are noisy, busy places. Until I woke up in your guest bedroom, I don't ever remember being alone before. I didn't like it."

It took him a moment to reply. "There's an easy fix to that. From now on, you sleep here with me and we leave a light on."

A hint of uncertainty swept across her expressive features. "Are you sure you don't mind?"

"Not even a little."

He continued to hold her until she drifted off, calling himself six kinds of fool. He watched as she slept, memorizing every curve and angle of her face. She was out cold, no faking that, so relaxed and trusting within his embrace.

She'd regained some of her color, her cheeks carrying a light flush instead of that frightening waxy pallor she'd worn during her hospital visit. And her hair fell in heavy curls across her shoulders and his bared chest, the soft, springy feel of it sheer torture.

Her lips were parted ever so slightly, making him long to sample them again, to delve inward and invade that honeyed warmth. To see if she tasted as sweet and rich as before or if he'd imagined it.

How could someone who looked so innocent be so amoral? Every instinct he possessed insisted she was telling the truth. That her amnesia was real. If he only had himself to consider, he'd take the risk. But his responsibilities encompassed far more than himself, and that meant he needed to use extreme caution. He had to remain on his guard every second, especially during moments like these. Intimate, private, vulnerable moments that someone experienced in running a con could turn to her advantage.

He closed his eyes, wishing he had the ability to trust. Wishing that he could believe in things like The Inferno and second chances and the goodness of human nature. But in his capacity as Dantes' troubleshooter he'd experienced far too much of the opposite to ever take such a leap of faith.

Even as the thought lingered in his mind, he settled her more firmly within his hold, his embrace equal parts possessive and protective. And as he joined her in sleep, one word sounded louder than all the others.

Mine.

Three endless days passed before Kiley received the official okay from Dr. Ruiz to resume normal activities. He also gave her the name of a doctor who specialized in retrograde amnesia, though she hoped she wouldn't need his services. Instead, she preferred to trust that with her husband's help, her memory would return on its own. It was just a matter of when.

She wished she could explain how disoriented she felt. Nicolò knew everything about her, while she knew nothing. Nothing about herself. Nothing about her likes and dislikes. Nothing about her personality or hopes or dreams. It put her in a position of reacting to all that went on around her instead of driving or controlling events. It also forced her to trust implicitly, which filled her with uncertainty and fear.

Every aspect of her life ended in a giant question mark. And every time she had to ask a question about herself and the appropriateness of her actions, or about mist-shrouded events from her past, or unremembered plans for her future, it left her both dependent and vulnerable.

Well, at least she could state two things with absolute certainty. First, she didn't like feeling either dependent or vulnerable. So, with each day that passed, she intended to make strides to put some distance between herself and those particular characteristics. To find a way to win back control over her life.

And second, despite her inability to recall the details of her previous life, her feelings toward her husband hadn't changed. It offered untold relief she felt such a powerful hunger toward the man at her side. That she couldn't wait to be with him, held safe within his arms. To kiss him again. To relive that joy of loving and being loved. And to uncover all the secrets he kept hidden from the rest of the world, secrets he'd probably shared with her, and her alone, if only she could remember.

She wanted him. Needed him. And she had little doubt that they'd act on those desires before very much longer. Soon she'd experience anew those soul-stirring emotions when he made love to her for the first time. Maybe in those intensely intimate moments her memory would return.

She could only hope.

"I'm sure everything will come back to me if we recreate our dates," she told Nicolò. "It's bound to spark something, right?"

"It's quite possible."

Her enthusiasm dimmed. "Do you think the fact I haven't had any flashes of recall so far means it won't return?"

He instantly wrapped his arms around her. "Not at all. And now that you've been given the all-clear, we'll see what memories we can shake loose."

They decided to skip their first meeting in the park and move on to their first "real" date. To Kiley's dismay, it didn't go quite the way she'd hoped. The day started off well enough. Her excitement at their implementing her plan carried her through the first couple hours as they toured the delights of San Francisco.

Nicolò took her to all the top tourist spots—Fisherman's Wharf and Ghirardelli Square with its view of Alcatraz Island, for a ride on the cable cars that rumbled through Chinatown and past Lombard Street, topped with a drive through Golden Gate Park. It was an exhausting array of sights and sounds, odors and impressions. Unfortunately, not one place incited more than a faint glimmer of recognition in the murky recesses of her mind, an awareness she'd read about or seen pictures of the city at some point.

And with every stop, she glanced toward Nicolò, hoping against hope to gain some clue as to that first time. Despite her promise to him, she wanted to ask if this occasion matched the one from the past. Had they said the same things? Had they laughed or talked or shared confidences then, all the important tidbits they weren't sharing this time around because she was too empty to have anything worth contributing?

Eventually, he became aware of her growing silence and sideways looks. "What's wrong?" he asked.

She collapsed on a park bench with a weary sigh. "This isn't working quite the way I'd thought it would."

He joined her on the bench. "You don't remember anything? Not necessarily our time together, but I hoped you might remember one of the places we've been. That it might spark some vague memory."

She shook her head, frustrated beyond belief. "I don't remember a blessed thing," she confessed. "Not any of the tourist spots." She spared him a swift, reluctant glance. "Not being with you. Ever."

He lowered his head. "I'm sorry, Kiley."

She covered his hand with hers. "None of this is your fault." He opened his mouth to argue and she cut him off. "I know you want to take responsibility for my accident. But you have to admit that if I'd been less impulsive, I wouldn't have been in the middle of a busy intersection where I could be hit by a cab."

She watched him struggle with that for a moment. "Why don't we agree to disagree on that particular subject?" he suggested with a grim smile.

Her return smile attempted to tease away his seriousness. "I can live with that." His hand tightened on hers, tugging her close. She slid into his hold with the ease of familiarity and tilted her head to one side in consideration. "What next? Do we continue with our tour? Or can you think of something else that might help me remember?"

He hesitated, before nodding. "There's one more place that might prompt a memory."

"And where's that?"

He gave her the sort of grin that threatened to melt her bones. No doubt it was the same smile he'd used during those earlier dates, if only she could recall. All he had to do was switch it on her and she could feel everything soft and feminine surrendering to him, softening, urging her to agree to anything he might ask of her.

"Come on. I'd rather it be a surprise."

He drove them from the park into the heart of the city toward the financial district and Embarcadero. Beneath one of the towering skyscrapers, he pulled into an underground parking lot and escorted her to a private elevator that shot them straight to a penthouse suite. When the doors parted, they stepped out into a massive room, which at first glance appeared to be someone's private residence.

Kiley entered ahead of Nicolò, sinking into the thick, plush carpet, the soft dove-gray color lending the area an opulent, yet intimate feel. There were several divans decorated in a subtle pinstripe of gray and white, accented with a narrow band of black, and silk chairs in a rich ruby red. The pieces were simple, yet exquisite.

Glass tables were arranged in front of the divans and chairs, sitting slightly higher than conventional coffee tables. The lighting also struck her as different, overhead spots creating blazing puddles of brilliance that struck the various tables, while the seats remained in soft shadow. Plants and elaborate fresh flower arrangements gave the area an added warmth.

"What is this place?" she whispered.

"Dantes Exclusive." Was it her imagination or did his gaze grow as intense as the spotlights?

"Dantes? I don't . . ." She shook her head in confusion. "Is this your family business?"

"You haven't heard of Dantes?"

She blinked. "Are you talking about the jewelry firm?" He simply continued to watch her and her breath escaped in a soft gasp. "You're one of *those* Dantes?"

"You remember us?"

She regarded him uneasily, regarding her husband in an entirely different light. She'd sensed his power, witnessed his affluence. But it never occurred to her that he moved in such elite circles. Or that she did. How could she possibly live up to what would be expected of a Dante wife?

"I wouldn't say I remember, exactly," she finally responded. "I know about Dantes the same way I know who the current president is. I retain general knowledge, just not specific memories about my past. I've heard of Dantes. I mean, who hasn't?"

He appeared to accept her comment at face value, though it troubled her he continued to question her amnesia. She kept feeling as though he was concealing something from her. Was it something he hoped she'd remember? Or something he preferred remain forgotten?

"Dantes Exclusive is the part of our retail operation for our high-end clients. It's by appointment only. I thought you might enjoy seeing some of our more select designs."

She managed a smile. Had he sprung this on her last time? Is that why he'd brought her here, today? "I'd enjoy that. Thank you."

He led her through the sitting area, past an impressive glass-and-mirror wet bar offering every possible libation, to a barely visible door set into the wall and protected by an elaborate security system. Nicolò removed a card from his wallet and swiped it across the device, before unlocking the mechanism with a combination of voice and thumbprint. The door clicked open and he escorted Kiley into a glittering fantasyland.

She stared around, wide-eyed. "Oh," she managed to murmur.

"Feel free to look around while I see if any of the family's here."

She looked at him in alarm. "Your family?"

"Don't panic. They won't hurt you. I promise." He started to leave, then hesitated. "Unless you want to be hermetically sealed in here, I'd look but not touch."

Kiley whipped her hands behind her back and interlaced her fingers. "I wouldn't dream of touching."

The minute he disappeared, she made a slow circuit of the room, feeling more overwhelmed with each step she took. Case after case displayed jewelry sets of stunning beauty. Not to mention astronomical expense. Is this the world to which she belonged? She shook her head. No, it didn't feel right. Surely, she didn't live a life of such wealth and opulence.

She paused in front of a particularly gorgeous display. Voices drifted to her from the doorway through which her husband had vanished. Nicolò's low murmur sent awareness rippling down her spine. Then came the higher-pitched reply of a woman. At first Kiley couldn't hear the actual words, but the contentious intonation came through loud and clear. Then the woman raised her voice.

"Forget it, Nicolò," she said. "I won't be party to—"

Nicolò interrupted, speaking at length in a soft, hard voice.

Then, "Okay, fine. But this is the one and only time."

Kiley hastened away from the doorway, worry balled in the pit of her stomach. What in the world did Nicolò want, and why wouldn't the woman he spoke to be party to whatever he'd suggested? Of even more concern, did their conversation involve her?

She paused by another display case, focusing all her attention on the glorious necklace, earrings, and bracelet. She was enthralled by their stunning appeal, despite her apprehension. A moment later, Nicolò entered the room, followed by a tall, elegant blonde with dark eyes.

She offered a forced smile that left Kiley feeling intensely uncomfortable.

"This is my sister-in-law, Francesca," Nicolò said. "She's Sev's wife and Dantes' top designer. You're looking at one of her designs."

"It's incredible," Kiley said as they shook hands. "Simple, yet elegant. And—and warm."

Her utter sincerity must have come through because Francesca's smile softened and the cool wariness eased from her gaze. "Thank you. It's part of a collection I created called Dante's Heart."

Kiley turned back to study the display case. "I think it's my favorite of all the ones I've seen here today."

"It's the fire diamonds," Francesca stated. "Working with them makes even the most ordinary piece extraordinary."

"Is that what you call those particular diamonds?" Kiley peered closer. "Oh, wow. I see it now. It is almost as though they're on fire."

She didn't know what alerted her. Perhaps it was the fierce stillness emanating from Francesca and Nicolò. Or perhaps she felt the intensity of their joint gaze. Kiley glanced up at them and slowly straightened.

"Could you please tell me what's going on?" she asked. "It's bad enough that I don't remember. But I also don't understand the silent subtext between you two." She focused on Nicolò. "Is there some reason I'm here other than your wanting to show me the family business and introduce me to Francesca?"

"I was hoping that seeing the fire diamonds might prompt a memory."

"What memory?"

"Any memory." He tilted his head to one side. "But it doesn't, does it?"

"Not even a little." She offered a strained smile. "I wish I had your talent, Francesca. It must give you such pleasure to create these spectacular—" And then a possibility struck her, one that left her trembling with excitement. "Oh, my God. Am I a jewelry designer, too? Is that why I'm here? Is that why you're acting so strangely? Am I supposed to recognize something I created?"

Struggling to contain a wild thrill of hope, she looked around with a hint of desperation before darting toward a wall full of display cases. She scanned them swiftly, praying that one of the sets would jump out and connect with her the same way she'd connected with Nicolò.

"I don't recognize anything. I'm trying. Really I am, but—" She glanced over her shoulder, her gaze clashing with Nicolò's. "Please. *Please* help me."

He reached her side before she'd even finished speaking and wrapped her up in a tight embrace. "Hell. I'm sorry, sweetheart." He held her close, comforting her with his warmth. "It's nothing like that."

"Oh." Kiley struggled to conceal the magnitude of her disappointment, praying she could blink back the tears before he saw them. She might have hidden them from Nicolò, but she had less luck with Francesca.

The other woman joined them and caught Kiley's hand in hers. "I am *so* sorry," Francesca said. "It didn't occur to me that you'd jump to that conclusion. Though now that you have, it seems such an obvious leap to make. I can't apologize enough for being so cruel."

"Don't—" Kiley could feel her emotions escaping her control. She waved a hand in front of her face. "Ignore me. I probably overdid today and it's all caught up with me at once."

"Nicolò," Francesca whispered fiercely, more than a hint of anger coloring her voice.

"This is my fault," he replied. "I'll deal with it."

He glanced down at Kiley. One look at her face had him swearing beneath his breath. She buried her face against the front of his shirt and he jerked his head at Francesca, who left without a word, though her infuriated expression spoke volumes.

"I'm sorry," he said. "I really screwed this up. I meant for you to look at some of the wedding ring sets and see if anything appealed."

"It's too much, Nicolò. Too overwhelming and way too soon."

"I realize that." He grimaced. "At least, I realize that now."

"Should I assume that our first date didn't end likc this?" she asked in a muffled voice.

"With you in tears? No, it didn't, thank God."

She released a watery laugh. "I'm relieved to hear it." She peeked up at him. "Just out of curiosity, how did it end?"

He closed his eyes, fighting an inner battle. A losing inner battle. "Like this . . ."

Chapter Five

He cupped her face, lifted it to his, and kissed her. She tasted of sweetness and tears, heat and hope, all mixed with white-hot desire. He shouldn't touch her. He sure as hell shouldn't kiss her. He'd thought by bringing her here, to the heart of Dantes' wealth and power, he'd catch a glimpse of something. Avarice. Delight. A quick hungry look she couldn't quite conceal.

But she hadn't shown a bit of that, not even after he'd left her alone in the room and watched her on the close-circuit cameras. If anything, she'd appeared nervous and uncomfortable, as though she'd rather have been almost anywhere other than stuck in a room with countless millions of dollars' worth of the world's most stunning jewelry.

She melted against him, her mouth parting beneath his. Unable to resist, he dipped inward. The flames from The Inferno roared to life, raging through him like wildfire. If they'd been anywhere else, he'd have said to hell with it and taken her right there and then. And based on the way she clung to him, wrapped herself around him, opened to him without hesitation, she wouldn't have lifted a finger to stop him.

"I'd like to see you in one of these designs," he told her between kisses. "Clothed in fire diamonds and black satin sheets."

She shivered against him. "That would still leave too much between us. Let's skip the diamonds and sheets. I'd rather be clothed in Dante. Or at least, one particular Dante."

"Much as I'd like to accommodate you, we can't. Not until you've had time to heal. Until then," He snatched another deep, penetrating kiss. "Let's go home."

Disappointment filled her, despite knowing he was being sensible. Cautious. Right now, she preferred reckless and passionate.

"Home it is," she reluctantly agreed. Though she remained tucked close by his side, she didn't speak again until they were in the elevator, returning to the underground garage. "So, what's your plan for tomorrow?"

An excellent question. Based on Francesca's reaction, he realized he needed to take Kiley away from San Francisco for a short time. Just long enough for Juice to complete his investigation. It would involve a quick phone call to an old family friend, Joc

Arnaud. But Nicolò didn't anticipate any problems from that end of things.

The Dantes and the billionaire financier had enjoyed a long-term friendship. They'd even designed his wife's wedding rings, as well as the jewelry set Joc had presented to Rosalyn on the birth of their son, Joshua. With luck, he'd assist Nicolò now, allowing him to stay on Joc's private island, Isla de los Deseos, while Nicolò decided how to handle the disastrous situation he'd created.

He pulled out of the garage, sparing Kiley a swift glance. She looked pale and exhausted. He'd pushed too hard today and could kick himself for his stupidity. "I have to call a friend in order to set something up. Fair warning, it might take a day or two."

"Is this another of our dates?"

He forced out the lie. "It preceded our marriage. In fact, it was what convinced you to marry me."

"You convinced me to marry you on our second date?"

"No. After today's disaster, I've decided to move our agenda forward a few weeks."

"A few weeks?" she repeated faintly. "You weren't kidding about our having a whirlwind affair, were you?"

"I did warn you that we didn't know each other very long."

She leaned back against the headrest and closed her eyes. "How strange. I must have been an impulsive person. Which explains the dash to beat out a cab."

"That explains you," he muttered. "Now try and explain me."

"I guess we have to blame it on The Inferno. It does seem to have a rather strong effect." She opened her eyes long enough to shoot him a look brimming with laughter. "On both of us."

"No question about that," he agreed.

She was right. The Inferno did have a strong effect on both of them. It also created a dozen problems. How did he put an end to the physical need clawing at him? Because when Juice found the evidence of Kiley's guilt, he'd have to put an end to their relationship. He couldn't—*wouldn't*—join himself with a woman he didn't trust. Not that it would be a problem. As soon as she regained her memory and discovered how he'd scammed her in return, she'd pour ice water on any remaining embers.

And if she didn't regain her memory? He refused to consider the possibility. It would come back. He didn't doubt it for a minute. And when it did, he'd watch a woman with a nature full of sweet generosity transform into a sly, devious creature who made a living by her wits and dishonesty. Perhaps that would put a rapid end to The Inferno.

He could only hope.

Kiley could barely contain her excitement when two days later Nicolò escorted her onto Dantes' corporate jet.

"Where are we going?" she demanded.

He regarded her with a lazy smile that made her long for them to be back in bed where maybe—just maybe—he'd surrender to the passion scorching them both with its relentless flames. So far that hadn't happened. He'd shown a disgusting amount of self-control, determined to wait until the right time and place before making love to her. She didn't have a clue when or where that might occur. As far as she was concerned, here and now would do just fine.

"We're going to Isla de los Deseos," he informed her.

Her tongue savored the syllables. "What a romantic name. What did we do there?"

As expected, he shook his head. "Not a chance. We're going to relax and enjoy ourselves. Nothing strenuous.

Nothing that will wear you out. This will give you the opportunity to recoup from your accident. Plus, we'll have the time and privacy we need to get to know each other better."

"We'll also get to reenact the dates that led up to our marriage." She nodded sagely. "I have to hand it to you, Nicolò. Recoup, reacquaint, and reenact. Not many are so adept at killing three birds with one stone."

"Four, but who's counting."

She tilted her head to one side, intrigued. "What's the fourth?"

His eyes grew uncomfortably direct. "Recover. As in, your memory."

"Oh, right."

For some reason that put a damper on her spirits. She didn't understand it. She wanted to recover her memory, didn't she? So, why did she shy away from the mere suggestion? Part of it resulted from a vague impression she picked up from Nicolò, as though he knew more than he'd told her.

No doubt there was. And no doubt when the time was right and she could handle the information, both physically and emotionally, he'd tell her whatever dark secrets he kept locked away. In the meantime, no matter how difficult she found it, she'd have to remain patient and wait until he felt comfortable sharing the information.

She slept for long periods of the flight to Deseos, wrapped in Nicolò's arms, held safe and secure. The rest of the time, they talked, their conversation quiet and intimate. He discussed his past while kneading his palm in an unconscious gesture, explained how he'd been taken in by his grandparents after the sailing accident that had claimed the lives of his mother and father. He spoke of Sev and how hard his eldest brother had worked to recover the family fortunes. He told her about the twins, Marco, the passionate charmer, who had tricked his bride into marriage by pretending to be his twin brother, and Lazz, the analytical loner. And he described his grandparents, how after The Inferno struck, Nonna had broken her engagement to another man and emigrated to California with Nicolò's grandfather, Primo.

She could picture Nicolò so clearly as a youth. Feel his pain. Sense his determination to solve the unsolvable, perhaps as a result of being unable to ease his family's sorrow after his parents' death. She suspected he possessed that same determination to fix her situation. The thought brought a misty smile to her mouth, a mouth he instantly captured with his own.

"I like it when you smile," he told her.

"You say that so reluctantly," she teased. "Are you afraid I'll use it against you?"

"Would you?"

"Yes." She tightened her arms around his neck. "If it made you kiss me again, I'd use it against you on an hourly basis."

She leaned forward to demonstrate when the flight attendant made an appearance, warning they'd be landing in a few minutes. Kiley released her husband with a disappointed sigh and buckled up just as the plane banked over a lush mountainous island dotting the surface of an aquamarine sea. They landed on a private airstrip and were driven to a secluded cabana sitting within the embrace of a stand of palm trees, steps from a private lagoon.

The cabana took Kiley's breath away. Decorated in vivid colors, typical of the Caribbean, it boasted a bamboo floor and every possible modern convenience. "How long are we staying here?" she asked.

Nicolò shrugged. "As long as we want."

She turned in alarm. "I only packed an overnight bag. I don't have enough clothes."

He shrugged. "Not to worry. They don't wear clothes here." He waited a beat before laughing at her expression. "I'm kidding."

"Thank goodness," she said faintly.

"We can buy anything you need."

Her brows drew together. "That seems rather excessive. If you'd just told me, I'd have been happy to—"

"You won't need much. A couple bathing suits. A couple dresses for the evening. We'll check out the shops in a little while."

First the wardrobe full of designer clothes, then Dantes Exclusive, and now this. She regarded him with a troubled expression. "I need to ask you a question and I'm not quite sure how to phrase it."

"Just be direct," he suggested.

"Are we . . . rich? Or rather, are you?"

"Yes."

So brutally frank. "Was—was I?"

He hesitated before shaking his head. "No."

She nodded in relief. "That makes sense. This feels . . ."

His scrutiny intensified. "What?"

"Different," she admitted with a shrug. Then she brightened. "But considering how short a time we've known each other, perhaps that explains it. I'm probably not accustomed to such a lavish lifestyle."

He turned to face her, folding his arms across his chest. She'd always been aware of his impressive size, especially in comparison with her own. But for some reason his current stance made her even more aware of it than usual. "You know that much about yourself, even though you have amnesia?" he asked.

The softness of the question captured her full attention. "It's not anything I remember," she hastened to explain. "It's just a feeling I have. Like I'm out of step or something. Like this isn't me."

"Not you?" He shook his head. "You seem to be operating under a misapprehension that I need to straighten out. You didn't have much money, but you thoroughly enjoyed the best life had to offer."

She couldn't conceal her shock. "I did?"

"Designer clothes and accessories. Five-star hotels." He caught her hands in his and turned them so she could see the lacquered tips. "Professional manicure and pedicure. An expert hairdresser. They were all part of your lifestyle when we first met."

For some reason his words impacted like a body blow. "I didn't know." Nor did she like hearing the truth. It felt wrong. Unappealing. Superficial. Was that the sort of person she'd been before? "If I was so shallow, why were you attracted to me?" she asked, troubled. "Why would you have married me?"

His fingers interlaced with hers until their palms joined. She could feel the heat from The Inferno build there, melding them together. "It's been like this from the beginning."

Oh, God. She stared at him in distress. "It's physical? Our entire relationship is based on this Inferno we feel for each other? That's it?"

"Would you like there to be more?"

"Of course!" She searched his expression. "Wouldn't you?"

"My grandparents have been married for five and a half decades. I'm well aware there has to be more to marriage than physical attraction. But that takes time to build."

"How do we build it when I know nothing about my background?" she protested, her distress increasing by the second. "Nothing about my history or experiences? How do we find common ground?"

"We start with this—"

He swept her into his arms and ravished her mouth with a kiss that stole every single thought from her head. Heat bloomed, a messy stream of need lapping through her veins and bringing a flush to cheeks and breasts before settling in the very core of her. He invaded her mouth, teasing her until she couldn't stand it any longer.

She fought back, deepening the kiss so it was his turn to catch fire, his turn to burn. His turn to lose control. She tugged his shirt free of his trousers and swept her hands underneath. The instant she hit skin she slowed, tracking a wayward path across his chest as she gathered all that heat in her palms. And then she dipped lower, over the rock-hard ripple of abs to the belt preventing her from a more intimate exploration. She settled for outlining the thick bulge she found there, cupping him as he'd once cupped her. At the last instant, he caught her hands in his and pulled them away.

"We start with this, the physical," he said, gritting out the words. "And we build on it. Together."

She collapsed against his chest and nodded. What a wonderful word. "Together," she whispered.

He made a visible effort to catch his breath. "And the first thing we're doing together is purchasing the clothes we'll need for our stay here."

Kiley wrinkled her nose at him. "That wasn't quite the togetherness I had in mind."

"It wasn't quite the togetherness I had in mind, either." Wry amusement gathered in his dark eyes. "But it'll have to do until—"

"Until when?" she couldn't resist asking.

She'd never seen Nicolò look so conflicted. "Until your memory returns. Until you can make an informed choice."

Iciness replaced the heat of only moments before. *An informed choice?* What did that mean? And of even greater concern, what had happened between them that prompted him to put that sort of condition on their current relationship? What happened the day of her accident that she no longer remembered?

When she first awoke in the hospital, Nicolò had told her they'd fought moments before she'd been injured. Whatever the cause of the argument, it had been serious enough to send her darting in front of a cab. Serious enough, her husband wouldn't make love to her until she remembered.

Was it also serious enough to end their marriage?

Kiley entered the restaurant, Ambrosia, feeling more awkward and uncomfortable than she could ever remember. Her mouth curved in a wry smile. Not that she had much basis for comparison.

At least her bruises were no longer visible, since in the gown Nicolò purchased, they would have stood out like a neon sign. She skated a hand down the pale green silk molded to her waist, hips and thighs before flaring outward in a short train, and struggled to appear poised and confident. It took every ounce of willpower not to tug at the strapless bodice, one that revealed more than it concealed.

She associated the elegant gown with "Old Kiley," a woman, based on her husband's description, she neither liked nor understood. Maybe that other version of herself enjoyed a life rich in sensual pleasure. The only sensual pleasure this Kiley cared about was the one she found in Nicolò's arms.

But did her preference match his? She searched his stunning profile. He was a Dante. A man who hobnobbed with billionaire financiers and jet-setters. He had a position to maintain. And he'd chosen that other Kiley for his life's mate. He'd been so patient with her, but maybe his patience would soon run out. Maybe he'd brought her here in an effort to change her back into the woman he'd first married.

She worried at another possibility, one that concerned her more than any other. Perhaps he chose her originally because she fit into his world, something no longer true. Without a memory of all the little turns of events that led her to develop into the person he married, she could only base her actions on what felt right. And though it broke her heart to admit it, this current getup felt completely wrong. No matter how hard she struggled to fit in, she simply didn't.

Since the moment she'd awoken in that hospital bed and been claimed by her husband, she'd been forced to rely on her instincts. And those instincts—straight down to the very core of her—told her she bore no relationship to this glossy woman he'd patchworked together for a dinner date with some fancy billionaire glamour couple.

Perhaps that had been true once upon a time. But not any longer. Not unless she regained her memory and lost her current self. If this version of Kiley wasn't good enough for Nicolò, she had a terrible feeling it doomed their relationship before it ever truly began.

The knowledge hung over her like the sword of Damocles, threatening with one swift plunge of the blade to sunder her from a man The Inferno insisted was her soul mate. A man she knew, deep in her heart of hearts, belonged to her every bit as much as she belonged to him.

Or did he belong to that other Kiley?

The maître d' appeared just then and showed them to a private dining alcove and a few minutes later Joc Arnaud and his wife, Rosalyn, appeared. To Kiley's surprise, Rosalyn proved to be a fellow redhead, although her hair gleamed a deep, rich auburn instead of Kiley's brighter shade. Of equal interest, Joc shared Nicolò's coloring.

The similarity ended there, of course. Rosalyn had the height and curves Kiley lacked and crossed the room with long, ground-eating strides that proclaimed her as comfortable on a Texas cattle ranch as in a ballroom. She stuck out her hand with equal forthrightness.

"I'm Rosalyn Arnaud," she announced. "Pleased to meet you. And this is my husband, Joc."

"Kiley O—Dante. Sorry." She released a quick laugh as they all exchanged handshakes. "I guess I'm still getting used to my name."

"Nicolò told us about your accident." Rosalyn took the seat Joc held for her and dropped her hand over Kiley's, giving it a gentle squeeze. "I'm really sorry you're going through such a difficult time."

"The doctors say I could get my memory back at any time."

"In the meanwhile, it must make it very difficult to take everything in. You must feel so dependent and vulnerable."

"That's exactly how I feel," Kiley confessed. "I don't know what I'd do if it weren't for Nicolò."

"Right." Rosalyn's gaze flashed in his direction and she smiled sweetly. "At least you have a husband who loves you and only has your best interests at heart. Someone you can trust to protect you."

Joc took the menu from their waiter and handed it to his wife. "Here you go, Red. See what trouble you can get into with this."

She shot a grin at Kiley and leaned in. "That means be quiet," she whispered in a voice that could be clearly heard by everyone at the table. "Not that I ever listen."

Kiley laughed. "How did you two meet?" she asked, intrigued by the unmistakable differences in attitude and polish between husband and wife.

"Joc sent some goons to my ranch in a vain attempt to buy it. I stormed his citadel and explained why that wasn't going to happen."

"And then?"

"Then he kidnapped me—"

"I most certainly did not," Joc argued. "I tendered an offer which you accepted with impressive alacrity."

"—and he brought me here and proceeded to seduce me." Rosalyn helped herself to a breadstick. "It was actually quite enjoyable."

"Coming here or being seduced?" Kiley asked.

Everyone laughed and Rosalyn gave Kiley a look of undisguised approval. "Since it resulted in our son, Joshua, I'd have to say that tips the scales ever so slightly toward the whole seduction number. What about you?"

"Oh, I'm hoping for a big seduction number, too." She waited for the laughter to die down again before asking, "How old is your son?"

"Not quite a year and walking already," Joc answered. "That's why we were late. We needed to settle him for the night and he wasn't in any hurry to settle. Then I had to talk Rosalyn into putting on the fancy duds."

"I'd live in jeans if it were up to me," she confessed.

"You don't—" Kiley broke off, searching for a more tactful way to phrase her question. "I assumed—"

"That we always live and dress like this?" Rosalyn shook her head. "Honey, if it were up to me, I'd never attend another fancy shindig for the rest of my natural born days. That's Joc's thing, not mine."

"A consequence of my position, I'm afraid." Joc glanced at Nicolò. "And of being a Dante, too, I presume."

Nicolò nodded and it wasn't until then that Kiley became aware of how quiet he'd remained all this time, content to sit back and observe. Observe her, she suddenly realized, while kneading his palm in a gesture that grew more habitual with each passing day.

"I'm not on the frontline quite as much as Sev or the twins," Nicolò conceded. "But I'm forced to do my fair share when the occasion demands."

"I doubt I'll ever get used to it," Kiley confessed. "I'm a nervous wreck right now."

Joc's brows pulled together. "Well, we can fix that easily enough." He shoved back his chair and stood. "I'll arrange for dinner to be delivered to our cabana. You and Nicolò can meet us there in say—" he twitched back a snowy cuff and checked his watch "—twenty minutes? Will that give you time to change into something casual? We'll send the nanny on her way and just relax and eat and have some wine. How does that sound?"

Before Kiley could interject, Nicolò nodded. "Sounds perfect, Joc. Thanks for understanding."

"Nothing to understand," he assured.

They met up twenty minutes later and Kiley thoroughly enjoyed every second of the evening from that point on. After dinner, a demanding wail sounded from one of the bedrooms and a few minutes later Rosalyn appeared with a sleepy baby held close in her arms. At first glance his hair seemed as dark as his father's, but as the two drew closer, Kiley saw it reflected a hint of Rosalyn's deep auburn. He'd also inherited his mother's eyes, the color an unusual violet-blue. He blinked at the assembled group for a moment, taking it all in, before offering a huge grin, proudly displaying a pair of bottom teeth.

Kiley couldn't resist. It was a night of new experiences and fate offered her one more she wanted to add to her collection. "May I?" she asked. "I can't remember ever holding a baby before."

Rosalyn instantly melted. "Joshua's still half-asleep, so I'm not sure how he'll take to you. Just don't be offended if he decides he wants to go to Joc. He's more of a guy's guy than a momma's boy."

Kiley took the baby into her arms, cradling him in her arms, barely daring to breathe. Joshua blinked up at her and she could tell he was weighing his options—scream his little head off or put up with her. To her delight, he gave her the benefit of the doubt.

"He's almost a year, and yet he still smells so new," she whispered to Nicolò.

He chuckled, joining her on the couch and wrapping an arm around her and the baby. "Try smelling him when he loads that diaper of his."

"Amen," Joc and Rosalyn said in unison.

The rest of the evening passed, possessing an almost dreamlike quality. Contentment settled over Kiley, along with a renewed self-confidence. Maybe she could handle this, especially if all Nicolò's friends were as nice as the Arnauds. She continued to hold Joshua, who promptly fell asleep against her breast.

"Lucky brat," Nicolò whispered in her ear.

"No," she whispered back. "Lucky me."

When the evening came to an end, Kiley reluctantly handed over Joshua and she and Nicolò made their farewells. They followed the lighted walkway from the Arnauds' cabana to their own, enjoying the exotic scents that filled the sultry night air. It gave Kiley a moment to think, to address the whispered concerns that had gradually grown to a shout during the course of the evening. She'd learned two very important facts this evening.

First, that she could act the part Nicolò required of her in order to fit into his world. And second, she didn't want to pretend to be anyone other than herself, the *real* woman she instinctively recognized as her true persona. Now, she had to convince her husband of that. Nicolò unlocked the door and waited for her to precede him into the darkened interior. She paused in the foyer and turned to face him.

"I can't continue this pretense any longer," she announced.

Chapter Six

Nicolò froze, Kiley's words causing bitter disappointment to clash with cynical triumph. *Gotcha.* He didn't know what about tonight had set her off, but she was finally going to admit the truth of who and what she was.

"Then end the pretense and put your cards on the table," he challenged.

"Okay, fine." She swiveled to face him, taking a step in his direction that shifted her from deep shadow into a pool of moonlight. "I can't continue living this sort of lifestyle. It feels wrong. *I* feel wrong," she emphasized.

Okay, not quite what he expected. "You didn't enjoy this evening?"

"This evening—or at least, the second half of the evening—was incredible. But not all the rest. Not the trappings and the facade I'd have to adopt." Worry filled her expression. "Is it necessary, Nicolò? Do I have to become the woman I was before in order for our relationship to work?"

"No." The word escaped before he could stop it. "You can be any sort of woman you wish."

She caught her bottom lip between her teeth, apprehension filling her expression. She sawed at her lip for a telling moment before the words burst from her. "And you'll still love me?"

The question burned like acid. "My feelings for you won't change."

"Even though I've changed?"

"Give it time, sweetheart."

She took another step in his direction, closing the gap between them. Her hands slipped across his chest and she gathered up handfuls of his shirt. "I don't want to be the Kiley you described to me earlier. How can I like or respect her if she's as shallow inside as she is on the outside? I just want to be who I am now. Can you live with that? Can you accept that?"

He wasn't the one who wouldn't accept it. She, herself, wouldn't. Couldn't. Not once she regained her memory. But how did he explain that to her, without telling her the rest?

"It's not my decision," he said, regret roughening his voice. "If your memory returns you'll be who you were before. Any events that occur since then may alter your perspective, somewhat. But you'll be the Kiley O'Dell I first met."

Tears filled her eyes and she shook her head. "I can almost hear the clock ticking down. Only in this version I don't know who or what Cinderella turns into when the clock strikes midnight. I'm afraid of that other woman, afraid I'll turn into something or someone I won't like."

"I don't understand. Don't you want to remember?"

"Yes. No. The way you act—" She shook her head, her tears catching on the end of her lashes. "The way everyone acts makes me wonder what you're not telling me. Even Rosalyn—"

Aw, hell. "What about her?"

"She was annoyed with you about something. Please don't deny it," Kiley added, before he had a chance to speak. "All that business about being vulnerable and having to trust you. I can read between the lines. I also overheard you and Francesca arguing at Dantes Exclusive. I'm not an idiot, Nicolò. You're keeping something from me. What is it?"

"It's nothing."

The tears fell then, each one impacting like a knife to the gut. "You're lying," she whispered, not even attempting to disguise her pain. "You said we fought right before my accident. Were we about to break up? Is that it? Is that what you can't bring yourself to tell me? Are you just waiting until my memory returns before you put an end to our marriage?"

"We did argue," he admitted. "And it's possible that when your memory returns you'll want to end our relationship."

"Why?"

He shook his head. "Call it irreconcilable differences."

"What happens if I never regain my memory?" she persisted. "If I never remember, do we continue to pretend there isn't a problem? For how long?"

"You'll get it back." He said it with such flat certainty, she flinched.

"What if I don't?" The question sounded more like a wish and a prayer. "What happens then?"

"I don't have an answer for you."

"That's why you initially put me in a separate bedroom. Why we haven't made love. Why you're insisting I regain my memory before we do. Because we were on the verge of divorce."

"It was an argument, Kiley. That's all."

She took a step back, releasing him. Her eyes glittered like crystal in the moonlight, leached of all color. She reached for the first button of her blouse and thumbed it through the hole. Then a second. And a third. The deep V of her neckline revealed the intricate heart-shaped locket on its thin silver chain.

It was almost identical to their first meeting at Le Premier when she'd tempted him with that tantalizing striptease. Only this time around, he didn't catch a flash of vibrant red. This time he couldn't tell what color provided such a sharp contrast between the milky whiteness of her skin and the unrelenting darkness of her blouse. This time her movements stuttered with a hint of clumsiness and sweet resolve, rather than cynical calculation.

His gaze shot to her face and he searched for some hint to her thoughts, some clue that she was playing him by reenacting their initial meeting. But he saw nothing other than a fierce determination.

She finished unbuttoning her blouse and shrugged it off. It crumpled to the floor behind her. She kicked aside her sandals before tugging at the snap of her jeans. Next came the rending of her zipper, the sound shattering in the dense silence of the foyer. She slipped the denim off her narrow hips, her no-nonsense movements in complete opposition to her provocative actions during their hotel room meeting.

She stood before him in bra and panties. They were much plainer than before, and for some reason far more tantalizing. When he made no attempt to touch her, she reached behind her back and unfastened her bra and tossed it to one side. And then her panties disappeared as simply and economically as her jeans.

Moonlight poured over her, silvering the creamy white of her skin and creating interesting shadows beneath the slight curve of her breasts, as well as in the nest of curls at the junction of her thighs. It also spotlighted a small birthmark riding the curve of her hip, one that reminded him of a flower in full bloom.

Some might have called her figure boyish. Nicolò found it anything but. Her arms and legs were sculpted with lean muscle with just enough curves to make them distinctly feminine in appearance. Her breasts were on the small side, certainly, but they were also round and pert, with the nipples forming perfect pearls that he longed to taste. She was so delicate, her ankles and wrists coltish-slender. And yet, she was all woman, an indomitable woman at that, determined to tempt him beyond endurance.

The Inferno woke with a roar, consuming him in huge greedy gulps, filling him with an insatiable hunger. In that moment he didn't care who she'd been before. All that mattered was here and now. They belonged together and he refused to deny the fact any longer. He'd deal with the fallout from his actions when Kiley regained her memory. In the meantime, he'd take what she so generously offered. Take it and be damned grateful because when she came to her senses, she'd make him pay.

Big-time.

In one swift stride he reached her and swept her into his arms. "I hope you know what you're doing," he told her.

Her arms whipped around his neck and clung. "Not even a little. Not that I care."

"I'll remind you of that at some point down the road."

"I won't forget." Her expression grew fierce. "Not this time."

He shouldered his way into their bedroom and dropped her onto the mattress. She came up on her knees, lost amid the flow of creamy silk covering the mile-wide bed. He didn't waste any time. He stripped out of his clothes and joined her.

And then he paused. Slowed. Allowed himself to savor the moment.

The moonlight had followed them in here and caught in the long curls of her hair. He could just make out a whisper of blush in the pale color, as well as the merest hint of green in the eyes she trained so steadily on him. "The light?"

he asked, remembering how she hated the dark.

"It's not necessary." She cupped his face and lifted upward, fitting her mouth to his. "Not any longer."

He sank into her, home at last. "Are you sure," he murmured between a series of long, drugging kisses.

"Positive."

"No regrets come morning?"

"No regrets, ever."

His smile held little humor. "Don't be so sure of that."

"And I'm guessing you aren't going to explain that particular remark, either."

"No." He lost his hands in the weight of her hair. "But there's one thing I want you to know and believe."

Her head tipped back giving him better access to the length of her neck. "And what's that?"

He slid his index finger along the pulse throbbing in her throat before following the same path with his tongue. "It was like this between us from the first moment we met. From the instant I set eyes on you, I wanted you."

"Was the feeling mutual?"

"You know the answer to that."

She smiled, the curve of her lips full of mystery and allure. "I responded the same way as I did at the hospital." It wasn't a question.

"Yes."

"I may have no memory," she whispered. "But I know you. I know your touch and your scent. I know the sound of your heartbeat and how it echoes my own. I know you were meant to be mine, just as I was meant to be yours."

He shook his head. "Kiley—"

She stopped his words with her hand. "I'm serious, Nicolò. On some level I must remember you. It's as if you imprinted yourself on my heart and soul. Can't we just start over, as though our fight never happened?"

He closed his eyes. "It won't change anything. Not in the long run. Not when you regain your memory."

She shifted, opening herself to him. "I'm willing to take the chance."

The last of his resistance vanished. He lowered himself to her, sliding over her. Skin burned against skin. Curves and angles collided before shaping themselves, one to the other. She was soft, so soft. It took every ounce of control to keep from burying himself in that softness. And then a stray thought took hold.

If her memory loss was real, if she couldn't remember anything of her life before, then she also didn't remember making love. For her this would be another new experience. And even if she regained her memory at some point, this night would, quite possibly, hold special meaning for her. How could he do anything other than make it as unique for her as possible?

He slowed the pace, taking her mouth in slow, deep kisses. And all the while he gave to her, gifted her with quiet caresses and teasing strokes. With whispered words that brought a flush of warmth to cheek and breast. He let her know with every touch, with every appreciative murmur, with every sweep of his hand that he found her the most beautiful woman he'd ever held in his arms. And she believed him, because it was the truth.

"Is this how it was the first time we were together?" she marveled at one point.

He couldn't lie. Not here. Not now. Not in such an intensely intimate moment when they were both stripped to their bare essence. "This isn't like any other time. This is new for both of us."

Her breath escaped in a happy sigh. "I'm glad. I want it to be different. I want it to be special."

And it would be. He'd see to that. He cupped her breasts, as tantalizing and perfect as the rest of her, and lathed the sensitive tips. She arched beneath him, pressing herself deeper into his mouth. He scraped the tight nipples with his teeth and heard the soft cry of pleasure it elicited. And then he tormented her other breast, feeling the pounding of her heart against his cheek.

The need to taste more of her drew him and he slid downward, sampling the soft indentation of her belly and the small birthmark at her hip, before finding the thick blush of curls concealing the heart of her. He parted the delicate folds and gave her the relief her body wept for. Her hips rose to meet his kiss, her thighs taut and trembling as she teetered on the knife's edge. He pushed, ever so slightly, and she went over with a cry, all fluid heat and gasping pleasure.

"We're not done, yet," he warned. "Not even close to done."

"I don't want this to ever end." Her hands curled in his hair and she tugged, drawing him up and over her. "I want this night to last forever."

She was so beautiful, still captured within the moon-silvered glow of her climax. "It's not within my power to make the night last forever." He traced her features, one by one. The winged arch of her brows, the wide, vivid eyes, her sculpted cheekbones and pert nose, right down to her sweetly lopsided smile. "But the memory of tonight will last forever."

Her smile faded. "What if I forget again?"

His gaze grew tender. "Then I'll remember for you."

Tears gathered in her eyes. "I'd like that."

He began again, building on what had gone before. Her reaction to him came quicker this time, her responses more natural and fluid. And she gave back in ways that threatened to send him straight out of his mind.

Her quick, clever hands stroked and gripped before flitting away to provoke a new sensation. And she moved—heaven help him, how she moved—with a sensual grace that drove him wild with desire. She flowed over his body like silk, cupping him, tracing a provocative finger of exploration across velvet and steel. By the time she finished she knew every inch of his body. But then, he knew every inch of hers.

Finally, the exploration ended in the ultimate discovery. Making short work of slipping on protection, he parted her thighs and forged deep inside. She wrapped herself around him, clinging to him as though she never intended to let go. And then she rocked upward, surging with him into a rhythm as old as mankind.

Nicolò could feel the white-hot forging of The Inferno, could feel the ultimate completion of the bond between them and the way it expanded until it filled him to overflowing. It didn't matter any longer whether Kiley was con artist or innocent. They belonged together, two parts of a whole. How their affair would ultimately end was a question for another time and place. All that mattered was here and now.

This moment.

This woman.

The creation of this memory, everlasting.

She shuddered beneath him. "No, not yet."

"Now, Kiley. Go over with me."

Their gazes locked, his demanding, hers so trusting it would haunt him forever. He cupped her head as he surged inward, watching her give in and take flight. Feeling her surrender radiate outward until it encompassed her entire body. And he soared with her, losing himself in her heat and warmth. Losing himself in that moment of ultimate completion. Losing himself, body and soul.

"How could I have forgotten that?" she whispered in the darkness. "How is it possible that something so—"

"Perfect?" The word escaped without thought.

"Yes. *Perfect.*" She didn't speak for a long moment, and then added, "I thought when we made love I'd remember. That the strength of it would bring the past back to me."

He couldn't help himself. He froze. "It didn't?"

Her breath escaped in a frustrated sigh. "No. I only have this one memory of us together. All the other times are—" Her hand fluttered through the air. "Gone."

Her voice broke on that last word and she curled into him, her tears biting into his skin. All he could do was hold her while she wept and allow the guilt to eat him alive. He couldn't doubt her any longer, at least not about her amnesia. Whatever she'd been before was currently trapped in the dark recesses of her mind, perhaps forever.

So where did the two of them go from here? He'd taken her on as his responsibility, claimed her as his own. Worse, he'd taken advantage of her vulnerability. If she'd been a scam artist, what did that make him?

He closed his eyes, flinching from the question. Up until now he could justify his actions. Could claim he was acting for the better good of his family. But what he'd done this night wasn't for anyone's benefit but his own. Hell, he could blame it on The Inferno, could claim their ending up in bed together was inevitable. But at least he knew all the facts, had taken this step with total awareness and understanding.

Kiley hadn't. Worse, she believed they were married, that when she'd given herself to him, it had been a wife to her husband. He pulled her close and kissed the top of her head. She murmured drowsily and snuggled closer. No question about what was going to happen as a result of his actions tonight, especially if his "wife" regained her memory anytime soon.

He was going straight to hell.

"What are you up to, Nicolò Dante?" Kiley faced her husband, her hands planted on her hips. Not that she appeared terribly intimidating, an impossible feat when dressed in a minuscule bikini, her modesty barely preserved by the paper thin floral *pareo*

she'd wrapped around her hips. "You have secret written all over you."

"A small deviation in plans."

"We're not reenacting another date?" she asked, unable to prevent a small twinge of disappointment.

He shook his head. "Since you ended up in tears the one time we attempted it, I'd rather not. Instead, I decided to try something else. You gave me the idea last night when you were holding Joshua."

She stared blankly. "I did?"

"You did." He adjusted her hat to ensure her pale skin remained shaded from the powerful rays of the sun. "You commented that holding a baby was a new experience for you. So, I've decided to give you a few more new experiences. They're waiting for you on the beach."

He led her toward the lagoon outside their cabana and she paused halfway across the sand, staring in amazement. A huge table had been assembled beneath a canvas tent, the linen-covered surface overflowing with food, drinks, and even flowers.

"What's all this?" she asked in astonishment.

"These are new memories." He gestured toward the table. "We're starting with appetizers and ending with dessert. There's a little of everything."

It took her a moment to reply, a series of emotions sweeping across her face. Surprise. Fascination. Curiosity. And sweet, utter delight. "And the flowers?"

"I had them gather up every variety they had in stock. You decide which ones you like best."

Her expression grew misty. "Oh, Nicolò, this is so thoughtful of you."

She threw her arms around him and lifted her mouth to his. He took his time with the kiss, sparking a return of the passion they'd shared the previous night. Before she could act on it, he caught her hand in his and drew her across the sand to the tent. Once inside, he considered the flowers and finally plucked one from the various arrangements, one she wouldn't have expected.

"Honeysuckle?" she asked. "Do I make you think of honeysuckle?"

He hesitated. "One of my earliest memories is wandering through my grandfather's garden. He has this beautiful pink honeysuckle growing along one of the fence lines. I couldn't have been much more than three, but that scent drew me. It was indescribable. I think I got drunk on the perfume."

She leaned in and inhaled the delicate sweetness. "It's wonderful."

"It was my first flower, or at least my first memory of one. My first floral scent."

"It's your favorite, isn't it? That's why you're sharing it with me."

"Yes. Though I learned to be cautious around a hedge of blooming honeysuckle."

"Uh-oh. Bees?" she hazarded a guess.

"'Fraid so. That day was also my first bee sting."

She frowned. "One of your favorite memories is also one of your most painful?"

He inclined his head. "I've discovered that's often the way life works."

"Why, Mr. Dante, you're a cynic."

"Comes with the territory, I'm afraid. As Dantes' troubleshooter I see all the problems. It's my job to fix them."

"Regardless of the cost?"

"Yes." He gave her a direct look, one that seemed to chill the humid warmth of the midday air. "And sometimes that cost is very high."

"You don't have to worry about that now," she told him, her tone taking on a fierce edge. "You don't have to troubleshoot a problem while we're on Deseos. Not here. Not with me. You can relax and enjoy yourself while we have fun playing."

Curls danced along her temples, tightened by the unrelenting humidity, and he tucked them behind her ear, anchoring them in place with the sprig of honeysuckle. "You, my dear, cause me nothing but trouble."

He said it with such a look of good humor she couldn't take offense. "Well, as long as I'm already trouble for you, why don't we see how much more I can cause you?" She shot him a flirtatious glance from beneath the brim of her hat. In response, heat flared to life in his dark eyes. "What do you say we dive into that table of new memories?"

The rest of the day was one of sheer delight and endless sensual pleasure. It wasn't just the food or flowers or drink, but who she shared them with. *Nicolò.* Nicolò, who left her in fits of laughter one minute and in the next moved her to tears with his poignant stories of family. Nicolò, who turned her life golden with a single smile. As the sun slipped away, and the shadows grew long, she went into his arms.

"Thank you for such an incredible day," she told him.

She lifted her mouth to his in order to sample the sweetest of all the desserts. This put the final touch on their time together. This made it perfect.

His reaction to her was instantaneous. He tugged her close, wrapping his arms around her with a power and strength that reminded her of their night together. He'd put those skillful hands on her the previous evening, used that strength and power—and gentleness—to drive her insane with desire.

She caught his lower lip between her teeth and tugged. With a groan, he opened to her and she slid into rich, lush warmth. Drowned in it. Drowned in him. "Please, Nicolò," she whispered against his mouth. "After all the new, I need something old. Not too old," she hastened to add. "Just a little old. A slight bit repetitive."

"One night old?" he suggested with a soft chuckle.

"Yeah. That should do it."

Without a word, he turned her toward the cabana and they walked hand-in-hand into the dusky interior. One by one, clothes were discarded, creating a pathway of color from doorway to bedroom. There was a different quality to their lovemaking this time. Less desperation. No, she decided with a muffled groan. She still felt desperate, in the best possible way. But there was less uncertainty. She had a better idea what to do and how to do it. And she put that knowledge to work.

Where before he'd taken charge, had guided the pace and rhythm, this time she took the lead. With each stroking caress, her confidence grew, as did her creativity. And then intent dissolved in the face of helpless passion. There was no follower or leader, just the two of them, lost in one another, drowning in glorious sensation. Reveling in touch and possession.

She took him in, hard and deep, moved with him, seeking that moment, that sweet, sweet moment when the melding would come, when two were mated into one. At last it hit, an uncontrollable rolling that crashed over her and sent her up and over. And as she tumbled, helpless beneath the hugeness of it, she realized she'd just experienced something else new, new and infinitely precious.

She'd just discovered how to love.

Chapter Seven

Nicolò and Kiley ended up spending five more delicious days and nights on Deseos; bright, shiny moments she treasured and held close to her heart. Although their original plan had been to duplicate the dates they'd enjoyed leading up to their island marriage—dates she still couldn't recall—she much preferred Nicolò's change of plan. Instead of repeating the old, he'd filled their time together with an endless tumble of new sensations, memories she'd always treasure.

Finally, the time came for their return to San Francisco and she packed away the memories with as much care as their various purchases. On the return trip, she and Nicolò curled up together, laughing softly over various highlights of their trip while exchanging deep, leisurely kisses.

Once they landed, they grabbed a cab that let them off in front of Nicolò's house. He carried the luggage they'd acquired on Deseos onto the broad, wraparound porch and stacked them to one side of the door before turning to address Kiley.

"My grandparents dropped Brutus off first thing this morning, which means he's going to need a walk. He has a fenced run out back, but it doesn't give him the amount of exercise he requires." He shot her a warning look. "You might want to stand back. Chances are, he'll be a bit exuberant."

Kiley decided to opt for the smarter course and wait on the sidewalk while Nicolò dealt with the massive animal. The instant he inserted the key in the lock she could feel the initial rumblings of the earthquake signaling the dog's approach. To her amusement instead of greeting Nicolò with their usual bonding ritual, Brutus shot past him and headed straight for her. Between his massive jaws he carried a much-abused tennis ball.

Kiley greeted the dog with a thorough scratch behind his ears and picked up the ball he dropped at her feet. "You want to play catch?" she asked.

Brutus spun around, barking in excitement. Then to Kiley's horror, he bounded into the street. Behind her, she heard Nicolò's shout of warning, a mirror to her own panicked cry. She saw the dog hesitate in confusion, then crouch down in his sphinxlike pose, holding perfectly still.

After that, events seemed to unravel in slow motion. Kiley swung her head to the left and saw a massive SUV heading for the motionless dog. Without a moment's hesitation, she charged toward the road, running on sheer instinct. Pelting toward Brutus, she grabbed for his collar. But even as she did so, she knew she'd reached him too late. She was nowhere near strong enough to drag the dog clear of danger before the SUV hit them.

She didn't see the vehicle's final approach, only heard the harsh blare of horn and the sickening squeal of brakes. She acted without thought, throwing herself across Brutus in a ridiculous attempt to protect him, not that she covered more than half the animal. Then she braced herself for the inevitable impact she knew would follow.

The horn and brakes continued their endless scream of warning and for a brief instant, something flashed through her mind. A memory. A memory that caused such pain and panic, every part of her cringed from it. In that split second of time she wasn't outside Nicolò's house, but found herself in the middle of a different street, where something bright yellow with blue fenders came barreling toward her. Before she could fully grasp the memory, it slipped away, along with all the foggy wisps of that other time and place, of that other Kiley.

The squeal of brakes seemed to last forever before the SUV slid to a stop mere inches from where Kiley had her head buried in Brutus's thick coat. The vehicle came so close she could feel the heat pouring off the engine hovering inches above her ear, and smell the distinctive oil and radiator stench that clogged her lungs and made it impossible to breath.

She vaguely heard the driver shout in a bizarre combination of anger and concern. Vaguely heard Nicolò's response before the driver took off with another punch of the car horn that left her trembling in reaction. Vaguely heard Brutus's whimper, as well as Nicolò's voice coming from somewhere above her.

She couldn't move. Couldn't process thought or any of the reassurances Nicolò offered in his soft, gentle rumble of a voice. She didn't even think she could feel, until Brutus washed the tears from her face and Nicolò lifted her from her prone position. Then she felt far, far too much. With a wordless cry, she dissolved against her husband, sobbing uncontrollably.

"Easy, sweetheart. You're okay. You're fine now."

"Bru-Brutus?" Her teeth were chattering so hard she could barely get the word out.

"He's fine." A snap of his fingers had the dog scurrying onto the porch, his tail between his legs. Nicolò followed, carrying her as though she were made of the most fragile porcelain. "What the hell were you thinking, running into the street after him like that?" He sounded angry, but even in her current state she understood the anger came from fear.

She sagged against him. "Wasn't thinking. Not even a little. I just . . ." The chatter of teeth hiccupped through her words. ". . . just reacted."

"That's obvious. Did you really believe you could protect Brutus by throwing yourself between him and a two-and-a-half ton SUV?"

She forced out a watery grin. "Haven't you figured it out, yet? I'm indestructible."

"Don't joke," he said, his voice tight and ragged. "You could have been killed. Again."

"But I wasn't. Again."

She pressed her mouth to his neck, inhaling the crisp, masculine scent of him. It stirred the oddest sensation, making her dizzy with need. How was that possible after what she'd just been through?

Nicolò put Kiley down long enough to toss their bags through the door before slamming it closed behind them.

Then he picked her up again, intent on taking her to the bedroom. He managed a single step before sagging onto the floor in a jumble of arms, legs, luggage, and dog.

"Aw, hell." He wrapped her up tight. Too tight. But he couldn't seem to control his response. *"Damn it,* Kiley. I thought I'd lost you."

"I'm sorry." Her words tumbled out, nearly incoherent. "I just reacted. All I could think about was saving Brutus. I'm fine. We're both fine now."

"That's twice." He lowered his head and inhaled her, her scent, her touch, her taste. He snatched a half-dozen urgent kisses. "Twice I've watched you come within an inch of dying. And both times I wasn't able to get to you before—"

"I'm okay. I'm safe." She caught hold of Brutus's collar and tugged the dog into their circle. "And so is Brutus."

It was time to face facts, he realized. He didn't know the woman he'd met that day at Le Premier. Whoever she was, she bore no relationship to the Kiley he held in his arms. That woman, the one prior to the accident, wouldn't have risked her perfectly manicured pinky to save his dog. That woman wouldn't have relished the scent of a simple sprig of honeysuckle, or reveled in the experience of holding a sleeping baby in her arms. That version of Kiley was gone, with luck permanently, and he could only thank God for it.

"Brutus, backyard," he ordered. As much as he adored his dog, right now he needed his wife.

No. Not his wife.

Not yet.

He cupped her face and covered her mouth in another kiss, only this one held a far different quality. Where before he'd been reassuring himself he'd reached her in time and she hadn't been harmed, this kiss was life-affirming. Fate had been kind to them both, had protected her not once, but twice. He'd see to it there wasn't a third incident. No matter what it took, he'd protect her from her own impulsiveness.

At the touch of his mouth, she opened to him, welcomed him home. Gave to him. He could feel his self-control slip as he lost himself in his desperate need for her.

"Now. I want you right here and right now."

She eased back and he snatched her into his arms again, unwilling to release her. "Wait," she said. Her laugh bubbled with happiness and desire and the sheer exhilaration of life. "I'm not going anywhere. You can have me wherever. Whenever. However."

"Here. Now. Naked."

Her laughter faded while her eyes heated. "In that case . . ."

Again she eased back and this time he let her go. Gripping the bottom of her shirt, she yanked it over her head and off. He didn't wait for her to remove her bra. His patience only stretched so far. No more than a few short seconds. With a flick of his fingers, he had the scrap of silk and lace open and swept aside.

She settled back onto his lap, back where she belonged, her legs cinching his waist. She started on the buttons of his shirt, but he didn't have the patience for that, either. In one button-spewing move, he shredded his shirt from stem to stern. Anything, if it meant having those clever hands of hers on his skin.

Heaven help him, but she was beautiful. Soft and tender and utterly edible. He cupped her bottom, gathered the slight weight of her in his palms. She tilted her head back with a groan, giving him total access to the elegant length of her throat and curve of her shoulders, long silken sweeps of skin that begged to be tasted and caressed. He gave her his full attention, finding every sensitive hollow and curve. And still it wasn't enough.

He tore at the snap and zip to her jeans, dragging them down her hips to reveal the flower-shaped birthmark stamped there, before peeling them off the pert curve of her backside. She wriggled clear of his lap just long enough for him to strip her. When he finished, she lay panting on the parquet floor, her skin sun-kissed gold against the dark wood, her hair full of red-hot flames. He ripped open his own jeans and took her hard and fast, sinking deep inside her in one powerful thrust while her cry of ecstasy echoed through the foyer.

He'd almost lost her. He might never have been able to hold her again. Kiss her. Make love to her. The mere thought left him crazed, gripped by a frenzy unlike anything he'd ever experienced before. He'd never been this desperate to have a woman. Never been so insane with desire that he hadn't cared about the where and when.

Until Kiley.

"Don't stop," she ordered. She clung to him, arms and legs wrapped tight around him, pulling him in until they were one flesh moving in unison. "Don't ever let go of me."

"Never. I swear I'm going to lock you away where no one can ever hurt you again."

She opened her mouth to reply, but instead arched upward, a keening cry ripped from her throat. She surrendered utterly to his possession, giving everything she had and holding nothing back. No hesitation, no subterfuge. Every stray thought and feeling there for him to see, his to accept or reject, more open and honest and giving than he believed it possible for a woman to be.

Her eyes turned a blinding shade of green, burning with an emotion so powerful and all-consuming it hurt to look at her. As he took her, as he sent her slamming into an endless climax, he realized it was love he saw in her eyes. A soul-deep commitment. And with that knowledge he went over the edge with her, lost to a moment that never should have happened.

It was a long time before he could move again. When he did, he realized nothing had changed. He had committed a crime beyond redemption and Kiley— He closed his eyes, utterly destroyed. Kiley had fallen in love with him. Gently, he lifted her in his arms and carried her to their bedroom. And all the while, two questions tormented him.

What the hell had he done?

And how could he fix it?

Kiley awoke the next morning, deliciously sore, yet thoroughly refreshed. On the pillow beside her, she found a businesslike note from Nicolò warning he'd be at the office all day.

Beneath the first note she found a second, and there was nothing businesslike at all about this one. The few short sentences left her in no doubt of Nicolò's feelings about the night before and caused a blush of delight to warm her cheeks.

She grinned like a loon over the second note, while fighting a wave of disappointment over the first. Well, what did she expect? Because of her accident, he'd been forced to take countless days off. He must have mountains of work piled up as a result.

Bouncing out of bed, she spent the morning on domestic chores, unpacking their bags and washing clothes. As the clock edged toward noon, she decided to surprise her husband for lunch. During their time together she'd gotten a fair idea of his tastes, and made up her mind to create a silly meal loaded with his favorites, everything from chicken Marsala to *panzanella*, pistachios to bitter chocolate, all easily available with just a few quick phone calls.

The instant the various treats arrived, she loaded them into a basket she found in a cupboard above the refrigerator and decorated it with a sprig of honeysuckle she found growing along the backyard fence. She liked to think Nicolò had started the hedge from a cutting he'd taken from his grandfather's garden, a tribute to that long-ago encounter with his first flower, not to mention his first bee sting.

Next, she called for a cab, relieved to discover the driver knew just where to find Dantes' corporate headquarters. The cabbie dropped her off in front of an impressively large office building and she entered through the revolving doors. Once inside she stumbled to a halt, staring in awe at the spectacular three-story glass foyer. She took her time, admiring everything from the elegant decor to the dance of sunlight off the sheets of tinted windows, to the impressive glass sculpture of dancing flames that hung above the receptionist's desk.

She'd just started toward the desk when an elderly man with a thick thatch of snowy hair approached. "Please, excuse me," he said, his deep voice carrying the lilting cadence of a Mediterranean heritage. "Are you Kiley O'Dell?"

She smiled warmly. "Actually, it's Kiley Dante."

"Yes, of course." He gazed at her with assessing gold eyes, eyes that cut straight through all pretense and yet held an unmistakable glint of kindness. "I believe, my dear, it is past time we met. I am Primo Dante."

Her smile grew and she regarded him in genuine delight. "You're Nicolò's grandfather. He told me all about you and how you helped raise him and his brothers."

"Nicolò, Severo, and the twins. Yes, Nonna and I took them in after the death of our son, Dominic, and his wife, Laura." He took her hand in his and leaned in to kiss first one of her cheeks, then the other. "You are on your way to visit Nicolò?"

She indicated the basket she carried. "I thought he'd enjoy some lunch."

Primo's gnarled fingers brushed the honeysuckle blossom decorating the handle. "And what have you brought him?" He listened intently while she listed the eclectic jumble of flavors. She petered out uncertainly and he gave her a reassuring smile. "It would seem you know my grandson's tastes quite well. And for yourself? Have you put nothing of your own in here? Or is all this for Nicolò's benefit alone?"

She looked momentarily abashed. "Tapioca pudding," she admitted. She couldn't help laughing at herself. "Who'd have figured I'd develop such a taste for it?"

He chuckled. "You may find it interesting to discover what things appeal when you permit yourself to give them a try without a history to influence your choices."

"Or what things no longer appeal?" she asked.

His gaze grew even more shrewd. "Excellent observation." He gestured toward the bank of elevators toward the rear of the foyer. "Shall I escort you?"

"Thank you. I'd appreciate that."

Primo used a key to access a private car. "You are recovered from your accident?" he asked politely.

"Physically, yes." A slight frown tugged at her brow as they entered the elevator. "I still haven't regained my memory. Although . . ."

"Although?"

She hesitated, for some reason tempted to confess something to Primo that she hadn't even told her husband. "I might have remembered something yesterday." She detailed her near-miss from the day before. "Right before I thought the SUV would hit us, I had a flash of memory."

"And what was this flash?"

"I suspect it was from that first accident."

Primo gave a slow nod. "That would make sense. The similarity between the two incidents might prompt a return of your memory."

She turned to face him, staring up at a compassionate face lined with a wealth of experience, both good and ill. "And yet, my memory didn't come back, even though for a split second I recalled . . . something. Pain. Fear. And . . ."

"And?" he prompted. "What are you afraid to see, Kiley O'Dell?"

"Dante," she corrected. "I know I wasn't certain I wanted to take the name when Nicolò and I first married, but I think it's probably like tapioca pudding. Things that might not have been to my taste before, are now."

"You are avoiding my question."

She grinned. "You're right, I am." Her smile faded. "I was afraid of whatever I saw. I guess of the accident, of the pain it caused me."

"Or maybe you were afraid of that other life. Maybe when you had the choice to remember or forget, you chose to forget."

His words caused her heart to kick up a beat, possibly because they held the weight of truth. She caught her bottom lip between her teeth and worried at it. "You think I don't want to remember?" she finally asked.

Primo shrugged. "The mind is a strange thing. Perhaps it is protecting you. Perhaps when you no longer need its protection, you will remember." Before she could reply, the door slid open and he gestured for her to precede him. "You will find Nicolò's office at the end of the corridor to the left. Tell him it is time for you to meet the family. Tell him it is past time, yes?"

"Yes, it is," she agreed.

He leaned down and kissed her cheeks again, then headed in the opposite direction. Taking a deep breath, she followed Primo's directions, pausing outside a door with Nicolò's name on it. Some jokester had added a shiny gold label beneath his name that read Chief Troublemaker. Her lips twitched and she lifted her fist to knock, hesitating at the last instant.

Was it possible? she couldn't help but wonder. Was she resisting remembering because she wanted to escape those memories? Could it all be tied in with the fight she'd had with Nicolò? Maybe if he told her what had happened it would cause her memory to return. Because despite how their marriage had functioned before her accident, they'd fully bonded since. And that meant they could find a way to work through whatever had divided them. She was convinced of it.

No matter what secret Nicolò kept from her, one thing was certain. The time had come for the two of them to be totally honest with one another, regardless of how painful the process. That decided, she rapped on the door, then turned the knob and walked in.

To her dismay, she found the room crowded with people. Three men stood in a pile, arguing at full throttle. None were Nicolò, though based on the fact that the three shared a physical similarity to her husband, and two of them were twins, they had to be his brothers. Off to one side sat a man with salt-and-pepper hair and a flushed complexion who silently seethed while he listened to the argument. He was flanked by yet another man, a huge tank-sized black man with black eyes that had been there and seen it all.

Finally, she located her husband, leaning against his desk, a grim expression darkening his face. At her entrance, his head jerked in her direction, and if anything, his expression turned blacker still.

He slowly straightened. "What are you doing here, Kiley?" he demanded in an undertone.

The salt-and-pepper-haired man glanced her way and leapt to his feet, pointing an accusing finger straight at her. "That's her! My God, you found the little bitch." He lunged toward her, his forward momentum stopped by the quick action of the three men Kiley had pegged as Nicolò's brothers. "Get out of my way," he roared. "I've waited a long time for this. Just give me five minutes of uninterrupted time alone with her and you can keep the money she owes me."

Kiley stumbled backward, relieved to find Nicolò planted in front of her, his stance clearly protective. "You shouldn't be here." He threw the comment over his shoulder. "Why did you come?"

"I—I brought you lunch. I wanted to surprise you." She swallowed, struggling to control the fear and tension tearing at her. "Surprise."

"Your timing couldn't have been worse."

"Who is that man? How does he know me? Why is he so angry?"

"The man is Jack Ferrell and he's leveled some accusations against you. The three by my desk are my brothers," he confirmed her guess by indicating the trio of men who'd been arguing when she'd first entered. "And Juice is Dantes head of security. We were trying to get to the bottom of the allegations when you arrived."

She stepped out from behind her husband, determined to face the accusations aimed at her head-on. The Dantes and Juice continued to restrain Ferrell while he ranted in undisguised fury. "What does he say I've done?"

Nicolò hesitated, then reluctantly explained, "He's accused you of scamming him out of a rather substantial sum of money."

"No." She shook her head. "That's not possible. I may not remember the past, but I do know myself. I wouldn't do anything so dishonest."

He turned to face her. "Kiley—"

"Oh, God." The lunch basket slipped from her fingers and hit the carpet, spilling its contents. The can of pistachios landed square on the honeysuckle, crushing the fragile blossoms. The sweet scent drifted up between them, sharp as a bee sting. "You believe him, don't you? You believe I ripped him off!"

Chapter Eight

To Kiley's horror, Nicolò didn't deny the accusation.

"Ferrell has proof, sweetheart," he said gently. "Granted, it's a bit on the sketchy side, but he insists you ran a con on him involving a fire diamond necklace, one you supposedly inherited from your grandfather."

"Fire diamonds?" For a split second she saw Francesca and Nicolò staring intently at her as she studied the fire diamonds at Dantes Exclusive, waiting . . . Waiting for what? For her to remember something about this necklace Ferrell referred to? Had they known about the accusations even then? "I don't understand any of this. What necklace does he mean?"

"I don't know. It's something we'll have to figure out together." She closed her eyes at his use of the word *together*. He must have understood how much it meant to her, because he traced his thumb along the curve of her cheek. "Until then, you need to go home."

"She's not going anywhere," Jack Ferrell protested. "I want my money. And I want her to pay for what she did to me. I insist you call the police and have her arrested."

Nicolò spun to face the man. "You signed a binding agreement, Ferrell. One that allows us to settle this matter quietly. It also requires you prove your claims. So far, all we have are accusations."

"She offered to sell me her grandfather's necklace. I put half the money down. But when I went to complete the transaction, she'd disappeared, along with my money and the necklace." He glared at Kiley. "You were slick, I'll give you that. But you won't get away this time."

Kiley shook her head, attempting to reason with the man. "I wouldn't do something like that. You must have me mixed up with someone else."

His lips pulled back in a snarl. "Not a chance in hell. You have a birthmark on your hip. It's shaped like a flower."

She felt every scrap of color drain from her face. Wordlessly, she shook her head.

"No? Come on, gorgeous. Strip down and show us the birthmark. Prove me wrong."

"Get out of here, Kiley," Nicolò interrupted. "I'll be home as soon as I resolve this."

"No. I'm not going anywhere. Not until the two of us discuss this." She spared a brief glance toward the other men. "Privately."

"Think you can sweet-talk your way around him?" Ferrell interrupted. "You're wasting your time. He's not the fool I was. With all the information his head of security has assembled, I'll bet he sees right through you. No way are you slipping out from under this one. Not this time."

Nicolò spun to face his brothers. "Shut him up, will you? I'll be right back." Without another word, he cupped Kiley's elbow and drew her from the room. "I can spare five minutes. We'll hash out the rest of it when I get home."

One look at his expression and everything went numb inside. This man wasn't her husband, wasn't the man who'd taken her with such crazed desperation on his foyer floor. This was the suspicious-eyed man from those first hours and days after her accident. Dear God. What had she done in that other life? What had she been?

She flinched from the possibility. Or maybe it was all some sort of colossal mistake. She'd never deliberately scam someone, would she? It didn't matter that Jack Ferrell knew about her birthmark. He could have found out about it somehow.

Kiley wrung her hands. If only she had her memory back, she could prove her innocence. Without it, she was utterly vulnerable. She spared the grim stranger at her side a quick glance, unremitting pain lancing through her.

And utterly alone.

She remained silent and heartsick while Nicolò ushered her into a small conference room. Like everything else she'd seen of Dantes so far, it was a lovely room, but one clearly designed for business. Is that what she'd become? Business? Based on his current attitude, she might as well be.

She fought to gather her self-control, to focus her confusion into some semblance of order, so that at least she'd know what questions to ask. She opened with the first one to come to mind.

"Why did you Dantes' head of security look into me?"

"I asked Juice to check into some things after your accident."

"That doesn't quite answer my question," she pointed out. "But let's start there. Did you make the request because of my accident or because of our fight?"

"Does it matter?"

"Is what that man was saying—" She gestured in the general direction of Nicolò's office. "The necklace and the money I supposedly took from him. Is that what our fight was about? The one before my accident?"

"Indirectly."

Anger ripped through her. "Stop it, Nicolò. Just stop all the cagey responses and give it to me straight. I'll believe whatever you tell me." She laughed, a hard, painful sound. "After all, I don't have any other choice. Since I don't remember, I have to accept your version of events."

"The truth?"

"If you don't mind."

"Your grandfather and your great-uncle jointly owned a fire diamond mine, a mine they sold to my grandfather, Primo. When we first met it was to discuss the legality of that sale. You claimed there was a problem with the transfer of title, that you still owned a portion of the mine."

She took a moment to absorb that. "Then, we didn't meet over a game of Frisbee?"

"No."

She shook her head in bewilderment. "Why would you make up a story? What difference does it make how or when we met?"

"It mattered."

Frustration ripped through her. "Why?"

He rubbed a spot between his brows where tension had formed a deep crease. "I didn't want to bring it up after your accident because I needed time to find out whether your claim on the mine was genuine. I needed time for Juice to unearth the truth while you recovered from your injuries. Time for us to get to know one another, to deal with The Inferno, without the mine coming between us."

She frowned in confusion. "I still don't understand. What has the sale of the mine got to do with this necklace Ferrell is going on about?"

"I have no idea. If there's a connection, I haven't found it, yet. Juice met Ferrell while investigating you and your claims regarding the mine."

"This man, Ferrell, he's convinced I've scammed him, isn't he?"

"Yes."

"And you? What do you believe?"

"We're still looking into it, Kiley," he said with a painful lack of intonation. All the while, a remote darkness swirled in his gaze.

She could feel her heart breaking at the distance he put between them. Despite that, she forced herself to ask the necessary questions. "But it's possible he's right?" She could see the answer in Nicolò's expression and something infinitely precious died inside. It took a moment before she could form her next question, one almost too painful to ask. "Do you believe I was trying to scam you about the diamond mine?"

"Don't do this, Kiley. Not now."

"Answer me, Nicolò. When we first met, did you think I was some sort of con artist?"

He hesitated, before reluctantly nodding. "I suspected you might be."

"Why?" It was a cry from the heart.

He lifted his shoulder in a shrug, his expression one of extreme weariness. "Nothing definitive. Just a feeling I had."

She wanted to go to him, to wrap her arms around him and reassure him that it would all work out. But she couldn't. Too much divided them right now, a chasm of doubt and suspicion she had no clue how to bridge. Had no way of bridging without her memory.

"If you suspected me of being that sort of person, why did you decide to date me? How did we end up falling in love? How did we end up married?"

He lifted his hand, palm out. "It would seem The Inferno doesn't worry about such minor details as—"

"As moral character?" she cut in.

"Kiley—"

She glanced toward the door, realizing she was poised to run, to escape an untenable situation. The urge nearly overwhelmed her. Was it gut instinct, or a pattern so much a part of her it didn't require memory? She fought it with every ounce of strength she possessed. "Is it true? What Ferrell accused me of? Did I do those things? Is that who I really am?"

"I don't know." She could hear the frustration ripping apart his words. "I don't want to believe it, Kiley."

"Then don't." She dared to approach, dared to splay her hands across his chest and gather that steady, life-affirming heartbeat in her palm. "I need you to believe in me, Nicolò. I need you to fight for me. Maybe everything Ferrell says is true. Maybe I am a horrible person."

"No." The word escaped without thought or hesitation and it gave her the first glimmer of hope.

"Okay, *was*. Maybe I *was* a horrible person. But what if it's all a mistake? Since I can't remember, I can't defend myself. I have to believe there's some other explanation, if we can only find it." She stared up at him, no longer interested in running, but determined to fight. "Please, Nicolò. I need to discover the truth."

"And if the truth isn't what you want to hear?"

"At least it'll be the truth."

She shouldn't kiss him, shouldn't put any more pressure on him. But she couldn't help herself. Just for a moment or two she needed her husband, needed to coax him out from under his troubleshooter persona.

She slid her arms around his neck and covered his mouth with hers, practically consuming him. She felt his momentary resistance, understood it even as it caused her unfathomable pain. And then she felt the give, the gentle slide from reluctance into acceptance, before it transformed into something desperate and greedy and urgent. The flutter of hope gained in strength. He hadn't given up on her. Not yet.

She snatched another kiss, a final one. "I need you to promise me something else," she said.

She could see the shutters slam back into place. "If I can."

"Promise me you'll tell me the truth from now on. When you're done here, we'll put all the cards on the table."

He gave a brief nod. "That's one promise I can make. Until then, go home and I'll join you there as soon as I'm able."

His eyes were dark with pain and haunted by secrets. He lowered his head and kissed her again. There was an unmistakable finality in the way he embraced her, as though acknowledging on some level that their relationship would never be the same again. This time when he released her, he took a step backward, distancing himself physically, as well as emotionally.

"Fair warning, Kiley. You won't like some of those cards I'm going to show you. They may very well end things between us."

There was nothing she could say to that, no way to reassure him or calm her own fears. He opened the conference room door for her and she sleepwalked through it. She headed for the elevators, but found herself continuing past them, unable to convince herself to leave. She never knew how long she wandered the corridors before Primo found her and gathered her up.

Murmuring in soothing Italian, he escorted her to a generous-sized office. He installed her in a large, deep-cushioned chair before crossing to a wet bar. Pouring her a drink, he handed it to her. She cupped her hands around the balloon of the snifter and inhaled the potent brandy before taking a generous swallow.

Primo didn't say anything to her, but resumed his seat at his desk and occupied himself with paperwork. She sat and sipped the brandy, losing track of time. It could have been minutes or hours. Time flowed in a confusing haze. But at long last she looked up.

"Lunch didn't go well," she announced in a low voice.

Primo set aside his papers and capped his pen. "I assumed as much."

"It's funny. For the past few weeks I've been enjoying so many new experiences. Until today. Today," She drew and deep breath and pushed out an unsteady smile. "Not so much."

"Sometimes we learn more from the bad experiences than the good."

She curled deeper in the chair. "I'm not sure I like that idea."

He cocked a head to one side in a gesture endearingly reminiscent of Nicolò. "Perhaps you have learned what you now must fix. Would that not allow some good to come from the bad?"

"I can fix being a con artist?"

His gaze sharpened. "So. You believe this man, Ferrell."

It shouldn't surprise her he'd heard about what had happened in Nicolò's office. The Dantes were a tight-knit family. "Ferrell knows things about me. Things he shouldn't—" Her voice broke and she struggled to control it. She met his golden gaze, caught the compassion gleaming there and allowed it to warm her. "What if he's right? What if I really am a scam artist?"

"Are you?" He paused a beat. "Or *were* you?"

Tears filled her eyes. "Is there a difference?"

"Very much so. One exists in a past you cannot recall. The other may be created in a future yet to come."

His words struck hard, restored the hope that had been so badly shaken. "Thank you, Primo." She uncurled from her chair and crossed the room to plant a kiss on his cheek. "I'm glad we finally met."

He stood and enfolded her in a tight embrace. "As am I."

Nicolò had told her to go home, but she couldn't bear the idea of returning there without him. Instead, she retraced her path to his office, hoping he'd now be available to leave with her. To her disappointment, the door stood open and the room deserted. She entered, intent on scribbling him a brief note. Crossing to his desk, she saw a folder bearing her name on the wooden surface. Curiosity got the better of her and she flipped it open.

And her world collapsed around her.

Nicolò had to be home, waiting for her, Kiley decided as she left Dantes. And when she arrived, she'd have him explain all she'd found in that damning file, a file currently tucked beneath her arm. There had to be an explanation, other than the obvious one. She couldn't be the person detailed between those pages. It wasn't possible.

To Kiley's disappointment, she arrived to find an empty house, empty except for Brutus, who seemed to sense her despair. He trailed behind her, whining softly, as she wandered from room to room, struggling to come to terms with all she'd learned. From deep within the house, she heard the doorbell ring and for a split second her heart leaped. *Nicolò.* He was home. Then common sense prevailed. Her husband would have used his key.

Leaving Brutus in the den, she crossed to the front door and opened it, surprised to discover a woman standing there, impatiently tapping her foot.

"About time," the woman announced, before sweeping inside. "Do you have any idea how long it's taken me to track you down? I finally tricked your address out of the hospital, though what the hell you were doing there, they wouldn't say."

"Who—" Kiley hesitated, taking a second, longer look.

The woman, a striking blonde, appeared to be in her late thirties, though something about the hardness around her carefully made up eyes and mouth hinted at a handful of years more than that. She matched Kiley's stature, or lack thereof, the only difference between them the extra few inches the older woman carried in the bust line and around the hips. She wore her hair in a short cap of curls that emphasized both her striking bone structure, as well as a pair of vivid blue eyes.

A possibility occurred to Kiley, one she could only pray was true. "I know this is going to sound like an odd question, but . . . Are you my mother?" she asked, fighting to control a wild surge of emotion.

A single eyebrow winged skyward. "Have you lost your mind? Of course, I'm your mother."

"Oh, my God." Kiley threw her arms around the woman, hugging her with tearful exuberance. She needed this, needed something to go right today. "Oh, Mom, you have no idea how happy I am to meet you."

"Now I know you've lost your mind." The woman pried herself free of Kiley's embrace. "What the hell do you mean you're happy to meet me? And—horror of horrors—since when have you called me 'Mom'? Try Lacey, you ungrateful brat. Now where's the damn necklace?"

Kiley fell back a step. "I—I call you Lacey?"

"If you don't pull yourself together, I swear I'm going to slap you, if only to knock an ounce of sense into that brain of yours. I mean, really, Kiley. What were you thinking? What made you believe for one tiny second that you could get away with it?"

"Get away with—" She shook her head. "You don't understand. I was in an accident. I lost my memory. I have no idea what you're talking about."

To Kiley's shock, Lacey burst out laughing. "Oh, that's a good one. You're always scheming, aren't you? Well? Come on." She folded her arms across her chest and set her foot to tapping again. "Explain how this latest one works. I'm all ears."

Kiley stared at her mother in horror. Didn't she believe her own daughter? But then, if the information in the file was correct, why would she? "You don't understand. I'm serious. I have no memory of you, or of my past, or—or anything."

"Oh, you poor dear." Lacey feigned a sympathetic look before spoiling it with a laugh. "I have to hand it to you, sweetie, you're really quite good at this. I'm actually starting to enjoy myself, which is rather miraculous considering my mood when I arrived." She crossed to Kiley's side and linked arms with her. "Now don't keep your dear momma standing in the hallway. Show me around the joint."

Every instinct Kiley possessed screamed a warning. "Why don't we go into the living room," she suggested instead. "Maybe I can give you a tour when Nicolò gets home. He's due any moment."

"Nicolò?"

"My husband."

Lacey's jaw dropped. "You're married?"

"Close to a month now." She gestured toward the sofa. "Can I fix you a drink?"

"The usual. Make it a double."

"And the usual is?"

Lacey shrugged. "I should have known you'd be too good to fall for that one. Double scotch. Neat." She waited until she'd been served before leaning forward with a wheedling expression.

"Come on, Kiley. Let me in on this one. I can play it anyway you want. Just give me the lowdown so I don't make any mistakes."

Kiley stared at her mother in disbelief. Oh, God. If this was the lifestyle she'd chosen before being hit by that cab, no wonder she didn't want to remember. How had she lived with herself? How had she justified such an unscrupulous existence? "This isn't a scam. I was hit by a cab and I'm suffering from something called retrograde amnesia."

Lacey waved that aside. "Whatever. At least tell me who your mark is."

Mark. With every word her mother uttered, she confirmed the information in the file—hideous, damning information that listed name after name, amount after amount, of people scammed and money taken. "There is no mark," Kiley stated numbly. "There's just my husband."

Lacey snapped her fingers. "Right. The husband. That's one I haven't pulled in a while. Too messy." She gestured for Kiley to continue. "Well? What's his name?"

"Nicolò Dante."

"Dante?" Lacey sat bolt upright. *"Nicolò Dante?* Have you lost your mind? You think you can take down a Dante?"

"I keep telling you," Kiley said wearily. "This isn't—"

"A scam. Right." Lacey slammed her drink onto the coffee table with such force it made the crystal sing and gathered up her purse. "Well, I don't want any part of whatever it isn't."

"Just answer a question first." Kiley crossed to where she'd left the file. Flipping it open, she removed one of the pages and offered it to Lacey. "Do you recognize these names? Is this information correct? Did I rip off all these people?"

With notable reluctance, Lacey set aside her purse and took the paper. Scanning it, she turned deathly pale as she read. "What the hell are you thinking, writing all this down?" she gritted out. "Do you have any idea what sort of trouble this could cause us?"

"All I want to know is whether or not it's accurate. Did I do those things?"

Lacey shot to her feet, shoving the list back into Kiley's hands. "That's it. I don't know what you're trying to pull, but I won't be party to it. I suggest you burn that paper before someone connects you with it. In the meantime, I'm out of here." She held out her hand. "Just give me the necklace and I'll be on my way."

Kiley stiffened. There it was again. The necklace. No doubt the same necklace Ferrell referred to. She carefully folded the list into fours and slipped it into her pocket. "What necklace?"

"Stop playing games." Lacey's voice could have cut glass. "Your grandfather Cameron's fire diamond necklace."

Kiley stilled. "Then, there really is a necklace?"

"Of course there really is a necklace. Now where is it?"

"I haven't got a clue." Kiley began to laugh. "Maybe when I get my memory back, I'll remember that, as well."

"The locket." Lacey's anger ebbed, replaced by a look of cunning. "If you don't have the necklace on you, you've got a safe deposit key hidden in the locket."

Kiley slipped her hand beneath her blouse and fisted her fingers protectively around the silver heart. "So, I'm not just a scam artist. I get top marks for deviousness, too. Lovely."

She remembered with painful amusement how crushed she'd been when Nicolò had informed her she didn't have a close relationship with her mother. How she'd longed for the sort of family ties the Dantes possessed. Right now, she'd have given almost anything to be an orphan.

Kiley fished the locket from beneath her blouse. "FYI, I don't know how to open it."

"Oh, would you please give this amnesia business a rest? You had me in stitches with it earlier, but enough's enough." She took another step in Kiley's direction, her face lined with grim intent. "Give me the locket. I'll open it if you won't."

Her hand fisted around the locket. "I'm not giving you anything."

"You are such a fool," she ranted. "Do you think I didn't consider setting up the Dantes years ago? Color me with a bit more common sense than you're currently showing. At least I knew better than to make a play in that direction, though I will admit the amnesia thing gives it an interesting twist."

"It's not—"

"I'm your mother, Kiley," Lacey bit out. "You can't fool me. Now, I want that key. Give it to me or I swear I'll take it from you. I'm not playing around here. I don't want to be anywhere in the vicinity when Dante discovers you're faking amnesia in order to scam him."

"To late, I'm afraid." Nicolò stepped into the room, Brutus at his heels. "It would seem that Dante found out a little sooner than you anticipated."

Chapter Nine

It took every ounce of self-control for Nicolò to hold his fury in check. At his appearance, Kiley and her mother both spun to face him, identical expressions of consternation on faces that bore a startling similarity. Or they would if Kiley ever acquired the bitter cunning that marked the older woman's features.

Here was the avarice he'd sought in Kiley's face during their visit to Dantes Exclusive. The slyness. The self-indulgence. Finally, he could see what she worked so hard to keep from him. He only had to meet the mother to uncover it. Beside him, Brutus checked out the newcomer and released a soft growl, one that had her taking a hasty step backward.

"You asked for the truth, Kiley." He stripped off his suit jacket and tossed it over a nearby chair. "I didn't realize you were the one who would provide it for me."

"No, Nicolò." Her cheeks turned every bit as waxen as they'd been during her hospital stay, a realization that gave him an unwanted pang of concern. "You misunderstood what we were saying."

He cut her off with a slice of his hand. "Drop the act, Kiley. I'm neither deaf nor a fool. I understood every word your mother . . . ?" He lifted an eyebrow in the older woman's direction, prompting her to confirm his assumption.

"Lacey O'Dell," she offered coolly. She took a step in his direction, hand outstretched, but stopped dead in her tracks when Brutus bristled. She cautiously lowered her arm to her side, and Nicolò couldn't help noting with some satisfaction that it took her a few seconds to recover her aplomb. "Call me Lacey."

He continued to address Kiley, tearing at the tie knotted at his throat. "I understood every word Lacey said. You've been faking amnesia in order to pull off a scam meant to garner you a share of the Dante fire diamond mine."

"I did warn you," Lacey said to Kiley, before fixing him with an assessing gaze.

The pale blue color struck him as ice-cold and lacked the humor and kindness—not to mention the fiery passion—so often reflected in her daughter's. Maybe the difference between the two came from Lacey's additional years of running scams.

Maybe this was how Kiley would appear a few years down such a rough and unforgiving road.

"I assume you're Nicolò Dante, Kiley's husband?" she asked.

"Is that what she told you?"

Lacey hesitated, disappointment flashing across her face. "Another lie?"

He stripped away his loosened tie and released the first few buttons of his shirt before it strangled him. "My lie, this time. Conning a con, I guess you'd call it."

Kiley caught her breath in a soft, disbelieving gasp. "No! No, that can't be. Tell me you didn't lie about that, Nicolò." She stared at him, her pleading look one of utter devastation. "Anything but that."

He met her gaze without saying a word. He simply waited. She knew the truth. She'd known from day one, minute one that they weren't married. And she'd chosen to play along every step of the way. No doubt her current performance was for her mother's benefit. Eventually she'd explain why she'd set this particular game in motion and what she hoped to gain from it. In the meantime, he was done playing.

At his continued silence, Kiley closed her eyes in abject surrender. The expression on her face absolutely gutted him, even though it had to be an act. It took her several seconds to regain her equilibrium and confront him again. When she did, her eyes were black with pain.

"We're not married? All those romantic dates you told me about, the seaside wedding, none of it ever happened?" When he didn't respond, she lifted a trembling hand to her mouth. "It's all a lie? *All of it?* Touring the city. Dantes Exclusive. Oh, God. Deseos. Those incredible, beautiful, romantic nights on Deseos. It was just a game to you?"

He didn't spare either of them. "It would seem we both lied, didn't we, Kiley?" But even that wasn't the complete truth. Because there had been times when he could have sworn there'd been nothing but honesty between them. "No doubt we each have our own special place reserved in hell."

"No! I don't believe you. Some of it had to be real."

Painfully aware of Lacey's keen interest, he cut Kiley off. He didn't want to remember any of it, remember what a fool he'd been. He especially refused to think about Deseos. "Enough. Just can the dramatics, will you? You've won your Oscar. I actually believed you had amnesia, if only for a few weeks."

Lacey blew out a sigh. "That's my daughter for you," she said with exaggerated sympathy. "Just one deception after another."

He turned on her next. "Like mother, like daughter?"

She stiffened, lifting her chin in defiance. "Not at all. Since you listened in on our conversation, you must have heard me say that I wanted no part in whatever scam Kiley's running."

"Very self-righteous of you," he said dryly. "I'd be a bit more impressed if I also hadn't heard you say you know better than to take on the Dantes. Still, I applaud your intelligence, as well as your keen sense of self-preservation."

She had the unmitigated gall to wink at him. "Thank you."

He removed his cufflinks and pocketed them before rolling up the sleeves of his shirt. Throughout the process, he continued to scrutinize her. "Just out of curiosity, what about the others?"

"What others?" Her movements slowed, stuttering to stillness, and she moistened her lips with the tip of her tongue. The "tell," the unconscious movement that warned him whenever she lied was painfully similar to the one he'd noticed Kiley use in the suite at Le Premier all those weeks ago. "I have no idea what you're talking about."

"I'm talking about the other men you've scammed over the years."

Lacey's eyes went flat and, if possible, even colder than before. "Hmm. I don't think I care for the direction this conversation has taken. So, if you don't mind, I think I'll opt out of it." She crossed to the sofa with a hip-swinging walk and gathered up her purse before confronting Kiley. "I believe you have something to give me."

The odd quality in her tone caused Brutus to leap to Kiley's defense. He muscled his way between the two women, appearing more ferocious and intimidating than Nicolò had ever seen him. With a muffled cry, Lacey stumbled back a few paces.

Kiley reached out and soothed the dog. "I have nothing for you. Do I, Brutus?"

He gave a sharp bark of agreement, one that had Lacey making a beeline for the doorway. Once she was satisfied, she stood a safe distance from the dog, she opened her mouth to argue. Sparing a swift glance toward Nicolò, she thought better of it. Apparently, he looked every bit as intimidating as his dog. It was a comforting thought.

"This isn't over," she warned. "Not by a long shot."

With that, she swept from the room escorted by Brutus, which no doubt explained why her heels tapped a frantic dance across the foyer. A few seconds later, the front door opened and slammed shut again. The silence hung in the air, thick and heavy. Nicolò could see Kiley struggling to find the right words to use on him. The best tack to explain away what he'd heard. He didn't give her the opportunity to settle on a strategy.

He approached, watching the wariness flare in her eyes. "When did you get your memory back? Or did you ever lose it in the first place?"

Her chin shot upward. "I lost it. I still don't remember anything before the accident, despite what you and my mother may think."

He couldn't help himself. He laughed, the sound harsh and ripe with disbelief. "Yeah, right."

She searched his face, no doubt looking for the chink in his armor, a chink he'd make very certain she never found. "There's nothing I can say to convince you I'm not faking amnesia, is there?"

"Not a thing."

Exhaustion settled over her, a visible blanket of weariness. "All right, fine, Nicolò. Have it your way. I'm lying about everything. I faked amnesia. Tell me what I've won. What's my consolation prize?"

He hesitated. "What are you talking about?"

"I must have faked amnesia for some reason." She spread her hands. "Tell me what I could possibly gain by such a pretense."

"Will half of Dantes' fire diamond mine do? I mean, when we first met at Le Premier that was your original scam, wasn't it?"

"For the sake of argument, let's say it was. Did it work?"

"You know it didn't."

"Why?"

His eyes narrowed in speculation. "What game are you playing now, Kiley?"

"Just answer the question. Why didn't it work?"

"Because your argument that day wasn't logical. You had all the documentation lined up, but it didn't make sense your family would have waited so many years before coming forward with the claim."

"Huh. Good point." It almost felt as though she were tiptoeing through her analysis, though he couldn't figure out why she bothered. "Okay, so I tried the con on you when we first met at Le Premier and it didn't work. Logically, what would I have done next?"

"Slipped away before I took legal action or involved the police."

"Then why didn't I? How would an amnesia scam work to my advantage? What do I gain by it?"

"You'd inveigle yourself into my life."

"Again, to what end? Money? I haven't asked and you haven't given me any. For the sex? Pretty damn good, I'll admit, but not worth the consequences when you found out about the scam. So, why would I assume such a risk? I had to know you'd take the precise steps you have and ask Juice to look into my background. If I were faking amnesia, that is."

He folded his arms across his chest. "You tell me. What could you possibly get out of pretending to lose your memory?"

"And there's the rub." For just an instant, humor lit her eyes before fading into something heartbreakingly bittersweet. "I haven't a clue. Maybe I fell in love with you when we first touched. Blame it on The Inferno, if that helps. Maybe I wanted a few days, a few precious weeks, to experience normalcy. No cons. No angle. Just a woman in love with a man with no strings attached."

He steeled himself not to reveal how her words had affected him. "And now?"

She lowered her head as though considering her options. Her hand slipped into her pocket, wrapping around something that crinkled. She froze, so still and silent, while conflict battled across her expression. And that's when it happened. She slowly looked up and he watched a hint of avarice grow in her eyes, watched them take on that hard, knowing look that had been so apparent in Lacey's gaze. She even managed to imitate her mother's flirtatious smile, the tip of her tongue tracing a tantalizing path along her lush mouth.

"I guess my little vacation from reality is over," she purred. "It's been fun. I got some designer clothes out of it, not to mention a trip to an island paradise. Of course, it didn't end as well as I'd hoped. But we'll just chalk that up to misfortune and move on."

"Kiley, what—"

"Don't," she said sharply, her breezy expression shattering for a telling moment. "It would never have worked, Nicolò. You must have known that as soon as you read my file. If we'd tried for anything more than a fling, my reputation would have ruined the Dante name. Just let me go. It's long past time I got back to my old life."

She was right and he knew it. "Fine. No point in dragging this out."

Without another word she headed for the foyer, picking up her purse from off the small hallway table where she'd left it. She hesitated with her hand on the front doorknob. "I appreciate you taking care of me after my accident."

Nicolò leaned against the archway between the living room and foyer. "Before you go, answer one question."

She shrugged without turning around. "Sure."

"Was any of it real?"

She swiveled to face him, but all he could see was Lacey staring at him through Kiley's eyes. "You mean, did I love you?"

"Did you?"

Her movements slowed, fluttering to stillness like a bird settling to its nest and she moistened her lips. "Sorry, Dante. I guess there was some sort of glitch in The Inferno that day at Le Premier. Our bond never took, at least not on my end of things. It may have been fun. But it wasn't true love." And with that, she walked out the door.

The instant it closed behind her, Brutus howled in anguish. "I'm right there with you, buddy," Nicolò whispered. "Right there with you."

Kiley never remembered the hours immediately following her flight from Nicolò's, where she went or what she did. She didn't awake to her surroundings until dusk had settled over the city and she found herself standing in front of a seedy little hotel somewhere in the Mission District.

A quick check of her wallet elicited five hundred dollars and a couple of credit cards. One was maxed out, so she used her precious cash, holding the second credit card in reserve. At least she now had a roof over her head. She huddled in the depressing little room she'd rented, her locket clutched in her hands, determined to come up with a game plan. The silver heart seemed to burn within her grasp, the lacey strips of silver pressing ridges into her palm, as though trying to imprint a message there.

But all she could think about was Nicolò. The expression on his face when he'd walked into the living room after overhearing her moth—No, *not* her mother—*Lacey*. That flash of emotion she'd seen in his eyes when he'd asked if any part of what they'd experienced over the past few weeks had been real. His shock when she'd shoved out the one lie she could ever remember telling.

She opened her hand and studied the locket, pushing absently at the intertwining strips of silver. She'd had to do it, had to lie to him. Once she'd absorbed that damning information from the file, she realized she couldn't stay. Couldn't allow her relationship with Nicolò to continue, assuming he'd have wanted such a thing. There'd been no other choice but to sever all remaining ties between them.

Even if Nicolò had been willing to overlook her past, she couldn't take the risk that one day her memory would come back and she'd transform into a younger version of Lacey. Couldn't risk the possibility she'd turn on him and use his wealth and position for her own personal gain. It didn't matter that walking away had broken her heart. After all she'd done to hurt others, it was a small price to pay.

And, regardless of what cost the sacrifice, she'd continue to pay until she put right all she'd set wrong in the past.

The instant she reached her decision one of the small strips of silver slid to one side and the locket clicked open. She stared in wonder at the small key she found nestled inside. If Lacey were right, it was the key to a safety deposit box, as well as the solution to her problem.

Because in that safety deposit box was the means for her to make amends to all those she'd injured over the years.

"Have you lost your mind?"

Nicolò glared at his brother, Lazz. "Why do you keep asking me that same question?"

"Because it bears repeating." He shoved a hand through his hair. "I mean, get serious. Did you not read her file?"

"Yes, I read her file."

"Did you not see the part that said scam artist in big red letters? Hell, it was hard to miss since Juice also put it in bolded caps."

"I saw it," Nicolò stated between gritted teeth.

"So then why the hesitation? She scammed every man she ever met, but she's not going to do the same to you because she's your Inferno soul mate?"

"That's part of it."

"And the other?"

"She's changed. She's not that person anymore."

Lazz's mouth dropped open and he floundered a moment before he could speak again. "You have got to be kidding me. You did not just say that."

Nicolò swore beneath his breath. He didn't know why it had taken him a full three hours after Kiley left before he caught the mistake within the lie. Maybe he'd been so focused on her claiming she didn't love him—and the "tell" which had given lie to that statement—that he hadn't fully processed her comment. But the instant it sank in, he realized she hadn't regained her memory at all, or she'd have known they never bonded at Le Premier.

As soon as he'd realized the truth, he'd gone charging out of the house. With Brutus at his side, he'd spent the entire night combing the city for her, but she'd disappeared as though she'd never existed. It was the first time in his entire life he hadn't been able to find a way out of a predicament. He was good at solving problems. The best. But this time he hit a brick wall and it was a wall he couldn't find a way over, under, or around, let alone through.

"She doesn't remember, Lazz," Nicolò insisted. "She still has amnesia."

"How can you possibly know?" Lazz argued.

"Because she slipped up right before she left. She said we first bonded at Le Premier. But we never did. We just spat sparks at each other. We weren't 'Infernoed' until I took her hand at the hospital."

"Hello. She's. A. Con. Artist. She hasn't changed. And it wasn't a slipup. It was an 'on purpose.' She was hoping you'd catch the mistake. Hoping you'd buy right back into the con. And damn it, Nicolò, you have, haven't you?"

"If that woman's still a con artist, then yeah, I'm buying it. And I'm going to keep buying it until I'm old and gray and we've been married for as many decades as Primo and Nonna." He leaned in, jaw set. "I'm going to find her, Lazz. And then I'm going to marry her. She's going to have my sons—and I say sons because, with the exception of our cousin, Gianna, the men in our family seem incapable of producing daughters. We're going to have four of them, in case you're interested. And anyone who has a problem with that can discuss it first with my right fist and then with my left hook."

He looked around with a hint of defiance, stunned when he caught Sev and Marco's nod of approval. Even better was the expression Primo wore, one that offered unconditional support. "Everyone should receive a second chance," his grandfather stated.

Nicolò turned on Lazz again, his determination rock-solid. "So, are you going to help me find her, or are you going to fight me over this?"

"You know I don't believe in the family curse," Lazz muttered.

"Blessing," the others chorused in unison.

Nicolò barked out a laugh, the first one since Kiley left him. "You better start believing in The Inferno, Lazz. So far, it's three down. You're the only one of us left."

"And that's the way it's going to stay." Lazz held up his hands before anyone could argue the point. "Fine. You want her, you got her."

Nicolò nodded. "Let's just hope it's that easy."

Chapter Ten

Of course, it wasn't easy at all. It took a team effort involving Juice and the entire Dante family to finally locate Kiley. Nicolò couldn't recall a rougher few weeks. Not that he had anyone to blame other than himself. He'd allowed her to walk out instead of stopping her, and that knowledge had haunted him every single minute since. When the call finally came in from Juice, he found it a struggle just to form a coherent sentence.

"Where is she?" he managed to ask.

"A small dive down in the Mission District bearing the delightful name of the Riff Raff Inn. Not one I'd recommend, especially not for a woman on her own."

Nicolò swore. "What the hell is she doing there?"

"I can't say. Might be all she could afford. Thank God she finally used plastic or we'd have had the devil's own time finding her."

Nicolò closed his eyes. Of course. She'd left with nothing in hand but the funds in her purse. Five hundred couldn't have kept her fed and housed for much longer than a couple weeks, if that. Not in San Francisco. What would she have done if she hadn't had another source of money? Would she have come back to him? Somehow he doubted it.

"Watch the motel in case she leaves," Nicolò instructed. "I'll be there in fifteen."

"You'd better make it ten."

Hell. "Why? What's wrong?"

"Our old buddy Ferrell just got out of a cab. He's making tracks toward the motel and looks like a man on a mission. Do you want me to intercept him?"

"Not unless there's trouble. It can't be a coincidence he's shown up, or much doubt who he's there to see. Follow him and call me back with a room number. I'm leaving now."

He was five minutes out when Juice called again. "More good news," came the head of security's gloomy voice. "By the look of things, Kiley's about to have another visitor."

"Who?"

"Based on the description you gave me, I'm guessing it's Lacey O'Dell. Blonde, blue eyes, five foot nothing. Looks a good bit like Kiley, except . . ."

"Harder," Nicolò supplied.

"I'd call her cold if she didn't look spitting mad. If I were a betting man, I'd say your wife, er, sorry—Ms. O'Dell has done something to seriously tick off Momma dearest."

"Which room is Kiley in?"

"Two-oh-nine. Up the stairs, hang a right. Middle of the hallway on the left. You'll find me near the stairwell. I can see the door, but I'm not close enough to hear anything. Don't want to attract too much attention from those inside."

"Will I have any trouble getting past the front desk?"

"I wasn't sure what sort of reception you might receive when you joined the party, so I dropped a Franklin on the manager. He's suddenly developed a severe case of deaf, dumb, and blind."

"Hang tight. I'm almost there."

A few minutes later, Nicolò swung into a parking space and hustled into the motel. Juice's bribe worked. The manager didn't so much as lift his head, just gestured toward a worn stairway carpeted in the remains of faded paisley. Nicolò came across Juice in the hallway, a few doors up from Kiley's room.

"In there," he muttered, pointing. "Decided I better move closer so I could step in if things turned nasty. Got a right little row going."

More than a row. Nicolò could hear Ferrell's voice raised in fury, as well as Lacey's. And then he heard Kiley's cry of alarm and didn't bother with a civilized knock on the door. He crashed against the hollow core panel and sent the door bursting inward.

It took only an instant to assess the situation. Ferrell and Lacey were in a furious struggle over something that glittered with unmistakable fire. A diamond necklace. Or rather, what remained of a diamond necklace. And then he saw Kiley. She was on the floor, a hand raised to her cheek, one that showed evidence of a rapidly growing bruise. He was at her side in an instant, lifting her in his arms and clear of the fray. He didn't know who had hit her or why, but someone would pay for hurting her.

"Are you okay?"

"I'm fine." She ran her hands across his chest while she ate him up with her eyes. "Don't think me ungrateful, but . . . What are you doing here?"

He pulled a slow smile. "I'm here to rescue you, of course. Isn't that how it's supposed to work?"

She shook her head, despite the hope dawning in her expression. "Only in fairy tales. Not in real life."

"In real life, too, sweetheart. Now, who hit you?"

"It was an accident."

"Uh-huh." He shot Lacey and Ferrell a grim look. "Don't go anywhere. I'll be right back."

"Forget it, Nicolò. This is my fight, too."

Together they waded into the fray, separating the two combatants. Lacey gave a squeak of surprise and broke away from Ferrell with only minor prompting from Kiley. The older man backed up several paces, the remains of a diamond necklace clutched in his hand.

"If you don't want to find yourself eating carpet with a bruise to match Kiley's, I suggest you hand over that necklace."

"I'm not handing over anything," Ferrell snarled. "The diamonds are mine."

"I paid you what you were owed," Nicolò bit out. "And a good deal more beside. Or have you forgotten that minor detail?"

Kiley balled her hands into fists. "Why, you lying piece of scum. You told me you didn't receive so much as a dime from the Dantes."

"Look who's calling who scum," he shot back. "I deserve the diamonds for the hell you put me through. You deserve to know what it feels like to get conned."

"I'm not going to warn you again," Nicolò interrupted. "Drop the necklace."

Ferrell glared in frustration. "You don't understand."

"No, you don't understand." Nicolò stalked closer, leaned in so the other man couldn't mistake his words. "I'm going to pretend that bruise on Kiley's cheek is a regrettable accident. That it didn't have anything to do with you. While I'm operating under that misapprehension, I suggest you get as far from this room as physically possible. You got me?"

Ferrell's hand clenched around the necklace, common sense in a pitched battle with greed. After an endless minute, sensibility won out, though it took on a vindictive edge. "Fine. I'll leave. But you're a fool, Dante. She's just going to use you the same way she's used every other man she's ever met." He shook his head in disgust. "You're going to wish you'd never met her before she's finished with you."

And with that, he threw down the remains of the necklace and stalked from the room. He attempted to slam the door behind him, but it listed drunkenly on its hinges and wouldn't close.

"Thank you for getting rid of him," Lacey said, offering Nicolò a beaming smile. "You can come to my rescue any time."

"My pleasure, though I'm here to rescue Kiley, not you."

He couldn't help but notice that Lacey's smile was absolutely symmetrical, no adorable tilt to disturb its perfection. She bent down and scooped up the necklace, allowing a brief frown to carve a network of lines between her brows and at the corners of her mouth.

"Damn," she muttered. "What the hell were you thinking, Kiley?"

Kiley shrugged. "You know what I was thinking. And FYI, my plans haven't changed just because of a bruised cheek."

"What happened to the necklace?" he asked. "Where are the rest of the diamonds?"

Lacey jumped in before Kiley could respond. "She grew a conscience, that's what." She shot a sour look at Nicolò. "Your bad influence, no doubt."

"I gather the necklace originally belonged to Cameron O'Dell?" At Lacey's nod, he held out his hand. "Do you mind?"

"Not much left of it." A wistful expression slipped through her gaze.

"You should have seen it before Kiley broke it up. It was spectacular."

He scrutinized the remaining diamonds. There were three of them, two single carat diamonds as well as a gorgeous five-carat stone that had to be one of the most exquisite fire diamonds he'd ever seen. "Magnificent."

"It was."

Unable to last another second without touching some part of Kiley, he drew her to the bed, and urged her down on the edge. Then he lifted her chin and tilted her face into the light. "That's quite a shiner you have there. I was right, wasn't I? Ferrell did this?"

"He didn't hit me on purpose," she conceded. "He and Lacey were fighting to get their hands on the necklace and my cheekbone got in the way of his elbow."

"Ouch." He glanced at Lacey and jerked his head toward the door. "Why don't you get your daughter some ice."

"Oh, of course. Right away." Not a trace of sarcasm rippled through her words, yet she managed to make her displeasure heard loud and clear. Quite a feat. "Only too happy to help."

As soon as she left the room, he asked, "What's going on, Kiley? How did you end up with the necklace?"

She shrugged. "I figured out how to open the locket."

He lifted an eyebrow. "And the necklace was inside?"

That won him a brief, endearingly lopsided smile. "No, but the key to a safety deposit box was. It took me a while to track down the right bank. But once I had, I found the necklace."

His eyes narrowed at that telling piece of information. Did she even realize what she'd said? By admitting she didn't know how to open the locket or where she'd stashed the necklace, she'd just confirmed she still had amnesia. He let it pass for now. "And after you found the necklace? What did you do then?"

"I used the list, the list from the file I found on your desk."

"What did you use it for?" he asked gently.

She focused on a spot over his shoulder, her face set in determined lines. "I gave the diamonds to the people I—" Her voice broke for an instant before she regained control over it. "To the people I scammed. Ferrell was the last one. I didn't realize you'd already paid him off or I'd never have contacted him."

"I gather he wasn't satisfied with a single diamond?"

"Even the little one was worth twice what I took from him. But he felt he deserved more for his pain and suffering. He wanted all three. Then Lacey arrived and . . ." She shrugged.

"Then I jumped into the fray. Got it."

Her gaze drifted to his face again. Clung. "How did you find me?"

The Inferno called to him, urging him to lean in and take her mouth, to drink her in like a man lost and parched and desperate for relief. He fought the sensation. Not yet. Not until they'd resolved all the remaining issues. "I've been searching for you almost from the moment you left."

"Almost," she repeated.

"Well, I had to come to my senses first," he admitted. "When I couldn't find you, I elicited some help from my family."

"Your family?" She shook her head in disbelief. "They were willing to help you find me?"

"Every last one of them," he confirmed.

She stared in wonder. "But why would they do that? Didn't they know what was in the file?"

"They knew."

"I don't understand any of this."

Before she could ask any more questions, Lacey returned with a bucket of ice. Playing the role of the concerned parent, she filled a washcloth with the cubes and offered it to Kiley. "There you go, sweetheart. This should help."

"Now it's your turn," Nicolò warned.

Lacey released a gusty sigh. "I had a feeling I wasn't going to get out of this unscathed."

"I'm surprised you came back. I half expected you to take off."

"Thought about it," she admitted.

"Why didn't you?"

She gave him a cheeky grin. "You have the diamonds."

Of course. Foolish to think she wouldn't make a final play for them. "Explain the necklace. And Kiley's scam with the fire diamond mine."

She lifted an eyebrow, a calculating expression sliding into her gaze. "What do I get in return?"

"Lacey!" Kiley protested.

"The two little ones," Nicolò offered.

"No way. I want the big one."

"That belongs to Kiley," he said in a voice that didn't brook any argument. "If you want the little ones, you're going to need to explain since Kiley can't."

Lacey made a face. "She really doesn't remember, does she? If she did, she'd never have given away the diamonds."

"I am still here, you know," Kiley objected.

Lacey patted her shoulder. "Of course you are, dear. I assume you showed Nicolò all of Cameron O'Dell's documentation? Birth certificate, death certificate, will?"

Nicolò waited while Kiley silently fumed, fully aware that she had no idea how to answer her mother's question. Satisfied Lacey's point had been made, he answered in Kiley's place, "Yes, I saw all that. What happened to Cameron's share of the mine?"

"He sold it to his brother before your grandfather, Primo, made his offer. He sold it in exchange—"

"For the necklace."

"Exactly. He thought the mine was played out. As did his brother, Seamus, for that matter."

"Got it. And you and Kiley have been using the necklace to run a series of scams. Selling and reselling it, I assume, then either substituting a fake or cutting out before the transaction was completed?"

She hesitated. "Well, not exactly." She shot a disgruntled look toward her daughter. "I guess since there's no more necklace, I can tell you the truth."

Kiley braced herself. "I'm not sure I can handle much more truth right now."

"Most of those things in the file?" Lacey shrugged. "It was me. I'm the one responsible."

"No." Kiley shook her head, adamant. "That's not possible. Those people identified me by name. Ferrell even knew about my birthmark.

"Yes, well." Lacey lowered her gaze and released a light laugh. "The others might have identified you because I was using your name and colored my hair to match. Ferrell knew about the birthmark because I have a matching one. Though, I suspect he knew damn well you weren't me. He probably figured out the connection between us and went with it, hoping the Dantes wouldn't figure out it was me, not you."

"You—" Kiley took a deep breath and tried again. "You would do that to your own daughter? Why?"

Lacey waved the question aside with a sweep of her well-manicured hand. "A girl's got to survive. And speaking of surviving . . ." She spun to face Nicolò. "Cough it up, handsome. I explained everything, now I want my diamonds."

"What about my scamming the Dantes?" Kiley pressed.

She spared her daughter a quick look. "Sorry, sweetie. That one's on you. I had no part in it." She spared Nicolò a quick look and made a gimme motion with her fingers.

He removed the largest of the stones from the band and pocketed it before handing her the remaining two. "I'll be watching to make sure that you don't use Kiley's name anytime in the future," he warned.

"Not a problem. And now, if you'll excuse me, I do believe I've outstayed my welcome. If there's one thing I've learned, it's how to make a graceful exit." She flashed a megawatt smile at them both. "Don't worry, I won't be in touch."

"I'll see you out," Nicolò insisted.

They didn't speak until they'd reached the foyer. He pulled a business card from his pocket and handed it to her. "I hope you won't need this, but just in case."

She regarded it in surprise. "I don't understand. Why are you giving this to me?"

"Two reasons. When all is said and done, you're still Kiley's mother. Family means a lot to the Dantes."

She shrugged that off as though it didn't count for much. Which, he supposed, it didn't. Not for her. "And the other?" she asked.

"The other is for the lie you just told in there. Although I wouldn't advise lying to me anytime in the future. I'll always know."

"That's so sweet." She twinkled up at him. "You're actually thanking me."

Before he could debate the point, his soon-to-be mother-in-law swept out the door and disappeared down the street with a jaunty hip-swinging stride. And wasn't the idea of a familial connection with Lacey a depressing thought? He didn't waste any further time on her. After giving Juice the money to pay for the damaged door, he sent the Dantes' head of security on his way. Then Nicolò returned to the room where he'd left his heart and soul.

Kiley stood by the motel window, staring in the direction her mother had taken. He joined her there, taking her hand in his. "I'm sorry, sweetheart. I'm sorry for doubting you. I'm sorry for allowing you to leave. And I'm even more sorry I didn't find you sooner."

"What do you want, Nicolò? I mean, really." She lifted her gaze to his and he flinched at the wealth of sorrow he found there. "As much as I appreciate your helping me out of a tight spot, what is there left to be said?"

"Just one more thing." He cupped her face. "I love you, Kiley O'Dell. I love you more than I believed it possible to love someone. I want to spend the rest of my life with you and I'm hoping that's what you want, too."

"I love you, Nicolò. I do." Her voice broke. "I always have."

"Marry me. For real this time. No more lies. No more deception. From this day on, cards on the table."

She shook her head, pain etched deep in her face. "Even now you're not leveling with me. After all we've been through, you still haven't put all your cards on the table."

"What are you—"

"Stop it, Nicolò. I know she lied. I'm not the victim she made me out to be."

He sucked in a deep breath. "How did you know?"

"I'm not a fool. I read the files. Every last word. Those men weren't describing my mother. They were describing me. When I met with them, when I made reparations, they recognized me. They—" She fought to gather her self-control. "They despised me. Me, not her."

"She's no innocent in all this."

"No, she's not. I suppose she tried to make amends by taking the blame for all those scams." Her mouth trembled, ripping him to shreds. "But I can't marry you. Not ever. It wouldn't be right."

He fought the panic turning his insides to ice water. "Don't do this, Kiley. The past doesn't matter."

"You're wrong. If it didn't matter, I wouldn't have given away those diamonds. Trust me. It matters. It matters even more when you have nothing left but your honor and self-respect."

"You're not the person you once were."

"I am that person," she insisted. "I'll always have to live with that knowledge. So will you, and so will your family. So will your friends and associates and customers. And they may not be as forgiving as you when they find out who—*what*—I am."

"Was, Kiley. *Was*. Don't you get it? I don't care. I love you. We belong together."

"Do you think I don't want to spend the rest of my life in your arms? Oh, Nicolò. I love you so much. But I can't be with you. I can't marry you."

"Why?"

The words burst out. "Because one day I'll wake up and I'll remember. And when that happens, I'll turn back into her. I won't have a choice. She's who I really am. Who I'm meant to be. I can't do that to you. I won't."

"Bullshit!" He broke off, drawing in a deep, calming breath. "Do you really believe you have no choice? Do you really believe that you can't change? Do you want to be the woman you were before?"

"No. *No.*"

"Then don't. It's that simple. When you remember—*if* you remember—you can choose. You can choose a life filled with love and family. Or you can choose to go back to your old lifestyle. I'm betting you'll like your new life far better than your old one."

"It's not that easy," she protested. "It can't be."

"It can and it is." He pulled her close, closing his eyes in relief when he felt the helpless give of her body. It told him he hadn't lost her, that he only had to find the right words to win her. Honest words. Words from the heart. "If someday you remember, if it becomes a struggle, I'll be there for you. I swear it. And so will my family. There's only one thing that matters, Kiley. Do you love me?"

"You know I do." Her breath shuddered from her lungs. "I don't want to be her, Nicolò. I don't *ever* want to be her."

He understood she didn't just mean her past self, but the sort of woman her mother had become, as well. "You're not. The person you are now, without the baggage from the past, that's the true woman. Your innate sweetness and strength, your intelligence and humor, your wit. All of those things are what exist at the core of you. That's the real you. That's the woman I fell in love with, the Kiley you would have been if your life had taken a different turn." His arms tightened around her and he put every ounce of grit and determination into his voice. "Well, it did make that turn, sweetheart. Call it fate. Call it divine intervention. Hell, call it The Inferno. But because of your accident, you've been given a chance to take your life in a new direction. With me."

He cupped her face and kissed his way past the tears, losing himself in her passionate warmth. This was the Kiley he knew. The Kiley he'd fallen in love with. The Inferno caught fire, blazing hotter than he'd ever felt it before. It was almost as though by their breaking through the final barriers separating them, by sharing those final pieces of themselves, The Inferno rewarded them with a connection so strong, so utterly complete, that nothing could ever divide them again.

He lifted his head and gazed down at her with unfettered honesty and trust.

"Marry me, Kiley. Take a chance. Create a brand-new life with me."

"Cards on the table from now on?"

"All fifty-two of them."

She smiled then, that beautiful, radiant, lopsided smile. "Take me home, Nicolò."

He didn't need any further prompting. Together they left behind the old and forgotten, the sordid and painful, and walked into a future shiny with possibility.

Epilogue

Kiley's memory did return, but not for another twenty years.

It came back on a hot summer day while she played baseball with her husband, her four strapping sons, and their various first and second cousins. Nicolò had suggested she play centerfield, "out of harm's way," but she'd insisted on covering third. What she hadn't anticipated was chasing an easy pop fly that took an unexpected curve into a nearby street.

It happened again as it had twice before in her life. She darted out into the street, her glove lifted skyward, only afterward realizing the sheer idiocy of her reckless actions. The driver of the oncoming car hit his brakes and horn at the exact same moment, skidding toward her at a frightening speed. She knew she wouldn't be able to avoid the impact this time, just as she hadn't on that very first occasion when she'd been struck by a cab outside of Le Premier. Ironically, this car was the same bright yellow as the cab had been all those years ago. This time it wouldn't miss her, just as it hadn't then. And this time she'd fully suffer the consequences of her impulsiveness.

At the last possible instant, an arm swooped around her waist like a band of iron and yanked her clear of the oncoming car. With a final blare of the horn, it swept past, leaving her trembling within Nicolò's embrace. Her husband growled out a string of Italian curses before kissing her senseless.

When she surfaced from the kiss, it was to find her sons grouped around her in a tight worried circle, and her husband gazing down at her with a combination of undisguised love and bone-deep terror. It felt as though time caught its breath for a brief instant, pausing just long enough for the rush of memories to finish cycling through her head, cascading over her in a dizzying flood.

In that odd timeless moment, she remembered it all. Those crazed early years with her mother. The childhood better off forgotten. The lessons she'd learned at the knee of an amoral parent more concerned with material possessions than character or soul. More concerned with money than the needs of a lonely child desperate for a proper mother. Kiley could see, as though through a thick glass, the string of scams she and her mother had pulled. Could feel the cold emptiness of that life, could feel the spirit draining out of her with each successive con.

"Mom?" Dominic, her eldest, touched her shoulder, fear evident in the deep black gaze he kept trained on her face. "You okay?

"I—"

The past tugged at her. Called to her. Tried to pull her back toward that other person. That person she'd been all those years ago. So many options opened themselves to her, options that for that long-ago Kiley would have been like hitting a multi-million dollar jackpot.

And then she began to laugh. She'd hit the jackpot long ago. She gazed up at her husband, a man she adored with all her heart and soul, a man who'd saved her from that other life. And she looked at each one of the children she'd given birth to, children she'd showered with love and attention, discipline and a strong moral character. And she laughed again, laughed for sheer joy. The diamond on her wedding ring flamed brighter than ever. It was the last diamond from Cameron O'Dell's fire diamond necklace, a diamond that symbolized an end to the old and the opportunity for a new beginning.

Go back?

Never.

She picked up the softball laying at her feet and tagged her son with it. "You're out," she told him. "Now, let's play ball."

Meet Day Leclaire

I love family first and foremost, which is why writing a family saga is so much fun. Maybe you can tell that from my books since they always feature the warmth and joy that comes from having a close-knit family. I also love animals and have taken in rescue dogs and cats and fostered dogs for the local animal shelter. And of course, I love writing. All I need is a functioning brain (batteries not included), a pen, and paper, and I can write anywhere. Please don't let a conversation with me lag because my imagination takes over and I. Am. Checked. Out!

USA Today bestselling author, Day Leclaire is the author of more than 60 novels and has received an impressive eleven nominations for the romance industry's most prestigious award, Romance Writers of America RITA© Award. Day lives in Charlotte, NC and spends her days obsessively writing while vaguely remembering to pay attention to her adorable husband, busy son and daughter-in-law, two tiny grandchildren, and two even tinier Teddy Bear dogs. Not to mention a whole lot of dust!

Thank you so much for taking the time to read **The Dante Inferno:** *The Dante Dynasty Series, books 1-3*. I hope you enjoy this very special Italian-American family. I love hearing from my readers. For a personal response, please contact me at Day@DayLeclaire.com. And be sure to visit my website at www.DayLeclaire.com, where you can sign up for my newsletter for my latest releases and insider info available nowhere else! Receive a FREE book as my thank you for joining.

I hope this boxset tempts to you to continue reading The Dante Dynasty Series.